THE TOWER OF
THE MAIMED GOD

Through the darkness of the City of Night, Belgarath the Sorcerer passed in the shape of a great wolf, leading Cherek and his sons to the iron tower of the Accursed God. There Belgarath changed again to a man and led the others up the rusted stairs that no man had climbed for two thousand years.

They came to the chamber where the God Torak lay in pain-haunted slumber, his hideously scarred face hidden behind an iron mask. They passed the God and came at last to the room where the Orb of Aldur lay concealed and safe within an iron cask.

Cherek motioned for Belgarath to take the Orb, but the Sorcerer refused. "I cannot touch it. If any man with even a trace of evil in his intent seizes it, it will destroy him as it burned Torak. Only a man of pure heart may take it up to save us from the Accursed One."

"But what man is entirely without evil intent in the silence of his soul?" Cherek asked.

By David Eddings

THE BELGARIAD

Published by Ballantine Books

*Forthcoming

"THEY'RE *GOOD*! IN FACT, THEY'RE FABULOUS. MORE! MORE! MORE!"
—Anne McCaffrey

"EDDINGS' *BELGARIAD* IS EXACTLY THE KIND OF FANTASY I LIKE. IT HAS MAGIC, ADVENTURE, HUMOR, MYSTERY AND A CERTAIN DELIGHTFUL HUMAN INSIGHT."
—Piers Anthony

Book One of The Belgariad

PAWN OF PROPHECY

DAVID EDDINGS

A Del Rey Book

BALLANTINE BOOKS · NEW YORK

A Del Rey Book
Published by Ballantine Books

Library of Congress Catalog Card Number: 81-68656

ISBN 0-345-32356-4

Manufactured in the United States of America

First Edition: April 1982
Tenth Printing: October 1984

Cover art by Laurence Schwinger

Front map of THE KINGDOMS OF THE WEST AND
THE ANGARAKS by Shelly Shapiro

Additional maps by Chris Barbieri

For Theone,
  who told me stories but could not stay for
  mine—
and for Arthur,
  who showed me the way to become a man—
  and who shows me still.

SEA OF
THE WINDS

CHEREK

ISLE
OF THE
WINDS

Gulf
of
Cherek

Kotu

The
Cherek
Bore

Drim

Mrin
Marsh

Val
Alorn

Aldur
Fens

Sendar

Medalia

Seline

Sulturn

Gar og Nadrak

SENDARIA

Great North Road

Camaar

Aldurford

Arendish
Forest

Darine

Vo Astur

Vo Mimbre

ULGOLAND

THE GREAT
WESTERN SEA

ARENDIA

Great Cardune River Road

Prolgu

Forest of
Vordue

TOLNEDRA

THE
KINGDOMS
OF THE
WEST
AND THE
ANGARAKS

Tol Vordue

Tol Honeth

Tol Borune

Tol Rane

Tol
Horb

Wood of the Dryads

Woods of the

Jungles of the

Snake People

Chtol Tsa

of the Serpent

NYISSA

Mar
Terin

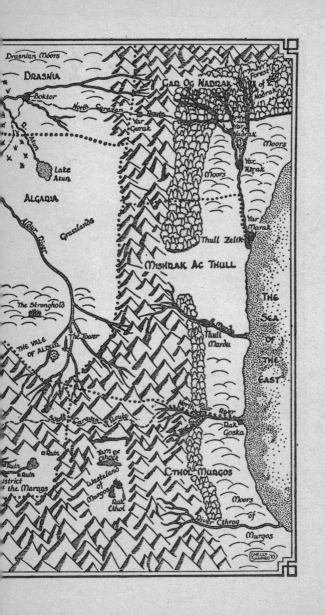

Prologue

Being a History of the War of the Gods and the Acts of Belgarath the Sorcerer
  —adapted from *The Book of Alorn*

WHEN THE WORLD was new, the seven Gods dwelt in harmony, and the races of man were as one people. Belar, youngest of the Gods, was beloved by the Alorns. He abode with them and cherished them, and they prospered in his care. The other Gods also gathered peoples about them, and each God cherished his own people.

But Belar's eldest brother, Aldur, was God over no people. He dwelt apart from men and Gods, until the day that a vagrant child sought him out. Aldur accepted the child as his disciple and called him Belgarath. Belgarath learned the secret of the Will and the Word and became a sorcerer. In the years that followed, others also sought out the solitary God. They joined in brotherhood to learn at the feet of Aldur, and time did not touch them.

Now it happened that Aldur took up a stone in the shape of a globe, no larger than the heart of a child, and he turned the stone in his hand until it became a living soul. The power of the living jewel, which men called the Orb of Aldur, was very great, and Aldur worked wonders with it.

Of all the Gods, Torak was the most beautiful, and his people were the Angaraks. They burned sacrifices before him, calling him Lord of Lords, and Torak found the smell of sacrifice and the words of adoration sweet. The day came, however, when he heard of the Orb of Aldur, and from that moment he knew no peace.

Finally, in a dissembling guise, he went to Aldur. "My brother," he said, "it is not fitting that thou shouldst absent thyself from our company and counsel. Put aside

1

this jewel which hath seduced thy mind from our fellowship."

Aldur looked into his brother's soul and rebuked him. "Why dost thou seek lordship and dominion, Torak? Is not Angarak enough for thee? Do not in thy pride seek to possess the Orb, lest it slay thee."

Great was Torak's shame at the words of Aldur, and he raised his hand and smote his brother. Taking the jewel, he fled.

The other Gods besought Torak to return the Orb, but he would not. Then the races of man rose up and came against the hosts of Angarak and made war on them. The wars of the Gods and of men raged across the land until, near the high places of Korim, Torak raised the Orb and forced its will to join with his to split the earth asunder. The mountains were cast down, and the sea came in. But Belar and Aldur joined their wills and set limits upon the sea. The races of man, however, were separated one from the others, and the Gods also.

Now when Torak raised the living Orb against the earth, its mother, it awoke and began to glow with holy flame. The face of Torak was seared by the blue fire. In pain he cast down the mountains; in anguish he cracked open the earth; in agony he let in the sea. His left hand flared and burned to ashes, the flesh on the left side of his face melted like wax, and his left eye boiled in its socket. With a great cry, he cast himself into the sea to quench the burning, but his anguish was without end.

When Torak rose from the water, his right side was still fair, but his left was burned and scarred hideously by the fire of the Orb. In endless pain, he led his people away to the east, where they built a great city on the plains of Mallorea, which they called *Cthol Mishrak*, City of Night, for Torak hid his maiming in darkness. The Angaraks raised an iron tower for their God and placed the Orb in an iron cask in the topmost chamber. Often Torak stood before the cask, then fled weeping, lest his yearning to look on the Orb overpower him and he perish utterly.

The centuries rolled past in the lands of the Angarak, and they came to call their maimed God Kal-Torak, both King and God.

Belar had taken the Alorns to the north. Of all men,

they were the most hardy and warlike, and Belar put
eternal hatred for Angarak in their hearts. With cruel
swords and axes they ranged the north, even to the fields
of eternal ice, seeking a way to their ancient enemies.

Thus it was until the time when Cherek Bear-shoulders,
greatest king of the Alorns, traveled to the Vale of Aldur
to seek out Belgarath the Sorcerer. "The way to the north
is open," he said. "The signs and the auguries are propiti-
ous. Now is the time ripe for us to discover the way to
the City of Night and regain the Orb from One-eye."

Poledra, wife of Belgarath, was great with child, and he
was reluctant to leave her. But Cherek prevailed. They
stole away one night to join Cherek's sons, Dras Bull-neck,
Algar Fleet-foot, and Riva Iron-grip.

Cruel winter gripped the northland, and the moors
glittered beneath the stars with frost and steel-gray ice.
To seek out their way, Belgarath cast an enchantment
and took the shape of a great wolf. On silent feet, he slunk
through the snow-floored forests where the trees cracked
and shattered in the sundering cold. Grim frost silvered
the ruff and shoulders of the wolf, and ever after the hair
and beard of Belgarath were silver.

Through snow and mist they crossed into Mallorea and
came at last to *Cthol Mishrak*. Finding a secret way into
the city, Belgarath led them to the foot of the iron tower.
Silently they climbed the rusted stairs which had known no
step for twenty centuries. Fearfully they passed through
the chamber where Torak tossed in pain-haunted slumber,
his maimed face hidden by a steel mask. Stealthily they
crept past the sleeping God in the smoldering darkness and
came at last to the chamber where lay the iron cask in
which rested the living Orb.

Cherek motioned for Belgarath to take the Orb, but
Belgarath refused. "I may not touch it," he said, "lest it
destroy me. Once it welcomed the touch of man or God,
but its will hardened when Torak raised it against its
mother. It will not be so used again. It reads our souls.
Only one without ill intent, who is pure enough to take it
and convey it in peril of his life, with no thought of power
or possession, may touch it now."

"What man has no ill intent in the silence of his soul?"
Cherek asked. But Riva Iron-grip opened the cask and

took up the Orb. Its fire shone through his fingers, but he was not burned.

"So be it, Cherek," Belgarath said. "Your youngest son is pure. It shall be his doom and the doom of all who follow him to bear the Orb and protect it." And Belgarath sighed, knowing the burden he had placed upon Riva.

"Then his brothers and I will sustain him," Cherek said, "for so long as this doom is upon him."

Riva muffled the Orb in his cloak and hid it beneath his tunic. They crept again through the chambers of the maimed God, down the rusted stairs, along the secret way to the gates of the city, and into the wasteland beyond.

Soon after, Torak awoke and went as always into the Chamber of the Orb. But the cask stood open, and the Orb was gone. Horrible was the wrath of Kal-Torak. Taking his great sword, he went down from the iron tower and turned and smote it once, and the tower fell. To the Angaraks he cried out in a voice of thunder: "Because you are become indolent and unwatchful and have let a thief steal that for which I paid so dear, I will break your city and drive you forth. Angarak shall wander the earth until *Cthrag Yaska*, the burning stone, is returned to me." Then he cast down the City of Night in ruins and drove the hosts of Angarak into the wilderness. *Cthol Mishrak* was no more.

Three leagues to the north, Belgarath heard the wailing from the city and knew that Torak had awakened. "Now will he come after us," he said, "and only the power of the Orb can save us. When the hosts are upon us, Iron-grip, take the Orb and hold it so they may see it."

The hosts of Angarak came, with Torak himself in the forefront, but Riva held forth the Orb so that the maimed God and his hosts might behold it. The Orb knew its enemy. Its hatred flamed anew, and the sky became alight with its fury. Torak cried out and turned away. The front ranks of the Angarak hosts were consumed by fire, and the rest fled in terror.

Thus Belgarath and his companions escaped from Mallorea and passed again through the marches of the north, bearing the Orb of Aldur once more into the Kingdoms of the West.

Now the Gods, knowing all that had passed, held council,

and Aldur advised them, "If we raise war again upon our brother Torak, our strife will destroy the world. Thus we must absent ourselves from the world so that our brother may not find us. No longer in flesh, but in spirit only may we remain to guide and protect our people. For the world's sake it must be so. In the day that we war again, the world will be unmade."

The Gods wept that they must depart. But Chaldan, Bull-God of the Arends, asked, "In our absence, shall not Torak have dominion?"

"Not so," Aldur replied. "So long as the Orb remains with the line of Riva Iron-grip, Torak shall not prevail."

So it was that the Gods departed, and only Torak remained. But the knowledge that the Orb in the hand of Riva denied him dominion cankered his soul.

Then Belgarath spoke with Cherek and his sons. "Here we must part, to guard the Orb and to prepare against the coming of Torak. Let each turn aside as I have instructed and make preparations."

"We will, Belgarath," vowed Cherek Bear-shoulders. "From this day, Aloria is no more, but the Alorns will deny dominion to Torak as long as one Alorn remains."

Belgarath raised his face. "Hear me, Torak One-eye," he cried. "The living Orb is secure against thee, and thou shalt not prevail against it. In the day that thou comest against us, I shall raise war against thee. I will maintain watch upon thee by day and by night and will abide against thy coming, even to the end of days."

In the wastelands of Mallorea, Kal-Torak heard the voice of Belgarath and smote about him in fury, for he knew that the living Orb was forever beyond his reach.

Then Cherek embraced his sons and turned away, to see them no more. Dras went north and dwelt in the lands drained by River Mrin. He built a city at Boktor and called his lands Drasnia. And he and his descendants stood athwart the northern marches and denied them to the enemy. Algar went south with his people and found horses on the broad plains drained by Aldur River. The horses they tamed and learned to ride for the first time in the history of man, mounted warriors appeared. Their country they called Algaria, and they became nomads, following their herds. Cherek returned sadly to Val Alorn and renamed

his kingdom Cherek, for now he was alone and without
sons. Grimly he built tall ships of war to patrol the seas
and deny them to the enemy.

Upon the bearer of the Orb, however, fell the burden
of the longest journey. Taking his people, Riva went to
the west coast of Sendaria. There he built ships, and he
and his people crossed to the Isle of the Winds. They
burned their ships and built a fortress and a walled city
around it. The city they called Riva and the fortress the
Hall of the Rivan King. Then Belar, God of the Alorns,
caused two iron stars to fall from the sky. Riva took up
the stars and forged a blade from one and a hilt from the
other, setting the Orb upon it as a pommel-stone. So large
was the sword that none but Riva could wield it. In the
wasteland of Mallorea, Kal-Torak felt in his soul the forging
of the sword and he tasted fear for the first time.

The sword was set against the black rock that stood at
the back of Riva's throne, with the Orb at the highest point,
and the sword joined to the rock so that none but Riva
could remove it. The Orb burned with cold fire when Riva
sat upon the throne. And when he took down his sword
and raised it, it became a great tongue of cold fire.

The greatest wonder of all was the marking of Riva's
heir. In each generation, one child in the line of Riva bore
upon the palm of his right hand the mark of the Orb. The
child so marked was taken to the throne chamber, and his
hand was placed upon the Orb, so that it might know him.
With each infant touch, the Orb waxed in brilliance, and
the bond between the living Orb and the line of Riva became stronger with each joining.

After Belgarath had parted from his companions, he
hastened to the Vale of Aldur. But there he found that
Poledra, his wife, had borne twin daughters and then had
died. In sorrow he named the elder Polgara. Her hair was
dark as the raven's wing. In the fashion of sorcerers, he
stretched forth his hand to lay it upon her brow, and a
single lock at her forehead turned frost-white at his touch.
Then he was troubled, for the white lock was the mark
of the sorcerers, and Polgara was the first female child to
be so marked.

His second daughter, fair-skinned and golden-haired, was
unmarked. He called her Beldaran, and he and her dark-

haired sister loved her beyond all else and contended with each other for her affection.

Now when Polgara and Beldaran had reached their sixteenth year, the Spirit of Aldur came to Belgarath in a dream, saying, "My beloved disciple, I would join thy house with the house of the guardian of the Orb. Choose, therefore, which of thy daughters thou wilt give to the Rivan King to be his wife and the mother of his line, for in that line lies the hope of the world, against which the dark power of Torak may not prevail."

In the deep silence of his soul, Belgarath was tempted to choose Polgara. But, knowing the burden which lay upon the Rivan King, he sent Beldaran instead, and wept when she was gone. Polgara wept also, long and bitterly, knowing that her sister must fade and die. In time, however, they comforted each other and came at last to know each other.

They joined their powers to keep watch over Torak. And some men say that they abide still, keeping their vigil through all the uncounted centuries.

Part One

SENDARIA

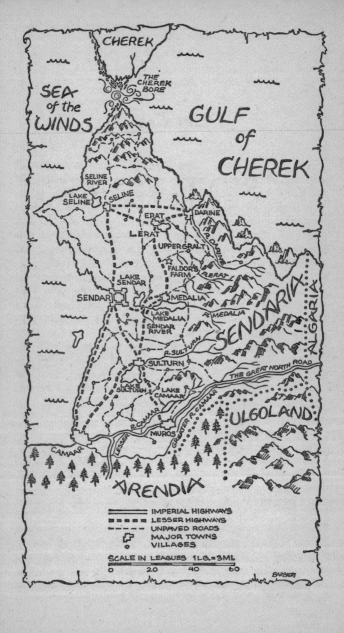

CHEREK

SEA
of the
WINDS

THE
CHEREK
BORE

GULF
of
CHEREK

SELINE
RIVER

LAKE
SELINE

SELINE

ERAT

L.ERAT

DARINE

R.DARINE

UPPER GRALT

FALDOR'S
FARM

R.ERAT

LAKE
SENDAR

SENDAR

MEDALIA

LAKE
MEDALIA

SENDARIA

R.MEDALIA

ALGARIA

SENDAR
RIVER

R.SULTURN

SULTURN

LAKE
SULTURN

LAKE
CAMAAR

THE GREAT NORTH ROAD

ULGOLAND

R.CAMAAR

MUROS

GREATER R.CAMAAR

LESSER R.CAMAAR

CAMAAR

ARENDIA

—————— IMPERIAL HIGHWAYS
▪▪▪▪▪▪▪▪ LESSER HIGHWAYS
– – – – UNPAVED ROADS
⌂ MAJOR TOWNS
∘ VILLAGES

SCALE IN LEAGUES 1 LG. = 3 MI.

0   20   40   60

BARBIERI

Chapter One

THE FIRST THING the boy Garion remembered was the kitchen at Faldor's farm. For all the rest of his life he had a special warm feeling for kitchens and those peculiar sounds and smells that seemed somehow to combine into a bustling seriousness that had to do with love and food and comfort and security and, above all, home. No matter how high Garion rose in life, he never forgot that all his memories began in that kitchen.

The kitchen at Faldor's farm was a large, low-beamed room filled with ovens and kettles and great spits that turned slowly in cavernlike arched fireplaces. There were long, heavy worktables where bread was kneaded into loaves and chickens were cut up and carrots and celery were diced with quick, crisp rocking movements of long, curved knives. When Garion was very small, he played under those tables and soon learned to keep his fingers and toes out from under the feet of the kitchen helpers who worked around them. And sometimes in the late afternoon when he grew tired, he would lie in a corner and stare into one of the flickering fires that gleamed and reflected back from the hundred polished pots and knives and long-handled spoons that hung from pegs along the whitewashed walls and, all bemused, he would drift off into sleep in perfect peace and harmony with all the world around him.

The center of the kitchen and everything that happened there was Aunt Pol. She seemed somehow to be able to be everywhere at once. The finishing touch that plumped a goose in its roasting pan or deftly shaped a rising loaf or garnished a smoking ham fresh from the oven was always hers. Though there were several others who worked in the kitchen, no loaf, stew, soup, roast, or vegetable ever went out of it that had not been touched at least once by Aunt

11

Pol. She knew by smell, taste, or some higher instinct what each dish required, and she seasoned them all by pinch or trace or a negligent-seeming shake from earthenware spice pots. It was as if there was a kind of magic about her, a knowledge and power beyond that of ordinary people. And yet, even at her busiest, she always knew precisely where Garion was. In the very midst of crimping a pie crust or decorating a special cake or stitching up a freshly stuffed chicken she could, without looking, reach out a leg and hook him back out from under the feet of others with heel or ankle.

As he grew a bit older, it even became a game. Garion would watch until she seemed far too busy to notice him, and then, laughing, he would run on his sturdy little legs toward a door. But she would always catch him. And he would laugh and throw his arms around her neck and kiss her and then go back to watching for his next chance to run away again.

He was quite convinced in those early years that his Aunt Pol was quite the most important and beautiful woman in the world. For one thing, she was taller than the other women on Faldor's farm—very nearly as tall as a man—and her face was always serious—even stern—except with him, of course. Her hair was long and very dark—almost black—all but one lock just above her left brow which was white as new snow. At night when she tucked him into the little bed close beside her own in their private room above the kitchen, he would reach out and touch that white lock; she would smile at him and touch his face with a soft hand. Then he would sleep, content in the knowledge that she was there, watching over him.

Faldor's farm lay very nearly in the center of Sendaria, a misty kingdom bordered on the west by the Sea of the Winds and on the east by the Gulf of Cherek. Like all farmhouses in that particular time and place, Faldor's farmstead was not one building or two, but rather was a solidly constructed complex of sheds and barns and hen roosts and dovecotes all facing inward upon a central yard with a stout gate at the front. Along the second story gallery were the rooms, some spacious, some quite tiny, in which lived the farmhands who tilled and planted and weeded the extensive fields beyond the walls. Faldor himself lived in quarters in the square tower above the central dining hall where his workers assembled three times a day—sometimes four during harvest time—to feast on the bounty of Aunt Pol's kitchen.

All in all, it was quite a happy and harmonious place. Farmer Faldor was a good master. He was a tall, serious man with a long nose and an even longer jaw. Though he seldom laughed or even smiled, he was kindly to those who worked for him and seemed more intent on maintaining them all in health and well-being than extracting the last possible ounce of sweat from them. In many ways he was more like a father than a master to the sixty-odd people who lived on his freeholding. He ate with them—which was unusual, since many farmers in the district sought to hold themselves aloof from their workers—and his presence at the head of the central table in the dining hall exerted a restraining influence on some of the younger ones who tended sometimes to be boisterous. Farmer Faldor was a devout man, and he invariably invoked with simple eloquence the blessing of the Gods before each meal. The people of his farm, knowing this, filed with some decorum into the dining hall before each meal and sat in the semblance at least of piety before attacking the heaping platters and bowls of food that Aunt Pol and her helpers had placed before them.

Because of Faldor's good heart—and the magic of Aunt Pol's deft fingers—the farm was known throughout the district as the finest place to live and work for twenty leagues in any direction. Whole evenings were spent in the tavern in the nearby village of Upper Gralt in minute descriptions of the near-miraculous meals served regularly in Faldor's dining hall. Less fortunate men who worked at other farms were frequently seen, after several pots of ale, to weep openly at descriptions of one of Aunt Pol's roasted geese, and the fame of Faldor's farm spread wide throughout the district.

The most important man on the farm, aside from Faldor, was Durnik the smith. As Garion grew older and was allowed to move out from under Aunt Pol's watchful eye, he found his way inevitably to the smithy. The glowing iron that came from Durnik's forge had an almost hypnotic attraction for him. Durnik was an ordinary-looking man with plain brown hair and a plain face, ruddy from the heat of his forge. He was neither tall nor short, nor was he thin or stout. He was sober and quiet, and like most men who follow his trade, he was enormously strong. He wore a rough leather jerkin and an apron of the same material. Both were spotted with burns from the sparks which flew from his forge. He also wore tight-fitting hose and soft leather boots as was the custom in that part of Sendaria. At first Durnik's only words to Garion were warnings to keep his fingers away from the forge and the glowing metal which came from it. In time, however, he and the boy became friends, and he spoke more frequently.

"Always finish what you set your hand to," he would advise. "It's bad for the iron if you set it aside and then take it back to the fire more than is needful."

"Why is that?" Garion would ask.

Durnik would shrug. "It just is."

"Always do the very best job you can," he said on another occasion as he put a last few finishing touches with a file on the metal parts of a wagon tongue he was repairing.

"But that piece goes underneath," Garion said. "No one will ever see it."

"But *I* know it's there," Durnik said, still smoothing the metal. "If it isn't done as well as I can do it, I'll be ashamed every time I see this wagon go by—and I'll see the wagon every day."

And so it went. Without even intending to, Durnik instructed the small boy in those solid Sendarian virtues of work, thrift, sobriety, good manners, and practicality which formed the backbone of the society.

At first Aunt Pol worried about Garion's attraction to the smithy with its obvious dangers; but after watching from her kitchen door for a while, she realized that Durnik was almost as watchful of Garion's safety as she was herself and she became less concerned.

"If the boy becomes pestersome, Goodman Durnik, send him away," she told the smith on one occasion when she had brought a large copper kettle to the smithy to be patched, "or tell me, and I'll keep him closer to the kitchen."

"He's no bother, Mistress Pol," Durnik said, smiling. "He's a sensible boy and knows enough to keep out of the way."

"You're too good-natured, friend Durnik," Aunt Pol said. "The boy is full of questions. Answer one and a dozen more pour out."

"That's the way of boys," Durnik said, carefully pouring bubbling metal into the small clay ring he'd placed around the tiny hole in the bottom of the kettle. "I was question-some myself when I was a boy. My father and old Barl, the smith who taught me, were patient enough to answer what they could. I'd repay them poorly if I didn't have the same patience with Garion."

Garion, who was sitting nearby, had held his breath dur-ing this conversation. He knew that one wrong word on either side would have instantly banished him from the smithy. As Aunt Pol walked back across the hard-packed dirt of the yard toward her kitchen with the new-mended kettle, he noticed the way that Durnik watched her, and an idea began to form in his mind. It was a simple idea, and the beauty of it was that it provided something for every-one.

"Aunt Pol," he said that night, wincing as she washed one of his ears with a rough cloth.

"Yes?" she said, turning her attention to his neck.

"Why don't you marry Durnik?"

She stopped washing. "What?" she asked.

"I think it would be an awfully good idea."

"Oh, do you?" Her voice had a slight edge to it, and Garion knew he was on dangerous ground.

"He likes you," he said defensively.

"And I suppose you've already discussed this with him?"

"No," he said. "I thought I'd talk to you about it first."

"At least *that* was a good idea."

"I can tell him about it tomorrow morning, if you'd like."

His head was turned around quite firmly by one ear. Aunt Pol, Garion felt, found his ears far too convenient.

"Don't you so much as breathe one word of this non-sense to Durnik or anyone else," she said, her dark eyes burning into his with a fire he had never seen there before.

"It was only a thought," he said quickly.

"A very bad one. From now on leave thinking to grown-ups." She was still holding his ear.

"Anything you say," he agreed hastily.

Later that night, however, when they lay in their beds in the quiet darkness, he approached the problem obliquely.

"Aunt Pol?"

"Yes?"

"Since you don't want to marry Durnik, whom *do* you want to marry?"

"Garion," she said.

"Yes?"

"Close your mouth and go to sleep."

"I think I've got a right to know," he said in an injured tone.

"*Garion!*"

"All right. I'm going to sleep, but I don't think you're being very fair about all this."

She drew in a deep breath. "Very well," she said. "I'm not thinking of getting married. I have never thought of getting married and I seriously doubt that I'll ever think of getting married. I have far too many important things to attend to for any of that."

"Don't worry, Aunt Pol," he said, wanting to put her mind at ease. "When I grow up, *I'll* marry you."

She laughed then, a deep, rich laugh, and reached out to touch his face in the darkness. "Oh no, my Garion," she said. "There's another wife in store for you."

"Who?" he demanded.

"You'll find out," she said mysteriously. "Now go to sleep."

"Aunt Pol?"

"Yes?"

"Where's my mother?" It was a question he had been meaning to ask for quite some time.

There was a long pause, then Aunt Pol sighed. "She died," she said quietly.

Garion felt a sudden wrenching surge of grief, an unbearable anguish. He began to cry.

And then she was beside his bed. She knelt on the floor and put her arms around him. Finally, a long time later, after she had carried him to her own bed and held him close until his grief had run its course, Garion asked brokenly, "What was she like? My mother?"

"She was fair-haired," Aunt Pol said, "and very young and very beautiful. Her voice was gentle, and she was very happy."

"Did she love me?"

"More than you could imagine."

And then he cried again, but his crying was quieter now, more regretful than anguished.

Aunt Pol held him closely until he cried himself to sleep.

There were other children on Faldor's farm, as was only natural in a community of sixty or so. The older ones on the farm all worked, but there were three other children of about Garion's age on the freeholding. These three became his playmates and his friends.

The oldest boy was named Rundorig. He was a year or two older than Garion and quite a bit taller. Ordinarily, since he was the eldest of the children, Rundorig would have been their leader; but because he was an Arend, his sense was a bit limited and he cheerfully deferred to the younger ones. The kingdom of Sendaria, unlike other kingdoms, was inhabited by a broad variety of racial stocks. Chereks, Algars, Drasnians, Arends, and even a substantial number of Tolnedrans had merged to form the elemental Sendar. Arends, of course, were very brave, but were also notoriously thick-witted.

Garion's second playmate was Doroon, a small, quick boy whose background was so mixed that he could only be called a Sendar. The most notable thing about Doroon was the fact that he was always running; he never walked if he could run. Like his feet, his mind seemed to tumble over itself, and his tongue as well. He talked continually and very fast and he was always excited.

The undisputed leader of the little foursome was the girl Zubrette, a golden-haired charmer who invented their games, made up stories to tell them, and set them to stealing apples and plums from Faldor's orchard for her. She ruled them as a little queen, playing one against the other and inciting them into fights. She was quite heartless, and each of the three boys at times hated her even while remaining helpless thralls to her tiniest whim.

In the winter they slid on wide boards down the snowy hillside behind the farmhouse and returned home, wet and snow-covered, with chapped hands and glowing cheeks as evening's purple shadows crept across the snow. Or, after Durnik the smith had proclaimed the ice safe, they would slide endlessly across the frozen pond that lay glittering frostily in a little dale just to the east of the farm buildings along the road to Upper Gralt. And, if the weather was too cold or on toward spring when rains and warm winds had made the snow slushy and the pond unsafe, they would gather in the hay barn and leap by the hour from the loft into the soft hay beneath, filling their hair with chaff and their noses with dust that smelled of summer.

In the spring they caught polliwogs along the marshy edges of the pond and climbed trees to stare in wonder at the tiny blue eggs the birds had laid in twiggy nests in the high branches.

It was Doroon, naturally, who fell from a tree and broke his arm one fine spring morning when Zubrette urged him into the highest branches of a tree near the edge of the pond. Since Rundorig stood helplessly gaping at his injured friend and Zubrette had run away almost before he hit the ground, it fell to Garion to make certain necessary decisions. Gravely he considered the situation for a few moments, his young face seriously intent beneath his shock of sandy hair. The arm was obviously broken, and Doroon, pale and frightened, bit his lip to keep from crying.

A movement caught Garion's eye, and he glanced up quickly. A man in a dark cloak sat astride a large black horse not far away, watching intently. When their eyes met, Garion felt a momentary chill, and he knew that he had seen the man before—that indeed that dark figure had hovered on the edge of his vision for as long as he could remember, never speaking, but always watching. There was in that silent scrutiny a kind of cold animosity curiously mingled with something that was almost, but not quite, fear. Then Doroon whimpered, and Garion turned back.

Carefully he bound the injured arm across the front of Doroon's body with his rope belt, and then he and Rundorig helped the injured boy to his feet.

"At least he could have helped us," Garion said resentfully.

"Who?" Rundorig said, looking around.

Garion turned to point at the dark-cloaked man, but the rider was gone.

"I didn't see anyone," Rundorig said.

"It hurts," Doroon said.

"Don't worry," Garion said. "Aunt Pol will fix it."

And so she did. When the three appeared at the door of her kitchen, she took in the situation with a single glance. "Bring him over here," she told them, her voice not even excited. She set the pale and violently trembling boy on a stool near one of the ovens and mixed a tea of several herbs taken from earthenware jars on a high shelf in the back of one of her pantries.

"Drink this," she instructed Doroon, handing him a steaming mug.

"Will it make my arm well?" Doroon asked, suspiciously eyeing the evil-smelling brew.

"Just drink it," she ordered, laying out some splints and linen strips.

"Ick! It tastes awful," Doroon said, making a face.

"It's supposed to," she told him. "Drink it all."

"I don't think I want any more," he said.

"Very well," she said. She pushed back the splints and took down a long, very sharp knife from a hook on the wall.

"What are you going to do with that?" he demanded shakily.

"Since you don't want to take the medicine," she said blandly, "I guess it'll have to come off."

"Off?" Doroon squeaked, his eyes bulging.

"Probably about right there," she said, thoughtfully touching his arm at the elbow with the point of the knife.

Tears coming to his eyes, Doroon gulped down the rest of the liquid and a few minutes later he was nodding, almost drowsing on his stool. He screamed once, though, when Aunt Pol set the broken bone, but after the arm had been wrapped and splinted, he drowsed again. Aunt Pol spoke briefly with the boy's frightened mother and then had Durnik carry him up to bed.

"You wouldn't really have cut off his arm," Garion said.

Aunt Pol looked at him, her expression unchanging.

"Oh?" she said, and he was no longer sure. "I think I'd like to have a word with Mistress Zubrette now," she said then.

"She ran away when Doroon fell out of the tree," Garion said.

"Find her."

"She's hiding," Garion protested. "She always hides when something goes wrong. I wouldn't know where to look for her."

"Garion," Aunt Pol said, "I didn't ask you if you knew where to look. I told you to find her and bring her to me."

"What if she won't come?" Garion hedged.

"Garion!" There was a note of awful finality in Aunt Pol's tone, and Garion fled.

"I didn't have anything to do with it," Zubrette lied as soon as Garion led her to Aunt Pol in the kitchen.

"You," Aunt Pol said, pointing at a stool, "sit!"

Zubrette sank onto the stool, her mouth open and her eyes wide.

"You," Aunt Pol said to Garion, pointing at the kitchen door, "out!"

Garion left hurriedly.

Ten minutes later a sobbing little girl stumbled out of the kitchen. Aunt Pol stood in the doorway looking after her with eyes as hard as ice.

"Did you thrash her?" Garion asked hopefully.

Aunt Pol withered him with a glance. "Of course not," she said. "You don't thrash girls."

"*I* would have," Garion said, disappointed. "What did you do to her?"

"Don't you have anything to do?" Aunt Pol asked.

"No," Garion said, "not really." That, of course, was a mistake.

"Good," Aunt Pol said, finding one of his ears. "It's time you started to earn your way. You'll find some dirty pots in the scullery. I'd like to have them scrubbed."

"I don't know why you're angry with me," Garion objected, squirming. "It wasn't my fault that Doroon went up that tree."

"The scullery, Garion," she said. "Now."

The rest of that spring and the early part of the summer were quiet. Doroon, of course, could not play until his arm mended, and Zubrette had been so shaken by whatever it was that Aunt Pol had said to her that she avoided the two other boys. Garion was left with only Rundorig to play with, and Rundorig was not bright enough to be much fun. Because there was really nothing else to do, the boys often went into the fields to watch the hands work and listen to their talk.

As it happened, during that particular summer the men on Faldor's farm were talking about the Battle of Vo Mimbre, the most cataclysmic event in the history of the west. Garion and Rundorig listened, enthralled, as the men unfolded the story of how the hordes of Kal Torak had quite suddenly struck into the west some five hundred years before.

It had all begun in 4865, as men reckoned time in that part of the world, when vast multitudes of Murgos and Nadraks and Thulls had struck down across the mountains of the eastern escarpment into Drasnia, and behind them in endless waves had come the uncountable numbers of the Malloreans.

After Drasnia had been brutally crushed, the Angaraks had turned southward onto the vast grasslands of Algaria and had laid siege to that enormous fortress called the Algarian Stronghold. The siege had lasted for eight years until finally, in disgust, Kal Torak had abandoned it. It was not until he turned his army westward into Ulgoland that the other kingdoms became aware that the Angarak invasion was directed not only against the Alorns but against all of the west. In the summer of 4875 Kal Torak had come down upon the Arendish plain before the city of Vo Mimbre, and it was there that the combined armies of the west awaited him.

The Sendars who participated in the battle were a part of the force under the leadership of Brand, the Rivan Warder. That force, consisting of Rivans, Sendars and Asturian Arends, assaulted the Angarak rear after the left had been engaged by Algars, Drasnians and Ulgos; the right by Tolnedrans and Chereks; and the front by the legendary charge of the Mimbrate Arends. For hours the battle had raged until, in the center of the field, Brand had met in a single combat with Kal Torak himself. Upon that duel had hinged the outcome of the battle.

Although twenty generations had passed since that titanic encounter, it was still as fresh in the memory of the Sendarian farmers who worked on Faldor's farm as if it had happened only yesterday. Each blow was described, and each feint and parry. At the final moment, when it seemed that he must inevitably be overthrown, Brand had removed the covering from his shield, and Kal Torak, taken aback by some momentary confusion, had lowered his guard and had been instantly struck down.

For Rundorig, the description of the battle was enough to set his Arendish blood seething. Garion, however, found that certain questions had been left unanswered by the stories.

"Why was Brand's shield covered?" he asked Cralto, one of the older hands.

Cralto shrugged. "It just was," he said. "Everyone I've ever talked with about it agrees on that."

"Was it a magic shield?" Garion persisted.

"It may have been," Cralto said, "but I've never heard anyone say so. All I know is that when Brand uncovered his shield, Kal Torak dropped his own shield, and Brand stabbed his sword into Kal Torak's head—through the eye, or so I am told."

Garion shook his head stubbornly. "I don't understand," he said. "How would something like that have made Kal Torak afraid?"

"I can't say," Cralto told him. "I've never heard anyone explain it."

Despite his dissatisfaction with the story, Garion quite quickly agreed to Rundorig's rather simple plan to re-enact the duel. After a day or so of posturing and banging at each other with sticks to simulate swords, Garion decided that they needed some equipment to make the game more enjoyable. Two kettles and two large pot lids mysteriously disappeared from Aunt Pol's kitchen; and Garion and Rundorig, now with helmets and shields, repaired to a quiet place to do war upon each other.

It was all going quite splendidly until Rundorig, who was older, taller and stronger, struck Garion a resounding whack on the head with his wooden sword. The rim of the kettle cut into Garion's eyebrow, and the blood began to flow. There was a sudden ringing in Garion's ears, and a kind of boiling exaltation surged up in his veins as he rose to his feet from the ground.

He never knew afterward quite what happened. He had only sketchy memories of shouting defiance at Kal Torak in words which sprang to his lips and which even he did not understand. Rundorig's familiar and somewhat foolish face was no longer the face before him but rather was replaced by something hideously maimed and ugly. In a fury Garion struck at that face again and again with fire seething in his brain.

And then it was over. Poor Rundorig lay at his feet, beaten senseless by the enraged attack. Garion was horrified at what he had done, but at the same time there was the fiery taste of victory in his mouth.

Later, in the kitchen, where all injuries on the farm were routinely taken, Aunt Pol tended their wounds with only minimal comments about them. Rundorig seemed not to be seriously hurt, though his face had begun to swell and turn purple in several places and he had difficulty focusing his eyes at first. A few cold cloths on his head and one of Aunt Pol's potions quickly restored him.

The cut on Garion's brow, however, required a bit more attention. She had Durnik hold the boy down and then she took needle and thread and sewed up the cut as calmly as she would have repaired a rip in a sleeve, all the while ignoring the howls from her patient. All in all, she seemed much more concerned about the dented kettles and battered pot lids than about the war wounds of the two boys.

When it was over, Garion had a headache and was taken up to bed.

"At least I beat Kal Torak," he told Aunt Pol somewhat drowsily.

She looked at him sharply. "Where did you hear about Torak?" she demanded.

"It's *Kal* Torak, Aunt Pol," Garion explained patiently.

"Answer me."

"The farmers were telling stories—old Cralto and the others—about Brand and Vo Mimbre and Kal Torak and all the rest. That's what Rundorig and I were playing. I was Brand and he was Kal Torak. I didn't get to uncover my shield, though. Rundorig hit me on the head before we got that far."

"I want you to listen to me, Garion," Aunt Pol said, "and I want you to listen carefully. You are never to speak the name of Torak again."

"It's *Kal* Torak, Aunt Pol," Garion explained again, "not just Torak."

Then she hit him—which she had never done before. The slap across his mouth surprised him more than it hurt, for she did not hit very hard. "You will *never* speak the name of Torak again. *Never!*" she said. "This is important, Garion. Your safety depends on it. I want your promise."

"You don't have to get so angry about it," he said in an injured tone.

"Promise."

"All right, I promise. It was only a game."

"A very foolish one," Aunt Pol said. "You might have killed Rundorig."

"What about *me?*" Garion protested.

"You were never in any danger," she told him. "Now go to sleep."

And as he dozed fitfully, his head light from his injury and the strange, bitter drink his aunt had given him, he seemed to hear her deep, rich voice saying, "Garion, my Garion, you're too young yet." And later, rising from deep sleep as a fish rises toward the silvery surface of the water, he seemed to hear her call, "Father, I need you." Then he plunged again into a troubled sleep, haunted by a dark figure of a man on a black horse who watched his every movement with a cold animosity and something that hovered very near the edge of fear; and behind that dark figure he had always known to be there but had never overtly acknowledged, even to Aunt Pol, the maimed and ugly face he had briefly seen or imagined in the fight with Rundorig loomed darkly, like the hideous fruit of an unspeakable evil tree.

Chapter Two

NOT LONG AFTER in the endless noon of Garion's boyhood, the storyteller appeared once again at the gate of Faldor's farm. The storyteller, who seemed not to have a proper name as other men do, was a thoroughly disreputable old man. The knees of his hose were patched and his mismatched shoes were out at the toes. His long-sleeved woolen tunic was belted about the waist with a piece of rope, and his hood, a curious garment not normally worn in that part of Sendaria and one which Garion thought quite fine with its loosely fitting yoke covering shoulders, back and chest, was spotted and soiled with spilled food and drink. Only his full cloak seemed relatively new. The old storyteller's white hair was cropped quite close, as was his beard. His face was strong, with a kind of angularity to it, and his features provided no clue to his background. He did not resemble Arend nor Cherek, Algar nor Drasnian, Rivan nor Tolnedran, but seemed rather to derive from some racial stock long since forgotten. His eyes were a deep and merry blue, forever young and forever full of mischief.

The storyteller appeared from time to time at Faldor's farm and was always welcome. He was in truth a rootless vagabond who made his way in the world by telling stories. His stories were not always new, but there was in his telling of them a special kind of magic. His voice could roll like thunder or hush down into a zepherlike whisper. He could imitate the voices of a dozen men at once; whistle so like a bird that the birds themselves would come to him to hear what he had to say; and when he imitated the howl of a wolf, the sound could raise the hair on the backs of his listeners' necks and strike a chill into their hearts like the depths of a Drasnian winter. He could make the sound of rain and of wind and even, most miraculously, the sound of snow falling. His stories were filled with sounds that made them come alive, and through the sounds and the words with which he wove the tales, sight and smell and the very *feel* of strange times and places seemed also to come to life for his spellbound listeners.

All of this wonder he gave freely in exchange for a few meals, a few tankards of ale, and a warm spot in the hay barn in which to sleep. He roamed about the world seemingly as free of possessions as the birds.

Between the storyteller and Aunt Pol there seemed to be a sort of hidden recognition. She had always viewed his coming with a kind of wry acceptance, knowing, it seemed, that the ultimate treasures of her kitchen were not safe so long as he lurked in the vicinity. Loaves and cakes had a way of disappearing when he was around, and his quick knife, always ready, could neatly divest the most carefully prepared goose of a pair of drumsticks and a generous slab of breast meat with three swift slices when her back was turned. She called him "Old Wolf," and his appearance at the gate of Faldor's farm marked the resumption of a contest which had obviously been going on for years. He flattered her outrageously even as he stole from her. Offered cookies or dark brown bread, he would politely refuse and then steal half a plateful before the platter had moved out of his reach. Her beer pantry and wine cellar might as well have been delivered into his hands immediately upon his appearance at the gate. He seemed to delight in pilferage, and if she watched him with steely eye, he found quite easily a dozen confederates willing to sack her kitchen in exchange for a single story.

Lamentably, among his most able pupils was the boy Garion. Often, driven to distraction by the necessity of watching at once an old thief and a fledgling one, Aunt Pol would arm herself with a broom and drive them both from her kitchen with hard words and resounding blows. And the old storyteller, laughing, would flee with the boy to some secluded place where they would feast on the fruits of their pilferage and the old man, tasting frequently from a flagon of stolen wine or beer, would regale his student with stories out of the dim past.

The best stories, of course, were saved for the dining

hall when, after the evening meal was over and the plates had been pushed back, the old man would rise from his place and carry his listeners off into a world of magical enchantment.

"Tell us of the beginnings, my old friend," Faldor, always pious, said one evening, "and of the Gods."

"Of the beginnings and the Gods," the old man mused. "A worthy subject, Faldor, but a dry and dusty one."

"I've noticed that you find all subjects dry and dusty, Old Wolf," Aunt Pol said, going to the barrel and drawing off a tankard of foamy beer for him.

He accepted the tankard with a stately bow. "It's one of the hazards of my profession, Mistress Pol," he explained. He drank deeply, then set the tankard aside. He lowered his head in thought for a moment, then looked directly, or so it seemed, at Garion. And then he did a strange thing which he had never before done when telling stories in Faldor's dining hall. He drew his cloak about him and rose to his full height.

"Behold," he said, his voice rich and sonorous, "at the beginning of days made the Gods the world and the seas and the dry land also. And cast they the stars across the night sky and did set the sun and his wife, the moon, in the heavens to give light unto the world.

"And the Gods caused the earth to bring forth the beasts, and the waters to bud with fish, and the skies to flower with birds.

"And they made men also, and divided men into Peoples.

"Now the Gods were seven in number and were all equal, and their names were Belar, and Chaldan, and Nedra, and Issa, and Mara, and Aldur, and Torak."

Garion knew the story, of course; everyone in that part of Sendaria was familiar with it, since the story was of Alorn origin and the lands on three sides of Sendaria were Alorn kingdoms. Though the tale was familiar, however, he had never before heard it told in such a way. His mind soared as in his imagination the Gods themselves strode the world in those dim, misty days when the world was first made, and a chill came over him at each mention of the forbidden name of Torak.

He listened intently as the storyteller described how each

God selected a people—for Belar the Alorns, for Issa the Nyissans, for Chaldan the Arends, for Nedra the Tolnedrans, for Mara the Marags which are no more, and for Torak the Angaraks. And he heard how the God Aldur dwelt apart and considered the stars in his solitude, and how some very few men he accepted as pupils and disciples.

Garion glanced at the others who were listening. Their faces were rapt with attention. Durnik's eyes were wide, and old Cralto's hands were clasped on the table in front of him. Faldor's face was pale, and tears stood in his eyes. Aunt Pol stood at the rear of the room. Though it was not cold, she too had drawn her mantle about her and stood very straight, her eyes intent.

"And it came to pass," the storyteller continued, "that the God Aldur caused to be made a jewel in the shape of a globe, and behold, in the jewel was captured the light of certain stars that did glitter in the northern sky. And great was the enchantment upon the jewel which men called the Orb of Aldur, for with the Orb could Aldur see that which had been, that which was, and that which was yet to be."

Garion realized he was holding his breath, for he was now completely caught up in the story. He listened in wonder as Torak stole the Orb and the other Gods made war on him. Torak used the Orb to sunder the earth and let in the sea to drown the land, until the Orb struck back against misuse by melting the left side of his face and destroying his left hand and eye.

The old man paused and drained his tankard. Aunt Pol, with her mantle still close about her, brought him another, her movements somehow stately and her eyes burning.

"I've never heard the story told so," Durnik said softly.

"It's *The Book of Alorn*.* It's only told in the presence of kings," Cralto said, just as softly. "I knew a man once who had heard it at the king's court at Sendar, and he remembered some of it. I've never heard it all before, though."

The story continued, recounting how Belgarath the Sor-

---

* Several shorter, less formal versions of the story existed, similar to the adaptation used here in the Prologue. Even *The Book of Alorn* was said to be an abridgment of a much older document.

cerer led Cherek and his three sons to regain the Orb two thousand years later, and how the western lands were settled and guarded against the hosts of Torak. The Gods removed from the world, leaving Riva to safeguard the Orb in his fortress on the Isle of the Winds. There he forged a great sword and set the Orb in its hilt. While the Orb remained there and the line of Riva sat on the throne, Torak could not prevail.

Then Belgarath sent his favorite daughter to Riva to be a mother to kings, while his other daughter remained with him and learned his art, for the mark of the sorcerers was upon her.

The old storyteller's voice was now very soft as his ancient tale drew to its close. "And between them," he said, "did Belgarath and his daughter, the Sorceress Polgara, set enchantments to keep watch against the coming of Torak. And some men say they shall abide against his coming even though it be until the very end of days, for it is prophesied that one day shall maimed Torak come against the kingdoms of the west to reclaim the Orb which he so dearly purchased, and battle shall be joined between Torak and the fruit of the line of Riva, and in that battle shall be decided the fate of the world."

And then the old man fell silent and let his mantle drop from about his shoulders, signifying that his story was at an end.

There was a long silence in the hall, broken only by a few faint cracks from the dying fire and the endless song of frogs and crickets in the summer night outside.

Finally Faldor cleared his throat and rose, his bench scraping loudly on the wooden floor. "You have done us much honor tonight, my old friend," he said, his voice thick with emotion. "This is an event we will remember all our lives. You have told us a kingly story, not usually wasted on ordinary people."

The old man grinned then, his blue eyes twinkling. "I haven't consorted with many kings of late, Faldor." He laughed. "They all seem to be too busy to listen to the old tales, and a story must be told from time to time if it is not to be lost—besides, who knows these days where a king might be hiding?"

They all laughed at that and began to push back their

benches, for it was growing late and time for those who must be up with the first light of the sun to seek their beds.

"Will you carry a lantern for me to the place where I sleep, boy?" the storyteller asked Garion.

"Gladly," Garion said, jumping up and running into the kitchen. He fetched down a square glass lantern, lighted the candle inside it from one of the banked kitchen fires, and went back into the dining hall.

Faldor was speaking with the storyteller. As he turned away, Garion saw a strange look pass between the old man and Aunt Pol, who still stood at the back of the hall.

"Are we ready then, boy?" the old man asked as Garion came up to him.

"Whenever you are," Garion replied, and the two of them turned and left the hall.

"Why is the story unfinished?" Garion asked, bursting with curiosity. "Why did you stop before we found out what happened when Torak met the Rivan King?"

"That's another story," the old man explained.

"Will you tell it to me sometime?" Garion pressed.

The old man laughed. "Torak and the Rivan King have not as yet met," he said, "so I can't very well tell it, can I?—at least not until after their meeting."

"It's *only* a story," Garion objected. "Isn't it?"

"Is it?" The old man removed a flagon of wine from under his tunic and took a long drink. "Who is to say what is only a story and what is truth disguised as a story?"

"It's only a story," Garion said stubbornly, suddenly feeling very hardheaded and practical like any good Sendar. "It can't really be true. Why, Belgarath the Sorcerer would be—would be I don't know how old—and people don't live that long."

"Seven thousand years," the old man said.

"What?"

"Belgarath the Sorcerer is seven thousand years old—perhaps a bit older."

"That's impossible," Garion said.

"Is it? How old are you?"

"Nine—next Erastide."

"And in nine years you've learned everything that's both possible and impossible? You're a remarkable boy, Garion."

Garion flushed. "Well," he said, somehow not quite so

sure of himself, "the oldest man I ever heard of is old Weldrik over on Mildrin's farm. Durnik says he's over ninety and that he's the oldest man in the district."

"And it's a very big district, of course," the old man said solemnly.

"How old are you?" Garion asked, not wanting to give up.

"Old enough, boy," the old man said.

"It's still only a story," Garion insisted.

"Many good and solid men would say so," the old man told him, looking up at the stars, "—good men who will live out their lives believing only in what they can see and touch. But there's a world beyond what we can see and touch, and that world lives by its own laws. What may be impossible in this very ordinary world is very possible there, and sometimes the boundaries between the two worlds disappear, and then who can say what is possible and impossible?"

"I think I'd rather live in the ordinary world," Garion said. "The other one sounds too complicated."

"We don't always have that choice, Garion," the story-teller told him. "Don't be too surprised if that other world someday chooses you to do something that must be done— some great and noble thing."

"Me?" Garion said incredulously.

"Stranger things have happened. Go to bed, boy. I think I'll look at the stars for a while. The stars and I are very old friends."

"The stars?" Garion asked, looking up involuntarily. "You're a very strange old man—if you don't mind my saying so."

"Indeed," the storyteller agreed. "Quite the strangest you'll likely meet."

"I like you all the same," Garion said quickly, not wanting to give offense.

"That's a comfort, boy," the old man said. "Now go to bed. Your Aunt Pol will be worried about you."

Later, as he slept, Garion's dreams were troubled. The dark figure of maimed Torak loomed in the shadows, and monstrous things pursued him across twisted landscapes where the possible and the impossible merged and joined as that other world reached out to claim him.

Chapter Three

SOME FEW MORNINGS later, when Aunt Pol had begun to scowl at his continued lurking in her kitchen, the old man made excuse of some errand to the nearby village of Upper Gralt.

"Good," Aunt Pol said, somewhat ungraciously. "At least my pantries will be safe while you're gone."

He bowed mockingly, his eyes twinkling. "Do you need anything, Mistress Pol?" he asked. "Some trifling thing I might purchase for you—as long as I'm going anyway?"

Aunt Pol thought a moment. "Some of my spice pots are a bit low," she said, "and there's a Tolnedran spice merchant in Fennel Lane just south of the Town Tavern. I'm sure you'll have no trouble finding the tavern."

"The trip is likely to be dry," the old man admitted pleasantly. "And lonely, too. Ten leagues with no one to talk to is a long way."

"Talk to the birds," Aunt Pol suggested bluntly.

"Birds listen well enough," the old man said, "but their speech is repetitious and quickly grows tiresome. Why don't I take the boy along for company?"

Garion held his breath.

"He's picking up enough bad habits on his own," Aunt Pol said tartly. "I'd prefer his not having expert instruction."

"Why, Mistress Pol," the old man objected, stealing a cruller almost absently, "you do me an injustice. Besides, a change will do the boy good—broaden his horizons, you might say."

"His horizons are quite broad enough, thank you," she said.

Garion's heart sank.

"Still," she continued, "at least I can count on him not to

32

forget my spices altogether or to become so fuddled with ale that he confuses peppercorns with cloves or cinnamon with nutmeg. Very well, take the boy along; but mind, I don't want you taking him into any low or disreputable places."

"Mistress Pol!" the old man said, feigning shock. "Would I frequent such places?"

"I know you too well, Old Wolf," she said dryly. "You take to vice and corruption as naturally as a duck takes to a pond. If I hear that you've taken the boy into any un-savory place, you and I will have words."

"Then I'll have to make sure that you don't hear of any-thing like that, won't I?"

Aunt Pol gave him a hard look. "I'll see which spices I need," she said.

"And I'll borrow a horse and cart from Faldor," the old man said, stealing another cruller.

In a surprisingly short time, Garion and the old man were bouncing along the rutted road to Upper Gralt behind a fast-trotting horse. It was a bright summer morning, and there were a few dandelion-puff clouds in the sky and deep blue shadows under the hedgerows. After a few hours, however, the sun became hot, and the jolting ride became tiresome. "Are we almost there?" Garion asked for the third time.

"Not for some time yet," the old man said. "Ten leagues is a goodly distance."

"I was there once before," Garion told him, trying to sound casual. "Of course I was only a child at the time, so I don't remember too much about it. It seemed to be quite a fine place."

The old man shrugged. "It's a village," he said, "much like any other." He seemed a bit preoccupied.

Garion, hoping to nudge the old man into a story to make the miles go faster, began asking questions.

"Why is it that you have no name—if I'm not being im-polite in asking?"

"I have many names," the old man said, scratching his white beard. "Almost as many names as I have years."

"I've only got one," Garion said.

"So far."

"What?"

"You only have one name so far," the old man explained. "In time you may get another—or even several. Some people collect names as they go along through their lives. Sometimes names wear out—just like clothes."

"Aunt Pol calls you Old Wolf," Garion said.

"I know," the old man said. "Your Aunt Pol and I have known each other for a very long time."

"Why does she call you that?"

"Who can say why a woman such as your Aunt does anything?"

"May I call you Mister Wolf?" Garion asked. Names were quite important to Garion, and the fact that the old storyteller did not seem to have one had always bothered him. That namelessness had made the old man seem somehow incomplete, unfinished.

The old man looked at him soberly for a moment, and then he burst out laughing. "Mister Wolf indeed. How very appropriate. I think I like that name better than any I've had in years."

"May I then?" Garion asked. "Call you Mister Wolf, I mean?"

"I think I'd like that, Garion. I think I'd like that very much."

"Now would you *please* tell me a story, Mister Wolf?" Garion asked.

The time and distance went by much faster then as Mister Wolf wove for Garion tales of glorious adventure and dark treachery taken from those gloomy, unending centuries of the Arendish civil wars.

"Why are the Arends like that?" Garion asked after a particularly grim tale.

"The Arends are very noble," Wolf said, lounging back in the seat of the cart with the reins held negligently in one hand. "Nobility is a trait that's not always trustworthy, since it sometimes causes men to do things for obscure reasons."

"Rundorig is an Arend," Garion said. "He sometimes seems to be—well, not too quick of thought, if you know what I mean."

"It's the effect of all that nobility," Wolf said. "Arends spend so much time concentrating on being noble that they don't have time to think of other things."

They came over the crest of a long hill, and there in the next valley lay the village of Upper Gralt. To Garion the tiny cluster of gray stone houses with slate roofs seemed disappointingly small. Two roads, white with thick dust, intersected there, and there were a few narrow, winding streets besides. The houses were square and solid, but seemed almost like toys set down in the valley below. The horizon beyond was ragged with the mountains of eastern Sendaria, and, though it was summer, the tops of most of the mountains were still wrapped in snow.

Their tired horse plodded down the hill toward the village, his hooves stirring little clouds of dust with each step, and soon they were clattering along the cobblestoned streets toward the center of the village. The villagers, of course, were all too important to pay any attention to an old man and a small boy in a farm cart. The women wore gowns and high-pointed hats, and the men wore doublets and soft velvet caps. Their expressions seemed haughty, and they looked with obvious disdain at the few farmers in town who respectfully stood aside to let them pass.

"They're very fine, aren't they?" Garion observed.

"They seem to think so," Wolf said, his expression faintly amused. "I think it's time that we found something to eat, don't you?"

Though he had not realized it until the old man mentioned it, Garion was suddenly ravenous. "Where will we go?" he asked. "They all seem so splendid. Would any of them let strangers sit at their tables?"

Wolf laughed and shook a jingling purse at his waist. "We should have no trouble making acquaintances," he said. "There are places where one may buy food."

Buy food? Garion had never heard of such a thing before. Anyone who appeared at Faldor's gate at mealtime was invited to the table as a matter of course. The world of the villagers was obviously very different from the world of Faldor's farm. "But I don't have any money," he objected.

"I've enough for us both," Wolf assured him, stopping their horse before a large, low building with a sign bearing a picture of a cluster of grapes hanging just above its door. There were words on the sign, but of course Garion could not read them.

"What do the words say, Mister Wolf?" he asked.

"They say that food and drink may be bought inside," Wolf told him, getting down from the cart.

"It must be a fine thing to be able to read," Garion said wistfully.

The old man looked at him, seemingly surprised. "You can't read, boy?" he asked incredulously.

"I've never found anyone to teach me," Garion said. "Faldor reads, I think, but no one else at the farm knows how."

"Nonsense," Wolf snorted. "I'll speak to your Aunt about it. She's been neglecting her responsibility. She should have taught you years ago."

"Can Aunt Pol read?" Garion asked, stunned.

"Of course she can," Wolf said, leading the way into the tavern. "She says she finds little advantage in it, but she and I had that particular argument out many years ago." The old man seemed quite upset by Garion's lack of education.

Garion, however, was far too interested in the smoky interior of the tavern to pay much attention. The room was large and dark with a low, beamed ceiling and a stone floor strewn with rushes. Though it was not cold, a fire burned in a stone pit in the center of the room, and the smoke rose errantly toward a chimney set above it on four square stone pillars. Tallow candles guttered in clay dishes on several of the long, stained tables, and there was a reek of wine and stale beer in the air.

"What have you to eat?" Wolf demanded of a sour, unshaven man wearing a grease-spotted apron.

"We've a bit of a joint left," the man said, pointing at a spit resting to one side of the fire pit. "Roasted only day before yesterday. And meat porridge fresh yesterday morning, and bread no more than a week old."

"Very well," Wolf said, sitting down. "And I'll have a pot of your best ale and milk for the boy."

"Milk?" Garion protested.

"Milk," Wolf said firmly.

"You have money?" the sour-looking man demanded.

Wolf jingled his purse, and the sour man looked suddenly less sour.

"Why is that man over there sleeping?" Garion asked, pointing at a snoring villager sitting with his head down on one of the tables.

"Drunk," Wolf said, scarcely glancing at the snoring man.

"Shouldn't someone take care of him?"

"He'd rather not be taken care of."

"Do you know him?"

"I know of him," Wolf said, "and many others like him. I've occasionally been in that condition myself."

"Why?"

"It seemed appropriate at the time."

The roast was dry and overdone, the meat porridge was thin and watery, and the bread was stale, but Garion was too hungry to notice. He carefully cleaned his plate as he had been taught, then sat as Mister Wolf lingered over a second pot of ale.

"Quite splendid," he said, more to be saying something than out of any real conviction. All in all he found that Upper Gralt did not live up to his expectations.

"Adequate." Wolf shrugged. "Village taverns are much the same the world over. I've seldom seen one I'd hurry to revisit. Shall we go?" He laid down a few coins, which the sour-looking man snatched up quickly, and led Garion back out into the afternoon sunlight.

"Let's find your Aunt's spice merchant," he said, "and then see to a night's lodging—and a stable for our horse." They set off down the street, leaving horse and cart beside the tavern.

The house of the Tolnedran spice merchant was a tall, narrow building in the next street. Two swarthy, thick-bodied men in short tunics lounged in the street at his front door near a fierce-looking black horse wearing a curious armored saddle. The two men stared with dull-eyed disinterest at passers-by in the lane.

Mister Wolf stopped when he caught sight of them.

"Is something wrong?" Garion asked.

"Thulls," Wolf said quietly, looking hard at the two men.

"What?"

"Those two are Thulls," the old man said. "They usually work as porters for the Murgos."

"What are Murgos?"

"The people of Cthol Murgos," Wolf said shortly. "Southern Angaraks."

"The ones we beat at the battle of Vo Mimbre?" Garion asked. "Why would they be here?"

"The Murgos have taken up commerce," Wolf said, frowning. "I hadn't expected to see one of them in so remote a village. We may as well go in. The Thulls have seen us, and it might look strange if we turned now and went back. Stay close to me, boy, and don't say anything."

They walked past the two heavyset men and entered the spice merchant's shop.

The Tolnedran was a thin, baldheaded man wearing a brown, belted gown that reached to the floor. He was nervously weighing several packets of pungent-smelling powder which lay on the counter before him.

"Good day to you," he said to Wolf. "Please have patience. I'll be with you shortly." He spoke with a slight lisp that Garion found peculiar.

"No hurry," Wolf said in a wheezy, cracking voice. Garion looked at him sharply and was astonished to see that his friend was stooped and that his head was nodding foolishly.

"See to their needs," the other man in the shop said shortly. He was a dark, burly man wearing a chain-mail shirt and a short sword belted to his waist. His cheekbones were high, and there were several savage-looking scars on his face. His eyes looked curiously angular, and his voice was harsh and thickly accented.

"No hurry," Wolf said in his wheezy cackle.

"My business here will take some time," the Murgo said coldly, "and I prefer not to be rushed. Tell the merchant here what you need, old man."

"My thanks, then," Wolf cackled. "I have a list somewhere about me." He began to fumble foolishly in his pockets. "My master drew it up. I do hope you can read it, friend merchant, for I cannot." He finally found the list and presented it to the Tolnedran.

The merchant glanced at the list. "This will only take a moment," he told the Murgo.

The Murgo nodded and stood staring stonily at Wolf and Garion. His eyes narrowed slightly, and his expression changed. "You're a seemly appearing boy," he said to Garion. "What's your name?"

Until that moment, in his entire life, Garion had been an honest and truthful boy, but Wolf's manner had opened before his eyes an entire world of deception and subterfuge. Somewhere in the back of his mind he seemed to hear a warning voice, a dry, calm voice advising him that the situation was dangerous and that he should take steps to protect himself. He hesitated only an instant before telling his first deliberate lie. He allowed his mouth to drop open and his face to assume an expression of vacant-headed stupidity. "Rundorig, your Honor," he mumbled.

"An Arendish name," the Murgo said, his eyes narrowing even more. "You don't look like an Arend."

Garion gaped at him.

"Are you an Arend, Rundorig?" the Murgo pressed.

Garion frowned as if struggling with a thought while his mind raced. The dry voice suggested several alternatives.

"My father was," he said finally, "but my mother is a Sendar, and people say I favor her."

"You say *was*," the Murgo said quickly. "Is your father dead, then?" His scarred face was intent.

Garion nodded foolishly. "A tree he was cutting fell on him," he lied. "It was a long time ago."

The Murgo suddenly seemed to lose interest. "Here's a copper penny for you, boy," he said, indifferently tossing a small coin on the floor at Garion's feet. "It has the likeness of the God Torak stamped on it. Perhaps it will bring you luck—or at least more wit."

Wolf stooped quickly and retrieved the coin, but the coin he handed to Garion was a common Sendarian penny.

"Thank the good man, Rundorig," he wheezed.

"My thanks, your Honor," Garion said, concealing the penny tightly in his fist.

The Murgo shrugged and looked away.

Wolf paid the Tolnedran merchant for the spices, and he and Garion left the shop.

"You played a dangerous game, boy," Wolf said once they were out of earshot of the two lounging Thulls.

"You seemed not to want him to know who we were," Garion explained. "I wasn't sure why, but I thought I ought to do the same. Was what I did wrong?"

"You're very quick," Wolf said approvingly. "I think we managed to deceive the Murgo."

"Why did you change the coin?" Garion asked.

"Sometimes Angarak coins are not what they seem," Wolf said. "It's better for you not to have any of. them. Let's fetch our horse and cart. It's a long way back to Faldor's farm."

"I thought we were going to take lodgings for the night."

"That's changed now. Come along, boy. It's time for us to leave."

The horse was very tired, and he moved slowly up the long hill out of Upper Gralt as the sun went down ahead of them.

"Why wouldn't you let me keep the Angarak penny, Mister Wolf?" Garion persisted. The subject still puzzled him.

"There are many things in this world that seem to be one thing and are in fact another," Wolf said somewhat grimly. "I don't trust Angaraks, and I particularly don't trust Murgos. It would be just as well, I think, if you never had in your possession anything that bears the likeness of Torak."

"But the war between the west and the Angaraks has been over for five hundred years now," Garion objected. "All men say so."

"Not all men," Wolf said. "Now take that robe out of the back of the cart and cover up. Your Aunt would never forgive me if you should take a chill."

"I will if you think I should," Garion said, "but I'm not a bit cold and not at all sleepy. I'll keep you company as we go."

"That'll be a comfort, boy," Wolf said.

"Mister Wolf," Garion said after some time, "did you know my mother and father?"

"Yes," Wolf said quietly.

"My father's dead too, isn't he?"

"I'm afraid so."

Garion sighed deeply. "I thought so," he said. "I wish I'd known them. Aunt Pol says I was only a baby when—" He couldn't bring himself to say it. "I've tried to remember my mother, but I can't."

"You were very small," Wolf said.

"What were they like?" Garion asked.

Wolf scratched at his beard. "Ordinary," he said. "So ordinary you wouldn't look twice at either one of them."

Garion was offended by that. "Aunt Pol says my mother was very beautiful," he objected.

"She was."

"Then how can you say she was ordinary?"

"She wasn't prominent or important," Wolf said. "Neither was your father. Anyone who saw them thought that they were just simple village people—a young man with a young wife and their baby—that's all anyone ever saw. That's all anyone was ever supposed to see."

"I don't understand."

"It's very complicated."

"What was my father like?"

"Medium size," Wolf said. "Dark hair. A very serious young man. I liked him."

"Did he love my mother?"

"More than anything."

"And me?"

"Of course."

"What kind of place did they live in?"

"It was a small place," Wolf said, "a little village near the mountains, a long way from any main roads. They had a cottage at the end of the street. It was a small, solid little house. Your father built it himself—he was a stonecutter. I used to stop by there once in a while when I was in the neighborhood." The old man's voice droned on, describing the village and the house and the two who lived there. Garion listened, not even realizing it when he fell asleep.

It must have been very late, almost on toward dawn. In a half drowse, the boy felt himself lifted from the cart and carried up a flight of stairs. The old man was surprisingly strong. Aunt Pol was there—he knew that without even opening his eyes. There was a particular scent about her that he could have found in a dark room.

"Just cover him up," Mister Wolf said softly to Aunt Pol. "Best not to wake him just now."

"What happened?" Aunt Pol asked, her voice as soft as the old man's.

"There was a Murgo in town—at your spice merchant's. He asked questions and he tried to give the boy an Angarak penny."

"In Upper Gralt? Are you certain he was only a Murgo?"

"It's impossible to tell. Not even I can distinguish between Murgo and Grolim with any certainty."

"What happened to the coin?"

"I was quick enough to get it. I gave the boy a Sendarian penny instead. If our Murgo was a Grolim, we'll let him follow me. I'm sure I can give him several months of entertainment."

"You'll be leaving, then?" Aunt Pol's voice seemed somehow sad.

"It's time," Wolf said. "Right now the boy is safe enough here, and I must be abroad. There are things afoot I must see to. When Murgos begin to appear in remote places, I begin to worry. We have a great responsibility and a great care placed upon us, and we mustn't allow ourselves to become careless."

"Will you be gone long?" Aunt Pol asked.

"Some years, I expect. There are many things I must look into and many people I'll have to see."

"I'll miss you," Aunt Pol said softly.

He laughed. "Sentimentality, Pol?" he said dryly. "That's hardly in character."

"You know what I mean. I'm not suited for this task you and the others have given me. What do I know about the raising of small boys?"

"You're doing well," Wolf said. "Keep the boy close, and don't let his nature drive you into hysterics. Be careful; he lies like a champion."

"Garion?" Her voice was shocked.

"He lied to the Murgo so well that even I was impressed."

"Garion?"

"He's also started asking questions about his parents," Wolf said. "How much have you told him?"

"Very little. Only that they're dead."

"Let's leave it at that for now. There's no point in telling him things he isn't old enough to cope with yet."

Their voices went on, but Garion drifted off into sleep again, and he was almost sure that it was all a dream.

But the next morning when he awoke, Mister Wolf was gone.

Chapter Four

THE SEASONS TURNED, as seasons will. Summer ripened into autumn; the blaze of autumn died into winter; winter grudgingly relented to the urgency of spring; and spring bloomed into summer again. With the turning of the seasons the years turned, and Garion imperceptibly grew older.

As he grew, the other children grew as well—all except poor Doroon, who seemed doomed to be short and skinny all his life. Rundorig sprouted like a young tree and was soon almost as big as any man on the farm. Zubrette, of course, did not grow so tall, but she developed in other ways which the boys began to find interesting.

In the early autumn just before Garion's fourteenth birthday, he came very close to ending his career. In response to some primal urge all children have—given a pond and a handy supply of logs—they had built a raft that summer. The raft was neither very large nor was it particularly well-built. It had a tendency to sink on one end if the weight aboard it were improperly distributed and an alarming habit of coming apart at unexpected moments.

Quite naturally it was Garion who was aboard the raft—showing off—on that fine autumn day when the raft quite suddenly decided once and for all to revert to its original state. The bindings all came undone, and the logs began to go their separate ways.

Realizing his danger only at the last moment, Garion made a desperate effort to pole for shore, but his haste only made the disintegration of his craft more rapid. In the end he found himself standing on a single log, his arms windmilling wildly in a futile effort to retain his balance. His eyes, desperately searching for some aid, swept the marshy shore. Some distance up the slope behind his play-

mates he saw the familiar figure of the man on the black
horse. The man wore a dark robe, and his burning eyes
watched the boy's plight. Then the spiteful log rolled under
Garion's feet, and he toppled and fell with a resounding
splash.

Garion's education, unfortunately, had not included instruction in the art of swimming; and while the water was
not really very deep, it was deep enough.

The bottom of the pond was very unpleasant, a kind of
dark, weedy ooze inhabited by frogs, turtles and a singu-
larly unsavory-looking eel that slithered away snakelike
when Garion plunged like a sinking rock into the weeds.
Garion struggled, gulped water and launched himself with
his legs toward the surface again. Like a broaching whale,
he rose from the depths, gasped a couple of quick, sputter-
ing breaths and heard the screams of his playmates. The
dark figure on the slope had not moved, and for a single
instant every detail of that bright afternoon was etched on
Garion's mind. He even observed that, although the rider
was in the open under the full glare of the autumn sun,
neither man nor horse cast any shadow. Even as his mind
grappled with that impossibility, he sank once more to the
murky bottom.

It occurred to him as he struggled, drowning, amongst
the weeds that if he could launch himself up in the vicinity
of the log, he might catch hold of it and so remain afloat.
He waved off a startled-looking frog and plunged upward
again. He came up, unfortunately, directly under the log.
The blow on the top of his head filled his eyes with light
and his ears with a roaring sound, and he sank, no longer
struggling, back toward the weeds which seemed to reach
up for him.

And then Durnik was there. Garion felt himself lifted
roughly by the hair toward the surface and then towed by
that same convenient handle toward shore behind Durnik's
powerfully churning strokes. The smith pulled the semi-
conscious boy out onto the bank, turned him over and
stepped on him several times to force the water out of his
lungs.

Garion's ribs creaked. "Enough, Durnik," he gasped finally. He sat up, and the blood from the splendid cut on
top of his head immediately ran into his eyes. He wiped the

blood clear and looked around for the dark, shadowless rider, but the figure had vanished. He tried to get up, but the world suddenly spun around him, and he fainted.

When he awoke, he was in his own bed with his head wrapped in bandages.

Aunt Pol stood beside his bed, her eyes blazing. "You stupid boy!" she cried. "What were you doing in that pond?"

"Rafting," Garion said, trying to make it sound quite ordinary.

"Rafting?" she said. "*Rafting?* Who gave you permission?"

"Well—" he said uncertainly. "We just—"

"You just what?"

He looked at her helplessly.

And then with a low cry she took him in her arms and crushed him to her almost suffocatingly.

Briefly Garion considered telling her about the strange, shadowless figure that had watched his struggles in the pond, but the dry voice in his mind that sometimes spoke to him told him that this was not the time for that. He seemed to know somehow that the business between him and the man on the black horse was something very private, and that the time would inevitably come when they would face each other in some kind of contest of will or deed. To speak of it now to Aunt Pol would involve her in the matter, and he did not want that. He was not sure exactly why, but he did know that the dark figure was an enemy, and though that thought was a bit frightening, it was also exciting. There was no question that Aunt Pol could deal with this stranger, but if she did, Garion knew that he would lose something very personal and for some reason very important. And so he said nothing.

"It really wasn't anything all that dangerous, Aunt Pol," he said instead, rather lamely. "I was starting to get the idea of how to swim. I'd have been all right if I hadn't hit my head on that log."

"But of course you *did* hit your head," she pointed out.

"Well, yes, but it wasn't that serious. I'd have been all right in a minute or two."

"Under the circumstances I'm not sure you *had* a minute or two," she said bluntly.

"Well—" he faltered, and then decided to let it drop.

That marked the end of Garion's freedom. Aunt Pol confined him to the scullery. He grew to know every dent and scratch on every pot in the kitchen intimately. He once estimated gloomily that he washed each one twenty-one times a week. In a seeming orgy of messiness, Aunt Pol suddenly could not even boil water without dirtying at least three or four pans, and Garion had to scrub every one. He hated it and began to think quite seriously of running away.

As autumn progressed and the weather began to deteriorate, the other children were also more or less confined to the compound as well, and it wasn't so bad. Rundorig, of course, was seldom with them anymore since his man's size had made him—even more than Garion—subject to more and more frequent labor.

When he could, Garion slipped away to be with Zubrette and Doroon, but they no longer found much entertainment in leaping into the hay or in the endless games of tag in the stables and barns. They had reached an age and size where adults rather quickly noticed such idleness and found tasks to occupy them. Most often they would sit in some out of the way place and simply talk—which is to say that Garion and Zubrette would sit and listen to the endless flow of Doroon's chatter. That small, quick boy, as unable to be quiet as he was to sit still, could seemingly talk for hours about a half-dozen raindrops, and his words tumbled out breathlessly as he fidgeted.

"What's that mark on your hand, Garion?" Zubrette asked one rainy day, interrupting Doroon's bubbling voice.

Garion looked at the perfectly round, white patch on the palm of his right hand.

"I've noticed it too," Doroon said, quickly changing subjects in midsentence. "But Garion grew up in the kitchen, didn't you, Garion? It's probably a place where he burned himself when he was little—you know, reached out before anyone could stop him and put his hand on something hot. I'll bet his Aunt Pol really got angry about that, because she can get angrier faster than anybody else I've ever seen, and she can really—"

"It's always been there," Garion said, tracing the mark on his palm with his left forefinger. He had never really looked closely at it before. It covered the entire palm of his hand and had in certain light a faint silvery sheen.

"Maybe it's a birthmark," Zubrette suggested.

"I'll bet that's it," Doroon said quickly. "I saw a man once that had a big purple one on the side of his face—one of those wagoneers that comes by to pick up the turnip crop in the fall—anyway, the mark was all over the side of his face, and I thought it was a big bruise at first and thought that he must have been in an awful fight—those wagoneers fight all the time—but then I saw that it wasn't really a bruise but—like Zubrette just said—it was a birthmark. I wonder what causes things like that."

That evening, after he'd gotten ready for bed, he asked his Aunt about it. "What's this mark, Aunt Pol?" he asked, holding his hand up, palm out.

She looked up from where she was brushing her long, dark hair. "It's nothing to worry about," she told him.

"I wasn't worried about it," he said. "I just wondered what it was. Zubrette and Doroon think it's a birthmark. Is that what it is?"

"Something like that," she said.

"Did either of my parents have the same kind of mark?"

"Your father did. It's been in the family for a long time."

A sudden strange thought occurred to Garion. Without knowing why, he reached out with the hand and touched the white lock at his Aunt's brow. "Is it like that white place in your hair?" he asked.

He felt a sudden tingle in his hand, and it seemed somehow that a window opened in his mind. At first there was only the sense of uncountable years moving by like a vast sea of ponderously rolling clouds, and then, sharper than any knife, a feeling of endlessly repeated loss, of sorrow. Then, more recent, there was his own face, and behind it more faces, old, young, regal or quite ordinary, and behind them all, no longer foolish as it sometimes seemed, the face of Mister Wolf. But more than anything there was a knowledge of an unearthly, inhuman power, the certainty of an unconquerable will.

Aunt Pol moved her head away almost absently. "Don't do that, Garion," she said, and the window in his mind shut.

"What was it?" he asked, burning with curiosity and wanting to open the window again.

"A simple trick," she said.

"Show me how."

"Not yet, my Garion," she said, taking his face between her hands. "Not yet. You're not ready yet. Now go to bed."

"You'll be here?" he asked, a little frightened now.

"I'll always be here," she said, tucking him in. And then she went back to brushing her long, thick hair, humming a strange song as she did in a deep, melodious voice; to that sound he fell asleep.

After that not even Garion himself saw the mark on his own palm very often. There suddenly seemed to be all kinds of dirty jobs for him to do which kept not only his hands, but the rest of him as well, very dirty.

The most important holiday in Sendaria—and indeed in the rest of the kingdoms of the west—was Erastide. It commemorated that day, eons before, when the seven Gods joined hands to create the world with a single word. The festival of Erastide took place in midwinter, and, because there was little to do on a farm like Faldor's at that season, it had by custom become a splendid two-week celebration with feasts and gifts and decorations in the dining hall and little pageants honoring the Gods. These last, of course, were a reflection of Faldor's piety. Faldor, though he was a good, simple man, had no illusions about how widely his sentiments were shared by others on the farm. He thought, however, that some outward show of devotional activity was in keeping with the season; and, because he was such a good master, the people on his farm chose to humor him.

It was also at this season, unfortunately, that Faldor's married daughter, Anhelda, and her husband, Eilbrig, made their customary annual visit to remain on speaking terms with her father. Anhelda had no intention of endangering her inheritance rights by seeming inattention. Her visits, however, were a trial to Faldor, who looked upon his daughter's somewhat overdressed and supercilious husband, a minor functionary in a commercial house in the capital city of Sendar, with scarcely concealed contempt.

Their arrival, however, marked the beginning of the Erastide festival at Faldor's farm; so, while no one cared for them personally, their appearance was always greeted with a certain enthusiasm.

The weather that year had been particularly foul—even for Sendaria. The rains had settled in early and were soon followed by a period of soggy snow—not the crisp, bright powder which came later in the winter, but a damp slush, always half-melting. For Garion, whose duties in the kitchen now prevented him from joining with his former playmates in their traditional preholiday orgy of anticipatory excitement, the approaching holiday seemed somehow flat and stale. He yearned back to the good old days and often sighed with regret and moped about the kitchen like a sandy-haired cloud of doom.

Even the traditional decorations in the dining hall, where Erastide festivities always took place, seemed decidedly tacky to him that year. The fir boughs festooning the ceiling beams were somehow not as green, and the polished apples carefully tied to the boughs were smaller and not as red. He sighed some more and reveled in his sullen moping.

Aunt Pol, however, was not impressed, and her attitude was firmly unsympathetic. She routinely checked his brow with her hand for signs of fever and then dosed him with the foulest-tasting tonic she could concoct. Garion was careful after that to mope in private and to sigh less audibly. That dry, secret part of his mind informed him matter-of-factly that he was being ridiculous, but Garion chose not to listen. The voice in his mind was much older and wiser than he, but it seemed determined to take all the fun out of life.

On the morning of Erastide, a Murgo and five Thulls appeared with a wagon outside the gate and asked to see Faldor. Garion, who had long since learned that no one pays attention to a boy and that many interesting things may be learned by placing himself in a position to casually overhear conversations, busied himself with some small, unimportant chore near the gate.

The Murgo, his face scarred much like the face of the one in Upper Gralt, sat importantly on the wagon seat, his chain-mail shirt clinking each time he moved. He wore a black, hooded robe, and his sword was much in evidence.

His eyes moved constantly, taking in everything. The Thulls, in muddy felt boots and heavy cloaks, lounged disinterestedly against the wagon, seemingly indifferent to the raw wind whipping across the snowy fields.

Faldor, in his finest doublet—it was after all Erastide— came across the yard, closely followed by Anhelda and Eilbrig.

"Good morrow, friend," Faldor said to the Murgo. "Joyous Erastide to you."

The Murgo grunted. "You are, I take it, the farmer Faldor?" he asked in his heavily accented voice.

"I am," Faldor replied.

"I understand you have a goodly number of hams on hand—well cured."

"The pigs did well this year," Faldor answered modestly.

"I will buy them," the Murgo announced, jingling his purse.

Faldor bowed. "First thing tomorrow morning," he said.

The Murgo stared.

"This is a pious household," Faldor explained. "We do not offend the Gods by breaking the sanctity of Erastide."

"Father," Anhelda snapped, "don't be foolish. This noble merchant has come a long way to do business."

"Not on Erastide," Faldor said stubbornly, his long face firm.

"In the city of Sendar," Eilbrig said in his rather high-pitched, nasal voice, "we do not let such sentimentality interfere with business."

"This is not the city of Sendar," Faldor said flatly. "This is Faldor's farm, and on Faldor's farm we do no work and conduct no business on Erastide."

"Father," Anhelda protested, "the noble merchant has gold. Gold, father, *gold!*"

"I will hear no more of it," Faldor announced. He turned to the Murgo. "You and your servants are welcome to join us in our celebration, friend," he said. "We can provide quarters for you and the promise of the finest dinner in all of Sendaria and the opportunity to honor the Gods on this special day. No man is made poorer by attending to his religious obligations."

"We do not observe this holiday in Cthol Murgos," the scar-faced man said coldly. "As the noble lady says, I have come a long way to do business and have not much time to tarry. I'm sure there are other farmers in the district with the merchandise I require."

"*Father!*" Anhelda wailed.

"I know my neighbors," Faldor said quietly. "Your luck today will be small, I fear. The observance of this day is a firm tradition in this area."

The Murgo thought for a moment. "It may be as you say," he said finally. "I will accept your invitation, provided that we can do business as early as possible tomorrow."

Faldor bowed. "I'll place myself at your service at first light tomorrow if you so desire."

"Done, then," the Murgo said, climbing down from his wagon.

That afternoon the feast was laid in the dining hall. The kitchen helpers and a half-dozen others who had been pressed into service for the special day scurried from kitchen to hall bearing smoking roasts, steaming hams and sizzling geese all under the lash of Aunt Pol's tongue. Garion observed sourly as he struggled with an enormous baron of beef that Faldor's prohibition of work on Erastide stopped at the kitchen door.

In time, all was ready. The tables were loaded, the fires in the fireplaces burned brightly, dozens of candles filled the hall with golden light, and torches flared in their rings on the stone pillars. Faldor's people, all in their best clothes, filed into the hall, their mouths watering in anticipation.

When all were seated, Faldor rose from his bench at the head of the center table. "Dear friends," he said, lifting his tankard, "I dedicate this feast to the Gods."

"The Gods," the people responded in unison, rising respectfully.

Faldor drank briefly, and they all followed suit. "Hear me, O Gods," he prayed. "Most humbly we thank you for the bounty of this fair world which you made on this day, and we dedicate ourselves to your service for yet another year." He looked for a moment as if he were going to say more, but then sat down instead. Faldor always labored for many hours over special prayers for occasions such as this, but the agony of speaking in public invariably erased the words so carefully prepared from his mind. His prayers, therefore, were always very sincere and very short.

"Eat, dear friends," he instructed. "Do not let the food grow cold."

And so they ate. Anhelda and Eilbrig, who joined them all at this one meal only at Faldor's insistence, devoted their conversational efforts to the Murgo, since he was the only one in the room who was worthy of their attention.

"I have long thought of visiting Cthol Murgos," Eilbrig stated rather pompously. "Don't you agree, friend merchant, that greater contact between east and west is the way to overcome those mutual suspicions which have so marred our relationships in the past?"

"We Murgos prefer to keep to ourselves," the scar-faced man said shortly.

"But you are here, friend," Eilbrig pointed out. "Doesn't that suggest that greater contact might prove beneficial?"

"I am here as a duty," the Murgo said. "I don't visit here out of preference." He looked around the room. "Are these then all of your people?" he asked Faldor.

"Every soul is here," Faldor told him.

"I was led to believe there was an old man here—with white hair and beard."

"Not here, friend," Faldor said. "I myself am the eldest here, and as you can see, my hair is far from white."

"One of my countrymen met such a one some years ago," the Murgo said. "He was accompanied by an Arendish boy—Rundorig, I believe his name was."

Garion, seated at the next table, kept his face to his plate and listened so hard that he thought his ears must be growing.

"We have a boy named Rundorig here," Faldor said. "That tall lad at the end of the far table over there." He pointed.

"No," the Murgo said, looking hard at Rundorig. "That isn't the boy who was described to me."

"It's not an uncommon name among the Arends," Faldor said. "Quite probably your friend met a pair from another farm."

"That must be it," the Murgo said, seeming to dismiss the affair. "This ham is excellent," he said, pointing at his plate with the point of the dagger with which he ate. "Are the ones in your smokehouse of similar quality?"

"Oh, no, friend merchant!" Faldor laughed. "You won't so easily trick me into talking business on this day."

The Murgo smiled briefly, the expression appearing strange on his scarred face. "One can always try," he said. "I would, however, compliment your cook."

"A compliment for you, Mistress Pol," Faldor said, raising his voice slightly. "Our friend from Cthol Murgos finds your cooking much to his liking."

"I thank him for his compliment," Aunt Pol said, somewhat coldly.

The Murgo looked at her, and his eyes widened slightly as if in recognition. "A noble meal, great lady," he said, bowing slightly in her direction. "Your kitchen is a place of magic."

"No," she said, her face suddenly very haughty, "not magic. Cooking is an art which anyone with patience may learn. Magic is quite something else."

"But magic is also an art, great lady," the Murgo said.

"There are many who think so," Aunt Pol said, "but true magic comes from within and is not the result of nimble fingers which trick the eye."

The Murgo stared at her, his face hard, and she returned his gaze with steely eyes. To Garion, sitting nearby, it seemed as if something had passed between them that had nothing to do with the words they spoke—a kind of challenge seemed to hang in the air. And then the Murgo looked away almost as if he feared to take up that challenge.

When the meal was over, it was time for the rather simple pageant which traditionally marked Erastide. Seven of the older farmhands who had slipped away earlier appeared in the doorway wearing the long, hooded robes and carefully carved and painted masks which represented the faces of the Gods. The costumes were old and showed the wrinkles which were the result of having been packed away in Faldor's attic for the past year. With a slow step, the robed and masked figures paced into the hall and lined up at the foot of the table where Faldor sat. Then each in turn spoke a short piece which identified the God he represented.

"I am Aldur," Cralto's voice came from behind the first mask, "the God who dwells alone, and I command this world to be."

"I am Belar," came another familiar voice from behind the second mask, "Bear-God of the Alorns, and I command this world to be."

And so it went down the line, Chaldan, Issa, Nedra, Mara and then finally the last figure, which, unlike the others, was robed in black and whose mask was made of steel instead of painted wood.

"I am Torak," Durnik's voice came hollowly from behind the mask, "Dragon-God of the Angaraks, and I command this world to be."

A movement caught Garion's eye, and he looked quickly. The Murgo had covered his face with his hands in a strange, almost ceremonial gesture. Beyond him, at the far table, the five Thulls were ashen-faced and trembling.

The seven figures at the foot of Faldor's table joined their hands. "We are the Gods," they said in unison, "and we command this world to be."

"Hearken unto the words of the Gods," Faldor declaimed. "Welcome are the Gods in the house of Faldor."

"The blessing of the Gods be upon the house of Faldor," the seven responded, "and upon all this company." And then they turned and, as slowly as they had come, they paced from the hall.

And then came the gifts. There was much excitement at this, for the gifts were all from Faldor, and the good farmer struggled long each year to provide the most suitable gift for each of his people. New tunics and hose and gowns and shoes were much in evidence, but Garion this year was nearly overwhelmed when he opened a smallish, cloth-wrapped bundle and found a neat, well-sheathed dagger.

"He's nearly a man," Faldor explained to Aunt Pol, "and a man always has need of a good knife."

Garion, of course, immediately tested the edge of his gift and quite promptly managed to cut his finger.

"It was inevitable, I suppose," Aunt Pol said, but whether she was speaking of the cut or the gift itself or the fact of Garion's growing up was not entirely clear.

The Murgo bought his hams the next morning, and he

and the five Thulls departed. A few days later Anhelda
and Eilbrig packed up and left on their return journey to
the city of Sendar, and Faldor's farm returned to normal.

The winter plodded on. The snows came and went, and
spring returned, as it always does. The only thing which
made that spring any different from any other was the arrival of Brill, the new hand. One of the younger farmers
had married and rented a small nearby croft and had left,
laden down with practical gifts and good advice from Faldor to begin his life as a married man. Brill was hired to
replace him.

Garion found Brill to be a definitely unattractive addition to the farm. The man's tunic and hose were patched
and stained, his black hair and scraggly beard were unkempt, and one of his eyes looked off in a different direction from its fellow. He was a sour, solitary man, and he
was none too clean. He seemed to carry with him an acrid
reek of stale sweat that hung in his vicinity like a miasma.
After a few attempts at conversation, Garion gave up and
avoided him.

The boy, however, had other things to occupy his mind
during that spring and summer. Though he had until then
considered her to be more an inconveniance than a genuine
playmate, quite suddenly he began to notice Zubrette. He
had always known that she was pretty, but until that particular season that fact had been unimportant, and he had
much preferred the company of Rundorig and Doroon. Now
matters had changed. He noticed that the two other boys
had also begun to pay more attention to her as well, and
for the first time he began to feel the stirrings of jealousy.

Zubrette, of course, flirted outrageously with all three of
them, and positively glowed when they glared at each other
in her presence. Rundorig's duties in the fields kept him
away most of the time, but Doroon was a serious worry to
Garion. He became quite nervous and frequently found ex-
cuses to go about the compound to make certain that Doroon and Zubrette were not alone together.

His own campaign was charmingly simple—he resorted
to bribery. Zubrette, like all little girls, was fond of sweets,
and Garion had access to the entire kitchen. In a short
period of time they had worked out an arrangement. Garion would steal sweets from the kitchen for his sunny-

haired playmate, and in return she would let him kiss her.
Things might perhaps have gone further if Aunt Pol had
not caught them in the midst of such an exchange one
bright summer afternoon in the seclusion of the hay barn.

"That's quite enough of that," she announced firmly
from the doorway.

Garion jumped guiltily away from Zubrette.

"I've got something in my eye," Zubrette lied quickly.
"Garion was trying to get it out for me."

Garion stood blushing furiously.

"Really?" Aunt Pol said. "How interesting. Come with
me, Garion."

"I—" he started.

"*Now,* Garion."

And that was the end of that. Garion's time thereafter
was totally occupied in the kitchen, and Aunt Pol's eyes
seemed to be on him every moment. He mooned about a
great deal and worried desperately about Doroon, who now
appeared hatefully smug, but Aunt Pol remained watchful,
and Garion remained in the kitchen.

Chapter Five

IN MIDAUTUMN that year, when the leaves had
turned and the wind had showered them down from the
trees like red and gold snow, when evenings were chill and
the smoke from the chimneys at Faldor's farm rose straight
and blue toward the first cold stars in a purpling sky, Wolf
returned. He came up the road one gusty afternoon under
a lowering autumn sky with the new-fallen leaves tumbling
about him and his great, dark cloak whipping in the wind.

Garion, who had been dumping kitchen slops to the pigs,
saw his approach and ran to meet him. The old man
seemed travel-stained and tired, and his face under his
gray hood was grim. His usual demeanor of happy-go-

lucky cheerfulness had been replaced by a somber mood Garion had never seen in him before.

"Garion," Wolf said by way of greeting. "You've grown, I see."

"It's been five years," Garion said.

"Has it been so long?"

Garion nodded, falling into step beside his friend.

"Is everyone well?" Wolf asked.

"Oh yes," Garion said. "Everything's the same here—except that Breldo got married and moved away, and the old brown cow died last summer."

"I remember the cow," Wolf said. Then he said, "I must speak with your Aunt Pol."

"She's not in a very good mood today," Garion warned. "It might be better if you rested in one of the barns. I can sneak some food and drink to you in a bit."

"We'll have to chance her mood," Wolf said. "What I have to say to her can't wait."

They entered the gate and crossed the courtyard to the kitchen door.

Aunt Pol was waiting. "You again?" she said tartly, her hands on her hips. "My kitchen still hasn't recovered from your last visit."

"Mistress Pol," Wolf said, bowing. Then he did a strange thing. His fingers traced an intricate little design in the air in front of his chest. Garion was quite sure that he was not intended to see those gestures.

Aunt Pol's eyes widened slightly, then narrowed, and her face became grim. "How do you—" she started, then caught herself. "Garion," she said sharply, "I need some carrots. There are still some in the ground at the far end of the kitchen garden. Take a spade and a pail and fetch me some."

"But—" he protested, and then, warned by her expression, he left quickly. He got a spade and pail from a nearby shed and then loitered near the kitchen door. Eavesdropping, of course, was not a nice habit and was considered the worst sort of bad manners in Sendaria, but Garion had long ago concluded that whenever he was sent away, the conversation was bound to be very interesting and would probably concern him rather intimately. He had wrestled briefly with his conscience about it; but, since he really saw no harm in the practice—as long as he didn't repeat anything he heard—conscience had lost to curiosity.

Garion's ears were very sharp, but it took him a moment or two to separate the two familiar voices from the other sounds in the kitchen.

"He will not leave you a trail," Aunt Pol was saying.

"He doesn't have to," Wolf replied. "The thing itself will make its trail known to me. I can follow it as easily as a fox can scent out the track of a rabbit."

"Where will he take it?" he asked.

"Who can say? His mind is closed to me. My guess is that he'll go north to Boktor. That's the shortest route to Gar og Nadrak. He'll know that I'll be after him, and he'll want to cross into the lands of the Angaraks as soon as possible. His theft won't be complete so long as he stays in the west."

"When did it happen?"

"Four weeks ago."

"He could already be in the Angarak kingdoms."

"That's not likely. The distances are great; but if he is, I'll have to follow him. I'll need your help."

"But how can I leave here?" Aunt Pol asked. "I have to watch over the boy."

Garion's curiosity was becoming almost unbearable. He edged closer to the kitchen door.

"The boy'll be safe enough here," Wolf said. "This is an urgent matter."

"No," Aunt Pol contradicted. "Even this place isn't safe. Last Erastide a Murgo and five Thulls came here. He posed as a merchant, but he asked a few too many questions—about an old man and a boy named Rundorig who had been seen in Upper Gralt some years ago. He may also have recognized me."

"It's more serious than I thought, then," Wolf said thoughtfully. "We'll have to move the boy. We can leave him with friends elsewhere."

"No," Aunt Pol disagreed again. "If I go with you, he'll have to go along. He's reaching an age where he has to be watched most carefully."

"Don't be foolish," Wolf said sharply.

Garion was stunned. Nobody talked to Aunt Pol that way.

"It's my decision to make," Aunt Pol said crisply. "We all agreed that he was to be in my care until he was grown. I won't go unless he goes with me."

Garion's heart leaped.

"Pol," Wolf said sharply, "think where we may have to go. You can't deliver the boy into those hands."

"He'd be safer in Cthol Murgos or in Mallorea itself than he would be here without me to watch him," Aunt Pol said. "Last spring I caught him in the barn with a girl about his own age. As I said, he needs watching."

Wolf laughed then, a rich, merry sound. "Is that all?" he said. "You worry too much about such things."

"How would you like it if we returned and found him married and about to become a father?" Aunt Pol demanded acidly. "He'd make an excellent farmer, and what matter if we'd all have to wait a hundred years for the circumstances to be right again?"

"Surely it hasn't gone that far. They're only children."

"You're blind, Old Wolf," Aunt Pol said. "This is back-country Sendaria, and the boy has been raised to do the proper and honorable thing. The girl is a bright-eyed little minx who's maturing much too rapidly for my comfort. Right now charming little Zubrette is a far greater danger than any Murgo could ever be. Either the boy goes along, or I won't go either. You have your responsibilities, and I have mine."

"There's no time to argue," Wolf said. "If it has to be this way, then so be it."

Garion almost choked with excitement. He felt only a passing, momentary pang at leaving Zubrette behind. He turned and looked exultantly up at the clouds scudding across the evening sky. And, because his back was turned, he did not see Aunt Pol approach through the kitchen door.

"The garden, as I recall, lies beyond the south wall," she pointed out.

Garion started guiltily.

"How is it that the carrots remain undug?" she demanded.

"I had to look for the spade," he said unconvincingly.

"Really? I see that you found it, however." Her eyebrows arched dangerously.

"Only just now."

"Splendid. Carrots, Garion—*now!*"

Garion grabbed his spade and pail and ran.

It was just dusk when he returned, and he saw Aunt Pol mounting the steps that led to Faldor's quarters. He might have followed her to listen, but a faint movement in the dark doorway of one of the sheds made him step instead into the shadow of the gate. A furtive figure moved from the shed to the foot of the stairs Aunt Pol had just climbed and silently crept up the stairs as soon as she went in Faldor's door. The light was fading, and Garion could not see exactly who followed his Aunt. He set down his pail and, grasping the spade like a weapon, he hurried quickly around the inner court, keeping to the shadows.

There came the sound of a movement inside the chambers upstairs, and the figure at the door straightened quickly and scurried down the steps. Garion slipped back out of sight, his spade still held at the ready. As the figure passed him, Garion briefly caught the scent of stale, musty clothing and rank sweat. As certainly as if he had seen the man's face, he knew that the figure that had followed his Aunt had been Brill, the new farmhand.

The door at the top of the stairs opened, and Garion heard his Aunt's voice. "I'm sorry, Faldor, but it's a family matter, and I must leave immediately."

"I would pay you more, Pol." Faldor's voice was almost breaking.

"Money has nothing to do with it," Aunt Pol replied. "You're a good man, Faldor, and your farm has been a haven to me when I needed one. I'm grateful to you—more than you can know—but I must leave."

"Perhaps when this family business is over, you can come back," Faldor almost pleaded.

"No, Faldor," she said. "I'm afraid not."

"We'll miss you, Pol," Faldor said with tears in his voice.

"And I'll miss you, dear Faldor. I've never met a better-hearted man. I'd take it kindly if you wouldn't mention my leaving until I've gone. I'm not fond of explanations or sentimental good-byes."

"Whatever you wish, Pol."

"Don't look so mournful, old friend," Aunt Pol said lightly. "My helpers are well-trained. Their cooking will be the same as mine. Your stomach will never know the difference."

"My heart will," Faldor said.

"Don't be silly," she said gently. "Now I must see to supper."

Garion moved quickly away from the foot of the stairs. Troubled, he put his spade back in the shed and fetched the pail of carrots he had left sitting by the gate. To reveal to his Aunt that he had seen Brill listening at the door would immediately raise questions about his own activities that he would prefer not to have to answer. In all probability Brill was merely curious, and there was nothing menacing or ominous about that. To observe the unsavory Brill duplicating his own seemingly harmless pastime, however, made Garion quite uncomfortable—even slightly ashamed of himself.

Although Garion was much too excited to eat, supper that evening seemed as ordinary as any meal on Faldor's farm had ever been. Garion covertly watched sour-faced Brill, but the man showed no outward sign of having in any way been changed by the conversation he had gone to so much trouble to overhear.

When supper was over, as was always the case when he visited the farm, Mister Wolf was prevailed upon to tell a story. He rose and stood for a moment deep in thought as the wind moaned in the chimney and the torches flickered in their rings on the pillars in the hall.

"As all men know," he began, "the Marags are no more, and the Spirit of Mara weeps alone in the wilderness and wails among the moss-grown ruins of Maragor. But also, as all men know, the hills and streams of Maragor are heavy with fine yellow gold. That gold, of course, was the cause of the destruction of the Marags. When a certain neighboring kingdom became aware of the gold, the temptation became too great, and the result—as it almost always is when gold is at issue between kingdoms—was war. The pretext for the war was the lamentable fact that the Marags were cannibals. While this habit is distasteful to civilized men, had there not been gold in Maragor it might have been overlooked.

"The war, however, was inevitable, and the Marags were

slain. But the Spirit of Mara and the ghosts of all the slaughtered Marags remained in Maragor, as those who went into that haunted kingdom soon discovered.

"Now it chanced to happen that about that time there lived in the town of Muros in southern Sendaria three adventuresome men, and, hearing of all that gold, they resolved to journey down to Maragor to claim their share of it. The men, as I said, were adventuresome and bold, and they scoffed at the tales of ghosts.

"Their journey was long, for it is many hundreds of leagues from Muros to the upper reaches of Maragor, but the smell of the gold drew them on. And so it happened, one dark and stormy night, that they crept across the border into Maragor past the patrols which had been set to turn back just such as they. That nearby kingdom, having gone to all the expense and inconvenience of war, was quite naturally reluctant to share the gold with anyone who chanced to pass by.

"Through the night they crept, burning with their lust for gold. The Spirit of Mara wailed about them, but they were brave men and not afraid of spirits—and besides, they told each other, the sound was not truly a spirit, but merely the moaning of the wind in the trees.

"As dim and misty morning seeped amongst the hills, they could hear, not far away, the rushing sound of a river. As all men know, gold is most easily found along the banks of rivers, and so they made quickly toward that sound.

"Then one of them chanced to look down in the dim light, and behold, the ground at his feet was strewn with gold—lumps and chunks of it. Overcome with greed, he remained silent and loitered behind until his companions were out of sight; then he fell to his knees and began to gather up gold as a child might pick flowers.

"He heard a sound behind him and he turned. What he saw it is best not to say. Dropping all his gold, he bolted.

"Now the river they had heard cut through a gorge just about there, and his two companions were amazed to see him run off the edge of that gorge and even continue to run as he fell, his legs churning insubstantial air. Then they turned, and they saw what had been pursuing him.

"One went quite mad and leaped with a despairing cry into the same gorge which had just claimed his companion, but the third adventurer, the bravest and boldest of all, told himself that no ghost could actually hurt a living man and stood his ground. That, of course, was the worst mistake of all. The ghosts encircled him as he stood bravely, certain that they could not hurt him."

Mister Wolf paused and drank briefly from his tankard. "And then," the old storyteller continued, "because even ghosts can become hungry, they divided him up and ate him."

Garion's hair stood on end at the shocking conclusion of Wolf's tale, and he could sense the others at his table shuddering. It was not at all the kind of story they had expected to hear.

Durnik the smith, who was sitting nearby, had a perplexed expression on his plain face. Finally he spoke. "I would not question the truth of your story for the world," he said to Wolf, struggling with the words, "but if they ate him—the ghosts, I mean—where did it go? I mean—if ghosts are insubstantial, as all men say they are, they don't have stomachs, do they? And what would they bite with?"

Wolf's face grew sly and mysterious. He raised one finger as if he were about to make some cryptic reply to Durnik's puzzled question, and then he suddenly began to laugh.

Durnik looked annoyed at first, and then, rather sheepishly, he too began to laugh. Slowly the laughter spread as they all began to understand the joke.

"An excellent jest, old friend," Faldor said, laughing as hard as any of the others, "and one from which much instruction may be gained. Greed is bad, but fear is worse, and the world is dangerous enough without cluttering it with imaginary hobgoblins." Trust Faldor to twist a good story into a moralistic sermon of some kind.

"True enough, good Faldor," Wolf said more seriously, "but there *are* things in this world which cannot be explained away or dismissed with laughter."

Brill, seated near the fire, had not joined in the laughter. "I have never seen a ghost," he said sourly, "nor ever met anyone who has, and I for one do not believe in any kind of magic or sorcery or such childishness." And he stood up and stamped out of the hall almost as if the story had been a kind of personal insult.

Later, in the kitchen, when Aunt Pol was seeing to the cleaning up and Wolf lounged against one of the work-tables with a tankard of beer, Garion's struggle with his conscience finally came into the open. That dry, interior voice informed him most pointedly that concealing what he had seen was not merely foolish, but possibly dangerous as well. He set down the pot he was scrubbing and crossed to where they were. "It might not be important," he said carefully, "but this afternoon, when I was coming back from the garden, I saw Brill following you, Aunt Pol."

She turned and looked at him. Wolf set down his tankard. "Go on, Garion," Aunt Pol said.

"It was when you went up to talk with Faldor," Garion explained. "He waited until you'd gone up the stairs and Faldor had let you in. Then he sneaked up and listened at the door. I saw him up there when I went to put the spade away."

"How long has this man Brill been at the farm?" Wolf asked, frowning.

"He came just last spring," Garion said, "after Breldo got married and moved away."

"And the Murgo merchant was here at Erastide some months before?"

Aunt Pol looked at him sharply. "You think—" She did not finish.

"I think it might not be a bad idea if I were to step around and have a few words with friend Brill," Wolf said grimly. "Do you know where his room is, Garion?"

Garion nodded, his heart suddenly racing.

"Show me." Wolf moved away from the table against which he had been lounging, and his step was no longer the step of an old man. It was curiously as if the years had suddenly dropped away from him.

"Be careful," Aunt Pol warned.

Wolf chuckled, and the sound was chilling. "I'm always careful. You should know that by now."

Garion quickly led Wolf out into the yard and around to the far end where the steps mounted to the gallery that led to the rooms of the farmhands. They went up, their soft leather shoes making no sound on the worn steps.

"Down here," Garion whispered, not knowing exactly why he whispered.

Wolf nodded, and they went quietly down the dark gallery.

"Here," Garion whispered, stopping.

"Step back," Wolf breathed. He touched the door with his fingertips.

"Is it locked?" Garion asked.

"That's no problem," Wolf said softly. He put his hand to the latch, there was a click, and the door swung open. Wolf stepped inside with Garion close behind.

It was totally dark in the room, and the sour stink of Brill's unwashed clothes hung in the air.

"He's not here," Wolf said in a normal tone. He fumbled with something at his belt, and there was the scrape of flint against steel and a flare of sparks. A wisp of frayed rope caught the sparks and began to glow. Wolf blew on the spark for a second, and it flared into flame. He raised the burning wisp over his head and looked around the empty room.

The floor and bed were littered with rumpled clothes and personal belongings. Garion knew instantly that this was not simple untidiness, but rather was the sign of a hasty departure, and he did not know exactly how it was that he knew.

Wolf stood for a moment, holding his little torch. His face seemed somehow empty, as if his mind were searching for something.

"The stables," he said sharply. "Quickly, boy!"

Garion turned and dashed from the room with Wolf close behind. The burning wisp of rope drifted down into the yard, illuminating it briefly after Wolf discarded it over the railing as he ran.

There was a light in the stable. It was dim, partially covered, but faint beams shone through the weathered cracks in the door. The horses were stirring uneasily.

"Stay clear, boy," Wolf said as he jerked the stable door open.

Brill was inside, struggling to saddle a horse that shied from his rank smell.

"Leaving, Brill?" Wolf asked, stepping into the doorway with his arms crossed.

Brill turned quickly, crouched and with a snarl on his unshaven face. His off-center eye gleamed whitely in the half-muffled light of the lantern hanging from a peg on one of the stalls, and his broken teeth shone behind his pulled-back lips.

"A strange time for a journey," Wolf said dryly.

"Don't interfere with me, old man," Brill said, his tone menacing. "You'll regret it."

"I've regretted many things in my life," Wolf said. "I doubt that one more will make all that much difference."

"I warned you." Brill snarled, and his hand dove under his cloak and emerged with a short, rust-splotched sword.

"Don't be stupid," Wolf said in a tone of overwhelming contempt.

Garion, however, at the first flash of the sword, whipped his hand to his belt, drew his dagger, and stepped in front of the unarmed old man.

"Get back, boy," Wolf barked.

But Garion had already lunged forward, his bright dagger thrust out ahead of him. Later, when he had time to consider, he could not have explained why he reacted as he did. Some deep instinct seemed to take over.

"Garion," Wolf said, "get out of the way!"

"So much the better," Brill said, raising his sword.

And then Durnik was there. He appeared as if from nowhere, snatched up an ox yoke and struck the sword from Brill's hand. Brill turned on him, enraged, and Durnik's second blow took the cast-eyed man in the ribs, a little below the armpit. The breath whooshed from Brill's lungs, and he collapsed, gasping and writhing to the straw-littered floor.

"For shame, Garion," Durnik said reproachfully. "I didn't make that knife of yours for this kind of thing."

"He was going to kill Mister Wolf," Garion protested.

"Never mind that," Wolf said, bending over the gasping man on the floor of the stable. He searched Brill roughly and pulled a jingling purse out from under the stained tunic. He carried the purse to the lantern and opened it.

"That's mine," Brill gasped, trying to rise. Durnik raised the ox yoke, and Brill sank back again.

"A sizable sum for an ordinary farmhand to have, friend Brill," Wolf said, pouring the jingling coins from the purse into his hand. "How did you manage to come by it?"

Brill glared at him.

Garion's eyes grew wide at the sight of the coins. He had never seen gold before.

"You don't really need to answer, friend Brill," Wolf said, examining one of the coins. "Your gold speaks for you." He dumped the coins back in the purse and tossed the small leather pouch back to the man on the floor. Brill grabbed it quickly and pushed it back inside his tunic.

"I'll have to tell Faldor of this," Durnik said.

"No," Wolf said.

"It's a serious matter," Durnik said. "A bit of wrestling or a few blows exchanged is one thing, but drawing weapons is quite another."

"There's no time for all of that," Wolf said, taking a piece of harness strap from a peg on the wall. "Bind his hands behind him, and we'll put him in one of the grain bins. Someone will find him in the morning."

Durnik stared at him.

"Trust me, good Durnik," Wolf said. "The matter is urgent. Bind him and hide him someplace; then come to the kitchen. Come with me, Garion." And he turned and left the stable.

Aunt Pol was pacing her kitchen nervously when they returned. "Well?" she demanded.

"He was attempting to leave," Wolf said. "We stopped him."

"Did you—?" she left it hanging.

"No. He drew a sword, but Durnik chanced to be nearby and knocked the belligerence out of him. The intervention was timely. Your cub here was about to do battle. That little dagger of his is a pretty thing, but not really much of a match for a sword."

Aunt Pol turned on Garion, her eyes ablaze. Garion prudently stepped back out of reach.

"There's no time for that," Wolf said, retrieving the tankard he had set down before leaving the kitchen. "Brill had a pouchful of good red Angarak gold. The Murgos have set eyes to watching this place. I'd wanted to make our going less noticeable, but since we're already being watched, there's no point in that now. Gather what you and the boy will need. I want a few leagues between us and Brill before he manages to free himself. I don't want to be looking over my shoulder for Murgos every place I go."

Durnik, who had just come into the kitchen, stopped and stood staring at them. "Things aren't what they seem here," he said. "What manner of folk are you, and how is it that you have such dangerous enemies?"

"That's a long story, good Durnik," Wolf said, "but I'm afraid there's no time to tell it now. Make our apologies to Faldor, and see if you can't detain Brill for a day or so. I'd like our trail to be quite cold before he or his friends try to find it."

"Someone else is going to have to do that," Durnik said slowly. "I'm not sure what this is all about, but I am sure that there's danger involved in it. It appears that I'll have to go with you—at least until I've gotten you safely away from here."

Aunt Pol suddenly laughed. "You, Durnik? You mean to protect *us?*"

He drew himself up. "I'm sorry, Mistress Pol," he said. "I will not permit you to go unescorted."

"*Will not permit?*" she said incredulously.

"Very well," Wolf said, a sly look on his face.

"Have you totally taken leave of your senses?" Aunt Pol demanded, turning on him.

"Durnik has shown himself to be a useful man," Wolf said. "If nothing else, he'll give me someone to talk with along the way. Your tongue has grown sharper with the years, Pol, and I don't relish the idea of a hundred leagues or more with nothing but abuse for companionship."

"I see that you've finally slipped into your dotage, Old Wolf," she said acidly.

"That's exactly the sort of thing I meant," Wolf replied blandly. "Now gather a few necessary things, and let's be away from here. The night is passing rapidly."

She glared at him a moment and then stormed out of the kitchen.

"I'll have to fetch some things too," Durnik said. He turned and went out into the gusty night.

Garion's mind whirled. Things were happening far too fast.

"Afraid, boy?" Wolf asked.

"Well—" Garion said. "It's just that I don't understand. I don't understand any of this at all."

"You will in time, Garion," Wolf said. "For now it's better perhaps that you don't. There's danger in what we're doing, but not all that great a danger. Your Aunt and I—and good Durnik, of course—will see that no harm comes to you. Now help me in the pantry." He took a lantern into the pantry and began loading some loaves of bread, a ham, a round yellow cheese and several bottles of wine into a sack which he took down from a peg.

It was nearly midnight, as closely as Garion could tell, when they quietly left the kitchen and crossed the dark courtyard. The faint creak of the gate as Durnik swung it open seemed enormously loud.

As they passed through the gate, Garion felt a momentary pang. Faldor's farm had been the only home he had ever known. He was leaving now, perhaps forever, and such things had great significance. He felt an even sharper pang at the memory of Zubrette. The thought of Doroon and Zubrette together in the hay barn almost made him want to give the whole thing up altogether, but it was far too late now.

Beyond the protection of the buildings, the gusty wind was chill and whipped at Garion's cloak. Heavy clouds covered the moon, and the road seemed only slightly less dark than the surrounding fields. It was cold and lonely and more than a little frightening. He walked a bit closer to Aunt Pol.

At the top of the hill he stopped and glanced back. Faldor's farm was only a pale, dim blur in the valley behind. Regretfully, he turned his back on it. The valley ahead was very dark, and even the road was lost in the gloom before them.

Chapter Six

THEY HAD WALKED for miles, how many Garion could not say. He nodded as he walked, and sometimes stumbled over unseen stones on the dark road. More than anything now he wanted to sleep. His eyes burned, and his legs trembled on the verge of exhaustion.

At the top of another hill—there always seemed to be another hill, for that part of Sendaria was folded like a rumpled cloth—Mister Wolf stopped and looked about, his eyes searching the oppressive gloom.

"We turn aside from the road here," he announced.

"Is that wise?" Durnik asked. "There are woods hereabout, and I've heard that there may be robbers hiding there. Even if there aren't any robbers, aren't we likely to lose our way in the dark?" He looked up at the murky sky, his plain face, dimly seen, troubled. "I wish there was a moon."

"I don't think we need to be afraid of robbers," Wolf said confidently, "and I'm just as happy that there isn't a moon. I don't think we're being followed yet, but it's just as well that no one happens to see us pass. Murgo gold can buy most secrets." And with that he led them into the fields that lay beside the road.

For Garion the fields were impossible. If he had stumbled now and then on the road, the unseen furrows, holes, and clumps in the rough ground seemed to catch at his feet with every step. At the end of a mile, when they reached the black edge of the woods, he was almost ready to weep with exhaustion. "How can we find our way in there?" he demanded, peering into the utter darkness of the woods.

"There's a woodcutter's track not far to this side," Wolf said, pointing. "We only have a little farther to go." And he set off again, following the edge of the dark woods, with

Garion and the others stumbling along behind him. "Here we are," he said finally, stopping to allow them to catch up. "It's going to be very dark in there, and the track isn't wide. I'll go first, and the rest of you follow me."

"I'll be right behind you, Garion," Durnik said. "Don't worry. Everything will be all right." There was a note in the smith's voice, however, that hinted that his words were more to reassure himself than to calm the boy.

It seemed warmer in the woods. The trees sheltered them from the gusty wind, but it was so dark that Garion could not understand how Wolf could possibly find his way. A dreadful suspicion grew in his mind that Wolf actually did not know where he was going and was merely floundering along blindly, trusting to luck.

"Stop," a rumbling voice suddenly, shockingly, said directly ahead of them. Garion's eyes, accustomed slightly now to the gloom of the woods, saw a vague outline of something so huge that it could not possibly be a man.

"A giant!" he screamed in a sudden panic. Then, because he was exhausted and because everything that had happened that evening had simply piled too much upon him all at one time, his nerve broke and he bolted into the trees.

"Garion!" Aunt Pol's voice cried out after him, "come back!"

But panic had taken hold of him. He ran on, falling over roots and bushes, crashing into trees and tangling his legs in brambles. It seemed like some endless nightmare of blind flight. He ran full tilt into a low-hanging, unseen branch, and sparks flared before his eyes with the sudden blow to his forehead. He lay on the damp earth, gasping and sobbing, trying to clear his head.

And then there were hands on him, horrid, unseen hands. A thousand terrors flashed through his mind at once, and he struggled desperately, trying to draw his dagger.

"Oh, no," a voice said. "None of that, my rabbit." His dagger was taken from him.

"Are you going to eat me?" Garion babbled, his voice breaking.

His captor laughed. "On your feet, rabbit," he said, and Garion felt himself pulled up by a strong hand. His arm was taken in a firm grasp, and he was half-dragged through the woods.

Somewhere ahead there was a light, a winking fire among the trees, and it seemed that he was being taken that way. He knew that he must think, must devise some means of escape, but his mind, stunned by fright and exhaustion, refused to function.

There were three wagons sitting in a rough half-circle around the fire. Durnik was there, and Wolf, and Aunt Pol, and with them a man so huge that Garion's mind simply refused to accept the possibility that he was real. His tree-trunk sized legs were wrapped in furs cross-tied with leather thongs, and he wore a chain-mail shirt that reached to his knees, belted at the waist. From the belt hung a ponderous sword on one side and a short-handled axe on the other. His hair was in braids, and he had a vast, bristling red beard.

As they came into the light, Garion was able to see the man who had captured him. He was a small man, scarcely taller than Garion himself, and his face was dominated by a long pointed nose. His eyes were small and squinted, and his straight, black hair was raggedly cut. The face was not the sort to inspire confidence, and the man's stained and patched tunic and short, wicked-looking sword did little to contradict the implications of the face.

"Here's our rabbit," the small, weasel-like man announced as he pulled Garion into the circle of the firelight. "And a merry chase he led me, too."

Aunt Pol was furious. "Don't you *ever* do that again," she said sternly to Garion.

"Not so quick, Mistress Pol," Wolf said. "It's better for him to run than to fight just yet. Until he's bigger, his feet are his best friends."

"Have we been captured by robbers?" Garion asked in a quavering voice.

"Robbers?" Wolf laughed. "What a wild imagination you have, boy. These two are our friends."

"Friends?" Garion asked doubtfully, looking suspiciously at the red-bearded giant and the weasel-faced man beside him. "Are you sure?"

The giant laughed then too, his voice rumbling like an

earthquake. "The boy seems mistrustful," he boomed. "Your face must have warned him, friend Silk."

The smaller man looked sourly at his burly companion.

"This is Garion," Wolf said, pointing at the boy. "You already know Mistress Pol." His voice seemed to stress Aunt Pol's name. "And this is Durnik, a brave smith who has decided to accompany us."

"Mistress Pol?" the smaller man said, laughing suddenly for no apparent reason.

"I am known so," Aunt Pol said pointedly.

"It shall be my pleasure to call you so then, great lady," the small man said with a mocking bow.

"Our large friend here is Barak," Wolf went on. "He's useful to have around when there's trouble. As you can see, he's not a Sendar, but a Cherek from Val Alorn."

Garion had never seen a Cherek before, and the fearful tales of their prowess in battle became suddenly quite believable in the presence of the towering Barak.

"And I," the small man said with one hand to his chest, "am called Silk—not much of a name, I'll admit, but one which suits me—and I am from Boktor in Drasnia. I am a juggler and an acrobat."

"And also a thief and a spy," Barak rumbled good-naturedly.

"We all have our faults," Silk admitted blandly, scratching at his scraggly whiskers.

"And I'm called Mister Wolf in this particular time and place," the old man said. "I'm rather fond of the name, since the boy there gave it to me."

"Mister Wolf?" Silk asked, and then he laughed again. "What a merry name for you, old friend."

"I'm delighted that you find it so, old friend," Wolf said flatly.

"Mister Wolf it shall be, then," Silk said. "Come to the fire, friends. Warm yourselves, and I'll see to some food."

Garion was still uncertain about the oddly matched pair. They obviously knew Aunt Pol and Mister Wolf—and just as obviously by different names. The fact that Aunt Pol might not be whom he had always thought she was was very disturbing. One of the foundation stones of his entire life had just disappeared.

The food which Silk brought was rough, a turnip stew with thick chunks of meat floating in it and crudely hacked off slabs of bread, but Garion, amazed at the size of his appetite, fell into it as if he had not eaten for days.

And then, his stomach full and his feet warmed by the crackling campfire, he sat on a log, half-dozing.

"What now, Old Wolf?" he heard Aunt Pol ask. "What's the idea behind these clumsy wagons?"

"A brilliant plan," Wolf said, "even if I do say it myself. There are, as you know, wagons going every which way in Sendaria at this time of year. Harvests are moving from field to farm, from farm to village and from village to town. Nothing is more unremarkable in Sendaria than wagons. They're so common that they're almost invisible. This is how we're going to travel. We're now honest freight haulers."

"We're *what?*" Aunt Pol demanded.

"Wagoneers," Wolf said expansively. "Hard-working transporters of the goods of Sendaria—out to make our fortunes and seek adventure, bitten by the desire to travel, incurably infected by the romance of the road."

"Have you any idea how long it takes to travel by wagon?" Aunt Pol asked.

"Six to ten leagues a day," he told her. "Slow, I'll grant you, but it's better to move slowly than to attract attention."

She shook her head in disgust.

"Where first, Mister Wolf?" Silk asked.

"To Darine," Wolf announced. "If the one we're following went to the north, he'll have to have passed through Darine on his way to Boktor and beyond."

"And what exactly are we carrying to Darine?" Aunt Pol asked.

"Turnips, great lady," Silk said. "Last morning my large friend and I purchased three wagonloads of them in the village of Winold."

"Turnips?" Aunt Pol asked in a tone that spoke volumes.

"Yes, great lady, turnips," Silk said solemnly.

"Are we ready, then?" Wolf asked.

"We are," the giant Barak said shortly, rising with his mail shirt clinking.

"We should look the part," Wolf said carefully, eyeing

Barak up and down. "Your armor, my friend, is not the sort of garb an honest wagoneer would wear. I think you should change it for stout wool."

Barak's face looked injured. "I could wear a tunic over it," he suggested tentatively.

"You rattle," Silk pointed out, "and armor has a distinctive fragrance about it. From the downwind side you smell like a rusty ironworks, Barak."

"I feel undressed without a mail shirt," Barak complained.

"We must all make sacrifices," Silk said.

Grumbling, Barak went to one of the wagons, jerked out a bundle of clothes and began to pull off his mail shirt. His linen undertunic bore large, reddish rust stains.

"I'd change tunics as well," Silk suggested. "Your shirt smells as bad as the armor."

Barak glowered at him. "Anything else?" he demanded. "I hope, for decency's sake, you don't plan to strip me entirely."

Silk laughed.

Barak pulled off his tunic. His torso was enormous and covered with thick red hair.

"You look like a rug," Silk observed.

"I can't help that," Barak said. "Winters are cold in Cherek, and the hair helps me to stay warm." He put on a fresh tunic.

"It's just as cold in Drasnia," Silk said. "Are you absolutely sure your grandmother didn't dally with a bear during one of those long winters?"

"Someday your mouth is going to get you into a great deal of trouble, friend Silk," Barak said ominously.

Silk laughed again. "I've been in trouble most of my life, friend Barak."

"I wonder why," Barak said ironically.

"I think all this could be discussed later," Wolf said pointedly. "I'd rather like to be away from here before the week's out, if I can."

"Of course, old friend," Silk said, jumping up. "Barak and I can amuse each other later."

Three teams of sturdy horses were picketed nearby, and they all helped to harness them to the wagons.

"I'll put out the fire," Silk said and fetched two pails of

water from a small brook that trickled nearby. The fire hissed when the water struck it, and great clouds of steam boiled up toward the low-hanging tree limbs.

"We'll lead the horses to the edge of the wood," Wolf said. "I'd rather not pick my teeth on a low branch."

The horses seemed almost eager to start and moved without urging along a narrow track through the dark woods. They stopped at the edge of the open fields, and Wolf looked around carefully to see if anyone was in sight.

"I don't see anybody," he said. "Let's get moving."

"Ride with me, good smith," Barak said to Durnik. "Conversation with an honest man is much preferable to a night spent enduring the insults of an over-clever Drasnian."

"As you wish, friend," Durnik said politely.

"I'll lead," Silk said. "I'm familiar with the back roads and lanes hereabouts. I'll put us on the high road beyond Upper Gralt before noon. Barak and Durnik can bring up the rear. I'm sure that between them they can discourage anyone who might feel like following us."

"All right," Wolf said, climbing up onto the seat of the middle wagon. He reached down his hand and helped up Aunt Pol.

Garion quickly climbed up onto the wagon bed behind them, a trifle nervous that someone might suggest that he ride with Silk. It was all very well for Mister Wolf to say that the two they had just met were friends, but the fright he had suffered in the wood was still too fresh in his mind to make him quite comfortable with them.

The sacks of musty-smelling turnips were lumpy, but Garion soon managed to push and shove a kind of half-reclining seat for himself among them just behind Aunt Pol and Mister Wolf. He was sheltered from the wind, Aunt Pol was close, and his cloak, spread over him, kept him warm. He was altogether comfortable, and, despite the excitement of the night's events, he soon drifted into a half-drowse. The dry voice in his mind suggested briefly that he had not behaved too well back in the wood, but it too soon fell silent, and Garion slept.

It was the change of sound that woke him. The soft thud of the horses' hooves on the dirt road became a clatter as they came to the cobblestones of a small village sleeping in the last chill hours of the autumn night. Garion opened his eyes and looked sleepily at the tall, narrow houses with their tiny windows all dark.

A dog barked briefly, then retreated back to his warm place under some stairs. Garion wondered what village it might be and how many people slept under those steep-peaked tile roofs, unaware of the passage of their three wagons.

The cobbled street was very narrow, and Garion could almost have reached out and touched the weathered stones of the houses as they passed.

And then the nameless village was behind them, and they were back on the road again. The soft sound of the horses' hooves lured him once more toward sleep.

"What if he hasn't passed through Darine?" Aunt Pol asked Mister Wolf in a low tone.

It occurred to Garion that in all the excitement he had never actually found out exactly what it was that they were seeking. He kept his eyes closed and listened.

"Don't start with the 'what ifs,' " Wolf said irritably. "If we sit around saying 'what if,' we'll never do anything."

"I was merely asking," Aunt Pol said.

"If he hasn't gone through Darine, we'll turn south—to Muros. He may have joined a caravan there to take the Great North Road to Boktor."

"And if he hasn't gone through Muros?"

"Then we go on to Camaar."

"And then?"

"We'll see when we get to Camaar." His tone was final, as if he no longer wished to discuss the matter.

Aunt Pol drew in a breath as if she were about to deliver some final retort, but apparently she decided against it and settled back instead on the wagon seat.

To the east, ahead of them, the faint stain of dawn touched the lowering clouds, and they moved on through the tattered, windswept end of the long night in their search for something which, though he could not yet even identify it, was so important that Garion's entire life had been uprooted in a single day because of it.

Chapter Seven

IT TOOK THEM FOUR DAYS to reach Darine on the north coast. The first day went quite well, since, though it was cloudy and the wind kept blowing, the air was dry and the roads were good. They passed quiet farmsteads and an occasional farmer bent to his labor in the middle of a field. Inevitably each man stopped his work to watch them pass. Some waved, but some did not.

And then there were villages, clusters of tall houses nestled in valleys. As they passed, the children came out and ran after the wagons, shouting with excitement. The villagers watched, idly curious, until it became obvious that the wagons were not going to stop, and then they sniffed and went back to their own concerns.

As afternoon of that first day lowered toward evening, Silk led them into a grove of trees at the roadside, and they made preparations for the night. They ate the last of the ham and cheese Wolf had filched from Faldor's pantry and then spread their blankets on the ground beneath the wagons. The ground was hard and cold, but the exciting sense of being on some great adventure helped Garion to endure the discomfort.

The next morning, however, it began to rain. It was a fine, misty rain at first, scattering before the wind, but as the morning wore on, it settled into a steady drizzle. The musty smell of the turnips in their wet sacks became stronger, and Garion huddled miserably with his cloak pulled tightly around him. The adventure was growing much less exciting.

The road became muddy and slick, and the horses struggled their way up each hill and had to be rested often. On the first day they had covered eight leagues; after that they were lucky to make five.

Aunt Pol became waspish and short-tempered. "This is idiocy," she said to Mister Wolf about noon on the third day.

"Everything is idiocy if you choose to look at it in the proper light," he replied philosophically.

"Why wagoneers?" she demanded. "There are faster ways to travel—a wealthy family in a proper carriage, for instance, or Imperial messengers on good horses—either way would have put us in Darine by now."

"And left a trail in the memories of all these simple people we've passed so wide that even a Thull could follow it," Wolf explained patiently. "Brill has long since reported our departure to his employers. Every Murgo in Sendaria is looking for us by now."

"Why are we hiding from the Murgos, Mister Wolf?" Garion asked, hesitant to interrupt, but impelled by curiosity to try to penetrate the mystery behind their flight. "Aren't they just merchants—like the Tolnedrans and the Drasnians?"

"The Murgos have no real interest in trade," Wolf explained. "Nadraks are merchants, but the Murgos are warriors. The Murgos pose as merchants for the same reason that we pose as wagoneers—so that they can move about more or less undetected. If you simply assumed that all Murgos are spies, you wouldn't be too far from the truth."

"Haven't you anything better to do than ask all these questions?" Aunt Pol asked.

"Not really," Garion said, and then instantly knew that he'd made a mistake.

"Good," she said. "In the back of Barak's wagon you'll find the dirty dishes from this morning's meal. You'll also find a bucket. Fetch the bucket and run to that stream ahead for water, then return to Barak's wagon and wash the dishes."

"In cold water?" he objected.

"*Now,* Garion," she said firmly.

Grumbling, he climbed down off the slowly moving wagon.

In the late afternoon of the fourth day they came over a high hilltop and saw below the city of Darine and beyond the city the leaden gray sea. Garion caught his breath. To his eyes the city looked very large. Its surrounding walls were thick and high, and there were more buildings within those walls than he had seen in all his life. But it was to the sea that his eyes were drawn. There was a sharp tang to the air. Faint hints of that smell had been coming to him on the wind for the past league or so, but now, inhaling deeply, he breathed in that perfume of the sea for the first time in his life. His spirit soared.

"Finally," Aunt Pol said.

Silk had stopped the lead wagon and came walking back. His hood was pulled back slightly, and the rain ran down his long nose to drip from its pointed tip. "Do we stop here or go on down to the city?" he asked.

"We go to the city," Aunt Pol said. "I'm not going to sleep under a wagon when there are inns so close at hand."

"Honest wagoneers would seek out an inn," Mister Wolf agreed, "and a warm taproom."

"I might have guessed that," Aunt Pol said.

"We have to try to look the part." Wolf shrugged.

They went on down the hill, the horses' hooves slipping and sliding as they braced back against the weight of the wagons.

At the city gate two watchmen in stained tunics and wearing rust-spotted helmets came out of the tiny watch house just inside the gate.

"What's your business in Darine?" one of them asked Silk.

"I am Ambar of Kotu," Silk lied pleasantly, "a poor Drasnian merchant hoping to do business in your splendid city."

"Splendid?" one of the watchmen snorted.

"What have you in your wagons, merchant?" the other inquired.

"Turnips," Silk said deprecatingly. "My family has been in the spice trade for generations, but I'm reduced to ped- dling turnips." He sighed. "The world is a topsy-turvy place, is it not, good friend?"

"We're obliged to inspect your wagons," the watchman said. "It'll take some time, I'm afraid."

"And a wet time at that," Silk said, squinting up into the rain. "It would be much more pleasant to devote the time to wetting one's inside in some friendly tavern."

"That's difficult when one doesn't have much money," the watchman suggested hopefully.

"I'd be more than pleased if you'd accept some small token of friendship from me to aid you in your wetting," Silk offered.

"You're most kind," the watchman replied with a slight bow.

Some coins changed hands, and the wagons moved on into the city uninspected.

From the hilltop Darine had looked quite splendid, but Garion found it much less so as they clattered through the wet streets. The buildings all seemed the same with a kind of self-important aloofness about them, and the streets were littered and dirty. The salt tang of the sea was tainted here with the smell of dead fish, and the faces of the people hurrying along were grim and unfriendly. Garion's first excitement began to fade.

"Why are the people all so unhappy?" he asked Mister Wolf.

"They have a stern and demanding God," Wolf replied.

"Which God is that?" Garion asked.

"Money," Wolf said. "Money is a worse God than Torak himself."

"Don't fill the boy's head with nonsense," Aunt Pol said. "The people aren't really unhappy, Garion. They're just all in a hurry. They have important affairs to attend to and they're afraid they'll be late. That's all."

"I don't think I'd like to live here," Garion said. "It seems like a bleak, unfriendly kind of place." He sighed. "Sometimes I wish we were all back at Faldor's farm."

"There are worse places than Faldor's," Wolf agreed.

The inn Silk chose for them was near the docks, and the smell of the sea and the rank detritus of the meeting of sea and land was strong there. The inn, however, was a stout building with stables attached and storage sheds for the wagons. Like most inns, the main floor was given over to the kitchen and the large common room with its rows of tables and large fireplaces. The upper floors provided sleeping chambers for the guests.

"It's a suitable place," Silk announced as he came back out to the wagons after speaking at some length with the innkeeper. "The kitchen seems clean, and I saw no bugs when I inspected the sleeping chambers."

"I will inspect it," Aunt Pol said, climbing down from the wagon.

"As you wish, great lady," Silk said with a polite bow.

Aunt Pol's inspection took much longer than Silk's, and it was nearly dark when she returned to the courtyard. "Adequate," she sniffed, "but only barely."

"It's not as if we planned to settle in for the winter, Pol," Wolf said. "At most we'll only be here a few days."

She ignored that. "I've ordered hot water sent up to our chambers," she announced. "I'll take the boy up and wash him while you and the others see to the wagons and horses. Come along, Garion." And she turned and went back into the inn.

Garion wished fervently that they would all stop referring to him as the boy. He did, after all, he reflected, have a name, and it was not that difficult a name to remember. He was gloomily convinced that even if he lived to have a long gray beard, they would still speak of him as the boy.

After the horses and wagons had been attended to and they had all washed up, they went down again to the common room and dined. The meal certainly didn't match up to Aunt Pol's, but it was a welcome change from turnips. Garion was absolutely certain that he'd never be able to look a turnip in the face again for the rest of his life.

After they had eaten, the men loitered over their ale pots, and Aunt Pol's face registered her disapproval. "Garion and I are going up to bed now," she said to them. "Try not to fall down too many times when you come up."

Wolf, Barak and Silk laughed at that, but Durnik, Garion thought, looked a bit shamefaced.

The next day Mister Wolf and Silk left the inn early and were gone all day. Garion had positioned himself in a strategic place in hopes that he might be noticed and asked to go along, but he was not; so when Durnik went down to look after the horses, he accompanied him instead.

"Durnik," he said after they had fed and watered the animals and the smith was examining their hooves for cuts or stone bruises, "does all this seem strange to you?"

Durnik carefully lowered the leg of the patient horse he

was checking. "All what, Garion?" he asked, his plain face sober.

"Everything," Garion said rather vaguely. "This journey, Barak and Silk, Mister Wolf and Aunt Pol—all of it. They all talk sometimes when they don't think I can hear them. This all seems terribly important, but I can't tell if we're running away from someone or looking for something."

"It's confusing to me as well, Garion," Durnik admitted. "Many things aren't what they seem—not what they seem at all."

"Does Aunt Pol seem different to you?" Garion asked. "What I mean is, they all treat her as if she were a noblewoman or something, and she acts differently too, now that we're away from Faldor's farm."

"Mistress Pol is a great lady," Durnik said. "I've always known that." His voice had that same respectful tone it always had when he spoke of her, and Garion knew that it was useless to try to make Durnik perceive anything unusual about her.

"And Mister Wolf," Garion said, trying another tack. "I always thought he was just an old storyteller."

"He doesn't seem to be an ordinary vagabond," Durnik admitted. "I think we've fallen in with important people, Garion, on important business. It's probably better for simple folk such as you and I not to ask too many questions, but to keep our eyes and ears open."

"Will you be going back to Faldor's farm when this is all over?" Garion asked carefully.

Durnik considered that, looking out across the rainswept courtyard of the inn. "No," he said finally in a soft voice. "I'll follow as long as Mistress Pol allows me to."

On an impulse Garion reached out and patted the smith's shoulder. "Everything is going to turn out for the best, Durnik."

Durnik sighed. "Let's hope so," he said and turned his attention back to the horses.

"Durnik," Garion asked, "did you know my parents?"

"No," Durnik said. "The first time I saw you, you were a baby in Mistress Pol's arms."

"What was she like then?"

"She seemed angry," Durnik said. "I don't think I've ever seen anyone quite so angry. She talked with Faldor for a while and then went to work in the kitchen—you know Faldor. He never turned anyone away in his whole life. At first she was just a helper, but that didn't last too long. Our old cook was getting fat and lazy, and she finally went off to live with her youngest daughter. After that, Mistress Pol ran the kitchen."

"She was a lot younger then, wasn't she?" Garion asked.

"No," Durnik said thoughtfully. "Mistress Pol never changes. She looks exactly the same now as she did that first day."

"I'm sure it only seems that way," Garion said. "Everybody gets older."

"Not Mistress Pol," Durnik said.

That evening Wolf and his sharp-nosed friend returned, their faces somber. "Nothing," Wolf announced shortly, scratching at his snowy beard.

"I might have told you that," Aunt Pol sniffed.

Wolf gave her an irritated look, then shrugged. "We had to be certain," he said.

The red-bearded giant, Barak, looked up from the mail shirt he was polishing. "No trace at all?" he asked.

"Not a hint," Wolf said. "He hasn't gone through here."

"Where now, then?" Barak asked, setting his mail shirt aside.

"Muros," Wolf said.

Barak rose and went to the window. "The rain is slacking," he said, "but the roads are going to be difficult."

"We won't be able to leave tomorrow anyway," Silk said, lounging on a stool near the door. "I have to dispose of our turnips. If we carry them out of Darine with us, it will seem curious, and we don't want to be remembered by anyone who might have occasion to talk to any wandering Murgo."

"I suppose you're right," Wolf said. "I hate to lose the time, but there's no help for it."

"The roads will be better after a day's drying," Silk pointed out, "and wagons travel faster empty."

"Are you sure you can sell them, friend Silk?" Durnik asked.

"I am a Drasnian," Silk replied confidently. "I can sell anything. We might even make a good profit."

"Don't worry about that," Wolf said. "The turnips have

served their purpose. All we need to do now is to get rid of them."

"It's a matter of principle," Silk said airily. "Besides, if I don't try to strike a hard bargain, that too would be remembered. Don't be concerned. The business won't take long and won't delay us."

"Could I go along with you, Silk?" Garion asked hopefully. "I haven't seen any part of Darine except for this inn."

Silk looked inquiringly at Aunt Pol.

She considered for a moment. "I don't suppose it would do any harm," she said, "and it'll give me time to attend to some things."

The next morning after breakfast Silk and Garion set out with Garion carrying a bag of turnips. The small man seemed to be in extraordinarily good spirits, and his long, pointed nose seemed almost to quiver. "The whole point," he said as they walked along the littered, cobblestoned streets, "is not to appear too eager to sell—and to know the market, of course."

"That sounds reasonable," Garion said politely.

"Yesterday I made a few inquiries," Silk went on. "Turnips are selling on the docks of Kotu in Drasnia for a Drasnian silver link per hundredweight."

"A what?" Garion asked.

"It's a Drasnian coin," Silk explained, "about the same as a silver imperial—not quite, but close enough. The merchant will try to buy our turnips for no more than a quarter of that, but he'll go as high as half."

"How do you know that?"

"It's customary."

"How many turnips do we have?" Garion asked, stepping around a pile of refuse in the street.

"We have thirty hundredweight," Silk said.

"That would be—" Garion's face contorted in an effort to make the complex calculation in his head.

"Fifteen imperials," Silk supplied. "Or three gold crowns."

"Gold?" Garion asked. Because gold coins were so rare in country dealings, the word seemed to have an almost magic quality.

Silk nodded. "It's always preferable," he said. "It's easier to carry. The weight of silver becomes burdensome."

"And how much did we pay for the turnips?"

"Five imperials," Silk said.

"The farmer gets five, we get fifteen, and the merchant gets thirty?" Garion asked incredulously. "That hardly seems fair."

Silk shrugged. "It's the way things are," he said. "There's the merchant's house." He pointed at a rather imposing building with broad steps. "When we go in, he'll pretend to be very busy and not at all interested in us. Later, while he and I are bargaining, he'll notice you and tell you what a splendid boy you are."

"Me?"

"He'll think that you're some relation of mine—a son or a nephew perhaps—and he'll think to gain advantage over me by flattering you."

"What a strange notion," Garion said.

"I'll tell him many things," Silk went on, talking very rapidly now. His eyes seemed to glitter, and his nose was actually twitching. "Pay no attention to what I say, and don't let any surprise show on your face. He'll be watching us both very closely."

"You're going to lie?" Garion was shocked.

"It's expected," Silk said. "The merchant will also lie. The one of us who lies the best will get the better of the bargain."

"It all seems terribly involved," Garion said.

"It's a game," Silk said, his ferretlike face breaking into a grin. "A very exciting game that's played all over the world. Good players get rich, and bad players don't."

"Are you a good player?" Garion asked.

"One of the best," Silk replied modestly. "Let's go in." And he led Garion up the broad steps to the merchant's house.

The merchant wore an unbelted, fur-trimmed gown of a pale green color and a close-fitting cap. He behaved much as Silk had predicted that he would, sitting before a plain table and leafing through many scraps of parchment with a busy frown on his face while Silk and Garion waited for him to notice them.

"Very well, then," he said finally. "You have business with me?"

"We have some turnips," Silk said somewhat deprecatingly.

"That's truly unfortunate, friend," the merchant said, assuming a long face. "The wharves at Kotu groan with turnips just now. It would hardly pay me to take them off your hands at any price."

Silk shrugged. "Perhaps the Chereks or the Algars then," he said. "Their markets may not yet be so glutted as yours." He turned. "Come along, boy," he said to Garion.

"A moment, good friend," the merchant said. "I detect from your speech that you and I are countrymen. Perhaps as a favor I'll look at your turnips."

"Your time is valuable," Silk said. "If you aren't in the market for turnips, why should we trouble you further?"

"I might still be able to find a buyer somewhere," the merchant protested, "if the merchandise is of good quality." He took the bag from Garion and opened it.

Garion listened with fascination as Silk and the merchant fenced politely with each other, each attempting to gain the advantage.

"What a splendid boy this is," the merchant said, suddenly seeming to notice Garion for the first time.

"An orphan," Silk said, "placed in my care. I'm attempting to teach him the rudiments of business, but he's slow to learn."

"Ah," the merchant said, sounding slightly disappointed.

Then Silk made a curious gesture with the fingers of his right hand.

The merchant's eyes widened slightly, then he too gestured.

After that, Garion had no idea of what was going on. The hands of Silk and the merchant wove intricate designs in the air, sometimes flickering so rapidly that the eye could scarce follow them. Silk's long, slender fingers seemed to dance, and the merchant's eyes were fixed upon them, his forehead breaking into a sweat at the intensity of his concentration.

"Done, then?" Silk said finally, breaking the long silence in the room.

"Done," the merchant agreed somewhat ruefully.

"It's always a pleasure doing business with an honest man," Silk said.

"I've learned much today," the merchant said. "I hope you don't intend to remain in this business for long, friend. If you do, I might just as well give you the keys to my warehouse and strongroom right now and save myself the anguish I'll experience every time you appear."

Silk laughed. "You've been a worthy opponent, friend merchant," he said.

"I thought so at first," the merchant said, shaking his head, "but I'm no match for you. Deliver your turnips to my warehouse on Bedik wharf tomorrow morning." He scratched a few lines on a piece of parchment with a quill. "My overseer will pay you."

Silk bowed and took the parchment. "Come along, boy," he said to Garion, and led the way from the room.

"What happened?" Garion asked when they were outside in the blustery street.

"We got the price I wanted," Silk said, somewhat smugly.

"But you didn't say anything," Garion objected.

"We spoke at great length, Garion," Silk said. "Weren't you watching?"

"All I saw was the two of you wiggling your fingers at each other."

"That's how we spoke," Silk explained. "It's a separate language my countrymen devised thousands of years ago. It's called the secret language, and it's much faster than the spoken one. It also permits us to speak in the presence of strangers without being overheard. An adept can conduct business while discussing the weather, if he chooses."

"Will you teach it to me?" Garion asked, fascinated.

"It takes a long time to learn," Silk told him.

"Isn't the trip to Muros likely to take a long time?" Garion suggested.

Silk shrugged. "As you wish," he said. "It won't be easy, but it will help pass the time, I suppose."

"Are we going back to the inn now?" Garion asked.

"Not right away," Silk said. "We'll need a cargo to explain our entry into Muros."

"I thought we were going to leave with the wagons empty."

"We are."

"But you just said—"

"We'll see a merchant I know," Silk explained. "He buys farm goods all over Sendaria and has them held on the farms until the markets are right in Arendia and Tolnedra. Then he arranges to have them freighted either to Muros or Camaar."

"It sounds very complicated," Garion said doubtfully.

"It's not really," Silk assured him. "Come along, my boy, you'll see."

The merchant was a Tolnedran who wore a flowing blue robe and a disdainful expression on his face. He was talking with a grim-faced Murgo as Silk and Garion entered his counting room. The Murgo, like all of his race Garion had ever seen, had deep scars on his face, and his black eyes were penetrating.

Silk touched Garion's shoulder with a cautionary hand when they entered and saw the Murgo, then he stepped forward. "Forgive me, noble merchant," he said ingratiatingly. "I didn't know you were occupied. My porter and I will wait outside until you have time for us."

"My friend and I will be busy for most of the day," the Tolnedran said. "Is it something important?"

"I was just wondering if you might have a cargo for me," Silk replied.

"No," the Tolnedran said shortly. "Nothing." He started to turn back to the Murgo, then stopped and looked sharply at Silk. "Aren't you Ambar of Kotu?" he asked. "I thought you dealt in spices."

Garion recognized the name Silk had given the watchmen at the gates of the city. It was evident that the little man had used the name before.

"Alas," Silk sighed. "My last venture lies at the bottom of the sea just off the hook of Arendia—two full shiploads bound for Tol Honeth. A sudden storm and I am a pauper."

"A tragic tale, worthy Ambar," the Tolnedran master merchant said, somewhat smugly.

"I'm now reduced to freighting produce," Silk said morosely. "I have three rickety wagons, and that's all that's left of the empire of Ambar of Kotu."

"Reverses come to us all," the Tolnedran said philosophically.

"So this is the famous Ambar of Kotu," the Murgo said, his harshly accented voice quite soft. He looked Silk up and down, his black eyes probing. "It was a fortunate chance that brought me out today. I am enriched by meeting so illustrious a man."

Silk bowed politely. "You're too kind, noble sir," he said.

"I am Asharak of Rak Goska," the Murgo introduced himself. He turned to the Tolnedran. "We can put aside our discussion for a bit, Mingan," he said. "We will accrue much honor by assisting so great a merchant to begin recouping his losses."

"You're too kind, worthy Asharak," Silk said, bowing again.

Garion's mind was shrieking all kinds of warnings, but the Murgo's sharp eyes made it impossible for him to make the slightest gesture to Silk. He kept his face impassive and his eyes dull even as his thoughts raced.

"I would gladly help you, my friend," Mingan said, "but I have no cargo in Darine at the moment."

"I'm already committed from Darine to Medalia," Silk said quickly. "Three wagonloads of Cherek iron. And I also have a contract to move furs from Muros to Camaar. It's the fifty leagues from Medalia to Muros that concerns me. Wagons traveling empty earn no profit."

"Medalia." Mingan frowned. "Let me examine my records. It seems to me that I do have something there." He stepped out of the room.

"Your exploits are legendary in the kingdoms of the east, Ambar," Asharak of Rak Goska said admiringly. "When last I left Cthol Murgos there was still a kingly price on your head."

Silk laughed easily. "A minor misunderstanding, Asharak," he said. "I was merely investigating the extent of Tolnedran intelligence gathering activities in your kingdom. I took some chances I probably shouldn't have, and the Tolnedrans found out what I was up to. The charges they leveled at me were fabrications."

"How did you manage to escape?" Asharak asked. "The soldiers of King Taur Urgas nearly dismantled the kingdom searching for you."

"I chanced to meet a Thullish lady of high station," Silk said. "I managed to prevail upon her to smuggle me across the border into Mishrak ac Thull."

"Ah," Asharak said, smiling briefly. "Thullish ladies are notoriously easy to prevail upon."

"But most demanding," Silk said. "They expect full repayment for any favors. I found it more difficult to escape from her than I did from Cthol Murgos."

"Do you still perform such services for your government?" Asharak asked casually.

"They won't even talk to me," Silk said with a gloomy expression. "Ambar the spice merchant is useful to them, but Ambar the poor wagoneer is quite another thing."

"Of course," Asharak said, and his tone indicated that he obviously did not believe what he had been told. He glanced briefly and without seeming interest at Garion, and Garion felt a strange shock of recognition. Without knowing exactly how it was that he knew, he was instantly sure that Asharak of Rak Goska had known him for all of his life. There was a familiarity in that glance, a familiarity that had grown out of the dozen times or more that their eyes had met while Garion was growing up and Asharak, muffled always in a black cloak and astride a black horse, had stopped and watched and then moved on. Garion returned the gaze without expression, and the faintest hint of a smile flickered across Asharak's scarred face.

Mingan returned to the room then. "I have some hams on a farm near Medalia," he announced. "When do you expect to arrive in Muros?"

"Fifteen or twenty days," Silk told him.

Mingan nodded. "I'll give you a contract to move my hams to Muros," he offered. "Seven silver nobles per wagonload."

"Tolnedran nobles or Sendarian?" Silk asked quickly.

"This is Sendaria, worthy Ambar."

"We're citizens of the world, noble merchant," Silk pointed out. "Transactions between us have always been in Tolnedran coin."

Mingan sighed. "You were ever quick, worthy Ambar," he said. "Very well, Tolnedran nobles—because we are old friends, and I grieve for your misfortunes."

"Perhaps we'll meet again, Ambar," Asharak said.

"Perhaps," Silk said, and he and Garion left the counting room.

"Skinflint," Silk muttered when they reached the street. "The rate should have been *ten*, not seven."

"What about the Murgo?" Garion asked. Once again there was the familiar reluctance to reveal too much about the strange, unspoken link that had existed between him and the figure that now at least had a name.

Silk shrugged. "He knows I'm up to something, but he doesn't know exactly what—just as I know that he's up to something. I've had dozens of meetings like that. Unless our purposes happen to collide, we won't interfere with each other. Asharak and I are both professionals."

"You're a very strange person, Silk," Garion said.

Silk winked at him.

"Why were you and Mingan arguing about the coins?" Garion asked.

"Tolnedran coins are a bit purer," Silk told him. "They're worth more."

"I see," Garion said.

The next morning they all mounted the wagons again and delivered their turnips to the warehouse of the Drasnian merchant. Then, their wagons rumbling emptily, they rolled out of Darine, bound toward the south.

The rain had ceased, but the morning was overcast and blustery. On the hill outside town Silk turned to Garion, who rode beside him. "Very well," he said, "let's begin." He moved his fingers in front of Garion's face. "This means 'Good morning.'"

Chapter Eight

AFTER THE FIRST DAY the wind blew itself out, and the pale autumn sun reappeared. Their route southward led them along the Darine River, a turbulent stream that rushed down from the mountains on its way to the Gulf of Cherek. The country was hilly and timbered but, since the wagons were empty, their horses made good time.

Garion paid scant attention to the scenery as they trundled up the valley of the Darine. His attention was riveted almost totally on Silk's flickering fingers.

"Don't shout," Silk instructed as Garion practiced.

"Shout?" Garion asked, puzzled.

"Keep your gestures small. Don't exaggerate them. The idea is to make the whole business inconspicuous."

"I'm only practicing," Garion said.

"Better to break bad habits before they become too strong," Silk said. "And be careful not to mumble."

"Mumble?"

"Form each phrase precisely. Finish one before you go on to the next. Don't worry about speed. That comes with time."

By the third day their conversations were half in words and half in gestures, and Garion was beginning to feel quite proud of himself. They pulled off the road into a grove of tall cedars that evening and formed up their usual half-circle with the wagons.

"How goes the instruction?" Mister Wolf asked as he climbed down.

"It progresses," Silk said. "I expect it will go more rapidly when the boy outgrows his tendency to use baby talk."

Garion was crushed.

Barak, who was also dismounting, laughed. "I've often thought that the secret language might be useful to know,"

he said, "but fingers built to grip a sword are not nimble
enough for it." He held out his huge hand and shook his
head.

Durnik lifted his face and sniffed at the air. "It's going
to be cold tonight," he said. "We'll have frost before morning."

Barak also sniffed, and then he nodded. "You're right,
Durnik," he rumbled. "We'll need a good fire tonight." He
reached into the wagon and lifted out his axe.

"There are riders coming," Aunt Pol announced, still
seated on the wagon.

They all stopped talking and listened to the faint drum-
ming sound on the road they had just left.

"Three at least," Barak said grimly. He handed the axe
to Durnik and reached back into the wagon for his sword.

"Four," Silk said. He stepped to his own wagon and took
his own sword out from under the seat.

"We're far enough from the road," Wolf said. "If we
stay still, they'll pass without seeing us."

"That won't hide us from Grolims," Aunt Pol said.
"They won't be searching with their eyes." She made two
quick gestures to Wolf which Garion did not recognize.

No, Wolf gestured back. *Let us instead*—He also made
an unrecognizable gesture.

Aunt Pol looked at him for a moment and then nodded.

"All of you stay quite still," Wolf instructed them. Then
he turned toward the road, his face intent.

Garion held his breath. The sound of the galloping
horses grew nearer.

Then a strange thing happened. Though Garion knew he
should be fearful of the approaching riders and the threat
they seemed to pose, a kind of dreamy lassitude fell over
him. It was as if his mind had quite suddenly gone to sleep,
leaving his body still standing there watching incuriously
the passage of those dark-mantled horsemen along the
road.

How long he stood so he was not able to say; but when
he roused from his half-dream, the riders were gone and
the sun had set. The sky to the east had grown purple with
approaching evening, and there were tatters of sun-stained
clouds along the western horizon.

"Murgos," Aunt Pol said quite calmly, "and one Gro-lim." She started to climb down from the wagon.

"There are many Murgos in Sendaria, great lady," Silk said, helping her down, "and on many different missions."

"Murgos are one thing," Wolf said grimly, "but Grolims are quite something else. I think it might be better if we moved off the well-traveled roads. Do you know a back way to Medalia?"

"Old friend," Silk replied modestly, "I know a back way to every place."

"Good," Wolf said. "Let's move deeper into these woods. I'd prefer it if no chance gleam from our fire reached the road."

Garion had seen the cloaked Murgos only briefly. There was no way to be sure if one of them had been that same Asharak he had finally met after all the years of knowing him only as a dark figure on a black horse, but somehow he was almost certain that Asharak had been among them. Asharak would follow him, would be there wherever he went. It was the kind of thing one could count on.

Durnik had been right when he had spoken of frost. The ground was white with it the next morning, and the horses' breath steamed in the chill air as they set out. They moved along lanes and little-used tracks that were partially weed-choked. The going was slower than it might have been on the main road, but they all felt much safer.

It took them five more days to reach the village of Win-old, some twelve leagues to the north of Medalia. There, at Aunt Pol's insistence, they stopped overnight at a some-what rundown inn. "I refuse to sleep on the ground again," she announced flatly.

After they had eaten in the dingy common room of the inn, the men turned to their ale pots, and Aunt Pol went up to her chamber with instructions that hot water be brought to her for bathing. Garion, however, made some pretext about checking the horses and went outside. It was not that he was in the habit of being deliberately deceptive, but it had occurred to him in the last day or so that he had not had a single moment alone since they had left Faldor's farm. He was not by nature a solitary boy, but he had be-gun to feel quite keenly the restriction of always being in the presence of his elders.

The village of Winold was not a large one, and he explored it from one end to the other in less than half an hour, loitering along its narrow, cobblestoned streets in the crispness of the early evening air. The windows of the houses glowed with golden candlelight, and Garion suddenly felt a great surge of homesickness.

Then, at the next corner of the crooked street, in the brief light from an opening door, he saw a familiar figure. He could not be positive, but he shrank back against a rough stone wall anyway.

The man at the corner turned in irritation toward the light, and Garion caught the sudden white gleam from one of his eyes. It was Brill. The unkempt man moved quickly out of the light, obviously not wishing to be seen, then he stopped.

Garion hugged the wall, watching Brill's impatient pacing at the corner. The wisest thing would have been to slip away and hurry back to the inn, but Garion quickly dismissed that idea. He was safe enough here in the deep shadow beside the wall, and he was too caught up by curiosity to leave without seeing exactly what Brill was doing here.

After what seemed hours, but was really only a few more minutes, another shadowy shape came scurrying down the street. The man was hooded, so it was impossible to see his face, but the outline of his form revealed a figure dressed in the tunic, hose and calf-length boots of an ordinary Sendar. There was also, when he turned, the outline of a sword belted at his waist, and that was far from ordinary. While it was not precisely illegal for Sendars of the lower classes to bear arms, it was uncommon enough to attract notice.

Garion tried to edge close enough to hear what Brill said to the man with the sword, but they spoke only briefly. There was a clink as some coins changed hands, and then the two separated. Brill moved quietly off around the corner, and the man with the sword walked up the narrow, crooked street toward the spot where Garion stood.

There was no place to hide, and as soon as the hooded man came close enough, he would be able to see Garion. To turn and run would be even more dangerous. Since there was no alternative, Garion put on a bold front and marched determinedly toward the oncoming figure.

"Who's there?" the hooded man demanded, his hand going to his sword-hilt.

"Good evening, sir," Garion said, deliberately forcing his voice up into the squeaky registers of a much younger boy. "Cold night, isn't it?"

The hooded man grunted and seemed to relax.

Garion's legs quivered with the desire to run. He passed the man with the sword, and his back prickled as he felt that suspicious gaze follow him.

"Boy," the man said abruptly.

Garion stopped. "Yes, sir?" he said, turning.

"Do you live here?"

"Yes, sir," Garion lied, trying to keep his voice from trembling.

"Is there a tavern hereabouts?"

Garion had just explored the town, and he spoke confidently. "Yes, sir," he said. "You go on up this street to the next corner and turn to your left. There are torches out front. You can't miss it."

"My thanks," the hooded man said shortly, and walked on up the narrow street.

"Good night, sir," Garion called after him, made bold by the fact that the danger seemed past.

The man did not answer, and Garion marched on down to the corner, exhilarated by his brief encounter. Once he was around the corner, however, he dropped the guise of a simple village boy and ran.

He was breathless by the time he reached the inn and burst into the smoky common room where Mister Wolf and the others sat talking by the fire.

At the last instant, realizing that to blurt out his news in the common room where others might overhear would be a mistake, he forced himself to walk calmly to where his friends sat. He stood before the fire as if warming himself and spoke in a low tone. "I just saw Brill in the village," he said.

"Brill?" Silk asked. "Who's Brill?"

Wolf frowned. "A farmhand with too much Angarak gold in his purse to be entirely honest," he said. Quickly he told Silk and Barak about the adventure in Faldor's stable.

"You should have killed him," Barak rumbled.

"This isn't Cherek," Wolf said. "Sendars are touchy about casual killings." He turned to Garion. "Did he see you?" he asked.

"No," Garion said. "I saw him first and hid in the dark. He met another man and gave him some money, I think. The other man had a sword." Briefly he described the whole incident.

"This changes things," Wolf said. "I think we'll leave earlier in the morning than we'd planned."

"It wouldn't be hard to make Brill lose interest in us," Durnik said. "I could probably find him and hit him on the head a few times."

"Tempting." Wolf grinned. "But I think it might be better just to slip out of town early tomorrow and leave him with no notion that we've ever been here. We don't really have time to start fighting with everyone we run across."

"I'd like a closer look at this sword-carrying Sendar, however," Silk said, rising. "If it turns out that he's following us, I'd rather know what he looks like. I don't like being followed by strangers."

"Discreetly," Wolf cautioned.

Silk laughed. "Have you ever known me to be otherwise?" he asked. "This won't take long. Where did you say that tavern was, Garion?"

Garion gave him directions.

Silk nodded, his eyes bright and his long nose twitching. He turned, went quickly across the smoky common room and out into the chill night.

"I wonder," Barak considered. "If we're being followed this closely, wouldn't it be better to discard the wagons and this tiresome disguise, buy good horses and simply make straight for Muros at a gallop?"

Wolf shook his head. "I don't think the Murgos are all that certain where we are," he said. "Brill could be here for some other dishonesty, and we'd be foolish to start running from shadows. Better just to move on quietly. Even if Brill is still working for the Murgos, I'd rather just slip away and leave them all beating the bushes here in central Sendaria." He stood up. "I'm going to step upstairs and let

Pol know what's happened." He crossed the common room and mounted the stairs.

"I still don't like it," Barak muttered, his face dark.

They sat quietly then, waiting for Silk's return. The fire popped, and Garion started slightly. It occurred to him as he waited that he had changed a great deal since they'd left Faldor's farm. Everything had seemed simple then with the world neatly divided into friends and enemies. In the short time since they'd left, however, he'd begun to perceive complexities that he hadn't imagined before. He'd grown wary and distrustful and listened more frequently to that interior voice that always advised caution if not outright guile. He'd also learned not to accept anything at face value. Briefly he regretted the loss of his former innocence, but the dry voice told him that such regret was childish.

Then Mister Wolf came back down the stairs and rejoined them.

After about a half hour Silk returned. "Thoroughly disreputable-looking fellow," he said, standing in front of the fire. "My guess is that he's a common footpad."

"Brill's seeking his natural level," Wolf observed. "If he's still working for the Murgos, he's probably hiring ruffians to watch for us. They'll be looking for four people on foot, however, rather than six in wagons. If we can get out of Winold early enough in the morning, I think we can elude them altogether."

"I think Durnik and I should stand watch tonight," Barak said.

"Not a bad idea," Wolf agreed. "Let's plan to leave about the fourth hour after midnight. I'd like to have two or three leagues of back roads between us and this place when the sun comes up."

Garion scarcely slept that night; when he did, there were nightmares about a hooded man with a cruel sword chasing him endlessly down dark, narrow streets. When Barak woke them, Garion's eyes felt sandy, and his head was thick from the exhausting night.

Aunt Pol carefully drew the shutters in their chamber before lighting a single candle. "It's going to be colder now," she said, opening the large bundle she'd had him carry up from the wagons. She took out a pair of heavy woolen hose and winter boots lined with lambswool. "Put these on," she instructed Garion, "and your heavy cloak."

"I'm not a baby any more, Aunt Pol," Garion said.

"Do you enjoy being cold?"

"Well, no, but—" He stopped, unable to think of any words to explain how he felt. He began to dress. He could hear the faint murmur of the others talking softly in the adjoining chamber in that curious, hushed tone that men always assume when they rise before the sun.

"We're ready, Mistress Pol," Silk's voice came through the doorway.

"Let's leave then," she said, drawing up the hood of her cloak.

The moon had risen late that night and shone brightly on the frost-silvered stones outside the inn. Durnik had hitched the horses to the wagons and had led them out of the stable.

"We'll lead the horses out to the road," Wolf said very quietly. "I see no need of rousing the villagers as we pass."

Silk again took the lead, and they moved slowly out of the innyard.

The fields beyond the village were white with frost, and the pale, smoky-looking moonlight seemed to have leeched all color from them.

"As soon as we're well out of earshot," Wolf said, climbing up into his wagon, "let's put some significant distance between us and this place. The wagons are empty, and a little run won't hurt the horses."

"Truly," Silk agreed.

They all mounted their wagons and set off at a walk. The stars glittered overhead in the crisp, cold sky. The fields were very white in the moonlight, and the clumps of trees back from the road very dark.

Just as they went over the first hilltop, Garion looked back at the dark cluster of houses in the valley behind. A single flicker of light came from a window somewhere, a lone, golden pinpoint that appeared and then vanished.

"Someone's awake back there," he told Silk. "I just saw a light."

"Some early riser perhaps," Silk suggested. "But then again, perhaps not." He shook the reins slightly, and the horses increased their pace. He shook them again, and they began to trot.

"Hang on, boy," he instructed, reached forward and slapped the reins down smartly on the rumps of the horses.

The wagon bounced and clattered fearfully behind the running team, and the bitterly chill air rushed at Garion's face as he clung to the wagon seat.

At full gallop the three wagons plunged down into the next valley, rushing between the frost-white fields in the bright moonlight, leaving the village and its single light far behind.

By the time the sun rose, they had covered a good four leagues, and Silk reined in his steaming horses. Garion felt battered and sore from the wild ride over the iron-hard roads and was glad for the chance to rest. Silk handed him the reins and jumped down from the wagon. He walked back and spoke briefly to Mister Wolf and Aunt Pol, then returned to the wagon.

"We turn off at that lane just ahead," he told Garion as he massaged his fingers.

Garion offered him the reins.

"You drive," Silk told him. "My hands are frozen stiff. Just let the horses walk."

Garion clucked at the horses and shook the reins slightly. Obediently, the team started out again.

"The lane circles around to the back of that hill," Silk said, pointing with his chin since his hands were tucked inside his tunic. "On the far side there's a copse of fir trees. We'll stop there to rest the horses."

"Do you think we're being followed?" Garion asked.

"This'll be a good time to find out," Silk said.

They rounded the hill and drove on down to where the dark firs bordered the road. Then Garion turned the horses and moved in under the shadowy trees.

"This will do fine," Silk said, getting down. "Come along."

"Where are we going?"

"I want to have a look at that road behind us," Silk said. "We'll go up through the trees to the top of the hill and see if our back trail has attracted any interest." And he started up the hill, moving quite rapidly but making absolutely no sound as he went. Garion floundered along behind him, his

feet cracking the dead twigs underfoot embarrassingly until he began to catch the secret of it. Silk nodded approvingly once, but said nothing.

The trees ended just at the crest of the hill, and Silk
stopped there. The valley below with the dark road passing
through it was empty except for two deer who had come
out of the woods on the far side to graze in the frosty grass.

"We'll wait a while," Silk said. "If Brill and his hireling
are following, they shouldn't be far behind." He sat on a
stump and watched the empty valley.

After a while, a cart moved slowly along the road toward
Winold. It looked tiny in the distance, and its pace along
the scar of the road seemed very slow.

The sun rose a bit higher, and they squinted into its full
morning brightness.

"Silk," Garion said finally in a hesitant tone.

"Yes, Garion?"

"What's this all about?" It was a bold question to ask,
but Garion felt he knew Silk well enough now to ask it.

"All what?"

"What we're doing. I've heard a few things and guessed
a few more, but it doesn't really make any sense to me."

"And just what have you guessed, Garion?" Silk asked,
his small eyes very bright in his unshaven face.

"Something's been stolen—something very important—
and Mister Wolf and Aunt Pol—and the rest of us—are
trying to get it back."

"All right," Silk said. "That much is true."

"Mister Wolf and Aunt Pol are not at all what they seem
to be," Garion went on.

"No," Silk agreed, "they aren't."

"I think they can do things that other people can't do,"
Garion said, struggling with the words. "Mister Wolf can
follow this thing—whatever it is—without seeing it. And
last week in those woods when the Murgos passed, they did
something—I don't even know how to describe it, but it
was almost as if they reached out and put my mind to
sleep. How did they do that? And why?"

Silk chuckled. "You're a very observant lad," he said.
Then his tone became more serious. "We're living in momentous times, Garion. The events of a thousand years and
more have all focused on these very days. The world, I'm

told, is like that. Centuries pass when nothing happens, and then in a few short years events of such tremendous importance take place that the world is never the same again."

"I think that if I had my choice, I'd prefer one of those quiet centuries," Garion said glumly.

"Oh, no," Silk said, his lips drawing back in a ferretlike grin. "Now's the time to be alive—to see it all happen, to be a part of it. That makes the blood race, and each breath is an adventure."

Garion let that pass. "What is this thing we're following?" he asked.

"It's best if you don't even know its name," Silk told him seriously, "or the name of the one who stole it. There are people trying to stop us; and what you don't know, you can't reveal."

"I'm not in the habit of talking to Murgos," Garion said stiffly.

"It's not necessary to talk to them," Silk said. "There are some among them who can reach out and pick the thoughts right out of your mind."

"That isn't possible," Garion said.

"Who's to say what's possible and what isn't?" Silk asked. And Garion remembered a conversation he had once had with Mister Wolf about the possible and the impossible.

Silk sat on the stump in the newly risen sun looking thoughtfully down into the still-shadowy valley, an ordinary-looking little man in ordinary-looking tunic and hose and a rough brown shoulder cape with its hood turned up over his head. "You were raised as a Sendar, Garion," he said, "and Sendars are solid, practical men with little patience for such things as sorcery and magic and other things that can't be seen or touched. Your friend, Durnik, is a perfect Sendar. He can mend a shoe or fix a broken wheel or dose a sick horse, but I doubt that he could bring himself to believe in the tiniest bit of magic."

"I *am* a Sendar," Garion objected. The hint implicit in Silk's observation struck at the very center of his sense of his own identity.

Silk turned and looked at him closely. "No," he said, "you aren't. I know a Sendar when I see one—just as I can

recognize the difference between an Arend and a Tolnedran or a Cherek and an Algar. There's a certain set of the
head, a certain look about the eyes of Sendars that you
don't have. You're not a Sendar."

"What am I then?" Garion challenged.

"I don't know," Silk said with a puzzled frown, "and
that's very unusual, since I've been trained to know what
people are. It may come to me in time, though."

"Is Aunt Pol a Sendar?" Garion asked.

"Of course not." Silk laughed.

"That explains it then," Garion said. "I'm probably the
same thing she is."

Silk looked sharply at him.

"She's my father's sister, after all," Garion said. "At
first I thought it was my mother she was related to, but
that was wrong. It was my father; I know that now."

"That's impossible," Silk said flatly.

"Impossible?"

"Absolutely out of the question. The whole notion's un-
thinkable."

"Why?"

Silk chewed at his lower lip for a moment. "Let's go
back to the wagons," he said shortly.

They turned and went down through the dark trees with
the bright morning sunlight slanting on their backs in the
frosty air.

They rode the back lanes for the rest of the day. Late in
the afternoon when the sun had begun to drop into a purple bank of clouds toward the west, they arrived at the
farm where they were to pick up Mingan's hams. Silk
spoke with the stout farmer and showed him the piece of
parchment Mingan had given them in Darine.

"I'll be glad to get rid of them," the farmer said.
"They've been occupying storage space I sorely need."

"That's frequently the case when one has dealings with
Tolnedrans," Silk observed. "They're gifted at getting a bit
more than they pay for—even if it's only the free use of
someone else's storage sheds."

The farmer glumly agreed.

"I wonder," Silk said as if the thought had just occurred
to him, "I wonder if you might have seen a friend of

mine—Brill by name? A medium-sized man with black hair and beard and a cast to one eye?"

"Patched clothes and a sour disposition?" the stout farmer asked.

"That's him," Silk said.

"He's been about the area," the farmer said, "looking— or so he said—for an old man and a woman and a boy. He said that they stole some things from his master and that he'd been sent to find them."

"How long ago was that?" Silk asked.

"A week or so," the farmer said.

"I'm sorry to have missed him," Silk said. "I wish I had the leisure to look him up."

"I can't for my life think why," the farmer said bluntly. "To be honest with you, I didn't care much for your friend."

"I'm not overfond of him myself," Silk agreed, "but the truth is that he owes me some money. I could quite easily do without Brill's companionship, but I'm lonesome for the money, if you take my meaning."

The farmer laughed.

"I'd take it as a kindness if you happened to forget that I asked after him," Silk said. "He'll likely be hard enough to find even if he isn't warned that I'm looking for him."

"You can depend on my discretion," the stout man said, still laughing. "I have a loft where you and your wagoneers can put up for the night, and I'd take it kindly if you'd sup with my workers in the dining hall over there."

"My thanks," Silk said, bowing slightly. "The ground's cold, and it's been some time since we've eaten anything but the rough fare of the road."

"You wagoneers lead adventuresome lives," the stout man said almost enviously. "Free as birds with always a new horizon just beyond the next hilltop."

"It's much overrated," Silk told him, "and winter's a thin time for birds and wagoneers both."

The farmer laughed again, clapped Silk on the shoulder and then showed him where to put up the horses.

The food in the stout farmer's dining hall was plain, but there was plenty; and the loft was a bit drafty, but the hay was soft. Garion slept soundly. The farm was not Faldor's, but it was familiar enough, and there was that comforting

sense of having walls about him again that made him feel
secure.

The following morning, after a solid breakfast, they
loaded the wagons with the Tolnedran's salt-crusted hams
and bade the farmer a friendly good-bye.

The clouds that had begun to bank up in the west the
evening before had covered the sky during the night, and it
was cold and gray as they set out for Muros, fifty leagues
to the south.

Chapter Nine

THE ALMOST TWO WEEKS it took them to reach
Muros were the most uncomfortable Garion had ever
spent. Their route skirted the edge of the foothills through
rolling and sparsely settled country, and the sky hung gray
and cold overhead. There were occasional spits of snow,
and the mountains loomed black against the skyline to the
east.

It seemed to Garion that he would never be warm again.
Despite Durnik's best efforts to find dry firewood each
night, their fires always seemed pitifully small, and the
great cold around them enormously large. The ground
upon which they slept was always frozen, and the chill
seemed actually to seep into Garion's bones.

His education in the Drasnian secret language continued
and he became, if not adept, at least competent by the time
they passed Lake Camaar and began the long, downhill
grade that led to Muros.

The city of Muros in south-central Sendaria was a
sprawling, unattractive place that had been since time im-
memorial the site of a great annual fair. Each year in late
summer, Algar horsemen drove vast cattle herds through
the mountains along the Great North Road to Muros where

cattle buyers from all over the west gathered to await their coming. Huge sums changed hands, and, because the Algar clansmen also commonly made their yearly purchases of useful and ornamental articles at that time, merchants from as far away as Nyissa in the remote south gathered to offer their wares. A large plain which lay to the east of the city was given over entirely to the cattle pens that stretched for miles but were still inadequate to contain the herds which arrived at the height of the season. Beyond the pens to the east lay the more or less permanent encampment of the Algars.

It was to this city one midmorning at the tag end of the fair, when the cattle pens were nearly empty and most of the Algars had departed and only the most desperate merchants remained, that Silk led the three wagons laden with the hams of Mingan the Tolnedran.

The delivery of the hams took place without incident, and the wagons soon drew into an innyard near the northern outskirts of the city.

"This is a respectable inn, great lady," Silk assured Aunt Pol as he helped her down from the wagon. "I've stopped here before."

"Let's hope so," she said. "The inns of Muros have an unsavory reputation."

"Those particular inns lie along the eastern edge of town," Silk assured her delicately. "I know them well."

"I'm certain you do," she said with an arched eyebrow.

"My profession sometimes requires me to seek out places I might otherwise prefer to avoid," he said blandly.

The inn, Garion noted, was surprisingly clean, and its guests seemed for the most part to be Sendarian merchants. "I thought there'd be many different kinds of people here in Muros," he said as he and Silk carried their bundles up to the chambers on the second floor.

"There are," Silk said, "but each group tends to remain aloof from the others. The Tolnedrans gather in one part of town, the Drasnians in another, the Nyissans in yet another. The Earl of Muros prefers it that way. Tempers sometimes flare in the heat of the day's business, and it's best not to have natural enemies housed under the same roof."

Garion nodded. "You know," he said as they entered the

chambers they had taken for their stay in Muros, "I don't think I've ever seen a Nyissan."

"You're lucky," Silk said with distaste. "They're an unpleasant race."

"Are they like Murgos?"

"No," Silk said. "The Nyissans worship Issa, the Snake-God, and it's considered seemly among them to adopt the mannerisms of the serpent. I don't find it at all that attractive myself. Besides, the Nyissans murdered the Rivan King, and all Alorns have disliked them since then."

"The Rivans don't have a king," Garion objected.

"Not anymore," Silk said. "They did once, though—until Queen Salmissra decided to have him murdered."

"When was that?" Garion asked, fascinated.

"Thirteen hundred years ago," Silk said, as if it had only been yesterday.

"Isn't that sort of a long time to hold a grudge?" Garion asked.

"Some things are unforgivable," Silk said shortly.

Since there was still a good part of the day left, Silk and Wolf left the inn that afternoon to search the streets of Muros for those strange, lingering traces that Wolf could apparently see or feel and which would tell him whether the object they sought had passed this way. Garion sat near the fire in the chamber he shared with Aunt Pol, trying to bake the chill out of his feet. Aunt Pol also sat by the fire, mending one of his tunics, her shining needle flickering in and out of the fabric.

"Who was the Rivan King, Aunt Pol?" he asked her.

She stopped sewing. "Why do you ask?" she said.

"Silk was telling me about Nyissans," he said. "He told me that their queen murdered the Rivan King. Why would she do that?"

"You're full of questions today, aren't you?" she asked, her needle moving again.

"Silk and I talk about a lot of things as we ride along," Garion said, pushing his feet even closer to the fire.

"Don't burn your shoes," she told him.

"Silk says that I'm not a Sendar," Garion said. "He says that he doesn't know what I am, but that I'm not a Sendar."

"Silk talks too much," Aunt Pol observed.

"You never tell me anything, Aunt Pol," he said in irritation.

"I tell you everything you need to know," she said calmly. "Right now it's not necessary for you to know anything about Rivan kings or Nyissan queens."

"All you want to do is keep me an ignorant child," Garion said petulantly. "I'm almost a man, and I don't even know what I am—or who."

"I know who you are," she said, not looking up.

"Who am I then?"

"You're a young man who's about to catch his shoes on fire," she said.

He jerked his feet back quickly. "You didn't answer me," he accused.

"That's right," she said in that same infuriatingly calm voice.

"Why not?"

"It's not necessary for you to know yet. When it's time, I'll tell you, but not until."

"That's not fair," he objected.

"The world's full of injustice," she said. "Now, since you're feeling so manly, why don't you fetch some more firewood? That'll give you something useful to think about."

He glared at her and stamped across the room.

"Garion," she said.

"What?"

"Don't even *think* about slamming the door."

That evening when Wolf and Silk returned, the usually cheerful old man seemed impatient and irritable. He sat down at the table in the common room of the inn and stared moodily at the fire. "I don't think it passed this way," he said finally. "There are a few places left to try, but I'm almost certain that it hasn't been here."

"Then we go on to Camaar?" Barak rumbled, his thick fingers combing his bristling beard.

"We must," Wolf said. "Most likely we should have gone there first."

"There was no way to know," Aunt Pol told him. "Why would he go to Camaar if he's trying to carry it to the Angarak kingdoms?"

"I can't even be certain where he's going," Wolf said

irritably. "Maybe he wants to keep the thing for himself. He's always coveted it." He stared into the fire again.

"We're going to need some kind of cargo for the trip to Camaar," Silk said.

Wolf shook his head. "It slows us too much," he said. "It's not unusual for wagons to return to Camaar from Muros without cargo, and it's reaching the point where we'll have to gamble our disguise for the sake of speed. It's forty leagues to Camaar, and the weather's turning bad. A heavy snowstorm could stop the wagons entirely, and I don't have time to spend the whole winter mired down in a snowbank."

Durnik dropped his knife suddenly and started to scramble to his feet.

"What's amiss?" Barak asked quickly.

"I just saw Brill," Durnik said. "He was in that doorway."

"Are you sure?" Wolf demanded.

"I know him," Durnik said grimly. "It was Brill, all right."

Silk pounded his fist down on the table. "Idiot!" he accused himself. "I underestimated the man."

"That doesn't matter now," Mister Wolf said, and there was almost a kind of relief in his voice. "Our disguise is useless now. I think it's time for speed."

"I'll see to the wagons," Durnik said.

"No," Wolf said. "The wagons are too slow. We'll go to the camp of the Algars and buy good horses." He stood up quickly.

"What of the wagons?" Durnik persisted.

"Forget them," Wolf said. "They're only a hindrance now. We'll ride the wagon horses to the camp of the Algars and take only what we can conveniently carry. Let's get ready to leave immediately. Meet me in the innyard as soon as you can." He went quickly to the door and out into the cold night.

It was only a few minutes later that they all met near the door to the stable in the cobblestoned innyard, each carrying a small bundle. Hulking Barak jingled as he walked, and Garion could smell the oiled steel of his mail shirt. A few flakes of snow drifted down through the frosty air and settled like tiny feathers to the frozen ground.

Durnik was the last to join them. He came breathlessly out of the inn and pressed a small handful of coins upon Mister Wolf. "It was the best I could do," he apologized. "It's scarce half the worth of the wagons, but the innkeeper sensed my haste and bargained meanly." He shrugged then. "At least we're rid of them," he said. "It's not good to leave things of value behind. They nag at the mind and distract one from the business at hand."

Silk laughed. "Durnik," he said, "you're the absolute soul of a Sendar."

"One must follow one's nature," Durnik said.

"Thank you, my friend," Wolf said gravely, dropping the coins in his purse. "Let's lead the horses," he went on. "Galloping through these narrow streets at night would only attract attention."

"I'll lead," Barak announced, drawing his sword. "If there's any trouble, I'm best equipped to deal with it."

"I'll walk along beside you, friend Barak," Durnik said, hefting a stout cudgel of firewood.

Barak nodded, his eyes grimly bright, and led his horse out through the gate with Durnik closely at his side.

Taking his lead from Durnik, Garion paused momentarily as he passed the woodpile and selected a good oak stick. It had a comforting weight, and he swung it a few times to get the feel of it. Then he saw Aunt Pol watching him, and he hurried on without any further display.

The streets through which they passed were narrow and dark, and the snow had begun to fall a bit more heavily now, settling almost lazily through the dead calm air. The horses, made skittish by the snow, seemed to be fearful and crowded close to those who led them.

When the attack came, it was unexpected and swift. There was a sudden rush of footsteps and a sharp ring of steel on steel as Barak fended off the first blow with his sword.

Garion could see only shadowy figures outlined against the falling snow, and then, as once before when in his boyhood he had struck down his friend Rundorig in mock battle, his ears began to ring; his blood surged boilingly in his veins as he leaped into the fight, ignoring the single cry from Aunt Pol.

He received a smart rap on the shoulder, whirled and

struck with his stick. He was rewarded with a muffled grunt. He struck again—and then again, swinging his club at those parts of his shadowy enemy which he instinctively knew were most sensitive.

The main fight, however, surged around Barak and Durnik. The ring of Barak's sword and the thump of Durnik's cudgel resounded in the narrow street along with the groans of their assailants.

"There's the boy!" a voice rang out from behind them, and Garion whirled. Two men were running down the street toward him, one with a sword and the other with a wicked-looking curved knife. Knowing it was hopeless, Garion raised his club, but Silk was there. The small man launched himself from the shadows directly at the feet of the two, and all three crashed to the street in a tangle of arms and legs. Silk rolled to his feet like a cat, spun and kicked one of the floundering men solidly just below the ear. The man sank twitching to the cobblestones. The other scrambled away and half rose just in time to receive both of Silk's heels in his face as the rat-faced Drasnian leaped into the air, twisted and struck with both legs. Then Silk turned almost casually.

"Are you all right?" he asked Garion.

"I'm fine," Garion said. "You're awfully good at this kind of thing."

"I'm an acrobat," Silk said. "It's simple once you know how."

"They're getting away," Garion told him.

Silk turned, but the two he had just put down were dragging themselves into a dark alley.

There was a triumphant shout from Barak, and Garion saw that the rest of the attackers were fleeing.

At the end of the street in the snow-speckled light from a small window was Brill, almost dancing with fury. "Cowards!" he shouted at his hirelings. "Cowards!" And then Barak started for him, and he too turned and ran.

"Are you all right, Aunt Pol?" Garion said, crossing the street to where she stood.

"Of course I am," she snapped. "And don't do that again, young man. Leave street brawling to those better suited for it."

"I was all right," he objected. "I had my stick here."

"Don't argue with me," she said. "I didn't go to all the trouble of raising you to have you end up dead in a gutter."

"Is everyone all right?" Durnik asked anxiously, coming back to them.

"Of course we are," Aunt Pol snapped peevishly. "Why don't you see if you can help the Old Wolf with the horses?"

"Certainly, Mistress Pol," Durnik said mildly.

"A splendid little fight," Barak said, wiping his sword as he joined them. "Not much blood, but satisfying all the same."

"I'm delighted you found it so," Aunt Pol said acidly. "I don't much care for such encounters. Did they leave anyone behind?"

"Regrettably no, dear lady," Barak said. "The quarters were too narrow for good strokes, and these stones too slippery for good footing. I marked a couple of them quite well, however. We managed to break a few bones and dent a head or two. As a group, they were much better at running than at fighting."

Silk came back from the alley where he had pursued the two who had tried to attack Garion. His eyes were bright, and his grin was vicious. "Invigorating," he said, and then laughed for no apparent reason.

Wolf and Durnik had managed to calm their wild-eyed horses and led them back to where Garion and the others stood. "Is anyone hurt?" Wolf demanded.

"We're all intact," Barak rumbled. "The business was hardly worth drawing a sword for."

Garion's mind was racing; in his excitement, he spoke without stopping to consider the fact that it might be wiser to think the whole thing through first. "How did Brill know we were in Muros?" he asked.

Silk looked at him sharply, his eyes narrowing. "Perhaps he followed us from Winold," he said.

"But we stopped and looked back," Garion said. "He wasn't following when we left, and we've kept a watch behind us every day."

Silk frowned. "Go on, Garion," he said.

"I think he knew where we were going," Garion blurted, struggling against a strange compulsion not to speak what his mind saw clearly now.

"And what else do you think?" Wolf asked.

"Somebody told him," Garion said. "Somebody who knew we were coming here."

"Mingan knew," Silk said, "but Mingan's a merchant, and he wouldn't talk about his dealings to somebody like Brill."

"But Asharak the Murgo was in Mingan's counting room when Mingan hired us." The compulsion was so strong now that Garion's tongue felt stiff.

Silk shrugged. "Why should it concern him? Asharak didn't know who we were."

"But what if he did?" Garion struggled. "What if he isn't just an ordinary Murgo, but one of those others—like the one who was with those ones who passed us a couple days after we left Darine?"

"A Grolim?" Silk said, and his eyes widened. "Yes, I suppose that if Asharak is a Grolim, he'd have known who we are and what we're doing."

"And what if the Grolim who passed us that day was Asharak?" Garion fought to say. "What if he wasn't really looking for us, but just coming south to find Brill and send him here to wait for us?"

Silk looked very hard at Garion. "Very good," he said softly. "Very, very good." He glanced at Aunt Pol. "My compliments, Mistress Pol. You've raised a rare boy here."

"What did this Asharak look like?" Wolf asked quickly.

"A Murgo." Silk shrugged. "He said he was from Rak Goska. I took him to be an ordinary spy on some business that didn't concern us. My mind seems to have gone to sleep."

"It happens when one deals with Grolims," Wolf told him.

"Someone's watching us," Durnik said quietly, "from that window up there."

Garion looked up quickly and saw a dark shape at a second-story window outlined by a dim light. The shape was hauntingly familiar.

Mister Wolf did not look up, but his face turned blank as if he were looking inward, or his mind were searching for something. Then he drew himself up and looked at the figure in the window, his eyes blazing. "A Grolim," he said shortly.

"A dead one perhaps," Silk said. He reached inside his tunic and drew out a long, needle-pointed dirk. He took two quick steps away from the house where the Grolim stood watching, spun and threw the dirk with a smooth, overhand cast.

The dirk crashed through the window. There was a muffled shout, and the light went out. Garion felt a strange pang in his left arm.

"Marked him," Silk said with a grin.

"Good throw," Barak said admiringly.

"One has picked up certain skills," Silk said modestly. "If it was Asharak, I owed him that for deceiving me in Mingan's counting room."

"At least it'll give him something to think about," Wolf said. "There's no point in trying to creep through town now. They know we're here. Let's mount and ride." He climbed onto his horse and led the way down the street at a quick walk.

The compulsion was gone now, and Garion wanted to tell them about Asharak, but there was no chance for that as they rode.

Once they reached the outskirts of the city, they nudged their horses into a fast canter. The snow was falling more seriously now, and the hoof-churned ground in the vast cattle pens was already faintly dusted with white.

"It's going to be a cold night," Silk shouted as they rode.

"We could always go back to Muros," Barak suggested. "Another scuffle or two might warm your blood."

Silk laughed and put his heels to his horse again.

The encampment of the Algars was three leagues to the east of Muros. It was a large area surrounded by a stout palisade of poles set in the ground. The snow by now was falling thickly enough to make the camp look hazy and indistinct. The gate, flanked by hissing torches, was guarded by two fierce-looking warriors in leather leggings, snow-dusted jerkins of the same material, and pot-shaped steel helmets. The points of their lances glittered in the torchlight.

"Halt," one of the warriors commanded, leveling his lance at Mister Wolf. "What business have you here at this time of night?"

"I have urgent need of speaking with your herd master," Wolf replied politely. "May I step down?"

The two guards spoke together briefly.

"You may come down," one of them said. "Your companions, however, must withdraw somewhat—but not beyond the light."

"Algars!" Silk muttered under his breath. "Always suspicious."

Mister Wolf climbed down from his horse, and, throwing back his hood, approached the two guards through the snow.

Then a strange thing happened. The elder of the two guards stared at Mister Wolf, taking in his silver hair and beard. His eyes suddenly opened very wide. He quickly muttered something to his companion, and the two men bowed deeply to Wolf.

"There isn't time for that," Wolf said in annoyance. "Convey me to your herd master."

"At once, Ancient One," the elder guard said quickly and hurried to open the gate.

"What was that about?" Garion whispered to Aunt Pol.

"Algars are superstitious," she said shortly. "Don't ask so many questions."

They waited with snow settling down upon them and melting on their horses. After about a half hour, the gate opened again and two dozen mounted Algars, fierce in their rivet-studded leather vests and steel helmets, herded six saddled horses out into the snow.

Behind them Mister Wolf walked, accompanied by a tall man with his head shaved except for a flowing scalp lock.

"You have honored our camp by your visit, Ancient One," the tall man was saying, "and I wish you all speed on your journey."

"I have little fear of being delayed with Algar horses under us," Wolf replied.

"My riders will accompany you along a route they know which will put you on the far side of Muros within a few hours," the tall man said. "They will then linger for a time to be certain you are not followed."

"I cannot express my gratitude, noble herd master," Wolf said, bowing.

"It is I who am grateful for the opportunity to be of service," the herd master said, also bowing.

The change to their new horses took only a minute. With half of their contingent of Algars leading and the other half bringing up the rear, they turned and rode back toward the west through the dark, snowy night.

Chapter Ten

GRADUALLY, ALMOST IMPERCEPTIBLY, the darkness became paler as the softly falling snow made indistinct even the arrival of morning. Their seemingly inexhaustible horses pounded on through the growing light, the sound of their hooves muffled by the snow now lying fetlock-deep on the broad surface of the Great North Road. Garion glanced back once and saw the jumbled tracks of their passage stretching behind them and, already at the hazy gray limit of his vision, beginning to fill with concealing snow.

When it was fully light, Mister Wolf reined in his steaming horse and proceeded at a walk for a time. "How far have we come?" he asked Silk.

The weasel-faced man who had been shaking the snow out of the folds of his cloak looked around, trying to pick out a landmark in the misty veil of dropping flakes. "Ten leagues," he said finally. "Perhaps a bit more."

"This is a miserable way to travel," Barak rumbled, wincing slightly as he shifted his bulk in the saddle.

"Think of how your horse must feel." Silk grinned at him.

"How far is it to Camaar?" Aunt Pol asked.

"Forty leagues from Muros," Silk told her.

"We'll need shelter then," she said. "We can't gallop forty leagues without rest, no matter who's behind us."

"I don't think we need to worry about pursuit just now," Wolf said. "The Algars will detain Brill and his hirelings or even Asharak if they try to follow us."

"At least there's something Algars are good for," Silk said dryly.

"If I remember correctly, there should be an imperial hostel about five leagues farther to the west," Wolf said. "We ought to reach it by noon."

"Will we be allowed to stay there?" Durnik asked doubtfully. "I've never heard that Tolnedrans are noted for hospitality."

"Tolnedrans will sell anything for a price," Silk said. "The hostel would be a good place to stop. Even if Brill or Asharak should evade the Algars and follow us there, the legionnaires won't permit any foolishness within their walls."

"Why should there be Tolnedran soldiers in Sendaria?" Garion asked, feeling a brief surge of patriotic resentment at the thought.

"Wherever the great roads are, you'll find the legions," Silk said. "Tolnedrans are even better at writing treaties than they are at giving short weight to their customers."

Mister Wolf chuckled. "You're inconsistent, Silk," he said. "You don't object to their highways, but you dislike their legions. You can't have the one without the other."

"I've never pretended to be consistent," the sharp-nosed man said airily. "If we want to reach the questionable comfort of the imperial hostel by noon, hadn't we better move along? I wouldn't want to deny His Imperial Majesty the opportunity to pick my pocket."

"All right," Wolf said, "let's ride." And he put his heels to the flanks of the Algar horse which had already begun to prance impatiently under him.

The hostel, when they reached it in the full light of snowy noon, proved to be a series of stout buildings surrounded by an even stouter wall. The legionnaires who manned it were not the same sort of men as the Tolnedran merchants Garion had seen before. Unlike the oily men of commerce, these were hard-faced professional fighting men in burnished breastplates and plumed helmets. They carried themselves proudly, even arrogantly, each bearing the knowledge that the might of all Tolnedra was behind him.

The food in the dining hall was plain and wholesome, but dreadfully expensive. The tiny sleeping cubicles were scrupulously clean, with hard, narrow beds and thick woolen blankets, and were also expensive. The stables were neat, and they too reached deeply into Mister Wolf's purse. Garion wondered at the thought of how much their lodging was costing, but Wolf paid for it all with seeming indifference as if his purse were bottomless.

"We'll rest here until tomorrow," the white-bearded old man announced when they had finished eating. "Maybe it will snow itself out by morning. I'm not happy with all this plunging blindly through a snowstorm. Too many things can hide in our path in such weather."

Garion, who by now was numb with exhaustion, heard these words gratefully as he half-drowsed at the table. The others sat talking quietly, but he was too tired to listen to what they said.

"Garion," Aunt Pol said finally, "why don't you go to bed?"

"I'm all right, Aunt Pol," he said, rousing himself quickly, mortified once more at being treated like a child.

"*Now*, Garion," she said in that infuriating tone he knew so well. It seemed that all his life she had been saying "*Now*, Garion," to him. But he knew better than to argue.

He stood up and was surprised to feel that his legs were trembling. Aunt Pol also rose and led him from the dining hall.

"I can find my way by myself," he objected.

"Of course," she said. "Now come along."

After he had crawled into bed in his cubicle, she pulled his blankets up firmly around his neck. "Stay covered," she told him. "I don't want you taking cold." She laid her cool hand briefly on his forehead as she had done when he was a small child.

"Aunt Pol?" he asked drowsily.

"Yes, Garion?"

"Who were my parents? I mean, what were their names?"

She looked at him gravely. "We can talk about that later," she said.

"I want to know," he said stubbornly.

"All right. Your father's name was Geran; your mother's was Ildera."

Garion thought about that. "The names don't sound Sendarian," he said finally.

"They're not," Aunt Pol said.

"Why was that?"

"It's a very long story," she said, "and you're much too tired to hear it just now."

On a sudden impulse he reached out and touched the white lock at her brow with the mark on the palm of his right hand. As had sometimes happened before, a window seemed to open in his mind at the tingling touch, but this time that window opened on something much more serious. There was anger, and a single face—a face that was strangely like Mister Wolf's, but was not his face, and all the towering fury in the world was directed at that face.

Aunt Pol moved her head away. "I've asked you not to do that, Garion," she said, her tone very matter-of-fact. "You're not ready for it yet."

"You're going to have to tell me what it is someday," he said.

"Perhaps," she said, "but not now. Close your eyes and go to sleep."

And then, as if that command had somehow dissolved his will, he fell immediately into a deep, untroubled sleep.

By the next morning it had stopped snowing. The world outside the walls of the imperial hostel was mantled in thick, unbroken white, and the air was filmy with a kind of damp haze that was almost—but not quite—fog.

"Misty Sendaria," Silk said ironically at breakfast. "Sometimes I'm amazed that the entire kingdom doesn't rust shut."

They traveled all that day at a mile-eating canter, and that night there was another imperial hostel, almost identical to the one they had left that morning—so closely identical in fact that it almost seemed to Garion that they had ridden all day and merely arrived back where they had started. He commented on that to Silk as they were putting their horses in the stable.

"Tolnedrans are nothing if not predictable," Silk said. "All their hostels are exactly the same. You can find these same buildings in Drasnia, Algaria, Arendia and any place else their great roads go. It's their one weakness—this lack of imagination."

"Don't they get tired of doing the same thing over and over again?"

"It makes them feel comfortable, I guess." Silk laughed. "Let's go see about supper."

It snowed again the following day, but by noon Garion caught a scent other than that faintly dusty odor snow always seemed to have. Even as he had done when they had approached Darine, he began to smell the sea, and he knew their journey was almost at an end.

Camaar, the largest city in Sendaria and the major seaport of the north, was a sprawling place which had existed at the mouth of the Greater Camaar River since antiquity. It was the natural western terminus of the Great North Road which stretched to Boktor in Drasnia and the equally natural northern end of the Great West Road which reached down across Arendia into Tolnedra and the imperial capital at Tol Honeth. With some accuracy it could be said that all roads ended at Camaar.

Late on a chill, snowy afternoon, they rode down a gradual hill toward the city. Some distance from the gate, Aunt Pol stopped her horse. "Since we're no longer posing as vagabonds," she announced, "I see no further need for selecting the most disreputable inns, do you?"

"I hadn't really thought about it," Mister Wolf said.

"Well, I have," she said. "I've had more than enough of wayside hostels and seedy village inns. I need a bath, a clean bed and some decent food. If you don't mind, I'll choose our lodging this time."

"Of course, Pol," Wolf said mildly. "Whatever you say."

"Very well, then," she said and rode on toward the city gate with the rest of them trailing behind her.

"What is your business in Camaar?" one of the furmantled guards at the broad gate asked rather rudely.

Aunt Pol threw back her hood and fixed the man with a steely gaze. "I am the Duchess of Erat," she announced in ringing tones. "These are my retainers, and my business in Camaar is my own affair."

The guard blinked and then bowed respectfully. "Forgive me, your Grace," he said. "I didn't intend to give offense."

"Indeed?" Aunt Pol said, her tone still cold and her gaze still dangerous.

"I did not recognize your Grace," the poor man floundered, squirming under that imperious stare. "May I offer any assistance?"

"I hardly think so," Aunt Pol said, looking him up and down. "Which is the finest inn in Camaar?"

"That would be the Lion, my Lady."

"And—?" she said impatiently.

"And what, my Lady?" the man said, confused by her question.

"Where is it?" she demanded. "Don't stand there gaping like a dolt. Speak up."

"It lies beyond the customs houses," the guard replied, flushing at her words. "Follow this street until you reach Customs Square. Anyone there can direct you to the Lion."

Aunt Pol pulled her hood back up. "Give the fellow something," she said over her shoulder and rode on into the city without a backward glance.

"My thanks," the guard said as Wolf leaned down to hand him a small coin. "I must admit that I haven't heard of the Duchess of Erat before."

"You're a fortunate man," Wolf said.

"She's a great beauty," the man said admiringly.

"And has a temper to match," Wolf told him.

"I noticed that," the guard said.

"We noticed you noticing," Silk told him slyly.

They nudged their horses and caught up with Aunt Pol.

"The Duchess of Erat?" Silk asked mildly.

"The fellow's manner irritated me," Aunt Pol said loftily, "and I'm tired of putting on a poor face in front of strangers."

At Customs Square Silk accosted a busy-looking merchant trudging across the snow-covered paving. "You—fellow," he said in the most insulting way possible, pulling his horse directly in front of the startled merchant. "My mistress, the Duchess of Erat, requires directions to an inn called the Lion. Be so good as to provide them."

The merchant blinked, his face flushing at the rat-faced man's tone. "Up that street," he said shortly, pointing. "Some goodly way. It will be on your left. There's a sign of a Lion at the front."

Silk sniffed ungraciously, tossed a few coins into the snow at the man's feet and whirled his horse in a grand manner. The merchant, Garion noted, looked outraged, but he *did* grope in the snow for the coins Silk had thrown.

"I doubt that any of these people will quickly forget our passage," Wolf said sourly when they were some ways up the street.

"They'll remember the passage of an arrogant noblewoman," Silk said. "This is as good a disguise as any we've tried."

When they arrived at the inn, Aunt Pol commanded not just the usual sleeping chambers but an entire apartment. "My chamberlain there will pay you," she said to the innkeeper, indicating Mister Wolf. "Our baggage horses are some days behind with the rest of my servants, so I'll require the services of a dressmaker and a maid. See to it." And she turned and swept imperially up the long staircase that led to her apartment, following the servant who scurried ahead to show her the way.

"The duchess has a commanding presence, doesn't she?" the innkeeper ventured as Wolf began counting out coins.

"She has indeed," Wolf agreed. "I've discovered the wisdom of not countering her wishes."

"I'll be guided by you then," the innkeeper assured him. "My youngest daughter is a serviceable girl. I'll dispatch her to serve as her Grace's maid."

"Many thanks, friend," Silk told him. "Our Lady becomes most irritable when those things she desires are delayed, and we're the ones who suffer most from her displeasure."

They trooped up the stairs to the apartments Aunt Pol had taken and stepped into the main sitting room, a splendid chamber far richer than any Garion had seen before. The walls were covered by tapestries with intricate pictures woven into the fabric. A wealth of candles—real wax instead of smoky tallow—gleamed in sconces on the walls and in a massive candelabra on the polished table. A good warm fire danced merrily on the hearth, and a large carpet of curious design lay on the floor.

Aunt Pol was standing before the fire, warming her hands. "Isn't this better than some shabby, wharfside inn reeking of fish and unwashed sailors?" she asked.

"If the Duchess of Erat will forgive my saying so," Wolf said somewhat tartly, "this is hardly the way to escape notice, and the cost of these lodgings would feed a legion for a week."

"Don't grow parsimonious in your dotage, Old Wolf," she replied. "No one takes a spoiled noblewoman seriously, and your wagons weren't able to keep that disgusting Brill from finding us. This guise is at least comfortable, and it permits us to move more rapidly."

Wolf grunted. "I only hope we won't regret all this," he said.

"Stop grumbling, old man," she told him.

"Have it your way, Pol." He sighed.

"I intend to," she said.

"How are we to behave, Mistress Pol?" Durnik asked hesitantly. Her sudden regal manner had obviously confused him. "I'm not familiar with the ways of the gentry."

"It's quite simple, Durnik," she said. She eyed him up and down, noting his plain, dependable face and his solid competence. "How would you like to be chief groom to the Duchess of Erat? And master of her stables?"

Durnik laughed uncomfortably. "Noble titles for work I've done all my life," he said. "I could manage the work easily enough, but the titles might grow a bit heavy."

"You'll do splendidly, friend Durnik," Silk assured him. "That honest face of yours makes people believe anything you choose to tell them. If I had a face like yours, I could steal half the world." He turned to Aunt Pol. "And what role am I to play, my Lady?" he asked.

"You'll be my reeve," she said. "The thievery usually associated with the position should suit you."

Silk bowed ironically.

"And I?" Barak said, grinning openly.

"My man-at-arms," she said. "I doubt that any would believe you to be a dancing master. Just stand around looking dangerous."

"What of me, Aunt Pol?" Garion asked. "What do I do?"

"You can be my page."

"What does a page do?"

"You fetch things for me."

"I've always done that. Is that what it's called?"

"Don't be impertinent. You also answer doors and announce visitors; and when I'm melancholy, you may sing to me."

"Sing?" he said incredulously. "Me?"

"It's customary."

"You wouldn't make me do that, would you, Aunt Pol?"

"Your Grace," she corrected.

"You won't be very gracious if you have to listen to me sing," he warned. "My voice isn't very good."

"You'll do just fine, dear," she said.

"And I've already been appointed your Grace's chamberlain," Wolf said.

"My chief steward," she told him. "Manager of my estates and keeper of my purse."

"Somehow I knew that would be part of it."

There was a timid rap at the door.

"See who that is, Garion," Aunt Pol said.

When he opened the door, Garion found a young girl with light brown hair in a sober dress and starched apron and cap standing outside. She had very large brown eyes that looked at him apprehensively.

"Yes?" he asked.

"I've been sent to wait upon the duchess," she said in a low voice.

"Your maid has arrived, your Grace," Garion announced.

"Splendid," Aunt Pol said. "Come in, child."

The girl entered the room.

"What a pretty thing you are," Aunt Pol said.

"Thank you, my Lady," the girl answered with a brief curtsy and a rosy blush.

"And what is your name?"

"I am called Donia, my Lady."

"A lovely name," Aunt Pol said. "Now to important matters. Is there a bath on the premises?"

It was still snowing the next morning. The roofs of nearby houses were piled high with white, and the narrow streets were deep with it.

"I think we're close to the end of our search," Mister Wolf said as he stared intently out through the rippled glass of the window in the room with the tapestries.

"It's unlikely that the one we're after would stay in Camaar for long," Silk said.

"Very unlikely," Wolf agreed, "but once we've found his trail, we'll be able to move more rapidly. Let's go into the city and see if I'm right."

After Mister Wolf and Silk had left, Garion sat for a while talking with Donia, who seemed to be about his own age. Although she was not quite as pretty as Zubrette, Garion found her soft voice and huge brown eyes extremely attractive. Things were going along well between them until Aunt Pol's dressmaker arrived and Donia's presence was required in the chamber where the Duchess of Erat was being fitted for her new gowns.

Since Durnik, obviously ill at ease in the luxurious surroundings of their chambers, had adjourned to the stables after breakfast, Garion was left in the company of the giant Barak, who worked patiently with a small stone, polishing a nick out of the edge of his sword—a memento of the skirmish in Muros. Garion had never been wholly comfortable with the huge, red-bearded man. Barak spoke rarely, and there seemed to be a kind of hulking menace about him. So it was that Garion spent the morning examining the tapestries on the walls of the sitting room. The tapestries depicted knights in full armor and castles on hilltops and strangely angular-looking maidens moping about in gardens.

"Arendish," Barak said, directly behind him. Garion jumped. The huge man had moved up so quietly that Garion had not heard him.

"How can you tell?" Garion asked politely.

"The Arends have a fondness for tapestry," Barak rumbled, "and the weaving of pictures occupies their women while the men are off denting each other's armor."

"Do they really wear all that?" Garion asked, pointing at a heavily armored knight pictured on the tapestry.

"Oh yes." Barak laughed. "That and more. Even their horses wear armor. It's a silly way to make war."

Garion scuffed his shoe on the carpet. "Is this Arendish too?" he asked.

Barak shook his head. "Mallorean," he said.

"How did it get here all the way from Mallorea?" Garion asked. "I've heard that Mallorea's all the way on the other end of the world."

"It's a goodly way off," Barak agreed, "but a merchant

would go twice as far to make a profit. Such goods as this commonly move along the North Caravan Route out of Gar og Nadrak to Boktor. Mallorean carpets are prized by the wealthy. I don't much care for them myself, since I'm not fond of anything that has to do with the Angaraks."

"How many kinds of Angaraks are there?" Garion asked. "I know there are Murgos and Thulls, and I've heard stories about the Battle of Vo Mimbre and all, but I don't know much about them really."

"There are five tribes of them," Barak said, sitting back down and resuming his polishing, "Murgos and Thulls, Nadraks and Malloreans, and of course the Grolims. They live in the four kingdoms of the east—Mallorea, Gar og Nadrak, Mishrak ac Thull and Cthol Murgos."

"Where do the Grolims live?"

"They have no special place," Barak replied grimly. "The Grolims are the priests of Torak One-eye and are everywhere in the lands of the Angaraks. They're the ones who perform the sacrifices to Torak. Grolim knives have spilled more Angarak blood than a dozen Vo Mimbres."

Garion shuddered. "Why should Torak take such pleasure in the slaughter of his own people?" he asked.

"Who can say?" Barak shrugged. "He's a twisted and evil God. Some believe that he was made mad when he used the Orb of Aldur to crack the world and the Orb repaid him by burning out his eye and consuming his hand."

"How could the world be cracked?" Garion asked. "I've never understood that part of the story."

"The power of the Orb of Aldur is such that it can accomplish anything," Barak told him. "When Torak raised it, the earth was split apart by its power, and the seas came in to drown the land. The story's very old, but I think that it's probably true."

"Where is the Orb of Aldur now?" Garion asked suddenly.

Barak looked at him, his eyes icy blue and his face thoughtful, but he didn't say anything.

"Do you know what I think?" Garion said on a sudden impulse. "I think that it's the Orb of Aldur that's been stolen. I think it's the Orb that Mister Wolf is trying to find."

"And I think it would be better if you didn't think so much about such things," Barak warned.

"But I want to *know*," Garion protested, his curiosity driving him even in the face of Barak's words and the warning voice in his mind. "Everyone treats me like an ignorant boy. All I do is tag along with no idea of what we're doing. Who *is* Mister Wolf, anyway? Why did the Algars behave the way they did when they saw him? How can he follow something that he can't see? Please tell me, Barak."

"Not I." Barak laughed. "Your Aunt would pull out my beard whisker by whisker if I made that mistake."

"You're not afraid of her, are you?"

"Any man with good sense is afraid of her," Barak said, rising and sliding his sword into its sheath.

"Aunt Pol?" Garion asked incredulously.

"Aren't you afraid of her?" Barak asked pointedly.

"No," Garion said, and then realized that was not precisely true. "Well—not really afraid. It's more—" He left it hanging, not knowing how to explain it.

"Exactly," Barak said. "And I'm no more foolhardy than you, my boy. You're too full of questions I'd be far wiser not to answer. If you want to know about these things, you'll have to ask your Aunt."

"She won't tell me," Garion said glumly. "She won't tell me anything. She won't even tell me about my parents—not really."

Barak frowned. "That's strange," he said.

"I don't think they were Sendars," Garion said. "Their names weren't Sendarian, and Silk says that I'm not a Sendar—at least I don't look like one."

Barak looked at him closely. "No," he said finally. "Now that you mention it, you don't. You look more like a Rivan than anything else—but not quite that either."

"Is Aunt Pol a Rivan?"

Barak's eyes narrowed slightly. "I think we're getting to some more of those questions I hadn't better answer," he said.

"I'm going to find out someday," Garion said.

"But not today," Barak said. "Come along. I need some exercise. Let's go out into the innyard and I'll teach you how to use a sword."

"Me?" Garion said, all his curiosity suddenly melting away in the excitement of that thought.

"You're at an age where you should begin to learn," Barak said. "The occasion may someday arise when it will be a useful thing for you to know."

Late that afternoon when Garion's arm had begun to ache from the effort of swinging Barak's heavy sword and the whole idea of learning the skills of a warrior had become a great deal less exciting, Mister Wolf and Silk returned. Their clothes were wet from the snow through which they had trudged all day, but Wolf's eyes were bright, and his face had a curiously exultant expression as he led them all back up the stairs to the sitting room.

"Ask your Aunt to join us," he told Garion as he removed his sodden mantle and stepped to the fire to warm himself.

Garion sensed quickly that this was not the time for questions. He hurried to the polished door where Aunt Pol had been closeted with her dressmaker all day and rapped.

"What is it?" her voice came from inside.

"Mister—uh—that is, your chamberlain has returned, my Lady," Garion said, remembering at the last moment that she was not alone. "He requests a word with you."

"Oh, very well," she said. After a minute she came out, firmly closing the door behind her.

Garion gasped. The rich, blue velvet gown she wore made her so magnificent that she quite took his breath away. He stared at her in helpless admiration.

"Where is he?" she asked. "Don't stand and gape, Garion. It's not polite."

"You're *beautiful*, Aunt Pol," he blurted.

"Yes, dear," she said, patting his cheek, "I know. Now where's the Old Wolf?"

"In the room with the tapestries," Garion said, still unable to take his eyes from her.

"Come along, then," she said and swept down the short hall to the sitting room. They entered to find the others all standing by the fireplace.

"Well?" she asked.

Wolf looked up at her, his eyes still bright. "An excellent choice, Pol," he said admiringly. "Blue has always been your best color."

"Do you like it?" she asked, holding out her arms and turning almost girlishly so that they all might see how fine

she looked. "I hope it pleases you, old man, because it's
costing you a great deal of money."

Wolf laughed. "I was almost certain it would," he said.

The effect of Aunt Pol's gown on Durnik was painfully
obvious. The poor man's eyes literally bulged, and his face
turned alternately very pale and then very red, then finally
settled into an expression of such hopelessness that Garion
was touched to the quick by it.

Silk and Barak in curious unison both bowed deeply and
wordlessly to Aunt Pol, and her eyes sparkled at their silent
tribute.

"It's been here," Wolf announced seriously.

"You're certain?" Aunt Pol demanded.

He nodded. "I could feel the memory of its passage in
the very stones."

"Did it come by sea?" she asked.

"No. He probably came ashore with it in some secluded
cove up the coast and then traveled here by land."

"And took ship again?"

"I doubt that," Wolf said. "I know him well. He's not
comfortable on the sea."

"Besides which," Barak said, "one word to King Anheg
of Cherek would have put a hundred warships on his trail.
No one can hide on the sea from the ships of Cherek, and
he knows that."

"You're right," Wolf agreed, "I think he'll avoid the do-
mains of the Alorns. That's probably why he chose not to
pass along the North Road through Algaria and Drasnia.
The Spirit of Belar is strong in the kingdoms of the Alorns,
and not even this thief is bold enough to risk a confronta-
tion with the Bear-God."

"Which leaves Arendia," Silk said, "or the land of the
Ulgos."

"Arendia, I think," Wolf said. "The wrath of UL is even
more fearsome than that of Belar."

"Forgive me," Durnik said, his eyes still on Aunt Pol.
"This is all most confusing. I've never heard just exactly
who this thief is."

"I'm sorry, gentle Durnik," Wolf said. "It's not a good
idea to speak his name. He has certain powers which might
make it possible for him to know our every move if we

alert him to our location, and he can hear his name spoken a thousand leagues away."

"A sorcerer?" Durnik asked unbelievingly.

"The word isn't one I'd choose," Wolf said. "It's a term used by men who don't understand that particular art. Instead let's call him 'thief,' though there are a few other names I might call him which are far less kindly."

"Can we be certain that he'll make for the kingdoms of the Angaraks?" Silk asked, frowning. "If that's the case, wouldn't it be quicker to take a ship directly to Tol Honeth and pick up his trail on the South Caravan Route into Cthol Murgos?"

Wolf shook his head. "Better to stay with this trail now that we've found it. We don't know what he intends. Maybe he wants to keep the thing he's stolen for himself rather than deliver it over to the Grolims. He might even seek sanctuary in Nyissa."

"He couldn't do that without the connivance of Salmissra," Aunt Pol said.

"It wouldn't be the first time that the Queen of the Serpent People has tampered with things that are none of her concern," Wolf pointed out.

"If that turns out to be true," Aunt Pol said grimly, "I think I'll give myself the leisure to deal with the snakewoman permanently."

"It's too early to know," Wolf said. "Tomorrow we'll buy provisions and ferry across the river to Arendia. I'll take up the trail there. For the time being all we can do is follow that trail. Once we know for certain where it leads, we'll be able to consider our alternatives."

From the evening-darkened innyard outside there came suddenly the sound of many horses.

Barak stepped quickly to the window and glanced out. "Soldiers," he said shortly.

"Here?" Silk said, also hurrying to the window.

"They appear to be from one of the king's regiments," Barak said.

"They won't be interested in us," Aunt Pol said.

"Unless they aren't what they seem," Silk said. "Uniforms of one kind or another aren't that difficult to come by."

"They aren't Murgos," Barak said. "I'd recognize Murgos."

"Brill isn't a Murgo either," Silk said, staring down into the innyard.

"See if you can hear what they say," Wolf instructed.

Barak carefully opened one of the windows a crack, and the candles all flickered in the gust of icy wind. In the yard below the captain of the soldiers was speaking with the innkeeper. "He's a man of somewhat more than medium height, with white hair and a short white beard. He may be traveling with some others."

"There's such a one here, your Honor," the innkeeper said dubiously, "but I'm sure he isn't the one you seek. This one is chief steward to the Duchess of Erat, who honors my inn with her presence."

"The Duchess of where?" the captain asked sharply.

"Of Erat," the innkeeper replied. "A most noble lady of great beauty and a commanding presence."

"I wonder if I might have a word with her Grace," the captain said, climbing down from his horse.

"I'll ask her if she will receive your Honor," the innkeeper replied.

Barak closed the window. "I'll deal with this meddlesome captain," he said firmly.

"No," Wolf said. "He's got too many soldiers with him, and if they're who they seem to be, they're good men who haven't done us any harm."

"There's the back stairs," Silk suggested. "We could be three streets away before he reached our door."

"And if he stationed soldiers at the back of the inn?" Aunt Pol suggested. "What then? Since he's coming to speak with the Duchess of Erat, why don't we let the duchess deal with him?"

"What have you got in mind?" Wolf asked.

"If the rest of you stay out of sight, I'll speak with him," she said. "I should be able to put him off until morning. We can be across the river into Arendia before he comes back."

"Perhaps," Wolf said, "but this captain sounds like a determined man."

"I've dealt with determined men before," she said.

"We'll have to decide quickly," Silk said from the door. "He's on the stairs right now."

"We'll try it your way, Pol," Wolf said, opening the door to the next chamber.

"Garion," Aunt Pol said, "you stay here. A duchess wouldn't be unattended."

Wolf and the others quickly left the room.

"What do you want me to do, Aunt Pol?" Garion whispered.

"Just remember that you're my page, dear," she said, seating herself in a large chair near the center of the room and carefully arranging the folds of her gown. "Stand near my chair and try to look attentive. I'll take care of the rest."

"Yes, my Lady," Garion said.

The captain, when he arrived behind the innkeeper's knock, proved to be a tall, sober-looking man with penetrating gray eyes. Garion, trying his best to sound officious, requested the soldier's name and then turned to Aunt Pol.

"There's a Captain Brendig to see you, your Grace," he announced. "He says that it's a matter of importance."

Aunt Pol looked at him for a moment as if considering the request. "Oh, very well," she said finally. "Show him in."

Captain Brendig stepped into the room, and the innkeeper left hurriedly.

"Your Grace," the captain said, bowing deferentially to Aunt Pol.

"What is it, Captain?" she demanded.

"I would not trouble your Grace if my mission were not of such urgency," Brendig apologized. "My orders are directly from the king himself, and you of all people will know that we must defer to his wishes."

"I suppose I can spare you a few moments for the king's business," she said.

"There's a certain man the king wishes to have apprehended," Brendig said. "An elderly man with white hair and beard. I'm informed that you have such a one among your servants."

"Is the man a criminal?" she asked.

"The king didn't say so, your Grace," he told her. "I was only told that the man was to be seized and delivered to the palace at Sendar—and all who are with him as well."

"I am seldom at court," Aunt Pol said. "It's most unlikely that any of my servants would be of such interest to the king."

"Your Grace," Brendig said delicately, "in addition to my duties in one of the king's own regiments, I also have the honor to hold a baronetcy. I've been at court all my life and must confess that I've never seen you there. A lady of your striking appearance would not be soon forgotten."

Aunt Pol inclined her head slightly in acknowledgment of the compliment. "I suppose I should have guessed, my Lord Brendig," she said. "Your manners are not those of a common soldier."

"Moreover, your Grace," he continued, "I'm familiar with all the holdings of the kingdom. If I'm not mistaken, the district of Erat is an earldom, and the Earl of Erat is a short, stout man—my great uncle incidentally. There has been no duchy in that part of Sendaria since the kingdom was under the dominion of the Wacite Arends."

Aunt Pol fixed him with an icy stare.

"My Lady," Brendig said almost apologetically, "the Wacite Arends were exterminated by their Asturian cousins in the last years of the third millenium. There has been no Wacite nobility for over two thousand years."

"I thank you for the history lesson, my Lord," Aunt Pol said coldly.

"All of that, however, is hardly the issue, is it?" Brendig continued. "I am bidden by my king to seek out the man of whom I spoke. Upon your honor, Lady, do you know such a man?"

The question hung in the air between them, and Garion, knowing in sudden panic that they were caught, almost shouted for Barak.

Then the door to the next chamber opened, and Mister Wolf stepped into the room. "There's no need to continue with this," he said. "I'm the one you're looking for. What does Fulrach of Sendaria want with me?"

Brendig looked at him without seeming surprise. "His Majesty did not see fit to take me into his confidence," he said. "He will explain it himself, I have no doubt, as soon as we reach the palace at Sendar."

"The sooner the better then," Wolf said. "When do we leave?"

"We depart for Sendar directly after breakfast in the morning," Brendig said. "I will accept your word that none of you will attempt to leave this inn during the night. I'd prefer not to subject the Duchess of Erat to the indignity of confinement at the local barracks. The cells there are most uncomfortable, I'm told."

"You have my word," Mister Wolf said.

"Thank you," Brendig said, bowing slightly. "I must also advise you that I am obliged to post guards about this inn—for your protection, of course."

"Your solicitude overwhelms us, my Lord," Aunt Pol said dryly.

"Your servant, my Lady," Brendig said with a formal bow. And then he turned and left the room.

The polished door was only wood; Garion knew that, but as it closed behind the departing Brendig it seemed to have that dreadful, final clang of the door to a dungeon.

Chapter Eleven

THEY WERE NINE DAYS on the coast road from Camaar to the capital at Sendar, though it was only fifty-five leagues. Captain Brendig measured their pace carefully, and his detachment of soldiers was arranged in such fashion that even the thought of escape was impossible. Although it had stopped snowing, the road was still difficult, and the wind which blew in off the sea and across the broad, snow-covered salt marshes was raw and chill. They stayed each night in the evenly spaced Sendarian hostels which stood like mileposts along that uninhabited stretch of coast. The hostels were not quite so well appointed as were their Tolnedran counterparts along the Great North Road, but they were at least adequate. Captain Brendig seemed solicitous about their comfort, but he also posted guards each night.

On the evening of the second day, Garion sat near the fire with Durnik, staring moodily into the flames. Durnik was his oldest friend, and Garion felt a desperate need for friendship just then.

"Durnik," he said finally.

"Yes, lad?"

"Have you ever been in a dungeon?"

"What could I have done to be put in a dungeon?"

"I thought that you might have seen one sometime."

"Honest folk don't go near such places," Durnik said.

"I've heard they're awful—dark and cold and full of rats."

"What is this talk of dungeons?" Durnik asked.

"I'm afraid we may find out all about places like that very soon," Garion said, trying not to sound too frightened.

"We've done nothing wrong," Durnik said.

"Then why would the king have us seized like this? Kings don't do things like that without good reason."

"We haven't done anything wrong," Durnik repeated stubbornly.

"But maybe Mister Wolf has," Garion suggested. "The king wouldn't send all these soldiers after him without some reason—and we could all be thrown in the dungeon with him just because we happened to be his companions."

"Things like that don't happen in Sendaria," Durnik said firmly.

The next day the wind was very strong as it blew in off the sea; but it was a warm wind, and the foot-deep snow on the road began to turn slushy. By midday it had started to rain. They rode in sodden misery toward the next hostel.

"I'm afraid we'll have to delay our journey until this blows out," Captain Brendig said that evening, looking out one of the tiny windows of the hostel. "The road's going to be quite impassable by morning."

They spent the next day, and the next, sitting in the cramped main room of the hostel listening to the wind-driven rain slashing at the walls and roof, all the while under the watchful eyes of Brendig and his soldiers.

"Silk," Garion said on the second day, moving over to the bench where the rat-faced little man sat dozing.

"Yes, Garion?" Silk asked, rousing himself.

"What kind of man is the king?"

"Which king?"

"Of Sendaria."

"A foolish man—like all kings." Silk laughed. "The Sendarian kings are perhaps a bit more foolish, but that's only natural. Why do you ask?"

"Well—" Garion hesitated. "Let's suppose that somebody did something that the king didn't like, and there were some other people traveling with him, and the king had these people seized. Would the king just throw them all into the dungeon? Or would he let the others go and just keep the one who'd angered him?"

Silk looked at him for a moment and then spoke firmly. "That question is unworthy of you, Garion."

Garion flushed. "I'm afraid of dungeons," he said in a small voice, suddenly very ashamed of himself. "I don't want to be locked up in the dark forever when I don't even know what for."

"The kings of Sendaria are just and honest men," Silk told him. "Not too bright, I'm afraid, but always fair."

"How can they be kings if they aren't wise?" Garion objected.

"Wisdom's a useful trait in a king," Silk said, "but hardly essential."

"How do they get to be kings, then?" Garion demanded.

"Some are born to it," Silk said. "The stupidest man in the world can be a king if he has the right parents. Sendarian kings have a disadvantage because they started so low."

"Low?"

"They were elected. Nobody ever elected a king before—only the Sendars."

"How do you elect a king?"

Silk smiled. "Very badly, Garion. It's a poor way to select a king. The other ways are worse, but election is a very bad way to choose a king."

"Tell me how it was done," Garion said.

Silk glanced briefly at the rain-spattered window across the room and shrugged. "It's a way to pass the time," he said. And then he leaned back, stretched his feet toward the fire and began.

"It all started about fifteen hundred years ago," he said, his voice loud enough to reach the ears of Captain Brendig, who sat nearby writing on a piece of parchment. "Sendaria wasn't a kingdom then, nor even a separate country. It had belonged from time to time to Cherek, Algaria or the northern Arends—Wacite or Asturian, depending on the fortunes of the Arendish civil war. When that war finally came to an end and the Wacites were destroyed and the Asturians had been defeated and driven into the untracked reaches of the great forest in northern Arendia, the Emperor of Tolnedra, Ran Horb II, decided that there ought to be a kingdom here."

"How could a Tolnedran emperor make that kind of decision for Sendaria?" Garion asked.

"The arm of the Empire is very long," Silk said. "The Great North Road had been built during the Second Borune Dynasty—I think it was Ran Borune IV who started the construction, wasn't it, Captain?"

"The fifth," Brendig said somewhat sourly without looking up. "Ran Borune V."

"Thank you, Captain," Silk said. "I can never keep the Borune Dynasties straight. Anyway, there were already imperial legions in Sendaria to maintain the highway, and if one has troops in an area, one has a certain authority, wouldn't you say, Captain?"

"It's your story," Brendig said shortly.

"Indeed it is," Silk agreed. "Now it wasn't really out of any kind of generosity that Ran Horb made his decision, Garion. Don't misunderstand that. Tolnedrans never give anything away. It was just that the Mimbrate Arends had finally won the Arendish civil war—a thousand years of bloodshed and treachery—and Tolnedra couldn't afford to allow the Mimbrates to expand into the north. The creation of an independent kingdom in Sendaria would block Mimbrate access to the trade routes down out of Drasnia and prevent the seat of world power from moving to Vo Mimbre and leaving the imperial capital at Tol Honeth in a kind of backwater."

"It all sounds terribly involved," Garion said.

"Not really," Silk said. "It's only politics, and that's a very simple game, isn't it, Captain?"

"A game I do not play," Brendig said, not looking up.

"Really?" Silk asked. "So long at court and not a politician? You're a rare man, Captain. At any rate, the Sendars suddenly discovered that they had themselves a kingdom but that they had no genuine hereditary nobility. Oh, there were a few retired Tolnedran nobles living on estates here and there, assorted pretenders to this or that Wacite or Asturian title, a Cherek war chief or two with a few followers, but no genuine Sendarian nobility. And so it was that they decided to hold a national election—select a king, don't you see, and then leave the bestowing of titles up to him. A very practical approach, and typically Sendarian."

"How do you elect a king?" Garion asked, beginning to lose his dread of dungeons in his fascination with the story.

"Everybody votes," Silk said simply. "Parents, of course, probably cast the votes for their children, but it appears that there was very little cheating. The rest of the world stood around and laughed at all this foolishness, but the Sendars continued to cast ballot after ballot for a dozen years."

"Six years, actually," Brendig said with his face still down over his parchment. "3827 to 3833."

"And there were over a thousand candidates," Silk said expansively.

"Seven hundred and forty-three," Brendig said tightly.

"I stand corrected, noble Captain," Silk said. "It's an enormous comfort to have such an expert here to catch my errors. I'm but a simple Drasnian merchant with little background in history. Anyway, on the twenty-third ballot, they finally elected their king—a rutabaga farmer named Fundor."

"He raised more than just rutabagas," Brendig said, looking up with an angry face.

"Of course he did," Silk said, smacking his forehead with an open palm. "How could I have forgotten the cabbages? He raised cabbages, too, Garion. Never forget the cabbages. Well, everybody in Sendaria who thought he was important journeyed to Fundor's farm and found him vigorously fertilizing his fields, and they greeted him with a great cry, 'Hail, Fundor the Magnificent, King of Sendaria,' and fell on their knees in his august presence."

"Must we continue with this?" Brendig asked in a pained voice, looking up.

"The boy wants to know, Captain," Silk replied with an innocent face. "It's our duty as his elders to instruct him in the history of our past, wouldn't you say?"

"Say whatever you like," Brendig said in a stiff voice.

"Thank you for your permission, Captain," Silk said, inclining his head. "Do you know what the King of Sendaria said then, Garion?" he asked.

"No," Garion said. "What?"

" 'I pray you, your eminences,' the king said, 'have a care for your finery. I have just well manured the bed in which you are kneeling.' "

Barak, who was sitting nearby, roared with laughter, pounding his knee with one huge hand.

"I find this less than amusing, sir," Captain Brendig said coldly, rising to his feet. "I make no jokes about the King of Drasnia, do I?"

"You're a courteous man, Captain," Silk said mildly, "and a nobleman. I'm merely a poor man trying to make his way in the world."

Brendig looked at him helplessly and then turned and stamped from the room.

The following morning the wind had blown itself out and the rain had stopped. The road was very nearly a quagmire, but Brendig decided that they must continue. Travel that day was difficult, but the next was somewhat easier as the road began to drain.

Aunt Pol seemed unconcerned by the fact that they had been seized at the king's orders. She maintained her regal bearing even though Garion saw no real need to continue the subterfuge and wished fervently that she would abandon it. The familiar practical sensibility with which she had ruled her kitchen at Faldor's farm had somehow been replaced by a kind of demanding willfulness that Garion found particularly distressing. For the first time in his life he felt a distance between them, and it left a vacancy that had never been there before. To make matters worse, the gnawing uncertainty which had been steadily growing since Silk's unequivocal declaration on the hilltop outside Winold that Aunt Pol could not possibly be his Aunt sawed roughly at his sense of his own identity, and Garion often found himself staring at the awful question, "Who am I?"

Mister Wolf seemed changed as well. He seldom spoke

either on the road nor at night in the hostels. He spent a great deal of time sitting by himself with an expression of moody irritability on his face.

Finally, on the ninth day after their departure from Camaar, the broad salt marshes ended, and the land along the coast became more rolling. They topped a hill about midday just as the pale winter sun broke through the clouds, and there in the valley below them the walled city of Sendar lay facing the sea.

The detachment of guards at the south gate of the city saluted smartly as Captain Brendig led the little party through, and he returned their salute crisply. The broad streets of the city seemed filled with people in the finest clothing, all moving about importantly as if their errands were the most vital in the world.

"Courtiers." Barak, who chanced to be riding beside Garion, snorted with contempt. "Not a real man amongst them."

"A necessary evil, my dear Barak," Silk said back over his shoulder to the big man. "Little jobs require little men, and it's the little jobs that keep a kingdom running."

After they had passed through a magnificently large square, they moved up a wide avenue to the palace. It was a very large building with many stories and broad wings extending out on each side of the paved courtyard. The entire structure was surmounted by a round tower that was easily the highest edifice in the whole city.

"Where do you suppose the dungeons are?" Garion whispered to Durnik when they stopped.

"I would take it most kindly, Garion," Durnik said with a pained look, "if you would not speak so much of dungeons."

Captain Brendig dismounted and went to meet a fussy-looking man in an embroidered tunic and feathered cap who came down the wide steps at the front of the palace to meet them. They spoke for a few moments and seemed to be arguing.

"My orders are from the king himself," Brendig said, his voice carrying to where they sat. "I am commanded to deliver these people directly to him immediately upon our arrival."

"My orders are also from the king," the fussy-looking

man said, "and *I* am commanded to have them made presentable before they are delivered to the throne room. I will take charge of them."

"They will remain in my custody, Count Nilden, until they have been delivered to the king himself," Brendig said coldly.

"I will not have your muddy soldiers tracking through the halls of the palace, Lord Brendig," the Count replied.

"Then we will wait here, Count Nilden," Brendig said. "Be so good as to fetch his Majesty."

"Fetch?" The Count's face was aghast. "I am Chief Butler to his Majesty's household, Lord Brendig. I do not fetch anything or anybody."

Brendig turned as if to remount his horse.

"Oh, very well," Count Nilden said petulantly, "if you must have it your own way. At least have them wipe their feet."

Brendig bowed coldly.

"I won't forget this, Lord Brendig," Nilden threatened.

"Nor shall I, Count Nilden," Brendig replied.

Then they all dismounted and, with Brendig's soldiers drawn up in close order about them, they crossed the courtyard to a broad door near the center of the west wing.

"Be so good as to follow me," Count Nilden said, glancing with a shudder at the mud-spattered soldiers, and he led them into the wide corridor which lay beyond the door.

Apprehension and curiosity struggled in Garion's mind. Despite the assurances of Silk and Durnik and the hopeful implications of Count Nilden's announcement that he was going to have them made presentable, the threat of some clammy, rat-infested dungeon, complete with a rack and a wheel and other unpleasant things, still seemed very real. On the other hand, he had never been in a palace before, and his eyes tried to be everywhere at once. That part of his mind which sometimes spoke to him in dry detachment told him that his fears were probably groundless and that his gawking made him appear to be a doltish country bumpkin.

Count Nilden led them directly to a part of the corridor where there were a number of highly polished doors. "This one is for the boy," he announced, pointing at one of them.

One of the soldiers opened the door, and Garion reluctantly stepped through, looking back over his shoulder at Aunt Pol.

"Come along now," a somewhat impatient voice said.

Garion whirled, not knowing what to expect.

"Close the door, boy," the fine-looking man who had been waiting for him said. "We don't have all day, you know." The man was waiting beside a large wooden tub with steam rising from it. "Quickly, boy, take off those filthy rags and get into the tub. His Majesty is waiting."

Too confused to object or even answer, Garion numbly began to unlace his tunic.

After he had been bathed and the knots had been brushed out of his hair, he was dressed in clothes which lay on a nearby bench. His coarse woolen hose of serviceable peasant brown were exchanged for ones of a much finer weave in a lustrous blue. His scuffed and muddy boots were traded for soft leather shoes. His tunic was soft white linen, and the doublet he wore over it was a rich blue, trimmed with a silvery fur.

"I guess that's the best I can do on short notice," the man who had bathed and dressed him said, looking him up and down critically. "At least I won't be totally embarrassed when you're presented to the king."

Garion mumbled his thanks and then stood, waiting for further instructions.

"Well, go along, boy. You mustn't keep his Majesty waiting."

Silk and Barak stood in the corridor, talking quietly. Barak was hugely splendid in a green brocade doublet, but looked uncomfortable without his sword. Silk's doublet was a rich black, trimmed in silver, and his scraggly whiskers had been carefully trimmed into an elegant short beard.

"What does all of this mean?" Garion asked as he joined them.

"We're to be presented to the king," Barak said, "and our honest clothes might have given offense. Kings aren't accustomed to looking at ordinary men."

Durnik emerged from one of the rooms, his face pale with anger. "That overdressed fool wanted to give me a bath!" he said in choked outrage.

"It's the custom," Silk explained. "Noble guests aren't expected to bathe themselves. I hope you didn't hurt him."

"I'm not a noble, and I'm quite able to bathe myself," Durnik said hotly. "I told him that I'd drown him in his own tub if he didn't keep his hands to himself. After that, he didn't pester me anymore, but he did steal my clothes. I had to put these on instead." He gestured at his clothes which were quite similar to Garion's. "I hope nobody sees me in all this frippery."

"Barak says the king might be offended if he saw us in our real clothes," Garion told him.

"The king won't be looking at me," Durnik said, "and I don't like this business of trying to look like something I'm not. I'll wait outside with the horses if I can get my own clothes back."

"Be patient, Durnik," Barak advised. "We'll get this business with the king straightened out and then be on our way again."

If Durnik was angry, Mister Wolf was in what could best be described as a towering fury. He came out into the corridor dressed in a snowy white robe, deeply cowled at the back. "Someone's going to pay for this," he raged.

"It *does* become you," Silk said admiringly.

"Your taste has always been questionable, Master Silk," Wolf said in a frosty tone. "Where's Pol?"

"The lady has not yet made her appearance," Silk said.

"I should have known," Wolf said, sitting down on a nearby bench. "We may as well be comfortable. Pol's preparations usually take quite a while."

And so they waited. Captain Brendig, who had changed his boots and doublet, paced up and down as the minutes dragged by. Garion was totally baffled by their reception. They did not seem to be under arrest, but his imagination still saw dungeons, and that was enough to make him very jumpy.

And then Aunt Pol appeared. She wore the blue velvet gown that had been made for her in Camaar and a silver circlet about her head which set off the single white lock at her brow. Her bearing was regal and her face stern.

"So soon, Mistress Pol?" Wolf asked dryly. "I hope you weren't rushed."

She ignored that and examined each of them in turn. "Adequate, I suppose," she said finally, absently adjusting the collar of Garion's doublet. "Give me your arm, Old

Wolf, and let's find out what the King of the Sendars wants with us."

Mister Wolf rose from his bench, extended his arm, and the two of them started down the corridor. Captain Brendig hastily assembled his soldiers and followed them all in some kind of ragged order. "If you please, my Lady," he called out to Aunt Pol, "permit me to show you the way."

"We know the way, Lord Brendig," she replied without so much as turning her head.

Count Nilden, the Chief Butler, stood waiting for them in front of two massive doors guarded by uniformed men-at-arms. He bowed slightly to Aunt Pol and snapped his fingers. The men-at-arms swung the heavy doors inward.

Fulrach, the King of Sendaria, was a dumpy-looking man with a short brown beard. He sat, rather uncomfortably it appeared, on a high-backed throne which stood on a dais at one end of the great hall into which Count Nilden led them. The throne room was vast, with a high, vaulted ceiling and walls covered with what seemed acres of heavy, red velvet drapery. There were candles everywhere, and dozens of people strolled about in fine clothes and chatted idly in the corners, all but ignoring the presence of the king.

"May I announce you?" Count Nilden asked Mister Wolf.

"Fulrach knows who I am," Wolf replied shortly and strode down the long scarlet carpet toward the throne with Aunt Pol still on his arm. Garion and the others followed, with Brendig and his soldiers close behind, through the suddenly quiet crowd of courtiers and their ladies.

At the foot of the throne they all stopped, and Wolf bowed rather coldly. Aunt Pol, her eyes frosty, curtsied, and Barak and Silk bowed in a courtly manner. Durnik and Garion followed suit, though not nearly as gracefully.

"If it please your Majesty," Brendig's voice came from behind them, "these are the ones you sought."

"I knew you could be depended upon, Lord Brendig," the King replied in a rather ordinary-sounding voice. "Your reputation is well deserved. You have my thanks." Then he looked at Mister Wolf and the rest of them, his expression undecipherable.

Garion began to tremble.

"My dear old friend," the king said to Mister Wolf. "It's been too many years since we met last."

"Have you lost your wits entirely, Fulrach?" Mister Wolf snapped in a voice which carried no further than the king's ears. "Why do you choose to interfere with me—now, of all times? And what possessed you to outfit me in this absurd thing?" He plucked at the front of his white robe in disgust. "Are you trying to announce my presence to every Murgo from here to the hook of Arendia?"

The king's face looked pained. "I was afraid you might take it this way," he said in a voice no louder than Mister Wolf's had been. "I'll explain when we can speak more privately." He turned quickly to Aunt Pol as if trying to preserve the appearance at least of dignity. "It's been much too long since we have seen you, dear Lady. Layla and the children have missed you, and I have been desolate in your absence."

"Your Majesty is too kind," Aunt Pol said, her tone as cold as Wolf's.

The king winced. "Pray, dear Lady," he apologized, "don't judge me too hastily. My reasons were urgent. I hope that Lord Brendig's summons did not too greatly inconvenience you."

"Lord Brendig was the soul of courtesy," Aunt Pol said, her tone unchanged. She glanced once at Brendig, who had grown visibly pale.

"And you, my Lord Barak," the king hurried on as if trying to make the best of a bad situation, "how fares your cousin, our dear brother king, Anheg of Cherek?"

"He was well when last I saw him, your Majesty," Barak replied formally. "A bit drunk, but that's not unusual for Anheg."

The king chuckled a bit nervously and turned quickly to Silk. "Prince Kheldar of the Royal House of Drasnia," he said. "We are amazed to find such noble visitors in our realm, and more than a little injured that they chose not to call upon us so that we might greet them. Is the King of the Sendars of so little note that he's not even worth a brief stop?"

"We intended no disrespect, your Majesty," Silk replied, bowing, "but our errand was of such urgency that there was no time for the usual courtesies."

The king flickered a warning glance at that and surprisingly wove his fingers in the scarce perceptible gestures of the Drasnian secret language. *Not here. Too many ears about.* He then looked inquiringly at Durnik and Garion.

Aunt Pol stepped forward. "This is Goodman Durnik of the District of Erat, your Majesty," she said, "a brave and honest man."

"Welcome, Goodman Durnik," the king said. "I can only hope that men may also one day call *me* a brave and honest man."

Durnik bowed awkwardly, his face filled with bewilderment. "I'm just a simple blacksmith, your Honor," he said, "but I hope all men know that I am your Honor's most loyal and devoted subject."

"Well-spoken, Goodman Durnik," the king said with a smile, and then he looked at Garion.

Aunt Pol followed his glance. "A boy, your Majesty," she said rather indifferently. "Garion by name. He was placed in my care some years ago and accompanies us because I didn't know what else to do with him."

A terrible coldness struck at Garion's stomach. The certainty that her casual words were in fact the bald truth came crashing down upon him. She had not even tried to soften the blow. The indifference with which she had destroyed his life hurt almost more than the destruction itself.

"Also welcome, Garion," the king said. "You travel in noble company for one so young."

"I didn't know who they were, your Majesty," Garion said miserably. "Nobody tells me anything."

The king laughed in tolerant amusement. "As you grow older, Garion," he said, "you'll probably find that during these days such innocence is the most comfortable state in which to live. I've been told things of late that I'd much prefer not to know."

"May we speak privately now, Fulrach?" Mister Wolf said, his voice still irritated.

"In good time, my old friend," the king replied. "I've ordered a banquet prepared in your honor. Let's all go in and dine. Layla and the children are waiting for us. There will be time later to discuss certain matters." And with that he rose and stepped down from the dais.

Garion, sunk in his private misery, fell in beside Silk.

"Prince Kheldar?" he said, desperately needing to take his mind off the shocking reality that had just fallen upon him.

"An accident of birth, Garion," Silk said with a shrug. "Something over which I had no control. Fortunately I'm only the nephew of the King of Drasnia and far down in the line of succession. I'm not in any immediate danger of ascending the throne."

"And Barak is—?"

"The cousin of King Anheg of Cherek," Silk replied. He looked over his shoulder. "What is your exact rank, Barak?" he asked.

"The Earl of Trellheim," Barak rumbled. "Why do you ask?"

"The lad here was curious," Silk said.

"It's all nonsense anyway," Barak said, "but when Anheg became king, someone had to become Clan-Chief. In Cherek you can't be both. It's considered unlucky—particularly by the chiefs of the other clans."

"I can see why they might feel that way." Silk laughed.

"It's an empty title anyway," Barak observed. "There hasn't been a clan war in Cherek for over three thousand years. I let my youngest brother act in my stead. He's a simpleminded fellow and easily amused. Besides, it annoys my wife."

"You're married?" Garion was startled.

"If you want to call it that," Barak said sourly.

Silk nudged Garion warningly, indicating that this was a delicate subject.

"Why didn't you tell us?" Garion demanded accusingly. "About your titles, I mean."

"Would it have made any difference?" Silk asked.

"Well—no," Garion admitted, "but—" He stopped, unable to put his feelings about the matter into words. "I don't understand any of this," he concluded lamely.

"It will all become clear in time," Silk assured him as they entered the banquet hall.

The hall was almost as large as the throne room. There were long tables covered with fine linen cloth and once again candles everywhere. A servant stood behind each chair, and everything was supervised by a plump little woman with a beaming face and a tiny crown perched precariously atop her head. As they all entered, she came forward quickly.

"Dear Pol," she said, "you look just wonderful." She embraced Aunt Pol warmly, and the two began talking together animatedly.

"Queen Layla," Silk explained briefly to Garion. "They call her the Mother of Sendaria. The four children over there are hers. She has four or five others—older and probably away on state business, since Fulrach insists that his children earn their keep. It's a standard joke among the other kings that Queen Layla's been pregnant since she was fourteen, but that's probably because they're expected to send royal gifts at each new birth. She's a good woman, though, and she keeps King Fulrach from making too many mistakes."

"She knows Aunt Pol," Garion said, and that fact disturbed him for some reason.

"Everybody knows your Aunt Pol," Silk told him.

Since Aunt Pol and the queen were deep in conversation and already drifting toward the head of the table, Garion stayed close to Silk. *Don't let me make any mistakes,* he gestured, trying to keep the movements of his fingers inconspicuous.

Silk winked in reply.

Once they were all seated and the food began to arrive, Garion began to relax. He found that all he had to do was follow Silk's lead, and the intricate niceties of formal dining no longer intimidated him. The talk around him was dignified and quite incomprehensible, but he reasoned that no one was likely to pay much attention to him and that he was probably safe if he kept his mouth shut and his eyes on his plate.

An elderly nobleman with a beautifully curled silvery beard, however, leaned toward him. "You have traveled recently, I'm told," he said in a somewhat condescending tone. "How fares the kingdom, young man?"

Garion looked helplessly across the table at Silk. *What do I say?* he gestured with his fingers.

Tell him that the kingdom fares no better nor no worse than might be anticipated under the present circumstances, Silk replied.

Garion dutifully repeated that.

"Ah," the old nobleman said, "much as I had expected. You're a very observant boy for one so young. I enjoy talking with young people. Their views are so fresh."

Who is he? Garion gestured.

The Earl of Seline, Silk replied. *He's a tiresome old bore, but be polite to him. Address him as my Lord.*

"And how did you find the roads?" the earl inquired.

"Somewhat in disrepair, my Lord," Garion replied with Silk's prompting. "But that's normal for this time of year, isn't it?"

"Indeed it is," the earl said approvingly. "What a splendid boy you are."

The strange three-way conversation continued, and Garion even began to enjoy himself as the comments fed to him by Silk seemed to amaze the old gentleman.

At last the banquet was over, and the king rose from his seat at the head of the table. "And now, dear friends," he announced, "Queen Layla and I would like to visit privately with our noble guests, and so we pray you will excuse us." He offered his arm to Aunt Pol, Mister Wolf offered his to the plump little queen, and the four of them walked toward the far door of the hall.

The Earl of Seline smiled broadly at Garion and then looked across the table. "I've enjoyed our conversation, Prince Kheldar," he said to Silk. "I may indeed be a tiresome old bore as you say, but that can sometimes be an advantage, don't you think?"

Silk laughed ruefully. "I should have known that an old fox like you would be an adept at the secret language, my Lord."

"A legacy from a misspent youth." The earl laughed. "Your pupil is most proficient, Prince Kheldar, but his accent is strange."

"The weather was cold while he was learning, my Lord," Silk said, "and our fingers were a bit stiff. I'll correct the problem when we have leisure."

The old nobleman seemed enormously pleased with himself at having outsmarted Silk. "Splendid boy," he said, patting Garion's shoulder, and then he went off chuckling to himself.

"You knew he understood all along," Garion accused Silk.

"Of course," Silk said. "Drasnian intelligence knows every adept at our secret speech. Sometimes it's useful to permit certain carefully selected messages to be intercepted. Don't ever underestimate the Earl of Seline, however. It's not impossible that he's at least as clever as I am, but look how much he enjoyed catching us."

"Can't you ever do anything without being sly?" Garion asked. His tone was a bit grumpy, since he was convinced that somehow he had been the butt of the whole joke.

"Not unless I absolutely have to, my Garion." Silk laughed. "People such as I continually practice deception— even when it's not necessary. Our lives sometimes depend on how cunning we are, and so we need to keep our wits sharp."

"It must be a lonely way to live," Garion observed rather shrewdly at the silent prompting of his inner voice. "You never really trust anyone, do you?"

"I suppose not," Silk said. "It's a game we play, Garion. We're all very skilled at it—at least we are if we intend to live very long. We all know each other, since we're members of a very small profession. The rewards are great, but after a while we play our game only for the joy of defeating each other. You're right, though. It *is* lonely, and sometimes disgusting—but most of the time it's a great deal of fun."

Count Nilden came up to them and bowed politely. "His Majesty asks that you and the boy join him and your other friends in his private apartments, Prince Kheldar," he said. "If you'll be so good as to follow me."

"Of course," Silk said. "Come along, Garion."

The king's private apartments were much simpler than the ornate halls in the main palace. King Fulrach had removed his crown and state robes and now looked much like any other Sendar in rather ordinary clothes. He stood talking quietly with Barak. Queen Layla and Aunt Pol were seated on a couch deep in conversation, and Durnik was not far away, trying his best to look inconspicuous. Mister Wolf stood alone near a window, his face like a thundercloud.

"Ah, Prince Kheldar," the king said. "We thought perhaps you and Garion had been waylaid."

"We were fencing with the Earl of Seline, your

Majesty," Silk said lightly. "Figuratively speaking, of course."

"Be careful of him," the king cautioned. "It's quite possible that he's too shrewd even for one of your talents."

"I have a great deal of respect for the old scoundrel." Silk laughed.

King Fulrach glanced apprehensively at Mister Wolf, then squared his shoulders and sighed. "I suppose we'd better get this unpleasantness over with," he said. "Layla, would you entertain our other guests while I give our grim-faced old friend there and the Lady the opportunity to scold me. It's obvious that he's not going to be happy until they've said a few unkind things to me about some matters that weren't really my fault."

"Of course, dear," Queen Layla said. "Try not to be too long and please don't shout. The children have been put to bed and they need their rest."

Aunt Pol rose from the couch, and she and Mister Wolf, whose expression hadn't changed, followed the king into an adjoining chamber.

"Well, then," Queen Layla said pleasantly, "what shall we talk about?"

"I am instructed, your Highness, to convey the regards of Queen Porenn of Drasnia to you should the occasion arise," Silk said in a courtly manner. "She asks leave of you to broach a correspondence on a matter of some delicacy."

"Why, of course," Queen Layla beamed. "She's a dear child, far too pretty and sweet-natured for that fat old bandit, Rhodar. I hope he hasn't made her unhappy."

"No, your Highness," Silk said. "Amazing though it may seem, she loves my uncle to distraction, and he, of course, is delirious with joy over so young and beautiful a wife. It's positively sickening the way they dote on each other."

"Some day, Prince Kheldar, *you* will fall in love," the queen said with a little smirk, "and the twelve kingdoms will stand around and chortle over the fall of so notorious a bachelor. What is this matter Porenn wishes to discuss with me?"

"It's a question of fertility, your Highness," Silk said with a delicate cough. "She wants to present my uncle with an heir and she needs to seek your advice in the business.

The entire world stands in awe of your gifts in that particular area."

Queen Layla blushed prettily and then laughed. "I'll write to her at once," she promised.

Garion by now had carefully worked his way to the door through which King Fulrach had taken Aunt Pol and Mister Wolf. He began a meticulous examination of a tapestry on the wall to conceal the fact that he was trying to hear what was going on behind the closed door. It took him only a moment to begin to pick up familiar voices.

"Exactly what does all this foolishness mean, Fulrach?" Mister Wolf was saying.

"Please don't judge me too hastily, Ancient One," the King said placatingly. "Some things have happened that you might not be aware of."

"You know that I'm aware of everything that happens," Wolf said.

"Did you know that we are defenseless if the Accursed One awakens? That which held him in check has been stolen from off the throne of the Rivan King."

"As a matter of fact, I was following the trail of the thief when your noble Captain Brendig interrupted me in my search."

"I'm sorry," Fulrach said, "but you wouldn't have gone much farther anyway. All the Kings of Aloria have been searching for you for three months now. Your likeness, drawn by the finest artists, is in the hands of every ambassador, agent and official of the five kingdoms of the north. Actually, you've been followed since you left Darine."

"Fulrach, I'm busy. Tell the Alorn Kings to leave me alone. Why are they suddenly so interested in my movements?"

"They want to have council with you," the king said. "The Alorns are preparing for war, and even my poor Sendaria is being quietly mobilized. If the Accursed One arises now, we're all doomed. The power that's been stolen can very possibly be used to awaken him, and his first move will be to attack the west—you know that, Belgarath. And you also know that until the return of the Rivan King, the west has no real defense."

Garion blinked and started violently, then tried to cover the sudden movement by bending to look at some of the finer detail on the tapestry. He told himself that he had heard wrong. The name King Fulrach had spoken could not have really been Belgarath. Belgarath was a fairy-tale figure, a myth.

"Just tell the Alorn Kings that I'm in pursuit of the thief," Mister Wolf said. "I don't have time for councils just now. If they'll leave me alone, I should be able to catch up with him before he can do any mischief with the thing he's managed to steal."

"Don't tempt fate, Fulrach," Aunt Pol advised. "Your interference is costing us time we can't afford to lose. Presently I'll become vexed with you."

The king's voice was firm as he answered. "I know your power, Lady Polgara," he said, and Garion jumped again. "I don't have any choice, however," the king continued. "I'm bound by my word to deliver you all up at Val Alorn to the Kings of Aloria, and a king can't break his word to other kings."

There was a long silence in the other room while Garion's mind raced through a dozen possibilities.

"You're not a bad man, Fulrach," Mister Wolf said. "Not perhaps as bright as I might wish, but a good man nonetheless. I won't raise my hand against you—nor will my daughter."

"Speak for yourself, Old Wolf," Aunt Pol said grimly.

"No, Polgara," he said. "If we have to go to Val Alorn, let's go with all possible speed. The sooner we explain things to the Alorns, the sooner they'll stop interfering."

"I think age is beginning to soften your brain, Father," Aunt Pol said. "We don't have the time for this excursion to Val Alorn. Fulrach can explain to the Alorn Kings."

"It won't do any good, Lady Polgara," the king said rather ruefully. "As your father so pointedly mentioned, I'm not considered very bright. The Alorn Kings won't listen to me. If you leave now, they'll just send someone like Brendig to apprehend you again."

"Then that unfortunate man may suddenly find himself living out the remainder of his days as a toad or possibly a radish," Aunt Pol said ominously.

"Enough of that, Pol," Mister Wolf said. "Is there a ship ready, Fulrach?"

"It lies at the north wharf, Belgarath," the king replied. "A Cherek vessel sent by King Anheg."

"Very well," Mister Wolf said. "Tomorrow then we'll go to Cherek. It seems that I'm going to have to point out a few things to some thickheaded Alorns. Will you be going with us?"

"I'm obliged to," Fulrach said. "The council's to be general, and Sendaria's involved."

"You haven't heard the last of this, Fulrach," Aunt Pol said.

"Never mind, Pol," Mister Wolf said. "He's only doing what he thinks is right. We'll straighten it all out in Val Alorn."

Garion was trembling as he stepped away from the door. It was impossible. His skeptical Sendarian upbringing made him at first incapable of even considering such an absurdity. Reluctantly, however, he finally forced himself to look the idea full in the face.

What if Mister Wolf really *was* Belgarath the Sorcerer, a man who had lived for over seven thousand years? And what if Aunt Pol was really his daughter, Polgara the Sorceress, who was only slightly younger? All the bits and pieces, the cryptic hints, the half-truths, fell together. Silk had been right; she could not be his Aunt. Garion's orphaning was complete now. He was adrift in the world with no ties of blood or heritage to cling to. Desperately he wanted to go home, back to Faldor's farm, where he could sink himself in unthinking obscurity in a quiet place where there were no sorcerers or strange searches or anything that would even remind him of Aunt Pol and the cruel hoax she had made of his life.

Part Two

CHEREK

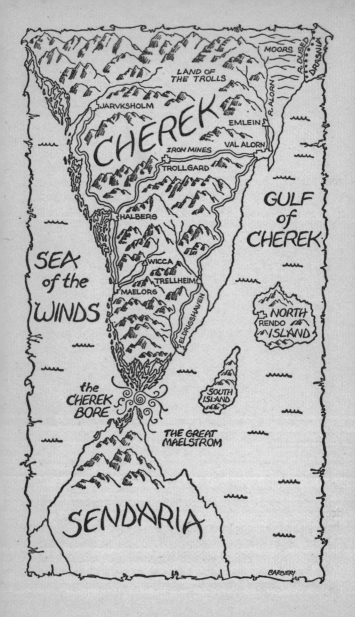

Chapter Twelve

IN THE GRAY FIRST LIGHT of early morning they rode through the quiet streets of Sendar to the harbor and their waiting ship. The finery of the evening before had been put aside, and they had all resumed their customary clothes. Even King Fulrach and the Earl of Seline had donned plain garb and now resembled nothing quite so much as two moderately prosperous Sendars on a business trip. Queen Layla, who was not to go with them, rode beside her husband, talking earnestly to him with an expression on her face that seemed almost to hover on the verge of tears. The party was accompanied by soldiers, cloaked against the raw, chill wind off the sea.

At the foot of the street which led down from the palace to the harbor, the stone wharves of Sendar jutted out into the choppy water, and there, rocking and straining against the hawsers which held her, was their ship. She was a lean vessel, narrow of beam and high-prowed, with a kind of wolfish appearance that did little to quiet Garion's nervousness about his first sea voyage. Lounging about on her deck were a number of savage-looking sailors, bearded and garbed in shaggy garments made of fur. With the exception of Barak, these were the first Chereks Garion had ever seen, and his first impression was that they would probably prove to be totally unreliable.

"Barak!" a burly man halfway up the mast shouted and dropped hand over hand down a steeply slanting rope to the deck and then jumped across to the wharf.

"Greldik!" Barak roared in response, swung down from his horse and clasped the evil-looking sailor in a bear hug.

"It would seem that Lord Barak is acquainted with our captain," the Earl of Seline observed.

"That's disquieting," Silk said wryly. "I was hoping for a

sober, sensible captain of middle years and a conservative disposition. I'm not fond of ships and sea travel to begin with."

"I'm told that Captain Greldik is one of the finest seamen in all of Cherek," the earl assured him.

"My Lord," Silk said with a pained look, "Cherek definitions can be deceptive." Sourly he watched Barak and Greldik toasting their reunion with tankards of ale that had been passed down to them from the ship by a grinning sailor.

Queen Layla had dismounted and she embraced Aunt Pol. "Please watch out for my poor husband, Pol," she said with a little laugh that quivered a bit. "Don't let those Alorn bullies goad him into doing anything foolish."

"Of course, Layla," Aunt Pol said comfortingly.

"Now, Layla," King Fulrach said in an embarrassed voice. "I'll be all right. I'm a grown man, after all."

The plump little queen wiped her eyes. "I want you to promise to wear warm clothes," she said, "and not to sit up all night drinking with Anheg."

"We're on serious business, Layla," the king said. "There won't be time for any of that."

"I know Anheg too well," the queen sniffed. She turned to Mister Wolf, stood on her tiptoes and kissed his bearded cheek. "Dear Belgarath," she said. "When this is over, promise that you and Pol will come back for a long visit."

"I promise, Layla," Mister Wolf said gravely.

"The tide is turning, Lord King," Greldik said, "and my ship is growing restless."

"Oh dear," the queen said. She put her arms around the king's neck and buried her face in his shoulder.

"Now, now," Fulrach said awkwardly.

"If you don't go now, I'm going to cry right here in public," she said, pushing him away.

The stones of the wharf were slippery, and the slim Cherek ship bobbed and rolled in the chop. The narrow plank they had to cross heaved and swayed dangerously, but they all managed to board without accident. The sailors slipped the hawsers and took their places at the oars. The lean vessel leaped away from the wharf and moved swiftly into the harbor past the stout and bulky merchantmen anchored nearby. Queen Layla stood forlornly on the wharf, surrounded by tall soldiers. She waved a few times and then stood watching, her chin lifted bravely.

Captain Greldik took his place at the tiller with Barak by his side and signaled to a squat, muscular warrior crouched nearby. The squat man nodded and pulled a ragged square of sailcloth off a hide-topped drum. He began a slow beat, and the oarsmen immediately took up the rhythm. The ship surged ahead and made for the open sea.

Once they were beyond the protection of the harbor, the swells grew so ponderous that the ship no longer rocked but ran instead down the back of each wave and up the face of the next. The long oars, dipping to the rhythm of the sullen drum, left little swirls on the surface of the waves. The sea was lead-gray beneath the wintry sky, and the low, snow-covered coastline of Sendaria slid by on their right, bleak and desolate-looking.

Garion spent most of the day shivering in a sheltered spot near the high prow, moodily staring out at the sea. The shards and shambles into which his life had fallen the night before lay in ruins around him. The idea that Wolf was Belgarath and Aunt Pol was Polgara was of course an absurdity. He was convinced, however, that a part of the whole thing at least was true. She might not be Polgara, but she was almost certainly not his Aunt. He avoided looking at her as much as possible, and did not speak to anyone.

They slept that night in cramped quarters beneath the stern deck of the ship. Mister Wolf sat talking for a long time with King Fulrach and the Earl of Seline. Garion covertly watched the old man whose silvery hair and short-cropped beard seemed almost to glow in the light from a swinging oil lamp hanging from one of the low beams. He still looked the same as always, and Garion finally turned over and went to sleep.

The next day they rounded the hook of Sendaria and beat northeasterly with a good following wind. The sails were raised, and the oarsmen were able to rest. Garion continued to wrestle with his problem.

On the third day out the weather turned stormy and bitterly cold. The rigging crackled with ice, and sleet hissed into the sea around them.

"If this doesn't break, it will be a rough passage through the Bore," Barak said, frowning into the sleet.

"The what?" Durnik asked apprehensively. Durnik was not at all comfortable on the ship. He was just recovering from a bout of seasickness, and he was obviously a bit edgy.

"The Cherek Bore," Barak explained. "It's a passage about a league wide between the northern tip of Sendaria and the southern end of the Cherek peninsula—riptides, whirlpools, that sort of thing. Don't be alarmed, Durnik. This is a good ship, and Greldik knows the secret of navigating the Bore. It may be a bit rough, but we'll be perfectly safe—unless we're unlucky, of course."

"That's a cheery thing to say," Silk observed dryly from nearby. "I've been trying for three days not to think about the Bore."

"Is it really that bad?" Durnik asked in a sinking voice.

"I make a special point of not going through it sober," Silk told him.

Barak laughed. "You ought to be thankful for the Bore, Silk," he said. "It keeps the Empire out of the Gulf of Cherek. All Drasnia would be a Tolnedran province if it wasn't there."

"I admire it politically," Silk said, "but personally I'd be much happier if I never had to look at it again."

On the following day they anchored near the rocky coast of northern Sendaria and waited for the tide to turn. In time it slackened and reversed, and the waters of the Sea of the Winds mounted and plunged through the Bore to raise the level of the Gulf of Cherek.

"Find something solid to hold on to, Garion," Barak advised as Greldik ordered the anchor raised. "With this following wind, the passage could be interesting." He strode along the narrow deck, his teeth gleaming in a broad grin.

It was foolish. Garion knew that, even as he stood up and began to follow the red-bearded man toward the prow, but four days of solitary brooding over a problem that refused to yield to any kind of logic made him feel almost belligerently reckless. He set his teeth together and took hold of a rusted iron ring embedded in the prow.

Barak laughed and clapped him a stunning blow on the shoulder. "Good boy," he said approvingly. "We'll stand together and look the Bore right down the throat."

Garion decided not to answer that.

With wind and tide behind her, Greldik's ship literally flew through the passage, yawing and shuddering as she was seized by the violent riptides. Icy spray stung their faces, and Garion, half-blinded by it, did not see the enormous whirlpool in the center of the Bore until they were almost upon it. He seemed to hear a vast roar and cleared his eyes just in time to see it yawning in front of him. "What's that?" he yelled over the noise.

"The Great Maelstrom," Barak shouted. "Hold on."

The Maelstrom was fully as large as the village of Upper Gralt and descended horribly down into a seething, mist-filled pit unimaginably far below. Incredibly, instead of guiding his vessel away from the vortex, Greldik steered directly at it.

"What's he doing?" Garion screamed.

"It's the secret of passing through the Bore," Barak roared. "We circle the Maelstrom twice to gain more speed. If the ship doesn't break up, she comes out like a rock from a sling, and we pass through the riptides beyond the Maelstrom before they can slow us down and drag us back."

"If the ship doesn't *what?*"

"Sometimes a ship is torn apart in the Maelstrom," Barak said. "Don't worry, boy. It doesn't happen very often, and Greldik's ship seems stout enough."

The ship's prow dipped hideously into the outer edges of the Maelstrom and then raced twice around the huge whirlpool with the oarsmen frantically bending their backs to the frenzied beat of the drum. The wind tore at Garion's face, and he clung to his iron ring, keeping his eyes averted from the seething maw gaping below.

And then they broke free and shot like a whistling stone through the churning water beyond the Maelstrom. The wind of their passage howled in the rigging, and Garion felt half-suffocated by its force.

Gradually the ship slowed in the swirling eddies, but the speed they had gained from the Maelstrom carried them on to calm water in a partially sheltered cove on the Sendarian side.

Barak was laughing gleefully and mopping spray from

his beard. "Well, lad," he said, "what do you think of the Bore?"

Garion didn't trust himself to answer and concentrated on trying to pry his numb fingers from the iron ring.

A familiar voice rang out from the stern. "Garion!"

"Now you've gone and got me in trouble," Garion said resentfully, ignoring the fact that standing in the prow had been his own idea.

Aunt Pol spoke scathingly to Barak about his irresponsibility and then turned her attention to Garion.

"Well?" she said. "I'm waiting. Would you like to explain?"

"It wasn't Barak's fault," Garion said. "It was my own idea." There was no point in their both being in trouble, after all.

"I see," she said. "And what was behind that?"

The confusion and doubt which had been troubling him made him reckless. "I felt like it," he said, half-defiantly. For the first time in his life he felt on the verge of open rebellion.

"You what?"

"I felt like it," he repeated. "What difference does it make why I did it? You're going to punish me anyway."

Aunt Pol stiffened, and her eyes blazed.

Mister Wolf, who was sitting nearby, chuckled.

"What's so funny?" she snapped.

"Why don't you let me handle this, Pol?" the old man suggested.

"I can deal with it," she said.

"But not well, Pol," he said. "Not well at all. Your temper's too quick, and your tongue's too sharp. He's not a child anymore. He's not a man yet, but he's not a child either. The problem needs to be dealt with in a special way. I'll take care of it." He stood up. "I think I insist, Pol."

"You *what?*"

"I insist." His eyes hardened.

"Very well," she said in an icy voice, turned, and walked away.

"Sit down, Garion," the old man said.

"Why's she so mean?" Garion blurted.

"She isn't," Mister Wolf said. "She's angry because you frightened her. Nobody likes to be frightened."

"I'm sorry," Garion mumbled, ashamed of himself.

"Don't apologize to me," Wolf said. "I wasn't frightened." He looked for a moment at Garion, his eyes penetrating. "What's the problem?" he asked.

"They call you Belgarath," Garion said as if that explained it all, "and they call her Polgara."

"So?"

"It's just not possible."

"Didn't we have this conversation before? A long time ago?"

"Are you Belgarath?" Garion demanded bluntly.

"Some people call me that. What difference does it make?"

"I'm sorry," Garion said. "I just don't believe it."

"All right," Wolf shrugged. "You don't have to if you don't want to. What's that got to do with your being impolite to your Aunt?"

"It's just—" Garion faltered. "Well—" Desperately he wanted to ask Mister Wolf that ultimate, fatal question, but despite his certainty that there was no kinship between himself and Aunt Pol, he could not bear the thought of having it finally and irrevocably confirmed.

"You're confused," Wolf said. "Is that it? Nothing seems to be like it ought to be, and you're angry with your Aunt because it seems like it has to be her fault."

"You make it sound awfully childish," Garion said, flushing slightly.

"Isn't it?"

Garion flushed even more.

"It's your own problem, Garion," Mister Wolf said. "Do you really think it's proper to make others unhappy because of it?"

"No," Garion admitted in a scarcely audible voice.

"Your Aunt and I are who we are," Wolf said quietly. "People have made up a lot of nonsense about us, but that doesn't really matter. There are things that have to be done, and we're the ones who have to do them. That's what matters. Don't make things more difficult for your Aunt just because the world isn't exactly to your liking. That's not only childish, it's ill-mannered, and you're a better boy than that. Now, I really think you owe her an apology, don't you?"

"I suppose so," Garion said.

"I'm glad we had this chance to talk," the old man said, "but I wouldn't wait too long before making up with her. You wouldn't believe how long she can stay angry." He grinned suddenly. "She's been angry with me for as long as I can remember, and that's so long that I don't even like to think about it."

"I'll do it right now," Garion said.

"Good," Wolf approved.

Garion stood up and walked purposefully to where Aunt Pol stood staring out at the swirling currents of the Cherek Bore.

"Aunt Pol," he said.

"Yes, dear?"

"I'm sorry. I was wrong."

She turned and looked at him gravely. "Yes," she said, "you were."

"I won't do it again."

She laughed then, a low, warm laugh, and ran her fingers through his tangled hair. "Don't make promises you can't keep, dear," she said, and she embraced him, and everything was all right again.

After the fury of the tide through the Cherek Bore had abated, they sailed north along the snow-muffled east coast of the Cherek peninsula toward the ancient city which was the ancestral home of all Alorns, Algar and Drasnian as well as Cherek and Rivan. The wind was chill and the skies threatening, but the remainder of the voyage was uneventful. After three more days their ship entered the harbor at Val Alorn and tied up at one of the ice-shrouded wharves.

Val Alorn was unlike any Sendarian city. Its walls and buildings were so incredibly ancient that they seemed more like natural rock formations than the construction of human hands. The narrow, crooked streets were clogged with snow, and the mountains behind the city loomed high and white against the dark sky.

Several horse-drawn sleighs awaited them at the wharf with savage-looking drivers and shaggy horses stamping impatiently in the packed snow. There were fur robes in the sleighs, and Garion drew one of them about him as he waited for Barak to conclude his farewells to Greldik and the sailors.

"Let's go," Barak told the driver as he climbed into the sleigh. "See if you can't catch up with the others."

"If you hadn't talked so long, they wouldn't be so far ahead, Lord Barak," the driver said sourly.

"That's probably true," Barak agreed.

The driver grunted, touched his horses with his whip, and the sleigh started up the street where the others had already disappeared.

Fur-clad Cherek warriors swaggered up and down the narrow streets, and many of them bellowed greetings to Barak as the sleigh passed. At one corner their driver was forced to halt while two burly men, stripped to the waist in the biting cold, wrestled savagely in the snow in the center of the street to the encouraging shouts of a crowd of onlookers.

"A common pastime," Barak told Garion. "Winter's a tedious time in Val Alorn."

"Is that the palace ahead?" Garion asked.

Barak shook his head. "The temple of Belar," he said. "Some men say that the Bear-God resides there in spirit. I've never seen him myself, though, so I can't say for sure."

Then the wrestlers rolled out of the way, and they continued.

On the steps of the temple an ancient woman wrapped in ragged woolen robes stood with a long staff clutched in one boney hand and her stringy hair wild about her face. "Hail, Lord Barak," she called in a cracked voice as they passed. "Thy Doom still awaits thee."

"Stop the sleigh," Barak growled at the driver, and he threw off his fur robe and jumped to the ground. "Martje," he thundered at the old woman. "You've been forbidden to loiter here. If I tell Anheg that you've disobeyed him, he'll have the priests of the temple burn you for a witch."

The old woman cackled at him, and Garion noted with a shudder that her eyes were milk-white blankness.

"The fire will not touch old Martje," she laughed shrilly. "That is not the Doom which awaits her."

"Enough of dooms," Barak said. "Get away from the temple."

"Martje sees what she sees," the old woman said. "The

mark of thy Doom is still upon thee, great Lord Barak.
When it comes to thee, thou shalt remember the words of
old Martje." And then she seemed to look at the sleigh
where Garion sat, though her milky eyes were obviously
blind. Her expression suddenly changed from malicious
glee to one strangely awestruck.

"Hail, greatest of Lords," she crooned, bowing deeply.
"When thou comest into thine inheritance, remember that
it was old Martje who first greeted thee."

Barak started toward her with a roar, but she scurried
away, her staff tapping on the stone steps.

"What did she mean?" Garion asked when Barak returned to the sleigh.

"She's a crazy woman," Barak replied, his face pale with
anger. "She's always lurking around the temple, begging
and frightening gullible housewives with her gibberish. If
Anheg had any sense, he'd have had her driven out of the
city or burned years ago." He climbed back into the sleigh.
"Let's go," he growled at the driver.

Garion looked back over his shoulder as they sped away,
but the old blind woman was nowhere in sight.

Chapter Thirteen

THE PALACE OF KING ANHEG of Cherek was a
vast, brooding structure near the center of Val Alorn. Huge
wings, many of them crumbled into decay with unpaned
windows staring emptily at the open sky through collapsed
roofs, stretched out from the main building in all directions. So far as Garion could tell there was no plan to the
palace whatsoever. It had, it seemed, merely grown over
the three thousand years and more that the kings of Cherek
had ruled there.

"Why is so much of it empty and broken down like that?" he asked Barak as their sleigh whirled into the snow-packed courtyard.

"What some kings build, other kings let fall down," Barak said shortly. "It's the way of kings." Barak's mood had been black since their encounter with the blind woman at the temple.

The others had all dismounted and stood waiting.

"You've been away from home too long if you can get lost on the way from the harbor to the palace," Silk said pleasantly.

"We were delayed," Barak grunted.

A broad, ironbound door at the top of the wide steps that led up to the palace opened then as if someone behind it had been waiting for them all to arrive. A woman with long flaxen braids and wearing a deep scarlet cloak trimmed with rich fur stepped out onto the portico at the top of the stairs and stood looking down at them. "Greetings, Lord Barak, Earl of Trellheim and husband," she said formally.

Barak's face grew even more somber. "Merel," he acknowledged with a curt nod.

"King Anheg granted me permission to greet you, my Lord," Barak's wife said, "as is my right and my duty."

"You've always been most attentive to your duties, Merel," Barak said. "Where are my daughters?"

"At Trellheim, my Lord," she said. "I didn't think it would be a good idea for them to travel so far in the cold." There was a faintly malicious note in her voice.

Barak sighed. "I see," he said.

"Was I in error, my Lord?" Merel asked.

"Let it pass," Barak said.

"If you and your friends are ready, my Lord," she said, "I'll escort you to the throne room."

Barak went up the stairs, briefly and rather formally embraced his wife, and the two of them went through the wide doorway.

"Tragic," the Earl of Seline murmured, shaking his head as they all went up the stairs to the palace door.

"Hardly that," Silk said. "After all, Barak got what he wanted, didn't he?"

"You're a cruel man, Prince Kheldar," the earl said.

"Not really," Silk said. "I'm a realist, that's all. Barak spent all those years yearning after Merel, and now he's got her. I'm delighted to see such steadfastness rewarded. Aren't you?"

The Earl of Seline sighed.

A party of mailed warriors joined them and escorted them through a maze of corridors, up broad stairs and down narrow ones, deeper and deeper into the vast pile.

"I've always admired Cherek architecture," Silk said sardonically. "It's so unanticipated."

"Expanding the palace gives weak kings something to do," King Fulrach observed. "It's not a bad idea, really. In Sendaria bad kings usually devote their time to street-paving projects, but all of Val Alorn was paved thousands of years ago."

Silk laughed. "It's always been a problem, your Majesty," he said. "How do you keep bad kings out of mischief?"

"Prince Kheldar," King Fulrach said, "I don't wish your uncle any misfortune, but I think it might be very interesting if the crown of Drasnia just happened to fall to you."

"Please, your Majesty," Silk said with feigned shock, "don't even suggest that."

"Also a wife," the Earl of Seline said slyly. "The prince definitely needs a wife."

"That's even worse," Silk said with a shudder.

The throne room of King Anheg was a vaulted chamber with a great fire pit in the center where whole logs blazed and crackled. Unlike the lushly draped hall of King Fulrach, the stone walls here were bare, and torches flared and smoked in iron rings sunk in the stone. The men who lounged near the fire were not the elegant courtiers of Fulrach's court, but rather were bearded Cherek warriors, gleaming in chain mail. At one end of the room sat five thrones, each surmounted by a banner. Four of the thrones were occupied, and three regal-looking women stood talking nearby.

"Fulrach, King of Sendaria!" one of the warriors who had escorted them boomed, striking the butt of his spear hollowly on the rush-strewn stone floor.

"Hail, Fulrach," a large, black-bearded man on one of the thrones called, rising to his feet. His long blue robe was wrinkled and spotted, and his hair was shaggy and unkempt. The gold crown he wore was dented in a place or two, and one of its points had been broken off.

"Hail, Anheg," the King of the Sendars replied, bowing slightly.

"Thy throne awaits thee, my dear Fulrach," the shaggy-haired man said, indicating the banner of Sendaria behind the one vacant throne. "The Kings of Aloria welcome the wisdom of the King of Sendaria at this council."

Garion found the stilted, archaic form of address strangely impressive.

"Which king is which, friend Silk?" Durnik whispered as they approached the thrones.

"The fat one in the red robe with the reindeer on his banner is my uncle, Rhodar of Drasnia. The lean-faced one in black under the horse banner is Cho-Hag of Algaria. The big, grim-faced one in gray with no crown who sits beneath the sword banner is Brand, the Rivan Warder."

"Brand?" Garion interrupted, startled as he remembered the stories of the Battle of Vo Mimbre.

"All Rivan Warders are named Brand," Silk explained.

King Fulrach greeted each of the other kings in the formal language that seemed to be customary, and then he took his place beneath the green banner with its golden sheaf of wheat that was the emblem of Sendaria.

"Hail Belgarath, Disciple of Aldur," Anheg said, "and hail Lady Polgara, honored daughter of immortal Belgarath."

"There's little time for all this ceremony, Anheg," Mister Wolf said tartly, throwing back his cloak and striding forward. "Why have the Kings of Aloria summoned me?"

"Permit us our little ceremonies, Ancient One," Rhodar, the grossly fat King of Drasnia said slyly. "We so seldom have the chance to play king. We won't be much longer at it."

Mister Wolf shook his head in disgust.

One of the three regal-looking women came forward then. She was a tall, raven-haired beauty in an elaborately cross-tied black velvet gown. She curtsied to King Fulrach and touched her cheek briefly to his. "Your Majesty," she said, "your presence honors our home."

"Your Highness," Fulrach replied, inclining his head respectfully.

"Queen Islena," Silk murmured to Durnik and Garion, "Anheg's wife." The little man's nose twitched with suppressed mirth. "Watch her when she greets Polgara."

The queen turned and curtsied deeply to Mister Wolf. "Divine Belgarath," she said, her rich voice throbbing with respect.

"Hardly divine, Islena," the old man said dryly.

"Immortal son of Aldur," she swept on, ignoring the interruption, "mightiest sorcerer in all the world. My poor house trembles at the awesome power you bring within its walls."

"A pretty speech, Islena," Wolf said. "A little inaccurate, but pretty all the same."

But the queen had already turned to Aunt Pol. "Glorious sister," she intoned.

"Sister?" Garion was startled.

"She's a mystic," Silk said softly. "She dabbles a bit in magic and thinks of herself as a sorceress. Watch."

With an elaborate gesture the queen produced a green jewel and presented it to Aunt Pol.

"She had it up her sleeve," Silk whispered gleefully.

"A royal gift, Islena," Aunt Pol said in a strange voice. "A pity that I can only offer this in return." She handed the queen a single deep red rose.

"Where did she get that?" Garion asked in amazement. Silk winked at him.

The queen looked at the rose doubtfully and cupped it between her two hands. She examined it closely, and her eyes widened. The color drained out of her face, and her hands began to tremble.

The second queen had stepped forward. She was a tiny blonde with a beautiful smile. Without ceremony she kissed King Fulrach and then Mister Wolf and embraced Aunt Pol warmly. Her affection seemed simple and unselfconscious.

"Porenn, Queen of Drasnia," Silk said, and his voice had an odd note to it. Garion glanced at him and saw the faintest hint of a bitter, self-mocking expression flicker across his face. In that single instant, as clearly as if it had suddenly been illuminated by a bright light, Garion saw the reason for Silk's sometimes strange manner. An almost suffocating surge of sympathy welled up in his throat.

The third queen, Silar of Algaria, greeted King Fulrach, Mister Wolf and Aunt Pol with a few brief words in a quiet voice.

"Is the Rivan Warder unmarried?" Durnik asked, looking around for another queen.

"He had a wife," Silk said shortly, his eyes still on Queen Porenn, "but she died some years ago. She left him four sons."

"Ah," Durnik said.

Then Barak, grim-faced and obviously angry, entered the hall and strode to King Anheg's throne.

"Welcome home, cousin," King Anheg said. "I thought perhaps you'd lost your way."

"Family business, Anheg," Barak said. "I had to have a few words with my wife."

"I see," Anheg said and let it drop.

"Have you met our friends?" Barak asked.

"Not as yet, Lord Barak," King Rhodar said. "We were involved with the customary formalities." He chuckled, and his great paunch jiggled.

"I'm sure you all know the Earl of Seline," Barak said, "and this is Durnik, a smith and a brave man. The boy's name is Garion. He's in Lady Polgara's care—a good lad."

"Do you suppose we could get on with this?" Mister Wolf asked impatiently.

Cho-Hag, King of the Algars, spoke in a strangely soft voice. "Art thou aware, Belgarath, of the misfortune which hath befallen us? We turn to thee for counsel."

"Cho-Hag," Wolf said testily, "you sound like a bad Arendish epic. Is all this theeing and thouing really necessary?"

Cho-Hag looked embarrassed and glanced at King Anheg.

"My fault, Belgarath," Anheg said ruefully. "I set scribes to work to record our meetings. Cho-Hag was speaking to history as well as to you." His crown had slipped a bit and perched precariously over one ear.

"History's very tolerant, Anheg," Wolf said. "You don't have to try to impress her. She'll forget most of what we say anyway." He turned to the Rivan Warder. "Brand," he said, "do you suppose you could explain all this without too much embellishment?"

"I'm afraid it's my fault, Belgarath," the gray-robed Warder said in a deep voice. "The Apostate was able to carry off his theft because of my laxity."

"The thing's supposed to protect itself, Brand," Wolf told him. "*I* can't even touch it. I know the thief, and there's no way you could have kept him out of Riva. What concerns me is how he was able to lay hands on it without being destroyed by its power."

Brand spread his hands helplessly. "We woke one morning, and it was gone. The priests were only able to divine the name of the thief. The Spirit of the Bear-God wouldn't say any more. Since we knew who he was, we were careful not to speak his name or the name of the thing he took."

"Good," Wolf said. "He has ways to pick words out of the air at great distances. I taught him how to do that myself."

Brand nodded. "We knew that," he said. "It made phrasing our message to you difficult. When you didn't come to Riva and my messenger didn't return, I thought something had gone wrong. That's when we sent men out to find you."

Mister Wolf scratched at his beard. "I guess it's my own fault that I'm here then," he said. "I borrowed your messenger. I had to get word to some people in Arendia. I suppose I should have known better."

Silk cleared his throat. "May I speak?" he asked politely.

"Certainly, Prince Kheldar," King Anheg said.

"Is it entirely prudent to continue these discussions in public?" Silk asked. "The Murgos have enough gold to buy ears in many places, and the arts of the Grolims can lift the thoughts out of the minds of the most loyal warriors. What isn't known can't be revealed, if you take my meaning."

"The warriors of Anheg aren't so easily bought, Silk," Barak said testily, "and there aren't any Grolims in Cherek."

"Are you also confident about the serving men and the kitchen wenches?" Silk suggested. "And I've found Grolims in some very unexpected places."

"There's something in what my nephew says," King Rhodar said, his face thoughtful. "Drasnia has centuries of experience in the gathering of information, and Kheldar is one of our best. If he thinks that our words might go further than we'd want them to, we might be wise to listen to him."

"Thank you, uncle," Silk said, bowing.

"Could *you* penetrate this palace, Prince Kheldar?" King Anheg challenged.

"I already have, your Majesty," Silk said modestly, "a dozen times or more."

Anheg looked at Rhodar with one raised eyebrow.

Rhodar coughed slightly. "It was some time ago, Anheg. Nothing serious. I was just curious about something, that's all."

"All you had to do was ask," Anheg said in a slightly injured tone.

"I didn't want to bother you," Rhodar said with a shrug. "Besides, it's more fun to do it the other way."

"Friends," King Fulrach said, "the issue before us is too important to chance compromising it. Wouldn't it be better to be overcautious rather than take any risks?"

King Anheg frowned and then shrugged. "Whatever you wish," he said. "We'll continue in private then. Cousin, would you clear old King Eldrig's hall for us and set guards in the hallways near it?"

"I will, Anheg," Barak said. He took a dozen warriors and left the hall.

The kings rose from their thrones—all except Cho-Hag. A lean warrior, very nearly as tall as Barak and with the shaved head and flowing scalp lock of the Algars, stepped forward and helped him up.

Garion looked inquiringly at Silk.

"An illness when he was a child," Silk explained softly. "It left his legs so weak that he can't stand unaided."

"Doesn't that make it kind of hard for him to be king?" Garion asked.

"Algars spend more time sitting on horses than they do standing on their feet," Silk said. "Once he's on a horse, Cho-Hag's the equal of any man in Algaria. The warrior who's helping him is Hettar, his adopted son."

"You know him?" Garion asked.

"I know everyone, Garion." Silk laughed softly. "Hettar and I have met a few times. I like him, though I'd rather he didn't know that."

Queen Porenn came over to where they stood. "Islena's taking Silar and me to her private quarters," she said to Silk. "Apparently women aren't supposed to be involved in matters of state here in Cherek."

"Our Cherek cousins have a few blind spots, your Highness," Silk said. "They're arch-conservatives, of course, and it hasn't occurred to them yet that women are human."

Queen Porenn winked at him with a sly little grin. "I'd hoped that we might get a chance to talk, Kheldar, but it doesn't look like it now. Did you get my message to Layla?"

Silk nodded. "She said she'd write to you immediately," he said. "If we'd known you were going to be here, I could have carried her letter myself."

"It was Islena's idea," she said. "She decided that it might be nice to have a council of queens while the kings were meeting. She'd have invited Layla too, but everyone knows how terrified she is of sea travel."

"Has your council produced anything momentous, Highness?" Silk asked lightly.

Queen Porenn made a face. "We sit around and watch Islena do tricks—disappearing coins, things up her sleeves, that kind of thing," she said. "Or she tells fortunes. Silar's too polite to object, and I'm the youngest, so I'm not supposed to say too much. It's terribly dull, particularly when she goes into trances over that stupid crystal ball of hers. Did Layla think she could help me?"

"If anyone can," Silk assured her. "I should warn you, though, that her advice is likely to be quite explicit. Queen Layla's an earthy little soul, and sometimes very blunt."

Queen Porenn giggled wickedly. "That's all right," she said. "I'm a grown woman, after all."

"Of course," Silk said. "I just wanted to prepare you, that's all."

"Are you making fun of me, Kheldar?" she asked.

"Would I do that, your Highness?" Silk asked, his face full of innocence.

"I think you would," she said.

"Coming, Porenn?" Queen Islena asked from not far away.

"At once, your Highness," the queen of Drasnia said. Her fingers flickered briefly at Silk. *What a bore.*

Patience, Highness, Silk gestured in reply.

Queen Porenn docilely followed the stately Queen of Cherek and the silent Queen of Algaria from the hall. Silk's eyes followed her, and his face had that same self-mocking expression as before.

"The others are leaving," Garion said delicately and pointed to the far end of the hall where the Alorn Kings were just going out the door.

"All right," Silk said and led the way quickly after them.

Garion stayed at the rear of the group as they all made their way through the drafty corridors toward King Eldrig's hall. The dry voice in his mind told him that if Aunt Pol saw him, she'd probably find a reason to send him away.

As he loitered along at the rear of the procession, a furtive movement flickered briefly far down one of the side corridors. He caught only one glimpse of the man, an ordinary-looking Cherek warrior wearing a dark green cloak, and then they had moved past that corridor. Garion stopped and stepped back to look again, but the man in the green cloak was gone.

At the door to King Eldrig's hall, Aunt Pol stood waiting with her arms crossed. "Where have you been?" she asked.

"I was just looking," he said as innocently as possible.

"I see," she said. Then she turned to Barak. "The council's probably going to last for a long time," she said, "and Garion's just going to get restless before it's over. Is there someplace where he can amuse himself until suppertime?"

"Aunt Pol!" Garion protested.

"The armory, perhaps?" Barak suggested.

"What would I do in an armory?" Garion demanded.

"Would you prefer the scullery?" Aunt Pol asked pointedly.

"On second thought, I think I might like to see the armory."

"I thought you might."

"It's at the far end of this corridor, Garion," Barak said. "The room with the red door."

"Run along, dear," Aunt Pol said, "and try not to cut yourself on anything."

Garion sulked slowly down the corridor Barak had pointed out to him, keenly feeling the injustice of the situa-

tion. The guards posted in the passageway outside King
Eldrig's hall even made eavesdropping impossible. Garion
sighed and continued his solitary way toward the armory.

The other part of his mind was busy, however, mulling
over certain problems. Despite his stubborn refusal to accept the possibility that Mister Wolf and Aunt Pol were
indeed Belgarath and Polgara, the behavior of the Alorn
Kings made it obvious that they at least *did* believe it. Then
there was the question of the rose Aunt Pol had given to
Queen Islena. Setting aside the fact that roses do not bloom
in the winter, how had Aunt Pol known that Islena would
present her with that green jewel and therefore prepared
the rose in advance? He deliberately avoided the idea that
his Aunt had simply created the rose on the spot.

The corridor along which he passed, deep in thought,
was dim, with only a few torches set in rings on the walls
to light the way. Side passages branched out from it here
and there, gloomy, unlighted openings that stretched back
into the darkness. He had almost reached the armory when
he heard a faint sound in one of those dark passages. Without knowing exactly why, he drew back into one of the
other openings and waited.

The man in the green cloak stepped out into the lighted
corridor and looked around furtively. He was an ordinary-
looking man with a short, sandy beard, and he probably
could have walked anywhere in the palace without attract-
ing much notice. His manner, however, and his stealthy
movements cried out louder than words that he was doing
something he was not supposed to be doing. He hurried up
the corridor in the direction from which Garion had come,
and Garion shrank back into the protective darkness of his
hiding place. When he carefully poked his head out into
the corridor again, the man had disappeared, and it was
impossible to know down which of those dark side passageways he had gone.

Garion's inner voice told him that even if he told anyone
about this, they wouldn't listen. He'd need more than just
an uneasy feeling of suspicion to report if he didn't want to
appear foolish. All he could do for the time being was to
keep his eyes open for the man in the green cloak.

Chapter Fourteen

IT WAS SNOWING the following morning, and Aunt Pol, Silk, Barak, and Mister Wolf again met for council with the kings, leaving Garion in Durnik's keeping. The two sat near the fire in the huge hall with the thrones, watching the two dozen or so bearded Cherek warriors who lounged about or engaged in various activities to pass the time. Some of them sharpened their swords or polished their armor; others ate or sat drinking—even though it was still quite early in the morning; several were engaged in a heated dice game; and some simply sat with their backs against the wall and slept.

"These Chereks seem to be very idle people," Durnik said quietly to Garion. "I haven't seen anyone actually working since we arrived, have you?"

Garion shook his head. "I think these are the king's own warriors," he said just as quietly. "I don't think they're supposed to do anything except sit around and wait for the king to tell them to go fight someone."

Durnik frowned disapprovingly. "It must be a terribly boring way to live," he said.

"Durnik," Garion asked after a moment, "did you notice the way Barak and his wife acted toward each other?"

"It's very sad," Durnik said. "Silk told me about it yesterday. Barak fell in love with her when they were both very young, but she was highborn and didn't take him very seriously."

"How does it happen that they're married, then?" Garion asked.

"It was her family's idea," Durnik explained. "After Barak became the Earl of Trellheim, they decided that a marriage would give them a valuable connection. Merel objected, but it didn't do her any good. Silk said that Barak

179

found out after they were married that she's really a very
shallow person, but of course it was too late by then. She
does spiteful things to try to hurt him, and he spends as
much time away from home as possible."

"Do they have any children?" Garion asked.

"Two," Durnik said. "Both girls—about five and seven.
Barak loves them very much, but he doesn't get to see
them very often."

Garion sighed. "I wish there was something we could
do," he said.

"We can't interfere between a man and his wife," Durnik said. "Things like that just aren't done."

"Did you know that Silk's in love with his aunt?" Garion
said without stopping to think.

"Garion!" Durnik's voice was shocked. "That's an un-
seemly thing to say."

"It's true all the same," Garion said defensively. "Of
course she's not really his aunt, I guess. She's his uncle's
second wife. It's not exactly like she was his real aunt."

"She's married to his uncle," Durnik said firmly. "Who
made up this scandalous story?"

"Nobody made it up," Garion said. "I was watching his
face when he talked to her yesterday. It's pretty plain the
way he feels about her."

"I'm sure you just imagined it," Durnik said disapprovingly. He stood up. "Let's look around. That will give us
something better to do than sit here gossiping about our
friends. It's really not the sort of thing decent men do."

"All right," Garion agreed quickly, a little embarrassed.
He stood up and followed Durnik across the smoky hall
and out into the corridor.

"Let's have a look at the kitchen," Garion suggested.

"And the smithy, too," Durnik said.

The royal kitchens were enormous. Entire oxen roasted
on spits, and whole flocks of geese simmered in lakes of
gravy. Stews bubbled in cart-sized cauldrons, and battalions
of loaves were marched into ovens big enough to stand in.
Unlike Aunt Pol's well-ordered kitchen at Faldor's farm,
everything here was chaos and confusion. The head cook
was a huge man with a red face who screamed orders
which everyone ignored. There were shouts and threats and
a great deal of horseplay. A spoon heated in a fire and left

where an unsuspecting cook would pick it up brought shrieks of mirth, and one man's hat was stolen and deliberately thrown into a seething pot of stew.

"Let's go someplace else, Durnik," he said. "This isn't what I expected at all."

Durnik nodded. "Mistress Pol would never tolerate all of this foolishness," he agreed disapprovingly.

In the hallway outside the kitchen a maid with reddish-blond hair and a pale green dress cut quite low at the bodice loitered.

"Excuse me," Durnik said to her politely, "could you direct us to the smithy?"

She looked him up and down boldly. "Are you new here?" she asked. "I haven't seen you before."

"We're just visiting," Durnik said.

"Where are you from?" she demanded.

"Sendaria," Durnik said.

"How interesting. Perhaps the boy could run this errand for you, and you and I could talk for a while." Her look was direct.

Durnik coughed, and his ears reddened. "The smithy?" he asked again.

The maid laughed lightly. "In the courtyard at the end on this corridor," she said. "I'm usually around here someplace. I'm sure you can find me when you finish your business with the smith."

"Yes," Durnik said, "I'm sure I could. Come along, Garion."

They went on down the corridor and out into a snowy inner courtyard.

"Outrageous!" Durnik said stiffly, his ears still flaming. "The girl has no sense of propriety whatsoever. I'd report her if I knew to whom."

"Shocking," Garion agreed, secretly amused by Durnik's embarrassment. They crossed the courtyard through the lightly sifting snow.

The smithy was presided over by a huge, black-bearded man with forearms as big as Garion's thighs. Durnik introduced himself and the two were soon happily talking shop to the accompaniment of the ringing blows of the smith's hammer. Garion noticed that instead of the plows, spades, and hoes that would fill a Sendarian smithy, the walls here were hung with swords, spears, and war axes. At one forge an apprentice was hammering out arrowheads, and at another, a lean, one-eyed man was working on an evil-looking dagger.

Durnik and the smith talked together for most of the remainder of the morning while Garion wandered about the inner courtyard watching the various workmen at their tasks. There were coopers and wheelwrights, cobblers and carpenters, saddlers and candlemakers, all busily at work to maintain the huge household of King Anheg. As he watched, Garion also kept his eyes open for the sandy-bearded man in the green cloak he'd seen the night before. It wasn't likely that the man would be here where honest work was being done, but Garion stayed alert all the same.

About noon, Barak came looking for them and led them back to the great hall where Silk lounged, intently watching a dice game.

"Anheg and the others want to meet privately this afternoon," Barak said. "I've got an errand to run, and I thought you might want to go along."

"That might not be a bad idea," Silk said, tearing his eyes from the game. "Your cousin's warriors dice badly, and I'm tempted to try a few rolls with them. It would probably be better if I didn't. Most men take offense at losing to strangers."

Barak grinned. "I'm sure they'd be glad to let you play, Silk," he said. "They've got just as much chance of winning as you do."

"Just as the sun has as much chance of coming up in the west as in the east," Silk said.

"Are you that sure of your skill, friend Silk?" Durnik asked.

"I'm sure of theirs." Silk chuckled. He jumped up. "Let's go," he said. "My fingers are starting to itch. Let's get them away from temptation."

"Anything you say, Prince Kheldar." Barak laughed.

They all put on fur cloaks and left the palace. The snow had almost stopped, and the wind was brisk.

"I'm a bit confused by all these names," Durnik said as they trudged toward the central part of Val Alorn. "I've been meaning to ask about it. You, friend Silk, are also Prince Kheldar and sometimes the merchant Ambar of

Kotu, and Mister Wolf is called Belgarath, and Mistress Pol is also Lady Polgara or the Duchess of Erat. Where I come from, people usually have one name."

"Names are like clothes, Durnik," Silk explained. "We put on what's most suitable for the occasion. Honest men have little need to wear strange clothes or strange names. Those of us who aren't so honest, however, occasionally have to change one or the other."

"I don't find it amusing to hear Mistress Pol described as not being honest," Durnik said stiffly.

"No disrespect intended," Silk assured him. "Simple definitions don't apply to Lady Polgara; and when I say that we're not honest, I simply mean that this business we're in sometimes requires us to conceal ourselves from people who are evil as well as devious."

Durnik looked unconvinced but let it pass.

"Let's take this street," Barak suggested. "I don't want to pass the Temple of Belar today."

"Why?" Garion asked.

"I'm a little behind in my religious duties," Barak said with a pained look, "and I'd rather not be reminded of it by the High Priest of Belar. His voice is very penetrating, and I don't like being called down in front of the whole city. A prudent man doesn't give either a priest or a woman the opportunity to scold him in public."

The streets of Val Alorn were narrow and crooked, and the ancient stone houses were tall and narrow with overhanging second stories. Despite the intermittent snow and the crisp wind, the streets seemed full of people, most of them garbed in furs against the chill.

There was much good-humored shouting and the exchange of bawdy insults. Two elderly and dignified men were pelting each other with snowballs in the middle of one street to the raucous encouragement of the bystanders.

"They're old friends," Barak said with a broad grin. "They do this every day all winter long. Pretty soon they'll go to an alehouse and get drunk and sing old songs together until they fall off their benches. They've been doing it for years now."

"What do they do in the summer?" Silk asked.

"They throw rocks," Barak said. "The drinking and

singing and falling off the benches stays the same, though."

"Hello, Barak," a green-eyed young woman called from an upper window. "When are you coming to see me again?"

Barak glanced up, and his face flushed, but he didn't answer.

"That lady's talking to you, Barak," Garion said.

"I heard her," Barak replied shortly.

"She seems to know you," Silk said with a sly look.

"She knows everyone," Barak said, flushing even more. "Shall we move along?"

Around another corner a group of men dressed in shaggy furs shuffled along in single file. Their gait was a kind of curious swaying from side to side, and people quickly made way for them.

"Hail, Lord Barak," their leader intoned.

"Hail, Lord Barak," the others said in unison, still swaying.

Barak bowed stiffly.

"May the arm of Belar protect thee," the leader said.

"All praise to Belar, Bear-God of Aloria," the others said.

Barak bowed again and stood until the procession had passed.

"Who were they?" Durnik asked.

"Bear-cultists," Barak said with distaste. "Religious fanatics."

"A troublesome group," Silk explained. "They have chapters in all the Alorn kingdoms. They're excellent warriors, but they're the instruments of the High Priest of Belar. They spend their time in rituals, military training, and interferring in local politics."

"Where's this Aloria they spoke of?" Garion asked.

"All around us," Barak said with a broad gesture. "Aloria used to be all the Alorn kingdoms together. They were all one nation. The cultists want to reunite them."

"That doesn't seem unreasonable," Durnik said.

"Aloria was divided for a reason," Barak said. "A certain thing had to be protected, and the division of Aloria was the best way to do that."

"Was this thing so important?" Durnik asked.

"It's the most important thing in the world," Silk said. "The Bear-cultists tend to forget that."

"Only now it's been stolen, hasn't it?" Garion blurted as that dry voice in his mind informed him of the connection between what Barak and Silk had just said and the sudden disruption of his own life. "It's this thing that Mister Wolf is following."

Barak glanced quickly at him. "The lad is wiser than we thought, Silk," he said soberly.

"He's a clever boy," Silk agreed, "and it's not hard to put it all together." His weasel face was grave. "You're right, of course, Garion," he said. "We don't know how yet, but somebody's managed to steal it. If Belgarath gives the word, the Alorn Kings will take the world apart stone by stone to get it back."

"You mean war?" Durnik said in a sinking voice.

"There are worse things than war," Barak said grimly. "It might be a good opportunity to dispose of the Angaraks once and for all."

"Let's hope that Belgarath can persuade the Alorn Kings otherwise," Silk said.

"The thing has to be recovered," Barak insisted.

"Granted," Silk agreed, "but there are other ways, and I hardly think a public street's the place to discuss our alternatives."

Barak looked around quickly, his eyes narrowing.

They had by then reached the harbor where the masts of the ships of Cherek rose as thickly as trees in a forest. They crossed an icy bridge over a frozen stream and came to several large yards where the skeletons of ships lay in the snow.

A limping man in a leather smock came from a low stone building in the center of one of the yards and stood watching their approach.

"Ho, Krendig," Barak called.

"Ho, Barak," the man in the leather smock replied.

"How does the work go?" Barak asked.

"Slowly in this season," Krendig said. "It's not a good time to work with wood. My artisans are fashioning the fittings and sawing the boards, but we won't be able to do much more until spring."

Barak nodded and walked over to lay his hand on the

new wood of a ship prow rising out of the snow. "Krendig
is building this for me," he said, patting the prow. "She'll
be the finest ship afloat."

"If your oarsmen are strong enough to move her," Krendig said. "She'll be very big, Barak, and very heavy."

"Then I'll man her with big men," Barak said, still gaz-
ing at the ribs of his ship.

Garion heard a gleeful shout from the hillside above the
shipyard and looked up quickly. Several young people were
sliding down the hill on smooth planks. It was obvious that
Barak and the others were going to spend most of the rest
of the afternoon discussing the ship. While that might be
all very interesting, Garion realized that he hadn't spoken
with anyone his own age for a long time. He drifted away
from the others and stood at the foot of the hill, watching.

One blond girl particularly attracted his eye. In some
ways she reminded him of Zubrette, but there were some
differences. Where Zubrette had been petite, this girl was
as big as a boy—though she was noticeably not a boy. Her
laughter rang out merrily, and her cheeks were pink in the
cold afternoon air as she slid down the hill with her long
braids flying behind her.

"That looks like fun," Garion said as her improvised sled
came to rest nearby.

"Would you like to try?" she asked, getting up and
brushing the snow from her woolen dress.

"I don't have a sled," he told her.

"I might let you use mine," she said, looking at him
archly, "if you give me something."

"What would you want me to give you?" he asked.

"We'll think of something," she said, eyeing him boldly.
"What's your name?"

"Garion," he said.

"What an odd name. Do you come from here?"

"No. I'm from Sendaria."

"A Sendar? Truly?" Her blue eyes twinkled. "I've never
met a Sendar before. My name is Maidee."

Garion inclined his head slightly.

"Do you want to use my sled?" Maidee asked.

"I might like to try it," Garion said.

"I might let you," she said, "for a kiss."

Garion blushed furiously, and Maidee laughed.

A large red-haired boy in a long tunic slid to a stop nearby and rose with a menacing look on his face. "Maidee, come away from there," he ordered.

"What if I don't want to?" she asked.

The red-haired boy swaggered toward Garion. "What are you doing here?" he demanded.

"I was talking with Maidee," Garion said.

"Who gave you permission?" the red-haired boy asked. He was a bit taller than Garion and somewhat heavier.

"I didn't bother to ask permission," Garion said.

The red-haired boy glowered, flexing his muscles threateningly. "I can thrash you if I like," he announced.

Garion realized that the redhead was feeling belligerent and that a fight was inevitable. The preliminaries—threats, insults and the like—would probably go on for several more minutes, but the fight would take place as soon as the boy in the long tunic had worked himself up to it. Garion decided not to wait. He doubled his fist and punched the larger boy in the nose.

The blow was a good one, and the redhead stumbled back and sat down heavily in the snow. He raised one hand to his nose and brought it away bright red. "It's bleeding!" he wailed accusingly. "You made my nose bleed."

"It'll stop in a few minutes," Garion said.

"What if it doesn't?"

"Nose bleeds don't last forever," Garion told him.

"Why did you hit me?" the redhead demanded tearfully, wiping his nose. "I didn't do anything to you."

"You were going to," Garion said. "Put snow on it, and don't be such a baby."

"It's still bleeding," the boy said.

"Put snow on it," Garion said again.

"What if it doesn't stop bleeding?"

"Then you'll probably bleed to death," Garion said in a heartless tone. It was a trick he had learned from Aunt Pol. It worked as well on the Cherek boy as it had on Doroon and Rundorig. The redhead blinked at him and then took a large handful of snow and held it to his nose.

"Are all Sendars so cruel?" Maidee asked.

"I don't know all the people in Sendaria," Garion said. The affair hadn't turned out well at all, and regretfully he turned and started back toward the shipyard.

"Garion, wait," Maidee said. She ran after him and caught him by the arm. "You forgot my kiss," she said, threw her arms around his neck and kissed him soundly on the lips.

"There," she said, and she turned and ran laughing back up the hill, her blond braids flying behind her.

Barak, Silk and Durnik were all laughing when he returned to where they stood.

"You were supposed to chase her," Barak said.

"What for?" Garion asked, flushing at their laughter.

"She wanted you to catch her."

"I don't understand."

"Barak," Silk said, "I think that one of us is going to have to inform the Lady Polgara that our Garion needs some further education."

"You're skilled with words, Silk," Barak said. "I'm sure you ought to be the one to tell her."

"Why don't we throw dice for the privilege?" Silk suggested.

"I've seen you throw dice before, Silk." Barak laughed.

"Of course we could simply stay here a while longer," Silk said slyly. "I rather imagine that Garion's new playmate would be quite happy to complete his education, and that way we wouldn't have to bother Lady Polgara about it."

Garion's ears were flaming. "I'm not as stupid as all that," he said hotly. "I know what you're talking about, and you don't have to say anything to Aunt Pol about it." He stamped away angrily, kicking at the snow.

After Barak had talked for a while longer with his shipbuilder and the harbor had begun to darken with the approach of evening, they started back toward the palace. Garion sulked along behind, still offended by their laughter. The clouds which had hung overhead since their arrival in Val Alorn had begun to tatter, and patches of clear sky began to appear. Here and there single stars twinkled as evening slowly settled in the snowy streets. The soft light of candles began to glow in the windows of the houses, and the few people left in the streets hurried to get home before dark.

Garion, still loitering behind, saw two men entering a wide door beneath a crude sign depicting a cluster of grapes. One of them was the sandy-bearded man in the green cloak that he had seen in the palace the night before. The other man wore a dark hood, and Garion felt a familiar tingle of recognition. Even though he couldn't see the hooded man's face, there was no need of that. They had looked at each other too often for there to be any doubt. As always before, Garion felt that peculiar restraint, almost like a ghostly finger touching his lips. The hooded man was Asharak, and, though the Murgo's presence here was very important, it was for some reason impossible for Garion to speak of it. He watched the two men only for a moment and then hurried to catch up with his friends. He struggled with the compulsion that froze his tongue, and then tried another approach.

"Barak," he asked, "are there many Murgos in Val Alorn?"

"There aren't any Murgos in Cherek," Barak said. "Angaraks aren't allowed in the kingdom on pain of death. It's our oldest law. It was laid down by old Cherek Bear-shoulders himself. Why do you ask?"

"I was just wondering," Garion said lamely. His mind shrieked with the need to tell them about Asharak, but his lips stayed frozen.

That evening, when they were all seated at the long table in King Anheg's central hall with a great feast set before them, Barak entertained them with a broadly exaggerated account of Garion's encounter with the young people on the hillside.

"A great blow it was," he said in expansive tones, "worthy of the mightiest warrior and truly struck upon the nose of the foe. The bright blood flew, and the enemy was dismayed and overcome. Like a hero, Garion stood over the vanquished, and, like a true hero, did not boast nor taunt his fallen opponent, but offered instead advice for quelling that crimson flood. With simple dignity then, he quit the field, but the bright-eyed maid would not let him depart unrewarded for his valor. Hastily, she pursued him and fondly clasped her snowy arms about his neck. And there she lovingly bestowed that single kiss that is the true hero's greatest reward. Her eyes flamed with admiration, and her chaste bosom heaved with newly wakened passion. But modest Garion innocently departed and tarried not to claim those other sweet rewards the gentle maid's fond demeanor so clearly offered. And thus the adventure ended with our hero tasting victory but tenderly declining victory's true compensation."

The warriors and kings at the long table roared with laughter and pounded the table and their knees and each others' backs in their glee. Queen Islena and Queen Silar smiled tolerantly, and Queen Porenn laughed openly. Lady Merel, however, remained stony-faced, her expression faintly contemptuous as she looked at her husband.

Garion sat with his face aflame, his ears besieged with shouted suggestions and advice.

"Is that really the way it happened, nephew?" King Rhodar demanded of Silk, wiping tears from his eyes.

"More or less," Silk replied. "Lord Barak's telling was masterly, though a good deal embellished."

"We should send for a minstrel," the Earl of Seline said. "This exploit should be immortalized in song."

"Don't tease him," Queen Porenn said, looking sympathetically at Garion.

Aunt Pol did not seem amused. Her eyes were cold as she looked at Barak. "Isn't it odd that three grown men can't keep one boy out of trouble?" she asked with a raised eyebrow.

"It was only one blow, my Lady," Silk protested, "and only one kiss, after all."

"Really?" she said. "And what's it going to be next time? A duel with swords, perhaps, and even greater foolishness afterward?"

"There was no real harm in it, Mistress Pol," Durnik assured her.

Aunt Pol shook her head. "I thought you at least had good sense, Durnik," she said, "but now I see that I was wrong."

Garion suddenly resented her remarks. It seemed that no matter what he did, she was ready to take it in the worst possible light. His resentment flared to the verge of open rebellion. What right had she to say anything about what he did? There was no tie between them, after all, and he could do anything he wanted without her permission if he felt like it. He glared at her in sullen anger.

She caught the look and returned it with a cool expression that seemed almost to challenge him. "Well?" she asked.

"Nothing," he said shortly.

Chapter Fifteen

THE NEXT MORNING dawned bright and crisp. The sky was a deep blue, and the sunlight was dazzling on the white mountaintops that rose behind the city. After breakfast, Mister Wolf announced that he and Aunt Pol would again meet privately that day with Fulrach and the Alorn Kings.

"Good idea," Barak said. "Gloomy ponderings are good for kings. Unless one has regal obligations, however, it's much too fine a day to be wasted indoors." He grinned mockingly at his cousin.

"There's a streak of cruelty in you that I hadn't suspected, Barak," King Anheg said, glancing longingly out a nearby window.

"Do the wild boars still come down to the edges of the forest?" Barak asked.

"In droves," Anheg replied even more disconsolately.

"I thought I might gather a few good men and go out and see if we can thin their numbers a bit," Barak said, his grin even wider now.

"I was almost sure you had something like that in mind," Anheg said moodily, scratching at his unkempt hair.

"I'm doing you a service, Anheg," Barak said. "You don't want your kingdom overrun with the beasts, do you?"

Rhodar, the fat King of Drasnia, laughed hugely. "I think he's got you, Anheg," he said.

"He usually does," Anheg agreed sourly.

"I gladly leave such activities to younger and leaner

men," Rhodar said. He slapped his vast paunch with both hands. "I don't mind a good supper, but I'd rather not have to fight with it first. I make too good a target. The blindest boar in the world wouldn't have much trouble finding me."

"Well, Silk," Barak said, "what do you say?"

"You're not serious," Silk said.

"You must go along, Prince Kheldar," Queen Porenn insisted. "Someone has to represent the honor of Drasnia in this venture."

Silk's face looked pained.

"You can be my champion," she said, her eyes sparkling.

"Have you been reading Arendish epics again, your Highness?" Silk asked acidly.

"Consider it a royal command," she said. "Some fresh air and exercise won't hurt you. You're starting to look dyspeptic."

Silk bowed ironically. "As you wish, your Highness," he said. "I suppose that if things get out of hand I can always climb a tree."

"How about you, Durnik?" Barak asked.

"I don't know much about hunting, friend Barak," Durnik said doubtfully, "but I'll come along if you like."

"My Lord?" Barak asked the Earl of Seline politely.

"Oh, no, Lord Barak." Seline laughed. "I outgrew my enthusiasm for such sport years ago. Thanks for the invitation, however."

"Hettar?" Barak asked the rangy Algar.

Hettar glanced quickly at his father.

"Go along, Hettar," Cho-Hag said in his soft voice. "I'm sure King Anheg will lend me a warrior to help me walk."

"I'll do it myself, Cho-Hag," Anheg said. "I've carried heavier burdens."

"I'll go with you then, Lord Barak," Hettar said. "And thanks for asking me." His voice was deep and resonant, but very soft, much like that of his father.

"Well, lad?" Barak asked Garion.

"Have you lost your wits entirely, Barak?" Aunt Pol snapped. "Didn't you get him into enough trouble yesterday?"

That was the last straw. The sudden elation he'd felt at Barak's invitation turned to anger. Garion gritted his teeth and threw away all caution. "If Barak doesn't think I'll just be in the way, I'll be glad to go along," he announced defiantly.

Aunt Pol stared at him, her eyes suddenly very hard.

"Your cub is growing teeth, Pol." Mister Wolf chuckled.

"Be still, father," Aunt Pol said, still glaring at Garion.

"Not this time, Miss," the old man said with a hint of iron in his voice. "He's made his decision, and you're not going to humiliate him by unmaking it for him. Garion isn't a child now. You may not have noticed, but he's almost man high and filling out now. He'll soon be fifteen, Pol. You're going to have to relax your grip sometime, and now's as good a time as any to start treating him like a man."

She looked at him for a moment. "Whatever you say, father," she said at last with deceptive meekness. "I'm sure we'll want to discuss this later, though—in private."

Mister Wolf winced.

Aunt Pol looked at Garion then. "Try to be careful, dear," she said, "and when you come back, we'll have a nice long talk, won't we?"

"Will my Lord require my aid in arming himself for the hunt?" Lady Merel asked in the stilted and insulting manner she always assumed with Barak.

"That won't be necessary, Merel," Barak said.

"I would not neglect any of my duties," she said.

"Leave it alone, Merel," Barak said. "You've made your point."

"Have I my Lord's permission then to withdraw?" she asked.

"You have," he said shortly.

"Perhaps you ladies would like to join me," Queen Islena said. "We'll cast auguries and see if we can predict the outcome of the hunt."

Queen Porenn, who stood somewhat behind the Queen of Cherek, rolled her eyes upward in resignation. Queen Silar smiled at her.

"Let's go then," Barak said. "The boars are waiting."

"Sharpening their tusks, no doubt," Silk said.

Barak led them down to the red door of the armory where they were joined by a grizzled man with enormously broad shoulders who wore a bullhide shirt with metal plates sewn on it.

"This is Torvik," Barak introduced the grizzled man, "Anheg's chief huntsman. He knows every boar in the forest by his first name."

"My Lord Barak is overkind," Torvik said, bowing.

"How does one go about this hunting of boars, friend Torvik?" Durnik asked politely. "I've never done it before."

"It's a simple thing," Torvik explained. "I take my huntsmen into the forest and we drive the beasts with noise and shouting. You and the other hunters wait for them with these." He gestured at a rack of stout, broad-headed boar spears. "When the boar sees you standing in his way, he charges you and tries to kill you with his tusks, but instead you kill him with your spear."

"I see," Durnik said somewhat doubtfully. "It doesn't sound very complicated."

"We wear mail shirts, Durnik," Barak said. "Our hunters are hardly ever injured seriously."

" 'Hardly ever' has an uncomfortable ring of frequency to it, Barak," Silk said, fingering a mail shirt hanging on a peg by the door.

"No sport is very entertaining without a certain element of risk." Barak shrugged, hefting a boar spear.

"Have you ever thought of throwing dice instead?" Silk asked.

"Not with your dice, my friend." Barak laughed.

They began pulling on mail shirts while Torvik's huntsmen carried several armloads of boar spears out to the sleighs waiting in the snowy courtyard of the palace.

Garion found the mail shirt heavy and more than a little uncomfortable. The steel rings dug at his skin even through his heavy clothes, and every time he tried to shift his posture to relieve the pressure of one of them, a half-dozen others bit at him. The air was very cold as they climbed into the sleighs, and the usual fur robes seemed hardly adequate.

They drove through the narrow, twisting streets of Val Alorn toward the great west gate on the opposite side of the city from the harbor. The breath of the horses steamed in the icy air as they rode.

The ragged old blind woman from the temple stepped

from a doorway as they passed in the bright morning sun. "Hail, Lord Barak," she croaked. "Thy Doom is at hand. Thou shalt taste of it before this day's sun finds its bed."

Without a word Barak rose in his sleigh, took up a boar spear and cast it with deadly accuracy full at the old woman.

With surprising speed, the witch-woman swung her staff and knocked the spear aside in midair. "It will avail thee not to try to kill old Martje." She laughed scornfully. "Thy spear shall not find her, neither shall thy sword. Go thou, Barak. Thy Doom awaits thee." And then she turned toward the sleigh in which Garion sat beside the startled Durnik. "Hail, Lord of Lords," she intoned. "Thy peril this day shall be great, but thou shalt survive it. And it is thy peril which shall reveal the mark of the beast which is the Doom of thy friend Barak." And then she bowed and scampered away before Barak could lay his hands on another spear.

"What was that about, Garion?" Durnik asked, his eyes still surprised.

"Barak says she's a crazy old blind woman," Garion said. "She stopped us when we arrived in Val Alorn after you and the others had already passed."

"What was all that talk about Doom?" Durnik asked with a shudder.

"I don't know," Garion said. "Barak wouldn't explain it."

"It's a bad omen so early in the day," Durnik said. "These Chereks are a strange people."

Garion nodded in agreement.

Beyond the west gate of the city were open fields, sparkling white in the full glare of the morning sun. They crossed the fields toward the dark edge of the forest two leagues away with great plumes of powdery snow flying out behind their racing sleighs.

Farmsteads lay muffled in snow along their track. The buildings were all made of logs and had high-peaked wooden roofs.

"These people seem to be indifferent to danger," Durnik said. "I certainly wouldn't want to live in a wooden house—what with the possibility of fire and all."

"It's a different country, after all," Garion said. "We can't expect the whole world to live the way we do in Sendaria."

"I suppose not," Durnik sighed, "but I'll tell you, Garion, I'm not very comfortable here. Some people just aren't meant for travel. Sometimes I wish we'd never left Faldor's farm."

"I do too, sometimes," Garion admitted, looking at the towering mountains that seemed to rise directly out of the forest ahead. "Someday it will be over, though, and we'll be able to go home again."

Durnik nodded and sighed once more.

By the time they had entered the woods, Barak had regained his temper and his good spirits, and he set about placing the hunters as if nothing had happened. He led Garion through the calf-deep snow to a large tree some distance from the narrow sleigh track. "This is a good place," he said. "There's a game trail here, and the boars may use it to try to escape the noise of Torvik and his huntsmen. When one comes, brace yourself and hold your spear with its point aimed at his chest. They don't see very well, and he'll run full into your spear before he even knows it's there. After that it's probably best to jump behind a tree. Sometimes the spear makes them very angry."

"What if I miss?" Garion asked.

"I wouldn't do that," Barak advised. "It's not a very good idea."

"I didn't mean that I was going to do it on purpose," Garion said. "Will he try to get away from me or what?"

"Sometimes they'll try to run," Barak said, "but I wouldn't count on it. More likely he'll try to split you up the middle with his tusks. At that point it's usually a good idea to climb a tree."

"I'll remember that," Garion said.

"I won't be far away if you have trouble," Barak promised, handing Garion a pair of heavy spears. Then he trudged back to his sleigh, and they all galloped off, leaving Garion standing alone under the large oak tree.

It was shadowy among the dark tree trunks, and bitingly cold. Garion walked around a bit through the snow, looking for the best place to await the boar. The trail Barak had pointed out was a beaten path winding back through the dark brush, and Garion found the size of the tracks imprinted in the snow on the path alarmingly large. The oak tree with low-spreading limbs began to look very inviting, but he dismissed that thought angrily. He was expected to stand on the ground and meet the charge of the boar, and he decided that he would rather die than hide in a tree like a frightened child.

The dry voice in his mind advised him that he spent far too much time worrying about things like that. Until he was grown, no one would consider him a man, so why should he go to all the trouble of trying to seem brave when it wouldn't do any good anyway?

The forest was very quiet now, and the snow muffled all sounds. No bird sang, and there was only the occasional padded thump of snow sliding from overloaded branches to the earth beneath. Garion felt terribly alone. What was he doing here? What business had a good, sensible Sendarian boy here in the endless forests of Cherek, awaiting the charge of a savage wild pig with only a pair of unfamiliar spears for company? What had the pig ever done to him? He realized that he didn't even particularly like the taste of pork.

He was some distance from the beaten forest track along which their sleighs had passed, and he set his back to the oak tree, shivered, and waited.

He didn't realize how long he had been listening to the sound when he became fully aware of it. It was not the stamping, squealing rush of a wild boar he had been expecting but was, rather, the measured pace of several horses moving slowly along the snow-carpeted floor of the forest, and it was coming from behind him. Cautiously he eased his face around the tree.

Three riders, muffled in furs, emerged from the woods on the far side of the sleigh-churned track. They stopped and sat waiting. Two of them were bearded warriors, little different from dozens of others Garion had seen in King Anheg's palace. The third man, however, had long, flaxen-colored hair and wore no beard. His face had the sullen, pampered look of a spoiled child, although he was a man of middle years, and he sat his horse disdainfully as if the company of the other two somehow offended him.

After a time, the sound of another horse came from near

the edge of the forest. Almost holding his breath, Garion waited. The other rider slowly approached the three who sat their horses in the snow at the edge of the trees. It was the sandy-bearded man in the green cloak whom Garion had seen creeping through the passageways of King Anheg's palace two nights before.

"My Lord," the green-cloaked man said deferentially as he joined the other three.

"Where have you been?" the flaxen-haired man demanded.

"Lord Barak took some of his guests on a boar hunt this morning. His route was the same as mine, and I didn't want to follow too closely."

The nobleman grunted sourly. "We saw them deeper in the wood," he said. "Well, what have you heard?"

"Very little, my Lord. The kings are meeting with the old man and the woman in a guarded chamber. I can't get close enough to hear what they're saying."

"I'm paying you good gold to get close enough. I have to know what they're saying. Go back to the palace and work out a way to hear what they're talking about."

"I'll try, my Lord," the green-cloaked man said, bowing somewhat stiffly.

"You'll do more than try," the flaxen-haired man snapped.

"As you wish, my Lord," the other said, starting to turn his horse.

"Wait," the nobleman commended. "Were you able to meet with our friend?"

"*Your* friend, my Lord," the other corrected with distaste. "I met him, and we went to a tavern and talked a little."

"What did he say?"

"Nothing very useful. His kind seldom do."

"Will he meet us as he said he would?"

"He told me that he would. If you want to believe him, that's your affair."

The nobleman ignored that. "Who arrived with the King of the Sendars?"

"The old man and the woman, another old man—some Sendarian noble, I think, Lord Barak and a weasel-faced Drasnian, and another Sendar—a commoner of some sort."

"That's all? Wasn't there a boy with them as well?"

The spy shrugged. "I didn't think the boy was important," he said.

"He's there then—in the palace?"

"He is, my Lord—an ordinary Sendarian boy of about fourteen, I'd judge. He seems to be some kind of servant to the woman."

"Very well. Go back to the palace and get close enough to that chamber to hear what the kings and the old man are saying."

"That may be very dangerous, my Lord."

"It'll be more dangerous if you don't. Now go, before that ape Barak comes back and finds you loitering here." He whirled his horse and, followed by his two warriors, plunged back into the forest on the far side of the snowy track that wound among the dark trees.

The man in the green cloak sat grimly watching for a moment, then he too turned his horse and rode back the way he had come.

Garion rose from his crouched position behind the tree. His hands were clenched so tightly around the shaft of his spear that they actually ached. This had gone entirely too far, he decided. The matter must be brought to someone's attention.

And then, some way off in the snowy depths of the wood, he heard the sound of hunting horns and the steely clash of swords ringing rhythmically on shields. The huntsmen were coming, driving all the beasts of the forest before them.

He heard a crackling in the bushes, and a great stag bounded into view, his eyes wild with fright and his antlers flaring above his head. With three huge leaps he was gone. Garion trembled with excitement.

Then there was a squealing rush, and a red-eyed sow plunged down the trail followed by a half-dozen scampering piglets. Garion stepped behind his tree and let them pass.

The next squeals were deeper and rang less with fright than with rage. It was the boar—Garion knew that before the beast even broke out of the heavy brush. When the boar appeared, Garion felt his heart quail. This was no fat, sleepy porker, but rather a savage, infuriated beast. The horrid tusks jutting up past the flaring snout were yellow, and bits of twigs and bark clung to them, mute evidence that the boar would slash at anything in his path—trees, bushes or a Sendarian boy without sense enough to get out of his way.

Then a peculiar thing happened. As in the long-ago fight with Rundorig or in the scuffle with Brill's hirelings in the dark streets of Muros, Garion felt his blood begin to surge, and there was a wild ringing in his ears. He seemed to hear a defiant, shouted challenge and could scarcely accept the fact that it came from his own throat. He suddenly realized that he was stepping into the middle of the trail and crouching with his spear braced and leveled at the massive beast.

The boar charged. Red-eyed and frothing from the mouth, with a deep-throated squeal of fury, he plunged at the waiting Garion. The powdery snow sprayed up from his churning hooves like foam from the prow of a ship. The snow crystals seemed to hang in the air, sparkling in a single ray of sunlight that chanced just there to reach the forest floor.

The shock as the boar hit the spear was frightful, but Garion's aim was good. The broad-bladed spearhead penetrated the coarsely haired chest, and the white froth dripping from the boar's tusks suddenly became bloody foam. Garion felt himself driven back by the impact, his feet slipping out from under him, and then the shaft of his spear snapped like a dry twig and the boar was on him.

The first slashing, upward-ripping blow of the boar's tusks took Garion full in the stomach, and he felt the wind whoosh out of his lungs. The second slash caught his hip as he tried to roll, gasping, out of the way. His chain-mail shirt deflected the tusks, saving him from being wounded, but the blows were stunning. The boar's third slash caught him in the back, and he was flung through the air and crashed into a tree. His eyes filled with shimmering light as his head banged against the rough bark.

And then Barak was there, roaring and charging through the snow—but somehow it seemed not to be Barak. Garion's eyes, glazed from the shock of the blow to his head, looked uncomprehendingly at something that could not be true. It was Barak, there could be no doubt of that, but it was also something else. Oddly, as if somehow occupying the same space as Barak, there was also a huge, hideous bear. The images of the two figures crashing through the snow were superimposed, their movements identical as if in sharing the same space they also shared the same thoughts.

Huge arms grasped up the wriggling, mortally wounded boar and crushed in upon it. Bright blood fountained from the boar's mouth, and the shaggy, half-man thing that seemed to be Barak and something else at the same time raised the dying pig and smashed it brutally to the ground. The man-thing lifted its awful face and roared in earth-shaking triumph as the light slid away from Garion's eyes and he felt himself drifting down into the gray well of unconsciousness.

There was no way of knowing how much time passed until he came to in the sleigh. Silk was applying a cloth filled with snow to the back of his neck as they flew across the glaring white fields toward Val Alorn.

"I see that you've decided to live." Silk grinned at him.

"Where's Barak?" Garion mumbled groggily.

"In the sleigh behind us," Silk said, glancing back.

"Is he—all right?"

"What could hurt Barak?" Silk asked.

"I mean—does he seem like himself?"

"He seems like Barak to me." Silk shrugged. "No, boy, lie still. That wild pig may have cracked your ribs." He place his hands on Garion's chest and gently held him down.

"My boar?" Garion demanded weakly. "Where is it?"

"The huntsmen are bringing it," Silk said. "You'll get your triumphal entry. If I might suggest it, however, you should give some thought to the virtue of constructive cowardice. These instincts of yours could shorten your life."

But Garion had already slipped back into unconsciousness.

And then they were in the palace, and Barak was carrying him, and Aunt Pol was there, white-faced at the sight of all the blood.

"It's not his," Barak assured her quickly. "He speared a boar, and it bled on him while they were tussling. I think the boy's all right—a little rap on the head is all."

"Bring him," Aunt Pol said curtly and led the way up the stairs toward Garion's room.

Later, with his head and chest wrapped and a foul-tasting cup of Aunt Pol's brewing making him light-headed and sleepy, Garion lay in his bed listening as Aunt Pol finally turned on Barak. "You great overgrown dolt," she raged. "Do you see what all your foolishness has done?"

"The lad is very brave," Barak said, his voice low and sunk in a kind of bleak melancholy.

"Brave doesn't interest me," Aunt Pol snapped. Then she stopped. "What's the matter with you?" she demanded. She reached out suddenly and put her hands on the sides of the huge man's head. She looked for a moment into his eyes and then slowly released him. "Oh," she said softly, "it finally happened, I see."

"I couldn't control it, Polgara," Barak said in misery.

"It'll be all right, Barak," she said, gently touching his bowed head.

"It'll never be all right again," Barak said.

"Get some sleep," she told him. "It won't seem so bad in the morning."

The huge man turned and quietly left the room.

Garion knew they were talking about the strange thing he had seen when Barak had rescued him from the boar, and he wanted to ask Aunt Pol about it; but the bitter drink she had given him pulled him down into a deep and dreamless sleep before he could put the words together to ask the question.

Chapter Sixteen

THE NEXT DAY Garion was too stiff and sore to even think about getting out of bed. A stream of visitors, however, kept him too occupied to think about his aches and pains. The visits from the Alorn Kings in their splendid robes were particularly flattering, and each of them praised his courage. Then the queens came and made a great fuss over his injuries, offering warm sympathy and gentle, stroking touches to his forehead. The combination of praise, sympathy and the certain knowledge that he was the absolute center of attention was overwhelming, and his heart was full.

The last visitor of the day, however, was Mister Wolf, who came when evening was creeping through the snowy streets of Val Alorn. The old man wore his usual tunic and cloak, and his hood was turned up as if he had been outside.

"Have you seen my boar, Mister Wolf?" Garion asked proudly.

"An excellent animal," Wolf said, though without much enthusiasm, "but didn't anyone tell you it's customary to jump out of the way after the boar has been speared?"

"I didn't really think about it," Garion admitted, "but wouldn't that seem—well—cowardly?"

"Were you that concerned about what a pig might think of you?"

"Well," Garion faltered, "not really, I guess."

"You're developing an amazing lack of good sense for one so young," Wolf observed. "It normally takes years and years to reach the point you seem to have arrived at overnight." He turned to Aunt Pol, who sat nearby. "Polgara, are you quite certain that there's no hint of Arendish blood in our Garion's background? He's been behaving most Arendish lately. First he rides the Great Maelstrom like a rocking horse, and then he tries to break a wild boar's tusks with his ribs. Are you sure you didn't drop him on his head when he was a baby?"

Aunt Pol smiled, but said nothing.

"I hope you recover soon, boy," Wolf said, "and try to give some thought to what I've said."

Garion sulked, mortally offended by Mister Wolf's words. Tears welled up in his eyes despite all his efforts to control them.

"Thank you for stopping by, Father," Aunt Pol said.

"It's always a pleasure to call on you, my daughter," Wolf said and quietly left the room.

"Why did he have to talk to me like that?" Garion burst out, wiping his nose. "Now he's gone and spoiled it all."

"Spoiled what, dear?" Aunt Pol asked, smoothing the front of her gray dress.

"All of it," Garion complained. "The kings all said I was very brave."

"Kings say things like that," Aunt Pol said. "I wouldn't pay too much attention, if I were you."

"I *was* brave, wasn't I?"

"I'm sure you were, dear," she said. "And I'm sure the pig was very impressed."

"You're as bad as Mister Wolf is," Garion accused.

"Yes, dear," she said, "I suppose I probably am, but that's only natural. Now, what would you like for supper?"

"I'm not hungry," Garion said defiantly.

"Really? You probably need a tonic then. I'll fix you one."

"I think I've changed my mind," Garion said quickly.

"I rather thought you might," Aunt Pol said. And then, without explanation, she suddenly put her arms around him and held him close to her for a long time. "What am I going to do with you?" she said finally.

"I'm all right, Aunt Pol," he assured her.

"This time perhaps," she said, taking his face between her hands. "It's a splendid thing to be brave, my Garion, but try once in a while to think a little bit first. Promise me."

"All right, Aunt Pol," he said, a little embarrassed by all this. Oddly enough she still acted as if she really cared about him. The idea that there could still be a bond between them even if they were not related began to dawn on him. It could never be the same, of course, but at least it was something. He began to feel a little better about the whole thing.

The next day he was able to get up. His muscles still ached a bit, and his ribs were somewhat tender, but he was young and was healing fast. About midmorning he was sitting with Durnik in the great hall of Anheg's palace when the silvery-bearded Earl of Seline approached them.

"King Fulrach wonders if you would be so kind as to join us in the council chamber, Goodman Durnik," he said politely.

"Me, your Honor?" Durnik asked incredulously.

"His Majesty is most impressed with your sensibility," the old gentleman said. "He feels that you represent the very best of Sendarian practicality. What we face involves all men, not just the Kings of the West, and so it's only proper that good, solid common sense be represented in our proceedings."

"I'll come at once, your Honor," Durnik said, getting up quickly, "but you'll have to forgive me if I say very little."

Garion waited expectantly.

"We've all heard of your adventure, my boy," the Earl of Seline said pleasantly to Garion. "Ah, to be young again," he sighed. "Coming, Durnik?"

"Immediately, your Honor," Durnik said, and the two of them made their way out of the great hall toward the council chamber.

Garion sat alone, wounded to the quick by his exclusion. He was at an age where his self-esteem was very tender, and inwardly he writhed at the lack of regard implicit in his not being invited to join them. Hurt and offended, he sulkily left the great hall and went to visit his boar which hung in an ice-filled cooling room just off the kitchen. At least the boar had taken him seriously.

One could, however, spend only so much time in the company of a dead pig without becoming depressed. The boar did not seem nearly so big as he had when he was alive and charging, and the tusks were impressive but neither so long nor so sharp as Garion remembered them. Besides, it was cold in the cooling room and sore muscles stiffened quickly in chilly places.

There was no point in trying to visit Barak. The red-bearded man had locked himself in his chamber to brood in blackest melancholy and refused to answer his door, even to his wife. And so Garion, left entirely on his own, moped about for a while and then decided that he might as well explore this vast palace with its dusty, unused chambers and dark, twisting corridors. He walked for what seemed hours, opening doors and following hallways that sometimes ended abruptly against blank stone walls.

The palace of Anheg was enormous, having been, as Barak had explained, some three thousand years and more in construction. One southern wing was so totally abandoned that its entire roof had fallen in centuries ago. Garion wandered there for a time in the second-floor corridors of the ruin, his mind filled with gloomy thoughts of mortality and transient glory as he looked into rooms where snow lay thickly on ancient beds and stools and the tiny tracks of mice and squirrels ran everywhere. And then he came to an unroofed corridor where there were other tracks, those of a man. The footprints were quite fresh, for there was no sign of snow in them and it had snowed heavily the night before. At first he thought the tracks might be his own and that he had somehow circled and come back to a corridor he had already explored, but the footprints were much larger than his.

There were a dozen possible explanations, of course, but Garion felt his breath quicken. The man in the green cloak was still lurking about the palace, Asharak the Murgo was somewhere in Val Alorn, and the flaxen-haired nobleman was hiding somewhere in the forest with obviously unfriendly intentions.

Garion realized that the situation might be dangerous and that he was unarmed except for his small dagger. He retraced his steps quickly to a snowy chamber he had just explored and took down a rusty sword from a peg where it had hung forgotten for uncountable years. Then, feeling a bit more secure, he returned to follow the silent tracks.

So long as the path of the unknown intruder lay in that roofless and long-abandoned corridor, following him was simplicity itself; the undisturbed snow made tracking easy. But once the trail led over a heap of fallen debris and into the gaping blackness of a dusty corridor where the roof was still intact, things became a bit more difficult. The dust on the floor helped, but it was necessary to do a great deal of stooping and bending over. Garion's ribs and legs were still sore, and he winced and grunted each time he had to bend down to examine the stone floor. In a very short while he was sweating and gritting his teeth and thinking about giving the whole thing up.

Then he heard a faint sound far down the corridor ahead. He shrank back against the wall, hoping that no light from behind him would filter dimly through to allow him to be seen. Far ahead, a figure passed stealthily through the pale light from a single tiny window. Garion caught a momentary flicker of green and knew finally whom he was following. He kept close to the wall and moved with catlike silence in his soft leather shoes, the rusty sword gripped tightly in his hand. If it had not been for the startling nearness of the voice of the Earl of Seline, however, he would probably have walked directly into the man he had been following.

"Is it at all possible, noble Belgarath, that our enemy can be awakened before all the conditions of the ancient prophecy are met?" the earl was asking.

Garion stopped. Directly ahead of him in a narrow embrasure in the wall of the corridor, he caught sight of a slight movement. The green-cloaked man lurked there, listening in the dimness to the words that seemed to come from somewhere beneath. Garion shrank back against the wall, scarcely daring to breathe. Carefully he stepped backward until he found another embrasure and drew himself into the concealing darkness.

"A most appropriate question, Belgarath," the quiet voice of Cho-Hag of the Algars said. "Can this Apostate use the power now in his hands to revive the Accursed One?"

"The power is there," the familiar voice of Mister Wolf said, "but he might be afraid to use it. If it isn't done properly, the power will destroy him. He won't rush into such an act, but will think very carefully before he tries it. It's that hesitation that gives us the little bit of time we have."

Then Silk spoke. "Didn't you say that he might want the thing for himself? Maybe he plans to leave his Master in undisturbed slumber and use the power he's stolen to raise himself as king in the lands of the Angaraks."

King Rhodar of Drasnia chuckled. "Somehow I don't see the Grolim Priesthood so easily relinquishing their power in the lands of Angarak and bowing down to an outsider. The High Priest of the Grolims is no mean sorcerer himself, I'm told."

"Forgive me, Rhodar," King Anheg said, "but if the power is in the thief's hands, the Grolims won't have any choice but to accept his dominion. I've studied the power of this thing, and if even half of what I've read is true, he can use it to rip down Rak Cthol as easily as you'd kick apart an anthill. Then, if they still resist, he could depopulate all

of Cthol Murgos from Rak Goska to the Tolnedran border.
No matter what, however, whether it's the Apostate or the
Accursed One who eventually raises that power, the An-
garaks will follow and they will come west."

"Shouldn't we inform the Arends and Tolnedrans—and
the Ulgos as well—what has happened then?" Brand, the
Rivan Warder, asked. "Let's not be taken by surprise
again."

"I wouldn't be in too much hurry to rouse our southern
neighbors," Mister Wolf said. "When Pol and I leave here,
we'll be moving south. If Arendia and Tolnedra are mobi-
lizing for war, the general turmoil would only hinder us.
The Emperor's legions are soldiers. They can respond
quickly when the need arises, and the Arends are always
ready for war. The whole kingdom hovers on the brink of
general warfare all the time."

"It's premature," Aunt Pol's familiar voice agreed. "Armies would just get in the way of what we're trying to do.
If we can apprehend my father's old pupil and return the
thing he pilfered to Riva, the crisis will be past. Let's not
stir up the southerners for nothing."

"She's right," Wolf said. "There's always a risk in a mo-
bilization. A king with an army on his hands often begins
to think of mischief. I'll advise the King of the Arends at
Vo Mimbre and the Emperor at Tol Honeth of as much as
they need to know as I pass through. But we should get
word through to the Gorim of Ulgo. Cho-Hag, do you
think you could get a messenger through to Prolgu at this
time of the year?"

"It's hard to say, Ancient One," Cho-Hag said. "The
passes into those mountains are difficult in the winter. I'll
try, though."

"Good," Wolf said. "Beyond that, there's not much more
we can do. For the time being it might not be a bad idea to
keep this matter in the family—so to speak. If worse comes
to worst and the Angaraks invade again, Aloria at least
will be armed and ready. There'll be time for Arendia and
the Empire to make their preparations."

King Fulrach spoke then in a troubled voice. "It's easy
for the Alorn Kings to talk of war," he said. "Alorns are
warriors; but my Sendaria is a peaceful kingdom. We don't

have castles or fortified keeps, and my people are farmers and tradesmen. Kal Torak made a mistake when he chose the battlefield at Vo Mimbre; and it's not likely that the Angaraks will make the same mistake again. I think they'll strike directly across the grasslands of northern Algaria and fall upon Sendaria. We have a lot of food and very few soldiers. Our country would provide an ideal base for a campaign in the west, and I'm afraid that we'd fall quite easily."

Then, to Garion's amazement, Durnik spoke. "Don't cheapen the men of Sendaria so, Lord King," he said in a firm voice. "I know my neighbors, and they'll fight. We don't know very much about swords and lances, but we'll fight. If Angaraks come to Sendaria, they won't find the taking as easy as some might imagine, and if we put torches to the fields and storehouses there won't be all that much food for them to eat."

There was a long silence, and then Fulrach spoke again in a voice strangely humble. "Your words shame me, Goodman Durnik," he said. "Maybe I've been king for so long that I've forgotten what it means to be a Sendar."

"One remembers that there are only a few passes leading through the western escarpment into Sendaria," Hettar, the son of King Cho-Hag, said quietly. "A few avalanches in the right places could make Sendaria as inaccessible as the moon. If the avalanches took place at the right times, whole armies of Angaraks might find themselves trapped in those narrow corridors."

"Now that's an entertaining thought." Silk chuckled. "Then we could let Durnik put his incendiary impulses to a better use than burning turnip patches. Since Torak One-eye seems to enjoy the smell of burning sacrifices so much, we might be able to accommodate him."

Far down the dusty passageway in which he was hiding, Garion caught the sudden flicker of a torch and heard the faint jingling of several mail shirts. He almost failed to recognize the danger until the last instant. The man in the green cloak also heard the sounds and saw the light of the torch. He stepped from his hiding place and fled back the way he had come—directly past the embrasure where Garion had concealed himself. Garion shrank back, clutching his rusty sword; but as luck had it, the man was looking back over his shoulder at the twinkling torch as he ran by on soft feet.

As soon as he had passed, Garion also slipped out of his hiding place and fled. The Cherek warriors were looking for intruders, and it might be difficult to explain what he was doing in the dark hallway. He briefly considered following the spy again, but decided that he'd had enough of that for one day. It was time to tell someone about the things he'd seen. Someone had to be told—someone to whom the kings would listen. Once he reached the more frequented corridors of the palace, he firmly began to make his way toward the chamber where Barak brooded in silent melancholy.

Chapter Seventeen

"BARAK," GARION CALLED through the door after he had knocked for several minutes without any answer.

"Go away," Barak's voice came thickly through the door.

"Barak, it's me, Garion. I have to talk with you."

There was a long silence inside the room, and finally a slow movement. Then the door opened.

Barak's appearance was shocking. His tunic was rumpled and stained. His red beard was matted, the long braids he usually wore were undone, and his hair was tangled. The haunted look in his eyes, however, was the worst. The look was a mixture of horror and self-loathing so naked that Garion was forced to avert his eyes.

"You saw it, didn't you, boy?" Barak demanded. "You saw what happened to me out there."

"I didn't really see anything," Garion said carefully. "I hit my head on that tree, and all I really saw were stars."

"You must have seen it," Barak insisted. "You must have seen my Doom."

"Doom?" Garion said. "What are you talking about? You're still alive."

"A Doom doesn't always mean death," Barak said morosely, flinging himself into a large chair. "I wish mine did. A Doom is some terrible thing that's fated to happen to a man, and death's not the worst thing there is."

"You've just let the words of that crazy old blind woman take over your imagination," Garion said.

"It's not only Martje," Barak said. "She's just repeating what everybody in Cherek knows. An augurer was called in when I was born—it's the custom here. Most of the time the auguries don't show anything at all, and nothing special is going to happen during the child's life. But sometimes the future lies so heavily on one of us that almost anyone can see the Doom."

"That's just superstition," Garion scoffed. "I've never seen any fortune-teller who could even tell for sure if it's going to rain tomorrow. One of them came to Faldor's farm once and told Durnik that he was going to die twice. Isn't that silly?"

"The augurers and soothsayers of Cherek have more skill," Barak said, his face still sunk in melancholy. "The Doom they saw for me was always the same—I'm going to turn into a beast. I've had dozens of them tell me the same thing. And now it's happened. I've been sitting here for two days now, watching. The hair on my body's getting longer, and my teeth are starting to get pointed."

"You're imagining things," Garion said. "You look exactly the same to me as you always have."

"You're a kind boy, Garion," Barak said. "I know you're just trying to make me feel better, but I've got eyes of my own. I know that my teeth are getting pointed and my body's starting to grow fur. It won't be long until Anheg has to chain me up in his dungeon so I won't be able to hurt anyone, or I'll have to run off into the mountains and live with the trolls."

"Nonsense," Garion insisted.

"Tell me what you saw the other day," Barak pleaded. "What did I look like when I changed into a beast?"

"All I saw were stars from banging my head on that tree," Garion said again, trying to make it sound true.

"I just want to know what kind of beast I'm turning

into," Barak said, his voice thick with self-pity. "Am I going to be a wolf or a bear or some kind of monster no one even has a name for?"

"Don't you remember anything at all about what happened?" Garion asked carefully, trying to blot the strange double image of Barak and the bear out of his memory.

"Nothing," Barak said. "I heard you shouting, and the next thing I remember was the boar lying dead at my feet and you lying under that tree with his blood all over you. I could feel the beast in me, though. I could even smell him."

"All you smelled was the boar," Garion said, "and all that happened was that you lost your head in all the excitement."

"Berserk, you mean?" Barak said, looking up hopefully. Then he shook his head. "No, Garion. I've been berserk before. It doesn't feel at all the same. This was completely different." He sighed.

"You're not turning into a beast," Garion insisted.

"I know what I know," Barak said stubbornly.

And then Lady Merel, Barak's wife, stepped into the room through the still-open door. "I see that my Lord is recovering his wits," she said.

"Leave me alone, Merel," Barak said. "I'm not in the mood for these games of yours."

"Games, my Lord?" she said innocently. "I'm simply concerned about my duties. If my Lord is unwell, I'm obliged to care for him. That's a wife's right, isn't it?"

"Quit worrying so much about rights and duties, Merel," Barak said. "Just go away and leave me alone."

"My Lord was quite insistent about certain rights and duties on the night of his return to Val Alorn," she said. "Not even the locked door of my bedchamber was enough to curb his insistence."

"All right," Barak said, flushing slightly. "I'm sorry about that. I hoped that things might have changed between us. I was wrong. I won't bother you again."

"Bother, my Lord?" she said. "A duty is not a bother. A good wife is obliged to submit whenever her husband requires it of her—no matter how drunk or brutal he may be when he comes to her bed. No one will ever be able to accuse me of laxity in that regard."

"You're enjoying this, aren't you?" Barak accused.

"Enjoying what, my Lord?" Her voice was light, but there was a cutting edge to it.

"What do you want, Merel?" Barak demanded bluntly.

"I want to serve my Lord in his illness," she said. "I want to care for him and watch the progress of his disease—each symptom as it appears."

"Do you hate me that much?" Barak asked with heavy contempt. "Be careful, Merel. I might take it into my head to insist that you stay with me. How would you like that? How would you like to be locked in this room with a raging beast?"

"If you grow unmanageable, my Lord, I can always have you chained to the wall," she suggested, meeting his enraged glare with cool unconcern.

"Barak," Garion said uncomfortably, "I have to talk to you."

"Not now, Garion," Barak snapped.

"It's important. There's a spy in the palace."

"A spy?"

"A man in a green cloak," Garion said. "I've seen him several times."

"Many men wear green cloaks," Lady Merel said.

"Stay out of this, Merel," Barak said. He turned to Garion. "What makes you think he's a spy?"

"I saw him again this morning," Garion said, "and I followed him. He was sneaking along a corridor that nobody seems to use. It passes above the hall where the kings are meeting with Mister Wolf and Aunt Pol. He could hear every word they said."

"How do you know what he could hear?" Merel asked, her eyes narrowing.

"I was up there too," Garion said. "I hid not far from him, and I could hear them myself—almost as if I were in the same room with them."

"What does he look like?" Barak asked.

"He has sandy-colored hair," Garion said, "and a beard and, as I said, he wears a green cloak. I saw him the day we went down to look at your ship. He was going into a tavern with a Murgo."

"There aren't any Murgos in Val Alorn," Merel said.

"There's one," Garion said. "I've seen him before. I

know who he is." He had to move around the subject carefully. The compulsion not to speak about his dark-robed
enemy was as strong as always. Even the hint he had given
made his tongue seem stiff and his lips numb.

"Who is he?" Barak demanded.

Garion ignored the question. "And then on the day of
the boar hunt I saw him in the forest."

"The Murgo?" Barak asked.

"No. The man in the green cloak. He met some other
men there. They talked for a while not far from where I
was waiting for the boar to come. They didn't see me."

"There's nothing suspicious about that," Barak said. "A
man can meet with his friends anywhere he likes."

"I don't think they were friends exactly," Garion said.
"The one in the green cloak called one of the other men
'my Lord,' and that one was giving him orders to get close
enough so that he could hear what Mister Wolf and the
kings were saying."

"That's more serious," Barak said, seeming to forget his
melancholy. "Did they say anything else?"

"The flaxen-haired man wanted to know about us," Garion
said. "You, me, Durnik, Silk—all of us."

"Flaxen-colored hair?" Merel asked quickly.

"The one he called 'my Lord,'" Garion explained. "He
seemed to know about us. He even knew about me."

"Long, pale-colored hair?" Merel demanded. "No beard?
A little older than Barak?"

"It couldn't be him," Barak said. "Anheg banished him
on pain of death."

"You're a child, Barak," she said. "He'd ignore that if it
suited him. I think we'd better tell Anheg about this."

"Do you know him?" Garion asked. "Some of the things
he said about Barak weren't very polite."

"I can imagine," Merel said ironically. "Barak was one
of those who said that he ought to have his head removed."

Barak was already pulling on his mail shirt.

"Fix your hair," Merel told him in a tone that oddly had
no hint of her former rancor in it. "You look like a hay-
stack."

"I can't stop to fool with it now," Barak said impatiently. "Come along, both of you. We'll go to Anheg at
once."

There was no time for any further questions, since Garion and Merel almost had to run to keep up with Barak. They swept through the great hall, and startled warriors scrambled out of their way after one look at Barak's face.

"My Lord Barak," one of the guards at the door of the council hall greeted the huge man.

"One side," Barak commanded and flung open the door with a crash.

King Anheg looked up, startled at the sudden interruption. "Welcome, cousin," he began.

"Treason, Anheg!" Barak roared. "The Earl of Jarvik has broken his banishment and set spies on you in your own palace."

"Jarvik?" Anheg said. "He wouldn't dare."

"He dared, all right," Barak said. "He's been seen not far from Val Alorn, and some of his plotting has been overheard."

"Who is this Jarvik?" the Rivan Warder asked.

"An earl I banished last year," Anheg said. "One of his men was stopped, and we found a message on him. The message was to a Murgo in Sendaria, and it gave the details of one of our most secret councils. Jarvik tried to deny that the message was his, even though it had his own seal on it and his strongroom bulged with red gold from the mines of Cthol Murgos. I'd have had his head on a pole, but his wife's a kinswoman of mine and she begged for his life. I banished him to one of his estates on the west coast instead." He looked at Barak. "How did you find out about this?" he asked. "Last I heard, you'd locked yourself in your room and wouldn't talk to anybody."

"My husband's words are true, Anheg," Lady Merel said in a voice that rang with challenge.

"I don't doubt him, Merel," Anheg said, looking at her with a faintly surprised expression. "I just wanted to know how he learned about Jarvik, that's all."

"This boy from Sendaria saw him," Merel said, "and heard him talk to his spy. I heard the boy's story myself, and I stand behind what my husband said, if anyone here dares to doubt him."

"Garion?" Aunt Pol said, startled.

"May I suggest that we hear from the lad?" Cho-Hag of the Algars said quietly. "A nobleman with a history of friendship for the Murgos who chooses this exact moment to break his banishment concerns us all, I think."

"Tell them what you told Merel and me, Garion," Barak ordered, pushing Garion forward.

"Your Majesty," Garion said, bowing awkwardly, "I've seen a man in a green cloak hiding here in your palace several times since we came here. He creeps along the passageways and takes a lot of trouble not to be seen. I saw him the first night we were here, and the next day I saw him going into a tavern in the city with a Murgo. Barak says there aren't any Murgos in Cherek, but I know that the man he was with was a Murgo."

"How do you know?" Anheg asked shrewdly.

Garion looked at him helplessly, unable to say Asharak's name.

"Well, boy?" King Rhodar asked.

Garion struggled with the words, but nothing would come out.

"Maybe you know this Murgo?" Silk suggested.

Garion nodded, relieved that someone could help him.

"You wouldn't know many Murgos," Silk said, rubbing his nose with one finger. "Was it the one we met in Darine, perhaps—and later in Muros? The one known as Asharak?"

Garion nodded again.

"Why didn't you tell us?" Barak asked.

"I—I couldn't," Garion stammered.

"Couldn't?"

"The words wouldn't come out," Garion said. "I don't know why, but I've never been able to talk about him."

"Then you've seen him before?" Silk said.

"Yes," Garion said.

"And you've never told anybody?"

"No."

Silk glanced quickly at Aunt Pol. "Is this the sort of thing you might know more about than we would, Polgara?" he asked.

She nodded slowly. "It's possible to do it," she said. "It's never been very reliable, so I don't bother with it myself. It is possible, however." Her expression grew grim.

"The Grolims think it's impressive," Mister Wolf said. "Grolims are easily impressed."

"Come with me, Garion," Aunt Pol said.

"Not yet," Wolf said.

"This is important," she said, her face hardening.

"You can do it later," he said. "Let's hear the rest of his story first. The damage has already been done. Go ahead, Garion. What else did you see?"

Garion took a deep breath. "All right," he said, relieved to be talking to the old man instead of the kings. "I saw the man in the green cloak again that day we all went hunting. He met in the forest with a yellow-haired man who doesn't wear a beard. They talked for a while, and I could hear what they were saying. The yellow-haired man wanted to know what all of you were saying in this hall."

"You should have come to me immediately," King Anheg said.

"Anyway," Garion went on, "I had that fight with the wild boar. I hit my head against a tree and was stunned. I didn't remember what I'd seen until this morning. After King Fulrach called Durnik here, I went exploring. I was in a part of the palace where the roof is all fallen in, and I found some footprints. I followed them, and then after a while I saw the man in the green cloak again. That was when I remembered all this. I followed him, and he went along a corridor that passes somewhere over the top of this hall. He hid up there and listened to what you were saying."

"How much do you think he could hear, Garion?" King Cho-Hag asked.

"You were talking about somebody called the Apostate," Garion said, "and you were wondering if he could use some power of some kind to awaken an enemy who's been asleep for a long time. Some of you thought you ought to warn the Arends and the Tolnedrans, but Mister Wolf didn't think so. And Durnik talked about how the men of Sendaria would fight if the Angaraks came."

They appeared startled.

"I was hiding not far from the man in the green cloak," Garion said. "I'm sure he could hear everything that I could. Then some soldiers came, and the man ran away. That's when I decided that I ought to tell Barak about all this."

"Up there," Silk said, standing near one of the walls and

pointing at a corner of the ceiling of the hall. "The mortar's crumbled away. The sound of our voices carries right up through the cracks between the stones into the upper corridor."

"This is a valuable boy you've brought with you, Lady Polgara," King Rhodar said gravely. "If he's looking for a profession, I think I might find a place for him. Gathering information is a rewarding occupation, and he seems to have certain natural gifts along those lines."

"He has some other gifts as well," Aunt Pol said. "He seems to be very good at turning up in places where he's not supposed to be."

"Don't be too hard on the boy, Polgara," King Anheg said. "He's done us a service that we may never be able to repay."

Garion bowed again and retreated from Aunt Pol's steady gaze.

"Cousin," Anheg said then to Barak, "it seems that we have an unwelcome visitor somewhere in the palace. I think I'd like to have a little talk with this lurker in the green cloak."

"I'll take a few men," Barak said grimly. "We'll turn your palace upside down and shake it and see what falls out."

"I'd like to have him more or less intact," Anheg cautioned.

"Of course," Barak said.

"Not too intact, however. As long as he's still able to talk, he'll serve our purposes."

Barak grinned. "I'll make sure that he's talkative when I bring him to you, cousin," he said.

A bleak answering grin touched Anheg's face, and Barak started toward the door.

Then Anheg turned to Barak's wife. "I'd like to thank you also, Lady Merel," he said. "I'm sure you had a significant part in bringing this to us."

"I don't need thanks, your Majesty," she said. "It was my duty."

Anheg sighed. "Must it always be duty, Merel?" he asked sadly.

"What else is there?" she asked.

"A very great deal, actually," the king said, "but you're going to have to find that out for yourself."

"Garion," Aunt Pol said, "come here."

"Yes, ma'am," Garion said and went to her a little nervously.

"Don't be silly, dear," she said. "I'm not going to hurt you." She put her fingertips lightly to his forehead.

"Well?" Mister Wolf asked.

"It's there," she said. "It's very light, or I'd have noticed it before. I'm sorry, Father."

"Let's see," Wolf said. He came over and also touched Garion's head with his hand. "It's not serious," he said.

"It could have been," Aunt Pol said. "And it was my responsibility to see that something like this didn't happen."

"Don't flog yourself about it, Pol," Wolf said. "That's very unbecoming. Just get rid of it."

"What's the matter?" Garion asked, alarmed.

"It's nothing to worry about, dear," Aunt Pol said. She took his right hand and touched it for a moment to the white lock at her brow.

Garion felt a surge, a welter of confused impressions, and then a tingling wrench behind his ears. A sudden dizziness swept over him, and he would have fallen if Aunt Pol had not caught him.

"Who is the Murgo?" she asked, looking into his eyes.

"His name is Asharak," Garion said promptly.

"How long have you known him?"

"All my life. He used to come to Faldor's farm and watch me when I was little."

"That's enough for now, Pol," Mister Wolf said. "Let him rest a little first. I'll fix something to keep it from happening again."

"Is the boy ill?" King Cho-Hag asked.

"It's not exactly an illness, Cho-Hag," Mister Wolf said. "It's a little hard to explain. It's cleared up now, though."

"I want you to go to your room, Garion," Aunt Pol said, still holding him by the shoulders. "Are you steady enough on your feet to get there by yourself?"

"I'm all right," he said, still feeling a little light-headed.

"No side trips and no more exploring," she said firmly.

"No, ma'am."

"When you get there, lie down. I want you to think back

and remember every single time you've seen this Murgo—
what he did, what he said."

"He never spoke to me," Garion said. "He just
watched."

"I'll be along in a little while," she went on, "and I'll
want you to tell me everything you know about him. It's
important, Garion, so concentrate as hard as you can."

"All right, Aunt Pol," he said.

Then she kissed him lightly on the forehead. "Run along
now, dear," she said.

Feeling strangely light-headed, Garion went to the door
and out into the corridor.

He passed through the great hall where Anheg's warriors were belting on swords and picking up vicious-
looking battle-axes in preparation for the search of the palace. Still bemused, he went through without stopping.

Part of his mind seemed half-asleep, but that secret, inner part was wide awake. The dry voice observed that
something significant had just happened. The powerful
compulsion not to speak about Asharak was obviously
gone. Aunt Pol had somehow pulled it out of his mind entirely. His feeling about that was oddly ambiguous. That
strange relationship between himself and dark-robed, silent
Asharak had always been intensely private, and now it was
gone. He felt vaguely empty and somehow violated. He
sighed and went up the broad stairway toward his room.

There were a half-dozen warriors in the hallway outside
his room, probably part of Barak's search for the man in
the green cloak. Garion stopped. Something was wrong,
and he shook off his half daze. This part of the palace was
much too populated to make it very likely that the spy
would be hiding here. His heart began racing, and step by
step he began to back away toward the top of the stairs he
had just climbed. The warriors looked like any other Chereks in the palace—bearded, dressed in helmets, mail shirts,
and furs, but something didn't seem exactly right.

A bulky man in a dark, hooded cloak stepped through
the doorway of Garion's room into the corridor. It was Asharak. The Murgo was about to say something, but then his
eyes fell on Garion. "Ah," he said softly. His dark eyes
gleamed in his scarred face. "I've been looking for you,
Garion," he said in that same soft voice. "Come here, boy."

Garion felt a tentative tug at his mind that seemed to slip away as if it somehow could not get a sure grip. He shook his head mutely and continued to back away.

"Come along now," Asharak said. "We've known each other far too long for this. Do as I say. You know that you must."

The tug became a powerful grasp that again slipped away.

"Come here, Garion!" Asharak commanded harshly.

Garion kept backing away, step by step. "No," he said.

Asharak's eyes blazed, and he drew himself up angrily. This time it was not a tug or a grasp, but a blow. Garion could feel the force of it even as it seemed somehow to miss or be deflected.

Asharak's eyes widened slightly, then narrowed. "Who did this?" he demanded. "Polgara? Belgarath? It won't do any good, Garion. I had you once, and I can take you again any time I want to. You're not strong enough to refuse me."

Garion looked at his enemy and answered out of some need for defiance. "Maybe I'm not," he said, "but I think you'll have to catch me first."

Asharak turned quickly to his warriors. "That's the boy I want," he barked sharply. "Take him!"

Smoothly, almost as if it were done without thought, one of the warriors raised his bow and leveled an arrow directly at Garion. Asharak swung his arm quickly and knocked the bow aside just as the steel-pointed shaft was loosed. The arrow sang in the air and clattered against the stones of the wall a few feet to Garion's left.

"Alive, idiot," Asharak snarled and struck the bowman a crushing blow to the side of the head. The bowman fell twitching to the stone floor.

Garion spun, dashed back to the stairs and plunged down three steps at a time. He didn't bother to look back. The sound of heavy feet told him that Asharak and his men were after him. At the bottom of the stairs, he turned sharply to the left and fled down a long, dark passageway that led back into the maze of Anheg's palace.

Chapter Eighteen

THERE WERE WARRIORS everywhere, and the sounds of fighting. In the first instant of his flight, Garion's plan had been simple. All he had to do was to find some of Barak's warriors, and he would be safe. But there were other warriors in the palace as well. The Earl of Jarvik had led a small army into the palace by way of the ruined wings to the south, and fighting raged in the corridors.

Garion quickly realized that there was no way he could distinguish friend from enemy. To him, one Cherek warrior looked the same as another. Unless he could find Barak or someone else he recognized, he did not dare reveal himself to any of them. The frustrating knowledge that he was running from friends as well as enemies added to his fright. It was altogether possible—even quite likely—that he would run from Barak's men directly into the arms of Jarvik's.

The most logical thing to do would be to go directly back to the council hall, but in his haste to escape from Asharak, he had run down so many dim passageways and turned so many corners that he had no idea where he was or how to get back to the familiar parts of the palace. His headlong flight was dangerous. Asharak or his men could wait around any corner to seize him, and he knew that the Murgo could quickly re-establish that strange bond between them that Aunt Pol had shattered with her touch. It was that which had to be avoided at any cost. Once Asharak had him again, he would never let go. The only alternative to him was to find some place to hide.

He dodged into another narrow passageway and stopped, panting and with his back pressed tightly against the stones of the wall. Dimly, at the far end of this hallway, he could see a narrow flight of worn stone steps twisting upward in the flickering light of a single torch. He quickly reasoned that the higher he went, the less likely he would be to encounter anyone. The fighting would most likely be concentrated on the lower floors. He took a deep breath and went swiftly to the foot of the stairs.

Halfway up he saw the flaw in his plan. There were no side passages on the stairs, no way to escape and no place to hide. He had to get to the top quickly or chance discovery and capture—or even worse.

"Boy!" a shout came from below.

Garion looked quickly over his shoulder. A grim-faced Cherek in mail and helmet was coming up the stairs behind him, his sword drawn.

Garion started to run, stumbling up the stairs.

There was another shout from above, and Garion froze. The warrior at the top was as grim as the one below and wielded a cruel-looking axe.

He was trapped between them. Garion shrank back against the stones, fumbling for his dagger, though he knew it would be of little use.

Then the two warriors saw each other. With ringing shouts they both charged. The one with the sword rushed up past Garion while the one with the axe lunged down.

The axe swung wide, missed and clashed a shower of sparks from the stones of the wall. The sword was more true. With his hair standing on end in horror, Garion saw it slide through the downward-plunging body of the axeman. The axe fell clattering down the stairs, and the axeman, still falling on top of his opponent, pulled a broad dagger from its sheath at his hip and drove it into the chest of his enemy. The impact as the two men came together tore them from their feet, and they tumbled, still grappled together down the stairs, their daggers flashing as each man struck again and again.

In helpless horror Garion watched as they rolled and crashed past him, their daggers sinking into each other with sickening sounds and blood spurting from their wounds like red fountains.

Garion retched once, clenched his teeth tightly, and ran

up the stairs, trying to close his ears to the awful sounds coming from below as the two dying men continued their horrid work on each other.

He no longer even considered stealth; he simply ran—fleeing more from that hideous encounter on the stairs than from Asharak or the Earl of Jarvik. At last, after how long he could not have said, gasping and winded, he plunged through the partially open door of a dusty, unused chamber. He pushed the door shut and stood trembling with his back against it.

There was a broad, sagging bed against one wall of the room and a small window set high in the same wall. Two broken chairs leaned wearily in corners and an empty chest, its lid open, in a third, and that was all. The chamber was at least a place out of the corridors where savage men were killing each other, but Garion quickly realized that the seeming safety here was an illusion. If anyone opened this door, he would be trapped. Desperately he began to look around the dusty room.

Hanging on the bare wall across from the bed were some drapes; and thinking that they might conceal some closet or adjoining chamber, Garion crossed the room and pulled them aside. There was an opening behind the drapes, though it did not lead into another room but instead into a dark, narrow hall. He peered into the passageway, but the darkness was so total that he could only see a short distance into it. He shuddered at the thought of groping through that blackness with armed men pounding along at his heels.

He glanced up at the single window and then dragged the heavy chest across the room to stand on so that he could see out. Perhaps he might be able to see something from the window that would give him some idea of his location. He climbed up on the chest, stood on his tiptoes and looked out.

Towers loomed here and there amid the long slate roofs of the endless galleries and halls of King Anheg's palace. It was hopeless. He saw nothing that he could recognize. He turned back toward the chamber and was about to jump down from the chest when he stopped suddenly. There, clearly in the dust which lay heavily on the floor, were his footprints.

He hopped quickly down and grabbed up the bolster from the long-unused bed. He spread it out on the floor and dragged it around the room, erasing the footprints. He knew that he could not completely conceal the fact that someone had been in the room, but he could obliterate the footprints which, because of their size, would immediately make it obvious to Asharak or any of his men that whoever had been hiding here was not yet full-grown. When he finished, he tossed the bolster back on the bed. The job wasn't perfect, but at least it was better than it had been.

Then there was a shout in the corridor outside and the ring of steel on steel.

Garion took a deep breath and plunged into the dark passageway behind the drapes.

He had gone no more than a few feet when the darkness in the narrow passage become absolute. His skin crawled at the touch of cobwebs on his face, and the dust of years rose chokingly from the uneven floor. At first he moved quite rapidly, wanting more than anything to put as much distance between himself and the fighting in the corridor as possible, but then he stumbled, and for one heart-stopping instant it seemed that he would fall. The picture of a steep stairway dropping down into the blackness flashed through his mind, and he realized that at his present pace there would be no possible way to catch himself. He began to move more cautiously, one hand on the stones of the wall and the other in front of his face to ward off the cobwebs which hung thickly from the low ceiling.

There was no sense of time in the dark, and it seemed to Garion that he had been groping for hours in this dark hallway that appeared to go on forever. Then, despite his care, he ran full into a rough stone wall. He felt a moment of panic. Did the passageway end here? Was it a trap?

Then, flickering at one corner of his vision, he saw dim light. The passageway did not end, but rather made a sharp turn to the right. There seemed to be a light at the far end, and Garion gratefully followed it.

As the light grew stronger, he moved more rapidly, and soon he reached the spot that was the source of the light. It was a narrow slot low in the wall. Garion knelt on the dusty stones and peered out.

The hall below was enormous, and a great fire burned in

a pit in the center with the smoke rising to the openings in the vaulted roof which lofted even above the place where Garion was. Though it looked much different from up here, he immediately recognized King Anheg's throne room. As he looked down, he saw the gross shape of King Rhodar and the smaller form of King Cho-Hag with the ever-present Hettar standing behind him. Some distance from the thrones, King Fulrach stood in conversation with Mister Wolf, and nearby was Aunt Pol. Barak's wife was talking with Queen Islena, and Queen Porenn and Queen Silar stood not far from them. Silk paced the floor nervously, glancing now and then at the heavily guarded doors. Garion felt a surge of relief. He was safe.

He was about to call down to them when the great door banged open, and King Anheg, mail-shirted and with his sword in his hand, strode into the hall, closely followed by Barak and the Rivan Warder, holding between them the struggling form of the flaxen-haired man Garion had seen in the forest on the day of the boar hunt.

"This treason will cost you dearly, Jarvik," Anheg said grimly over his shoulder as he strode toward his throne.

"Is it over, then?" Aunt Pol asked.

"Soon, Polgara," Anheg said. "My men are chasing the last of Jarvik's brigands in the furthest reaches of the palace. If we hadn't been warned, it might have gone quite differently, though."

Garion, his shout still hovering just behind his lips, decided at the last instant to stay silent for a few more moments.

King Anheg sheathed his sword and took his place on his throne. "We'll talk for a bit, Jarvik," he said, "before what must be done is done."

The flaxen-haired man gave up his hopeless struggle against Barak and the almost equally powerful Brand. "I don't have anything to say, Anheg," he said defiantly. "If the luck had gone differently, I'd be sitting on your throne right now. I took my chance, and that's the end of it."

"Not quite," Anheg said. "I want the details. You might as well tell me. One way or another, you're going to talk."

"Do your worst," Jarvik sneered. "I'll bite out my own tongue before I tell you anything."

"We'll see about that," Anheg said grimly.

"That won't be necessary, Anheg," Aunt Pol said, walking slowly toward the captive. "There's an easier way to persuade him."

"I'm not going to say anything," Jarvik told her. "I'm a warrior and I'm not afraid of you, witch-woman."

"You're a greater fool than I thought, Lord Jarvik," Mister Wolf said. "Would you rather I did it, Pol?"

"I can manage, Father," she said, not taking her eyes off Jarvik.

"Carefully," the old man cautioned. "Sometimes you go to extremes. Just a little touch is enough."

"I know what I'm doing, Old Wolf," she said tartly. She stared full into the captive's eyes.

Garion, still hidden, held his breath.

The Earl of Jarvik began to sweat and tried desperately to pull his eyes away from Aunt Pol's gaze, but it was hopeless. Her will commanded him, locking his eyes. He trembled, and his face grew pale. She made no move, no gesture, but merely stood before him, her eyes burning into his brain.

And then, after a moment, he screamed. Then he screamed again and collapsed, his weight sagging down in the hands of the two men who held him.

"Take it away," he whimpered, shuddering uncontrollably. "I'll talk, but please take it away."

Silk, now lounging near Anheg's throne, looked at Hettar. "I wonder what he saw," he said.

"I think it might be better not to know," Hettar replied.

Queen Islena had watched intently as if hoping to gain some hint of how the trick was done. She winced visibly when Jarvik screamed, pulling her eyes away.

"All right, Jarvik," Anheg said, his tone strangely subdued. "Begin at the beginning. I want it all."

"It was a little thing at first," Jarvik said in a shaking voice. "There didn't seem to be any harm in it."

"There never does," Brand said.

The Earl of Jarvik drew in a deep breath, glanced once at Aunt Pol and shuddered again. Then he straightened. "It started about two years ago," he said. "I'd sailed to Kotu in Drasnia, and I met a Nadrak merchant named Grashor there. He seemed to be a good enough fellow and after we'd gotten to know each other he asked me if I'd be interested in a profitable venture. I told him that I was an earl and not a common tradesman, but he persisted. He said he was nervous about the pirates who live on the islands in the Gulf of Cherek and an earl's ship manned by armed warriors was not likely to be attacked. His cargo was a single chest—not very large. I think it was some jewels he'd managed to smuggle past the customs houses in Boktor, and he wanted them delivered to Darine in Sendaria. I said that I wasn't really interested, but then he opened his purse and poured out gold. The gold was bright red, I remember, and I couldn't seem to take my eyes off it. I did need money—who doesn't after all?—and I really couldn't see any dishonor in doing what he asked.

"Anyway, I carried him and his cargo to Darine and met his associate—a Murgo named Asharak."

Garion started at the name, and he heard Silk's low whistle of surprise.

"As we'd agreed," Jarvik continued, "Asharak paid me a sum equal to what Grashor had given me, and I came away from the affair with a whole pouch of gold. Asharak told me that I'd done them a great favor and that if I ever needed more gold, he'd be happy to find ways for me to earn it.

"I now had more gold than I'd ever had at one time before, but it somehow seemed that it wasn't enough. For some reason I felt that I needed more."

"It's the nature of Angarak gold," Mister Wolf said. "It calls to its own. The more one has, the more it comes to possess him. That's why Murgos are so lavish with it. Asharak wasn't buying your services, Jarvik; he was buying your soul."

Jarvik nodded, his face gloomy. "At any rate," he continued, "it wasn't long before I found an excuse to sail to Darine again. Asharak told me that since Murgos are forbidden to enter Cherek, he'd developed a great curiosity about us and our kingdom. He asked me many questions and he gave me gold for every answer. It seemed to me to be a foolish way to spend money, but I gave him the answers and took his gold. When I came back to Cherek, I had another pouch full. I went to Jarviksholm and put the new gold with that I already had. I saw that I was a rich man, and I still hadn't done anything dishonorable. But now it seemed that there weren't enough hours in the day. I spent all my time locked in my strongroom, counting my gold over and over, polishing it until it gleamed red as blood and filling my ears with the sound of its tinkling.

"But after a while it seemed that I didn't really have very much, and so I went back to Asharak. He said he was still curious about Cherek and that he'd like to know Anheg's mind. He told me that he'd give me as much gold as I already had if I sent him word of what was said in the high councils here in the palace for a year. At first I said no, because I knew it would be dishonorable; but then he showed me the gold, and I couldn't say no any more."

From where he watched Garion could see the expressions of those in the hall below. Their faces had a curious mingling of pity and contempt as Jarvik's story continued.

"It was then, Anheg," he said, "that your men captured one of my messengers, and I was banished to Jarviksholm. At first I didn't mind, because I could still play with my gold. But again it wasn't long before it seemed that I didn't have enough. I sent a fast ship through the Bore to Darine with a message to Asharak begging him to find something else for me to do to earn more gold. When the ship came back, Asharak was aboard her, and we sat down and talked about what I could do to increase my hoard."

"You're doubly a traitor then, Jarvik," Anheg said in a voice that was almost sad. "You've betrayed me and you've broken the oldest law in Cherek. No Angarak has set foot on Cherek soil since the days of Bear-shoulders himself."

Jarvik shrugged. "I didn't really care by then," he said. "Asharak had a plan, and it seemed like a good one to me. If we could get through the city a few at a time, we could hide an army in the ruined southern wings of the palace. With surprise and a bit of luck we could kill Anheg and the other Alorn Kings, and I could take the throne of Cherek and maybe of all Aloria as well."

"And what was Asharak's price?" Mister Wolf demanded, his eyes narrowing. "What did he want in return for making you king?"

"A thing so small that I laughed when he told me what he wanted," Jarvik said. "But he said that he'd not only give me the crown but a roomful of gold if I'd get it for him."

"What was it?" Wolf repeated.

"He said that there was a boy—about fourteen—in the party of King Fulrach of Sendaria. He told me that as soon as that boy was delivered to him, he'd give me more gold than I could count and the throne of Cherek as well."

King Fulrach looked startled. "The boy Garion?" he asked. "Why would Asharak want him?"

Aunt Pol's single frightened gasp carried even up to where Garion was concealed. "Durnik!" she said in a ringing voice, but Durnik was already on his feet and racing toward the door with Silk close behind him. Aunt Pol spun with eyes blazing and the white lock at her brow almost incandescent in the midnight of her hair. The Earl of Jarvik flinched as her glare fell on him.

"If anything's happened to the boy, Jarvik, men will tremble at the memory of your fate for a thousand years," she told him.

It had gone far enough. Garion was ashamed and a little frightened by the fury of Aunt Pol's reaction.

"I'm all right, Aunt Pol," he called down to her through the narrow slot in the wall. "I'm up here."

"Garion?" She looked up, trying to see him. "Where are you?"

"Up here near the ceiling," he said, "behind the wall."

"How did you get up there?"

"I don't know. Some men were chasing me, and I ran. This is where I ended up."

"Come down here at once."

"I don't know how, Aunt Pol," he said. "I ran so far and took so many turns that I don't know how to get back. I'm lost."

"All right," she said, regaining her composure. "Stay where you are. We'll think of a way to get you down."

"I hope so," he said.

Chapter Nineteen

"WELL, IT HAS TO come out someplace," King Anheg said, squinting up toward the spot where Garion waited nervously. "All he has to do is follow it."

"And walk directly into the arms of Asharak the Murgo?" Aunt Pol asked. "He's better off staying where he is."

"Asharak's fleeing for his life," Anheg said. "He's nowhere in the palace."

"As I recall, he's not even supposed to be in the kingdom," she said pointedly.

"All right, Pol," Mister Wolf said. He called up, "Garion, which way does the passage run?"

"It seems to go on toward the back of the hall where the thrones are," Garion answered. "I can't tell for sure if it turns off or not. It's pretty dark up here."

"We'll pass you up a couple torches," Wolf said. "Set one at the spot where you are now and then go on down the passage with the other. As long as you can see the first one, you'll be going in a straight line."

"Very clever," Silk said. "I wish I were seven thousand years old so I could solve problems so easily."

Wolf let that pass.

"I still think the safest way would be to get some ladders and break a hole in the wall," Barak said.

King Anheg looked pained. "Couldn't we try Belgarath's suggestion first?" he asked.

Barak shrugged. "You're the king."

"Thanks," Anheg said dryly.

A warrior fetched a long pole and two torches were passed up to Garion.

"If the line of the passageway holds straight," Anheg

said, "he should come out somewhere in the royal apartments."

"Interesting," King Rhodar said with one raised eyebrow. "It would be most enlightening to know if the passage led *to* the royal chambers or *from* them."

"It's entirely possible that the passageway is just some long-forgotten escape route," Anheg said in an injured tone. "Our history, after all, has not been all that peaceful. There's no need to suspect the worst, is there?"

"Of course not," King Rhodar said blandly, "no need at all."

Garion set one of the torches beside the slot in the wall and followed the dusty passageway, looking back often to be sure that the torch was still in plain sight. Eventually he came to a narrow door which opened into the back of an empty closet. The closet was attached to a splendid-looking bedchamber, and outside there was a broad, well-lighted corridor.

Several warriors were coming down the corridor, and Garion recognized Torvik the huntsman among them. "Here I am," he said, stepping out with a surge of relief.

"You've been busy, haven't you?" Torvik said with a grin.

"It wasn't my idea," Garion said.

"Let's get you back to King Anheg," Torvik said. "The lady, your Aunt, seems concerned about you."

"She's angry with me, I suppose," Garion said, falling into step beside the broad-shouldered man.

"More than likely," Torvik said. "Women are almost always angry with us for one reason or another. It's one of the things you'll have to get used to as you get older."

Aunt Pol was waiting at the door to the throne room. There were no reproaches—not yet, at any rate. For one brief moment she clasped him fiercely to her and then looked at him gravely. "We've been waiting for you, dear," she said almost calmly; then she led him to where the others waited.

"In my grandmother's quarters, you say?" Anheg was saying to Torvik. "What an astonishing thing. I remember her as a crotchety old lady who walked with a cane."

"No one is born old, Anheg," King Rhodar said with a sly look.

"I'm sure there are many explanations, Anheg," Queen Porenn said. "My husband is just teasing you."

"One of the men looked into the passage, your Majesty," Torvik said tactfully. "The dust is very thick. It's possible that it hasn't been used for centuries."

"What an astonishing thing," Anheg said again.

The matter was then delicately allowed to drop, though King Rhodar's sly expression spoke volumes.

The Earl of Seline coughed politely. "I think young Garion here may have a story for us," he said.

"I expect he has," Aunt Pol said, turning toward Garion. "I seem to remember telling you to stay in your room."

"Asharak was in my room," Garion said, "and he had warriors with him. He tried to make me come to him. When I wouldn't, he said that he'd had me once and could get me again. I didn't understand exactly what he meant, but I told him that he'd have to catch me first. Then I ran."

Brand, the Rivan Warder, chuckled. "I don't see how you can find much fault with that, Polgara," he said. "I think that if I found a Grolim priest in my room, I'd probably run away too."

"You're sure it was Asharak?" Silk asked.

Garion nodded. "I've known him for a long time," he said. "All my life, I guess. And he knew me. He called me by name."

"I think I'd like to have a long talk with this Asharak," Anheg said. "I want to ask him some questions about all the mischief he's been stirring up in my kingdom."

"I doubt if you'll find him, Anheg," Mister Wolf said. "He seems to be more than just a Grolim priest. I touched his mind once—in Muros. It's not an ordinary mind."

"I'll amuse myself with the search for him," Anheg said with a bleak expression. "Not even a Grolim can walk on water, so I believe I'll just seal off all the ports in Cherek and then put my warriors to work searching the mountains and forests for him. They get fat and troublesome in the wintertime anyway, and it'll give them something to do."

"Driving fat, troublesome warriors into the snow in the dead of winter isn't going to make you a popular king, Anheg," Rhodar observed.

"Offer a reward," Silk suggested. "That way you get the job done and stay popular as well."

"That's an idea," Anheg said. "What kind of reward would you suggest, Prince Kheldar?"

"Promise to equal the weight of Asharak's head in gold," Silk said. "That should lure the fattest warrior away from the dice cup and the ale keg."

Anheg winced.

"He's a Grolim," Silk said. "They probably won't find him, but they'll take the kingdom apart looking. Your gold is safe, your warriors get a bit of exercise, you get a reputation for generosity, and, with every man in Cherek looking for him with an axe, Asharak's going to be much too busy hiding to stir up any more mischief. A man whose head is more valuable to others than it is to himself has little time for foolishness."

"Prince Kheldar," Anheg said gravely, "you're a devious man."

"I try, King Anheg," Silk said with an ironic bow.

"I don't suppose you'd care to come to work for me?" the King of Cherek offered.

"Anheg!" Rhodar protested.

Silk sighed. "Blood, King Anheg," he said. "I'm committed to my uncle by our bonds of kinship. I'd be interested to hear your offer, though. It might help in future negotiations about compensation for my services."

Queen Porenn's laughter was like a small silver bell, and King Rhodar's face became tragic. "You see," he said. "I'm absolutely surrounded by traitors. What's a poor fat old man to do?"

A grim-looking warrior entered the hall and marched up to Anheg. "It's done, King," he said. "Do you want to look at his head?"

"No," Anheg said shortly.

"Should we put it on a pole near the harbor?" the warrior asked.

"No," Anheg said. "Jarvik was a brave man once and my kinsman by marriage. Have him delivered to his wife for a proper burial."

The warrior bowed and left the hall.

"This problem of the Grolim, Asharak, interests me,"

Queen Islena said to Aunt Pol. "Might we not between us, Lady Polgara, devise a way to locate him?" Her expression had a certain quality of self-importance to it.

Mister Wolf spoke quickly before Aunt Pol could answer. "Bravely spoken, Islena," he said. "But we couldn't allow the Queen of Cherek to take such a risk. I'm sure your skills are formidable, but such a search opens the mind completely. If Asharak felt you looking for him, he'd retaliate instantly. Polgara wouldn't be in any danger, but I'm afraid your mind could be blown out like a candle. It would be a great shame to have the Queen of Cherek live out the rest of her life as a raving lunatic."

Islena turned suddenly very pale and did not see the sly wink Mister Wolf directed at Anheg.

"I couldn't permit it," Anheg said firmly. "My queen is far too precious for me to allow her to take such a terrible risk."

"I must accede to the will of my Lord," Islena said in a relieved tone. "By his command I withdraw my suggestion."

"The courage of my queen honors me," Anheg said with an absolutely straight face.

Islena bowed and backed away rather quickly. Aunt Pol looked at Mister Wolf with one raised eyebrow, but let it pass.

Wolf's expression became more serious as he rose from the chair in which he had been sitting. "I think that the time has come to make some decisions," he said. "Things are beginning to move too fast for any more delay." He looked at Anheg. "Is there some place where we can speak without risk of being overheard?"

"There's a chamber in one of the towers," Anheg said. "I thought about it before our first meeting, but—" He paused and looked at Cho-Hag.

"You shouldn't have let it concern you," Cho-Hag said. "I can manage stairs if I have to, and it would have been better for me to have been a little inconvenienced than to have had Jarvik's spy overhear us."

"I'll stay with Garion," Durnik said to Aunt Pol.

Aunt Pol shook her head firmly. "No," she said. "As long as Asharak is on the loose in Cherek, I don't want him out of my sight."

"Shall we go, then?" Mister Wolf said. "It's getting late, and I want to leave first thing in the morning. The trail I was following is getting colder."

Queen Islena, still looking shaken, stood to one side with Porenn and Silar and made no effort to follow as King Anheg led the way from the throne room.

I'll let you know what happens, King Rhodar signaled to his queen.

Of course, Porenn gestured back. Her face was placid, but the snap of her fingers as they spoke betrayed her irritability.

Calmly, child, Rhodar's fingers told her. *We're guests here and have to obey local customs.*

Whatever my Lord commands, she replied with a tilt of her hands that spoke whole volumes of sarcasm.

With Hettar's help, King Cho-Hag managed the stairs, although his progress was painfully slow. "I apologize for this," he puffed, stopping halfway up to catch his breath. "It's as tiresome for me as it is for you."

King Anheg posted guards at the foot of the stairs, then came up and closed the heavy door behind him. "Light the fire, cousin," he said to Barak. "We might as well be comfortable."

Barak nodded and put a torch to the wood in the fireplace.

The chamber was round and not too spacious, but there was adequate room for them all and chairs and benches to sit on.

Mister Wolf stood at one of the windows, looking down at the twinkling lights of Val Alorn below. "I've always been fond of towers," he said, almost to himself. "My Master lived in one like this, and I enjoyed the time I spent there."

"I'd give my life to have known Aldur," Cho-Hag said softly. "Was he really surrounded by light as some say?"

"He seemed quite ordinary to me," Mister Wolf said. "I lived with him for five years before I even knew who he was."

"Was he really as wise as we're told?" Anheg asked.

"Probably wiser," Wolf said. "I was a wild and errant boy when he found me dying in a snowstorm outside his tower. He managed to tame me—though it took him several hundred years to do it." He turned from the window with a deep sigh. "To work then," he said.

"Where will you go to take up the search?" King Fulrach asked.

"Camaar," Wolf said. "I found the trail there. I think it led down into Arendia."

"We'll send warriors with you," Anheg said. "After what's happened here, it looks like the Grolims may try to stop you."

"No," Wolf said firmly. "Warriors are useless in dealing with the Grolims. I can't move with an army underfoot, and I won't have time to explain to the King of Arendia why I'm invading his kingdom with a horde of troops at my back. It takes even longer to explain things to Arends than it does to Alorns—impossible as that sounds."

"Don't be uncivil, Father," Aunt Pol said. "It's their world too, and they're concerned."

"You wouldn't necessarily need an army, Belgarath," King Rhodar said, "but wouldn't it be prudent to take along a few good men?"

"There's very little that Polgara and I can't deal with by ourselves," Wolf said, "and Silk, Barak and Durnik are along to deal with more mundane problems. The smaller our group, the less attention we'll attract." He turned to Cho-Hag. "As long as we're on the subject, though, I'd like to have your son Hettar with us. We're likely to need his rather specialized talents."

"Impossible," Hettar said flatly. "I have to remain with my father."

"No, Hettar," Cho-Hag said. "I don't intend for you to live out your life as a cripple's legs."

"I've never felt any restriction in serving you, Father," Hettar said. "There are plenty of others with the same talents I have. Let the Ancient One choose another."

"How many Sha-Darim are there among the Algars?" Mister Wolf asked gravely.

Hettar looked at him sharply as if trying to tell him something with his eyes.

King Cho-Hag drew in his breath sharply. "Hettar," he asked, "is this true?"

Hettar shrugged. "It may be, Father," he said. "I didn't think it was important."

Cho-Hag looked at Mister Wolf.

Wolf nodded. "It's true," he said. "I knew it the first time I saw him. He's a Sha-Dar. He had to find out for himself, though."

Cho-Hag's eyes suddenly brimmed with tears. "My son!" he said proudly, pulling Hettar into a rough embrace.

"It's no great thing, Father," Hettar said quietly, as if suddenly embarrassed.

"What are they talking about?" Garion whispered to Silk.

"It's something the Algars take very seriously," Silk said softly. "They think that there are some people who can talk to horses with their thoughts alone. They call these people Sha-Darim—Clan-Chiefs of the horses. It's very rare—maybe only two or three in a whole generation. It's instant nobility for any Algar who has it. Cho-Hag's going to explode with pride when he gets back to Algaria."

"Is it that important?" Garion asked.

Silk shrugged. "The Algars seem to think so," he said. "All the clans gather at the Stronghold when they find a new Sha-Dar. The whole nation celebrates for six weeks. There are all kinds of gifts. Hettar'll be a rich man if he chooses to accept them. He may not. He's a strange man."

"You must go," Cho-Hag said to Hettar. "The pride of Algaria goes with you. Your duty is clear."

"As my father decides," Hettar said reluctantly.

"Good," Mister Wolf said. "How long will it take you to go to Algaria, pick up a dozen or so of your best horses and take them to Camaar?"

Hettar thought for a moment. "Two weeks," he said, "if there aren't any blizzards in the mountains of Sendaria."

"We'll all leave here in the morning then," Wolf said. "Anheg can give you a ship. Take the horses along the Great North Road to the place a few leagues east of Camaar where another road strikes off to the south. It fords the Greater Camaar River and runs down to join the Great West Road at the ruins of Vo Wacune in northern Arendia. We'll meet you there in two weeks."

Hettar nodded.

"We'll also be joined at Vo Wacune by an Asturian Arend," Wolf went on, "and somewhat later by a Mimbrate. They might be useful to us in the south."

"And will also fulfill the prophecies," Anheg said cryptically.

Wolf shrugged, his bright blue eyes twinkling suddenly. "I don't object to fulfilling prophecies," he said, "as long as it doesn't inconvenience me too much."

"Is there anything we can do to help in the search?" Brand asked.

"You'll have enough to do," Wolf said. "No matter how our search turns out, it's obvious that the Angaraks are getting ready for some kind of major action. If we're successful, they might hesitate, but Angaraks don't think the way we do. Even after what happened at Vo Mimbre, they may decide to risk an all-out attack on the west. It could be that they're responding to prophecies of their own that we don't know anything about. In any event, I think you should be ready for something fairly major from them. You'll need to make preparations."

Anheg grinned wolfishly. "We've been preparing for them for five thousand years," he said. "This time we'll purge the whole world of this Angarak infection. When Torak One-eye awakes, he'll find himself as alone as Mara—and just as powerless."

"Maybe," Mister Wolf said, "but don't plan the victory celebration until the war's over. Make your preparations quietly, and don't stir up the people in your kingdoms any more than you have to. The west is crawling with Grolims, and they're watching everything we do. The trail I'll be following could lead me into Cthol Murgos, and I'd rather not have to deal with an army of Murgos massed on the border."

"I can play the watching game too," King Rhodar said with a grim look on his plump face. "Probably even better than the Grolims. It's time to send a few more caravans to the east. The Angaraks won't move without help from the east, and the Malloreans will have to cross over into Gar og Nadrak before they deploy south. A bribe or two here and there, a few barrels of strong ale in the right mining camps—who knows what a bit of diligent corruption might turn up? A chance word or two could give us several months' warning."

"If they're planning anything major, the Thulls will be building supply dumps along the eastern escarpment," Cho-Hag said. "Thulls aren't bright, and it's easy to observe them without being seen. I'll increase my patrols along those mountains. With a little luck, we might be able to anticipate their invasion route. Is there anything else we can do to help you, Belgarath?"

Mister Wolf thought for a moment. Suddenly he grinned. "I'm certain that our thief is listening very hard, waiting for one of us to speak his name or the name of the thing he stole. Sooner or later someone's bound to make a slip; and once he locates us, he'll be able to hear every word we say. Instead of trying to gag ourselves, I think it might be better if we gave him something to listen to. If you can arrange it, I'd like to have every minstrel and storyteller in the north start retelling certain old stories—you know the ones. When those names start sounding in every village marketplace north of the Camaar River, it'll set up a roaring in his ears like a thunderstorm. If nothing else, it will give us freedom to speak. In time he'll get tired of it and stop listening."

"It's getting late, Father," Aunt Pol reminded him.

Wolf nodded. "We're playing a deadly game," he told them all, "but our enemies are playing one just as deadly. Their danger's as great as ours, and right now no one can predict what will finally happen. Make your preparations and send out men you can trust to keep watch. Be patient and don't do anything rash. That could be more dangerous than anything else right now. At the moment, Polgara and I are the only ones who can act. You're going to have to trust us. I know that sometimes some of the things we've done have seemed a bit strange, but there are reasons for what we do. Please don't interfere again. I'll get word to you now and then about our progress; if I need you to do anything else, I'll let you know. All right?"

The kings nodded gravely, and everyone rose to his feet.

Anheg stepped over to Mister Wolf. "Could you come to my study in an hour or so, Belgarath?" he said quietly. "I'd like to have a few words with you and Polgara before your departure."

"If you wish, Anheg," Mister Wolf said.

"Come along, Garion," Aunt Pol said. "We have packing to take care of."

Garion, a little awed by the solemnity of the discussions, rose quietly and followed her to the door.

Chapter Twenty

KING ANHEG'S STUDY was a large, cluttered room high in a square tower. Books bound in heavy leather lay everywhere, and strange devices with gears and pulleys and tiny brass chains sat on tables and stands. Intricately drawn maps, with beautiful illuminations were pinned up on the walls, and the floor was littered with scraps of parchment covered with tiny writing. King Anheg, his coarse black hair hanging in his eyes, sat at a slanted table in the soft glow of a pair of candles studying a large book written on thin sheets of crackling parchment.

The guard at the door let them enter without a word, and Mister Wolf stepped briskly into the center of the room. "You wanted to see us, Anheg?"

The King of Cherek straightened from his book and laid it aside. "Belgarath," he said with a short nod of greeting. "Polgara." He glanced at Garion who stood uncertainly near the door.

"I meant what I said earlier," Aunt Pol said. "I'm not going to let him out of my sight until I know for certain that he's out of the reach of the Grolim Asharak."

"Anything you say, Polgara," Anheg said. "Come in, Garion."

"I see that you're continuing your studies," Mister Wolf said approvingly, glancing at the littered room.

"There's so much to learn," Anheg said with a helpless gesture that included all the welter of books and papers and strange machines. "I have a feeling that I might have been happier if you'd never introduced me to this impossible task."

"You asked me," Wolf said simply.

"You could have said no." Anheg laughed. Then his brutish face turned serious. He glanced once at Garion and began to speak in an obviously oblique manner. "I don't want to interfere," he said, "but the behavior of this Asharak concerns me."

Garion moved away from Aunt Pol and began to study one of the strange little machines sitting on a nearby table, being careful not to touch it.

"We'll take care of Asharak," Aunt Pol said.

But Anheg persisted. "There have been rumors for centuries that you and your father have been protecting—" He hesitated, glanced at Garion, then continued smoothly. "—A certain thing that must be protected at all costs. Several of my books speak of it."

"You read too much, Anheg," Aunt Pol said.

Anheg laughed again. "It passes the time, Polgara," he said. "The alternative is drinking with my earls, and my stomach's getting a little delicate for that—and my ears as well. Have you any idea of how much noise a hall full of drunk Chereks can make? My books don't shout or boast and they don't fall down or slide under the tables and snore. They're much better company, really."

"Foolishness," Aunt Pol said.

"We're all foolish at one time or another," Anheg said philosophically. "But let's go back to this other matter. If those rumors I mentioned are true, aren't you taking some serious risks? Your search is likely to be very dangerous."

"No place is really safe," Mister Wolf said.

"Why take chances you don't have to?" Anheg asked. "Asharak isn't the only Grolim in the world, you know."

"I can see why they call you Anheg the sly," Wolf said with a smile.

"Wouldn't it be safer to leave this certain thing in my care until you return?" Anheg suggested.

"We've already found that not even Val Alorn is safe from the Grolims, Anheg," Aunt Pol said firmly. "The mines of Cthol Murgos and Gar og Nadrak are endless, and the Grolims have more gold at their disposal than you could even imagine. How many others like Jarvik have they bought? The Old Wolf and I are very experienced at protecting this certain thing you mentioned. It will be safe with us."

"Thank you for your concern, however," Mister Wolf said.

"The matter concerns us all," Anheg said.

Garion, despite his youth and occasional recklessness, was not stupid. It was obvious that what they were talking about involved him in some way and quite possibly had to do with the mystery of his parentage as well. To conceal the fact that he was listening as hard as he could, he picked up a small book bound in a strangely textured black leather. He opened it, but there were neither pictures nor illuminations, merely a spidery-looking script that seemed strangely repulsive.

Aunt Pol, who always seemed to know what he was doing, looked over at him. "What are you doing with that?" she said sharply.

"Just looking," he said. "I can't read."

"Put it down immediately," she told him.

King Anheg smiled. "You wouldn't be able to read it anyway, Garion," he said. "It's written in Old Angarak."

"What are you doing with that filthy thing anyway?" Aunt Pol asked Anheg. "You of all people should know that it's forbidden."

"It's only a book, Pol," Mister Wolf said. "It doesn't have any power unless it's permitted to."

"Besides," Anheg said, rubbing thoughtfully at the side of his face, "the book gives us clues to the mind of our enemy. That's always a good thing to know."

"You can't know Torak's mind," Aunt Pol said, "and it's dangerous to open yourself to him. He can poison you without your even knowing what's happening."

"I don't think there's any danger of that, Pol," Wolf said. "Anheg's mind is well-trained enough to avoid the traps in Torak's book. They're pretty obvious after all."

Anheg looked across the room at Garion and beckoned to him. Garion crossed and stood in front of the King of Cherek.

"You're an observant young man, Garion," Anheg said gravely. "You've done me a service today, and you can call on me at any time for service in return. Know that Anheg

of Cherek is your friend." He extended his right hand, and
Garion took it in his own without thinking.

King Anheg's eyes grew suddenly wide, and his face
paled slightly. He turned Garion's hand over and looked
down at the silvery mark on the boy's palm.

Then Aunt Pol's hands were also there, firmly closing
Garion's fingers and removing him from Anheg's grip.

"It's true, then," Anheg said softly.

"Enough," Aunt Pol said. "Don't confuse the boy." Her
hands were still firmly holding Garion's. "Come along,
dear," she said. "It's time to finish packing." And she
turned and led him from the room.

Garion's mind was racing. What was there about the
mark on his hand that had so startled Anheg? The birthmark, he knew, was hereditary. Aunt Pol had once told
him that his father's hand had had the same mark, but why
would that be of interest to Anheg? It had gone too far. His
need to know became almost unbearable. He had to know
about his parents, about Aunt Pol—about all of it. If the
answers hurt, then they'd just have to hurt. At least he
would know.

The next morning was clear, and they left the palace for
the harbor quite early. They all gathered in the courtyard
where the sleighs waited.

"There's no need for you to come out in the cold like
this, Merel," Barak told his fur-robed wife as she mounted
the sleigh beside him.

"I have a duty to see my Lord safely to his ship," she
replied with an arrogant lift of her chin.

Barak sighed. "Whatever you wish," he said.

With King Anheg and Queen Islena in the lead, the
sleighs whirled out of the courtyard and into the snowy
streets.

The sun was very bright, and the air was crisp. Garion
rode silently with Silk and Hettar.

"Why so quiet, Garion?" Silk asked.

"A lot of things have happened here that I don't understand," Garion said.

"No one can understand everything," Hettar said rather
sententiously.

"Chereks are a violent and moody people," Silk said.
"They don't even understand themselves."

"It's not just the Chereks," Garion said, struggling with the words. "It's Aunt Pol and Mister Wolf and Asharak—all of it. Things are happening too fast. I can't get it all sorted out."

"Events are like horses," Hettar told him. "Sometimes they run away. After they've run for a while, though, they'll start to walk again. Then there'll be time to put everything together."

"I hope so," Garion said dubiously and fell silent again.

The sleighs came around a corner into the broad square before the temple of Belar. The blind woman was there again, and Garion realized that he had been half-expecting her. She stood on the steps of the temple and raised her staff. Unaccountably, the horses which pulled the sleighs stopped, trembling, despite the urgings of the drivers.

"Hail, Great One," the blind woman said. "I wish thee well on thy journey."

The sleigh in which Garion was riding had stopped closest to the temple steps, and it seemed that the old woman was speaking to him. Almost without thinking he answered, "Thank you. But why do you call me that?"

She ignored the question. "Remember me," she commanded, bowing deeply. "Remember Martje when thou comest into thine inheritance."

It was the second time she'd said that, and Garion felt a sharp pang of curiosity. "What inheritance?" he demanded.

But Barak was roaring with fury and struggling to throw off the fur robe and draw his sword at the same time. King Anheg was also climbing down from his sleigh, his coarse livid face white with rage.

"No!" Aunt Pol said sharply from nearby. "I'll tend to this." She stood up. "Hear me, witch-woman," she said in a clear voice, casting back the hood of her cloak. "I think you see too much with those blind eyes of yours. I'm going to do you a favor so that you'll no longer be troubled by the darkness and these disturbing visions which grow out of it."

"Strike me down if it please thee, Polgara," the old woman said. "I see what I see."

"I won't strike you, Martje," Aunt Pol said. "I'm going to give you a gift instead." She raised her hand in a brief and curious gesture.

Garion saw it happen quite plainly, so there was no way

that he could later persuade himself that it had all been
some trick of the eye. He was looking directly at Martje's
face and saw the white film drain down off her eyes like
milk draining down the inside of a glass.

The old woman stood frozen to the spot as the bright
blue of her eyes emerged from the film which had covered
them. And then she screamed. She held up her hands,
looked at them and screamed again. There was in her
scream a wrenching note of indescribable loss.

"What did you do?" Queen Islena demanded.

"I gave her back her eyes," Aunt Pol said, sitting down
again and rearranging the fur robe about her.

"You can do that?" Islena asked, her face blanching and
her voice weak.

"Can't you? It's a simple thing, really."

"But," Queen Porenn objected, "with her eyes restored,
she'll lose that other vision, won't she?"

"I imagine so," Aunt Pol said, "but that's a small price
to pay, isn't it?"

"She'll no longer be a witch, then?" Porenn pressed.

"She wasn't really a very good witch anyway," Aunt Pol
said. "Her vision was clouded and uncertain. It's better this
way. She won't be disturbing herself and others with shadows any more." She looked at King Anheg who sat frozen
with awe beside his half-fainting queen. "Shall we continue?" she asked calmly. "Our ship is waiting."

The horses, as if released by her words, leaped forward,
and the sleighs sped away from the temple, spraying snow
from their runners.

Garion glanced back once. Old Martje stood on the steps
of the temple looking at her two outstretched hands and
sobbing uncontrollably.

"We've been privileged to witness a miracle, my
friends," Hettar said.

"I gather, however, that the beneficiary was not very
pleased with it," Silk said dryly. "Remind me not to offend
Polgara. Her miracles seem to have two edges to them."

Chapter Twenty-one

THE LOW-SLANTING RAYS of the morning sun glittered on the icy waters of the harbor as their sleighs halted near the stone quays. Greldik's ship rocked and strained at her hawsers, and a smaller ship nearby also waited with seeming impatience.

Hettar stepped down and went over to speak with Cho-Hag and Queen Silar. The three of them talked together quietly and seriously, drawing a kind of shell of privacy about them.

Queen Islena had partially regained her composure, and sat in her sleigh straight-backed and with a fixed smile on her face. After Anheg had gone to speak with Mister Wolf, Aunt Pol crossed the icy wharf and stopped near the sleigh of the Queen of Cherek.

"If I were you, Islena," she said firmly, "I'd find another hobby. Your gifts in the arts of sorcery are limited, and it's a dangerous area for dabbling. Too many things can go wrong if you don't know what you're doing."

The queen stared at her mutely.

"Oh," Aunt Pol said, "one other thing. It would be best, I think, if you broke off your connections with the Bear-cult. It's hardly proper for a queen to have dealings with her husband's political enemies."

Islena's eyes widened. "Does Anheg know?" she asked in a stricken voice.

"I wouldn't be surprised," Aunt Pol said. "He's much more clever than he looks, you know. You're walking very close to the edge of treason. You ought to have a few babies. They'd give you something useful to do with your time and keep you out of trouble. That's only a suggestion,

of course, but you might think it over. I've enjoyed our
visit, dear. Thank you for your hospitality." And with that
she turned and walked away.

Silk whistled softly. "That explains a few things," he
said.

"Explains what?" Garion asked.

"The High Priest of Belar's been dabbling in Cherek
politics lately. He's obviously gone a bit further than I'd
thought in penetrating the palace."

"The queen?" Garion asked, startled.

"Islena's obsessed with the idea of magic," Silk said.
"The Bear-cultists dabble in certain kinds of rituals that
might look sort of mystical to someone as gullible as she
is." He looked quickly toward where King Rhodar was
speaking with the other kings and Mister Wolf. Then he
drew in a deep breath. "Let's go talk to Porenn," he said
and led the way across the wharf to where the tiny blond
Queen of Drasnia stood looking out at the icy sea.

"Highness," Silk said deferentially.

"Dear Kheldar," she said, smiling at him.

"Could you give some information to my uncle for me?"
he asked.

"Of course."

"It seems that Queen Islena's been a bit indiscreet," Silk
said. "She's been involved with the Bear-cult here in
Cherek."

"Oh dear," Porenn said. "Does Anheg know?"

"It's hard to say," Silk told her. "I doubt if he'd admit it
if he did. Garion and I happened to hear Polgara tell her to
stop it."

"I hope that puts an end to it," Porenn said. "If it went
too far, Anheg would have to take steps. That could be
tragic."

"Polgara was quite firm," Silk said. "I think Islena will
do as she was told, but advise my uncle. He likes to be kept
aware of this kind of thing."

"I'll tell him about it," she said.

"You might also suggest that he keep his eyes on the
local chapters of the cult in Boktor and Kotu," Silk suggested. "This kind of thing isn't usually isolated. It's been
about fifty years since the last time the cult had to be suppressed."

Queen Porenn nodded gravely. "I'll see to it that he knows," she said. "I've got some of my own people planted in the Bear-cult. As soon as we get back to Boktor, I'll talk with them and see what's afoot."

"Your people? Have you gone that far already?" Silk asked in a bantering tone. "You're maturing rapidly, my Queen. It won't be long until you're as corrupt as the rest of us."

"Boktor is full of intrigue, Kheldar," the queen said primly. "It isn't just the Bear-cult, you know. Merchants from all over the world gather in our city, and at least half of them are spies. I have to protect myself—and my husband."

"Does Rhodar know what you're up to?" Silk asked slyly.

"Of course he does," she said. "He gave me my first dozen spies himself—as a wedding present."

"How typically Drasnian," Silk said.

"It's only practical, after all," she said. "My husband's concerned with matters involving other kingdoms. I try to keep an eye on things at home to leave his mind free for that kind of thing. My operations are a bit more modest than his, but I manage to stay aware of things." She looked at him slyly from beneath her eyelashes. "If you ever decide to come home to Boktor and settle down, I might just be able to find work for you."

Silk laughed. "The world seems to be full of opportunities lately," he said.

The queen looked at him seriously. "When *are* you coming home, Kheldar?" she asked. "When will you stop being this vagabond, Silk, and come back where you belong? My husband misses you very much, and you could serve Drasnia more by becoming his chief advisor than by all this flitting about the world."

Silk looked away, squinting into the bright wintry sun. "Not just yet, your Highness," he said. "Belgarath needs me too, and this is a very important thing we're doing just now. Besides, I'm not ready to settle down yet. The game is still entertaining. Perhaps someday when we're all much older it won't be anymore—who knows?"

She sighed. "I miss you too, Kheldar," she said gently.

"Poor, lonely little queen," Silk said, half-mockingly.

"You're impossible," she said, stamping her tiny foot.

"One does one's best." He grinned.

Hettar had embraced his father and mother and leaped across to the deck of the small ship King Anheg had provided him. "Belgarath," he called as the sailors slipped the stout ropes that bound the ship to the quay, "I'll meet you in two weeks at the ruins of Vo Wacune."

"We'll be there," Mister Wolf replied.

The sailors pushed the ship away from the quay and began to row out into the bay. Hettar stood on the deck, his long scalp lock flowing in the wind. He waved once, then turned to face the sea.

A long plank was run down over the side of Captain Greldik's ship to the snow-covered stones.

"Shall we go on board, Garion?" Silk said. They climbed the precarious plank and stepped out onto the deck.

"Give our daughters my love," Barak said to his wife.

"I will, my Lord," Merel said in the same stiffly formal tone she always used with him. "Have you any other instructions?"

"I won't be back for quite some time," Barak said. "Plant the south fields to oats this year, and let the west fields lie fallow. Do whatever you think best with the north fields. And don't move the cattle up to the high pastures until all the frost is out of the ground."

"I'll be most careful of my husband's lands and herds," she said.

"They're yours too," Barak said.

"As my husband wishes."

Barak sighed. "You never let it rest, do you, Merel?" he said sadly.

"My Lord?"

"Forget it."

"Will my Lord embrace me before he leaves?" she asked.

"What's the point?" Barak said. He jumped across to the ship and immediately went below.

Aunt Pol stopped on her way to the ship and looked gravely at Barak's wife. She looked as if she were about to say something. Then, without warning, she suddenly laughed.

"Something amusing, Lady Polgara?" Merel asked.

"Very amusing, Merel," Aunt Pol said with a mysterious smile.

"Might I be permitted to share it?"

"Oh, you'll share it, Merel," Aunt Pol promised, "but I wouldn't want to spoil it for you by telling you too soon." She laughed again and stepped onto the plank that led to the ship. Durnik offered his hand to steady her, and the two of them crossed to the deck.

Mister Wolf clasped hands with each of the kings in turn and then nimbly crossed to the ship. He stood for a moment on the deck looking at the ancient, snow-shrouded city of Val Alorn and the towering mountains of Cherek rising behind.

"Farewell, Belgarath," King Anheg called.

Mister Wolf nodded. "Don't forget about the minstrels," he said.

"We won't," Anheg promised. "Good luck."

Mister Wolf grinned and then walked forward toward the prow of Greldik's ship. Garion, on an impulse, followed him. There were questions which needed answers, and the old man would know if anyone would.

"Mister Wolf," he said when they both reached the high prow.

"Yes, Garion?"

He was not sure where to start, so Garion approached the problem obliquely. "How did Aunt Pol do that to old Martje's eyes?"

"The Will and the Word," Wolf said, his long cloak whipping about him in the stiff breeze. "It isn't difficult."

"I don't understand," Garion said.

"You simply will something to happen," the old man said, "and then speak the word. If your will's strong enough, it happens."

"That's all there is to it?" Garion asked, a little disappointed.

"That's all," Wolf said.

"Is the word a magic word?"

Wolf laughed, looking out at the sun glittering sharply on the winter sea. "No," he said. "There aren't any magic words. Some people think so, but they're wrong. Grolims use strange words, but that's not really necessary. Any word will do the job. It's the Will that's important, not the Word. The Word's just a channel for the Will."

"Could I do it?" Garion asked hopefully.

Wolf looked at him. "I don't know, Garion," he said. "I wasn't much older than you are the first time I did it, but I'd been living with Aldur for several years. That makes a difference, I suppose."

"What happened?"

"My Master wanted me to move a rock," Wolf said. "He seemed to think that it was in his way. I tried to move it, but it was too heavy. After a while I got angry, and I told it to move. It did. I was a little surprised, but my Master didn't seem to think it so unusual."

"You just said, 'move?' That's all?" Garion was incredulous.

"That's all." Wolf shrugged. "It seemed so simple that I was surprised I hadn't thought of it before. At the time I imagined that anybody could do it, but men have changed quite a bit since then. Maybe it isn't possible anymore. It's hard to say, really."

"I always thought that sorcery had to be done with long spells and strange signs and things like that," Garion said.

"Those are just the devices of tricksters and charlatans," Wolf said. "They make a fine show and impress and frighten simple people, but spells and incantations have nothing to do with the real thing. It's all in the Will. Focus the Will and speak the Word, and it happens. Sometimes a gesture of some sort helps, but it isn't really necessary. Your Aunt always seems to want to gesture when she makes something happen. I've been trying to break her of that habit for hundreds of years now."

Garion blinked. "*Hundreds* of years?" he gasped. "How old is she?"

"Older than she looks," Wolf said. "It isn't polite to ask questions about a lady's age, however."

Garion felt a sudden, shocking emptiness. The worst of his fears had just been confirmed. "Then she isn't really my Aunt, is she?" he asked sickly.

"What makes you say that?" Wolf asked.

"She couldn't be, could she? I always thought that she was my father's sister, but if she's hundreds and thousands of years old, it would be impossible."

"You're much too fond of that word, Garion," Wolf said. "When you get right down to it, nothing—or at least very little—is actually impossible."

"How could she be? My Aunt, I mean?"

"All right," Wolf said. "Polgara was not strictly speaking your father's sister. Her relationship to him is quite a bit more complex. She was the sister of his grandmother—his ultimate grandmother, if there is such a term—and of yours as well, of course."

"Then she'd be my great-aunt," Garion said with a faint spark of hope. It was something, at least.

"I don't know that I'd use that precise term around her." Wolf grinned. "She might take offense. Why are you so concerned about all of this?"

"I was afraid that maybe she'd just said that she was my Aunt, and that there wasn't really any connection between us at all," Garion said. "I've been afraid of that for quite a while now."

"Why were you afraid?"

"It's kind of hard to explain," Garion said. "You see, I don't really know who I am or what I am. Silk says I'm not a Sendar, and Barak says I look sort of like a Rivan—but not exactly. I always thought I was a Sendar—like Durnik—but I guess I'm not. I don't know anything about my parents or where they came from or anything like that. If Aunt Pol isn't related to me, then I don't have anybody in the world at all. I'm all alone, and that's a very bad thing."

"But now it's all right, isn't it?" Wolf said. "Your Aunt is really your Aunt—at least your blood and hers are the same."

"I'm glad you told me," Garion said. "I've been worried about it."

Greldik's sailors untied the hawsers and began to push the ship away from the quay.

"Mister Wolf," Garion said as a strange thought occurred to him.

"Yes, Garion?"

"Aunt Pol really is my Aunt—or my Great-Aunt?"

"Yes."

"And she's your daughter?"

"I have to admit that she is," Wolf said wryly. "I try to forget that sometimes, but I can't really deny it."

Garion took a deep breath and plunged directly into it. "If she's my Aunt and you're her father," he said, "wouldn't that sort of make you my Grandfather?"

Wolf looked at him with a startled expression. "Why yes," he said, laughing suddenly, "I suppose that in a way it does. I'd never thought of it exactly like that before."

Garion's eyes suddenly filled with tears, and he impulsively embraced the old man. "Grandfather," he said, trying the word out.

"Well, well," Wolf said, his own voice strangely thick. "What a remarkable discovery." Awkwardly he patted Garion's shoulder.

They were both a little embarrassed by Garion's sudden display of affection, and they stood silently, watching as Greldik's sailors rowed the ship out into the harbor.

"Grandfather," Garion said after a while.

"Yes?"

"What really happened to my mother and father? I mean, how did they die?"

Wolf's face became very bleak. "There was a fire," he said shortly.

"A fire?" Garion said weakly, his imagination lurching back from that awful thought—of the unspeakable pain. "How did it happen?"

"It's not very pleasant," Wolf said grimly. "Are you really sure you want to know?"

"I have to, Grandfather," Garion said quietly. "I have to know everything I can about them. I don't know why, but it's very important."

Mister Wolf sighed. "Yes, Garion," he said, "I guess it would be at that. All right, then. If you're old enough to ask the questions, you're old enough to hear the answers." He sat down on a sheltered bench out of the chilly wind. "Come over here and sit down." He patted the bench beside him.

Garion sat down and pulled his cloak around him.

"Let's see," Wolf said, scratching thoughtfully at his beard, "where do we start?" He pondered for a moment. "Your family's very old, Garion," he said finally, "and like so many old families, it has a certain number of enemies."

"Enemies?" Garion was startled. That particular idea hadn't occurred to him before.

"It's not uncommon," Wolf said. "When we do something someone else doesn't like, they tend to hate us. The hatred builds up over the years until it turns into something almost like a religion. They hate not only us, but everything connected with us. Anyway, a long time ago your family's enemies became so dangerous that your Aunt and I decided that the only way we could protect the family was to hide it."

"You aren't telling me everything," Garion said.

"No," Wolf said blandly, "I'm not. I'm telling you as much as it's safe for you to know for right now. If you knew certain things, you'd act differently, and people would notice that. It's safer if you stay ordinary for a while longer."

"You mean ignorant," Garion accused.

"All right, ignorant then. Do you want to hear the story, or do you want to argue?"

"I'm sorry," Garion said.

"It's all right," Wolf said, patting Garion's shoulder. "Since your Aunt and I are related to your family in a rather special way, we were naturally interested in your safety. That's why we hid your people."

"Can you actually hide a whole family?" Garion asked.

"It's never been that big a family," Wolf said. "It seems, for one reason or another, to be a single, unbroken line—no cousins or uncles or that kind of thing. It's not all that hard to hide a man and wife with a single child. We've been doing it for hundreds of years now. We've hidden them in Tolnedra, Riva, Cherek, Drasnia—all kinds of places. They've lived simple lives—artisans mostly, sometimes ordinary peasants—the kind of people nobody would ever look at twice. Anyway, everything had gone well until about twenty years ago. We moved your father, Geran, from a place in Arendia to a little village in eastern Sendaria, about sixty leagues southeast of Darine, up in the mountains. Geran was a stonecutter—didn't I tell you that once before?"

Garion nodded. "A long time ago," he said. "You said you liked him and used to visit him once in a while. Was my mother a Sendar, then?"

"No," Wolf said. "Ildera was an Algar, actually—the second daughter of a Clan-Chief. Your Aunt and I introduced her to Geran when they were about the right age. The usual sort of thing happened, and they got married. You were born a year or so afterward."

"When was the fire?" Garion asked.

"I'm getting to that," Wolf said. "One of the enemies of your family had been looking for your people for a long time."

"How long?"

"Hundreds of years, actually."

"That means that he was a sorcerer, too, doesn't it?" Garion asked. "I mean, only sorcerers live for that long, don't they?"

"He has certain capabilities along those lines," Wolf admitted. "Sorcerer is a misleading term, though. It's not the sort of thing we actually call ourselves. Other people do, but we don't exactly think of it that way. It's a convenient term for people who don't really understand what it's all about. Anyway, your Aunt and I happened to be away when this enemy finally tracked down Geran and Ildera. He came to their house very early one morning while they were still sleeping and he sealed up the doors and windows and then he set it on fire."

"I thought you said the house was made of stone."

"It was," Wolf said, "but you can make stone burn if you really want to. The fire just has to be hotter, that's all. Geran and Ildera knew that there was no way they could get out of the burning house, but Geran managed to knock one of the stones out of the wall, and Ildera pushed you out through the hole. The one who had set the fire was waiting for that. He picked you up and started out of the village. We could never be sure exactly what he had in mind—either he was going to kill you, or maybe he was going to keep you for some reason of his own. At any rate, that's when I got there. I put out the fire, but Geran and Ildera were already dead. Then I went after the one who'd stolen you."

"Did you kill him?" Garion demanded fiercely.

"I try not to do that any more than I have to," Wolf said. "It disrupts the natural course of events too much. I had some other ideas at the time—much more unpleasant than killing." His eyes were icy. "As it turned out, though, I never got the chance. He threw you at me—you were only a baby—and I had to try to catch you. It gave him time to get away. I left you with Polgara and then I went looking for your enemy. I haven't been able to find him yet, though."

"I'm glad you haven't," Garion said.

Wolf looked a little surprised at that.

"When I get older, *I'm* going to find him," Garion said. "I think I ought to be the one who pays him back for what he did, don't you?"

Wolf looked at him gravely. "It could be dangerous," he said.

"I don't care. What's his name?"

"I think that maybe I'd better wait a while before I tell you that," Wolf said. "I don't want you jumping into something before you're ready."

"But you will tell me?"

"When the time comes."

"It's very important, Grandfather."

"Yes," Wolf said. "I can see that."

"Do you promise?"

"If you insist. And if I don't, I'm sure your Aunt will. She feels the same way you do."

"Don't you?"

"I'm much older," Wolf said. "I see things a little differently."

"I'm not that old yet," Garion said. "I won't be able to do the kind of things you'd do, so I'll have to settle for just killing him." He stood up and began to pace back and forth, a rage boiling in him.

"I don't suppose I'll be able to talk you out of this," Wolf said, "but I really think you're going to feel differently about it after it's over."

"Not very likely," Garion said, still pacing.

"We'll see," Wolf said.

"Thank you for telling me, Grandfather," Garion said.

"You'd have found out sooner or later anyway," the old man said, "and it's better that I tell you than for you to get a distorted account from somebody else."

"You mean Aunt Pol?"

"Polgara wouldn't deliberately lie to you," Wolf said, "but she sees things in a much more personal way than I do. Sometimes that colors her perceptions. I try to take the long view of things." He laughed rather wryly. "I suppose that's the only view I could take—under the circumstances."

Garion looked at the old man whose white hair and beard seemed somehow luminous in the morning sun. "What's it like to live forever, Grandfather?" he asked.

"I don't know," Wolf said. "I haven't lived forever."

"You know what I mean."

"The quality of life isn't much different," Wolf said. "We all live as long as we need to. It just happened that I have something to do that's taken a very long time." He stood up abruptly. "This conversation's taken a gloomy turn," he said.

"This thing that we're doing is very important, isn't it, Grandfather?" Garion asked.

"It's the most important thing in the world right now," Wolf said.

"I'm afraid I'm not going to be very much help," Garion said.

Wolf looked at him gravely for a moment and then put one arm around his shoulders. "I think you may be surprised about that before it's all over, Garion," he said.

And then they turned and looked out over the prow of the ship at the snowy coast of Cherek sliding by on their right as the sailors rowed the ship south toward Camaar and whatever lay beyond.

Here ends Book One of *The Belgariad*.
Book Two, *Queen of Sorcery*,
will reveal Garion's own dangerous powers of sorcery and more on his heritage, which underlies their quest.

About the Author

David Eddings was born in Spokane, Washington, in 1931, and was raised in the Puget Sound area north of Seattle. He received a Bachelor of Arts degree from Reed College in Portland, Oregon, in 1954 and a Master of Arts degree from the University of Washington in 1961. He has served in the United States Army, worked as a buyer for the Boeing Company, has been a grocery clerk, and has taught college English. He has lived in many parts of the United States.

His first novel, *High Hunt* (published by Putnam in 1973), was a contemporary adventure story. The field of fantasy has always been of interest to him, however, and he turned to *The Belgariad* in an effort to develop certain technical and philosophical ideas concerning that genre.

Eddings currently resides with his wife, Leigh, in the northwest.

Enchanting fantasies from